The King's Return

www.transworldbooks.co.uk

Also by Andrew Swanston

The King's Spy
The King's Exile

The King's Return

Andrew Swanston

BANTAM PRESS

LONDON · TORONTO · SYDNEY · AUCKLAND · JOHANNESBURG

TRANSWORLD PUBLISHERS
61–63 Uxbridge Road, London W5 5SA
A Random House Group Company
www.transworldbooks.co.uk

First published in Great Britain
in 2014 by Bantam Press
an imprint of Transworld Publishers

A CIP catalogue record for this book
is available from the British Library.

ISBN 9780593068908

Addresses for Random House Group Ltd companies outside the UK
can be found at: www.randomhouse.co.uk
The Random House Group Ltd Reg. No. 954009

The Random House Group Limited supports the Forest Stewardship Council® (FSC®),
the leading international forest-certification organisation. Our books carrying the FSC label are
printed on FSC®-certified paper. FSC is the only forest-certification scheme supported by the
leading environmental organisations, including Greenpeace. Our paper procurement
policy can be found at www.randomhouse.co.uk/environment

Typeset in 12/16.5pt Classico by Falcon Oast Graphic Art Ltd.
Printed and bound in Great Britain by
Clays Ltd, Bungay, Suffolk

2 4 6 8 10 9 7 5 3 1

MIX
Paper from
responsible sources
FSC® C016897

For Isaac and Amelie

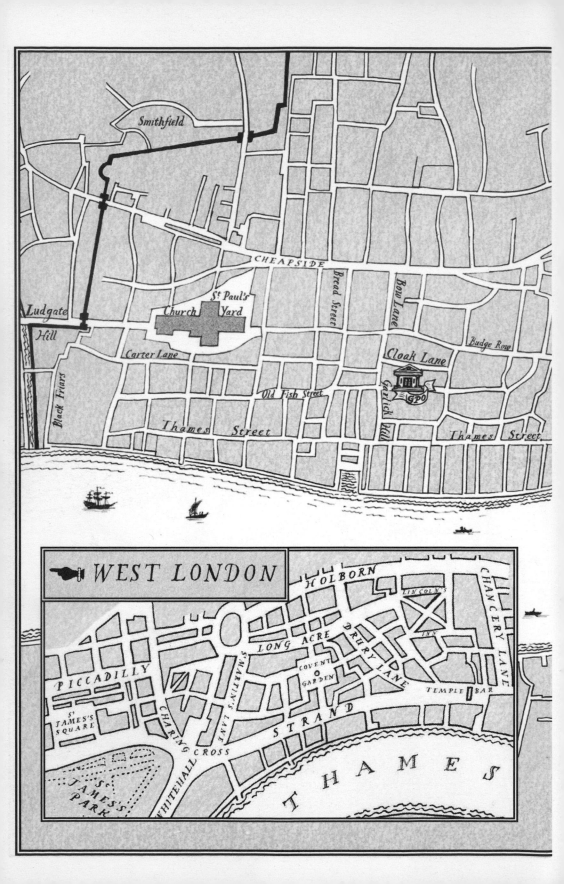

Smithfield

CHEAPSIDE

Bread Street

Bow Lane

Budge Row

Ludgate Hill

St Paul's Yard

Church

Carter Lane

Cloak Lane

Garlick Hill

GPO

Black Friars

Old Fish Street

Thames Street

Thames Street

WEST LONDON

HOLBORN

CHANCERY LANE

LINCOLN'S INN

LONG ACRE

DRURY LANE

PICCADILLY

ST MARTIN'S LANE

COVENT GARDEN

TEMPLE BAR

ST JAMES'S SQUARE

CHARING CROSS

STRAND

WHITEHALL

ST JAMES'S PARK

THAMES

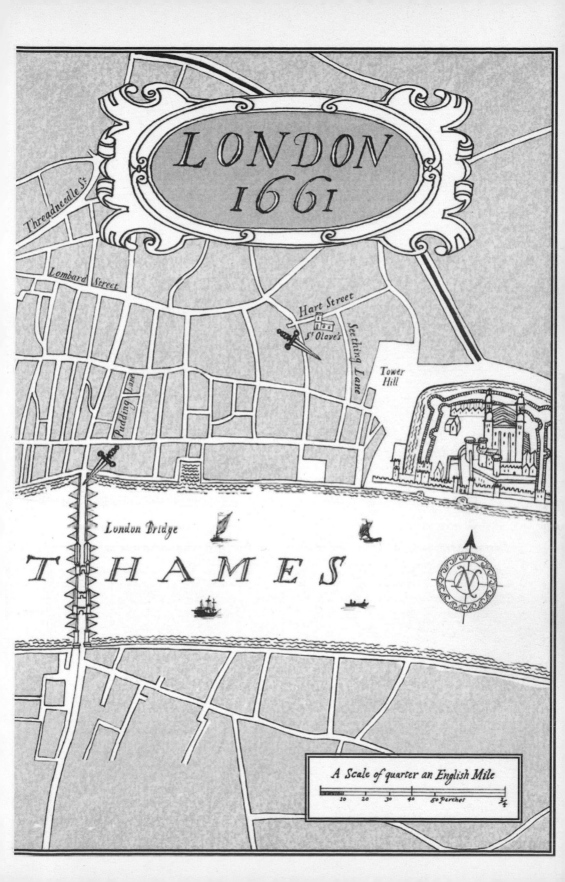

CHAPTER 1

April 1661

For an hour the Dutchman had been standing silent and unmoving in the doorway of a derelict house halfway down the lane. He was hooded and wore black leather gloves, a black coat and soft leather boots. Neither the waiting nor the chill of the night bothered him — he was used to such things — and he would stay there until midnight if he had to. Nor was he concerned at using this lane again. It had served well enough the first time, it was dark and quiet and he had taken up his position early to make sure that there was no one about and to accustom his eyes to the dark.

He had collected his instructions from the usual place behind a loose brick on the side of an inn in Bishopsgate that he checked at a different time every day. This was his second task since arriving from Holland at the end of March. He hoped there would be more.

The bells of a church somewhere in the city signalled ten o'clock. The mark was due. The Dutchman removed a long-bladed knife from inside his coat and carefully tested the edge with his thumb. Not that there was any need — he had whetted the blade himself and knew that it would cut almost anything short of steel — it was just a habit acquired over ten years of perfecting his craft. Ten years in which he had never failed to carry out a commission successfully.

From his left the Dutchman heard footsteps on the cobbles — not the brisk steps of a man returning home or a constable, more the shambling gait of a drinker trying to find his way without falling over, or an elderly man uncertain of his balance. His information was that the mark was elderly. A small man, he had been told, slightly stooped and poor of eyesight. Not a man likely to give him any trouble. He touched his damaged face and smiled. He liked easy money as much as he liked killing Englishmen.

The Dutchman lowered his head, backed into the doorway a little more and waited for the footsteps to pass him. When they did, he looked up from under his hood. A stooped man was shuffling down the other side of the lane towards the river. He knew that his mark would wait at the end of the lane for the man he expected to meet to emerge from the Honest Wherryman tavern. The mark would be watching the tavern door and would not see his attacker approaching from the shadows on the other side of the lane. He had no idea how an elderly man had been persuaded to come to such a place at night, nor did he care.

He slipped out of the doorway and down the lane, keeping ten yards or so behind the mark. He watched the man reach the tavern and stand outside it. For a moment he looked as if he was about to go inside, but then he moved on. The Dutchman closed the gap between them, glanced about to be sure there was no one else in the lane, and when he was no more than five yards away, darted forward, grabbed the old man's hair, pulled his head back to expose his throat and with one swift stroke opened his windpipe. A fountain of blood spurted from the wound. It was done so cleanly and so fast that the victim uttered not a sound. The Dutchman lowered the body on to the cobbles, then wiped his blade on the man's coat and patted his pockets. He extracted the dead man's purse and pocket watch and turned back up the lane. To the coroner the murder would look like the work of a robber.

The mark was dead and there was nothing to connect the Dutchman or his paymaster to his murder. Within thirty minutes he was back in the house in Wapping that had been provided for him.

CHAPTER 2

The carriage in which Thomas Hill sat — as a gentleman should, with his back to the coachman — rattled over the Southwark cobbles towards London Bridge. After three uncomfortable days Thomas's backside was sore and his temper short. Holding a lavender-scented handkerchief to his sensitive nose, he leaned out of the window and shouted at the coachman to stop. Among the beggars, urchins and street vendors, he had spotted a mercury selling news sheets. Thomas summoned the boy and handed over three pence.

The front page of the news sheet was devoted, unsurprisingly, to the coronation and the magnificent procession which would precede it. On the eve of his coronation, King Charles II would proceed with his knights and bishops from the Tower to Whitehall, under arches erected especially for the occasion, and past a naval display at the Royal Exchange, a Temple of Concord in Cheapside and a Garden of Plenty in Fleet Street. The king was a man who, like his devout Catholic mother, Queen Henrietta Maria, understood the importance of ceremony, the more extravagant the better. That tiny, formidable lady had led an army of three thousand men to Oxford and had dressed and lived as a soldier, yet could spend thousands on entertainments for the king. For her son, the streets had been cleaned and gravelled and rails erected to keep the crowd a suitable distance from the royal party. Thousands were expected to line the route.

As for the coronation itself, the writer described in fulsome detail what the new king would be wearing, who, with his brother James, would accompany him, and what the ceremony, designed by the Garter King of Arms himself, would entail. And he reminded his readers that, had he not died of smallpox six months earlier, the king's brother Henry would also have been at his side.

As Thomas read on, he learned who had made the royal shoes, the royal wig and each item of His Majesty's magnificent coronation robes. The people of London were about to witness the grandest ceremony the city had ever seen, as befitted a monarch restored to his rightful throne after twelve years of dreary Puritanism, and the great day, the day for which all of England had been waiting, would end with a wondrous display of fireworks. Thomas disliked fireworks and hoped that he would not be expected to attend. The coronation itself would be quite sufficient.

When he turned the page, Thomas's eye was immediately caught by the headline of the next story.

ANOTHER MURDER IN PUDDING LANE

Sir Montford Babb found dead

Coroner believes robbery again the motive

Thomas caught his breath. There used to be Babbs in Hampshire and he remembered Sir Montford as a rather vague, kindly man, not a man you would expect to find with his throat cut in a filthy London alley. And he was surprised to find the murder of a single unknown man reported in the news sheet, especially when those who had sat in judgement on the king's father or taken any part in his trial were being arrested and executed every week. Perhaps the writer thought it best to spare his readers' sensibilities. Hanging, drawing and quartering – a traitor's death – was a gruesome, sickening affair. Thomas read on.

Sir Montford's body had been found in Pudding Lane two nights earlier, near the Honest Wherryman alehouse. He had been attacked from behind and his throat cut. As his pockets were empty, the coroner, Master Seymour Manners, had concluded that the motive was robbery. It was not known why Sir Montford had been alone in a dark street best known for its low taverns and bakers' shops, but there were no witnesses and no other clues. This was the second such murder in the space of three weeks, the previous victim having been a Mr Matthew Smith, also robbed and found with his throat cut in Pudding Lane. The coroner had expressed the view that both victims died at the same hand.

Like Mr Smith, Sir Montford Babb was a respectable gentleman, well known in the coffee houses of the city. He had no known enemies and his distraught widow had been unable to shed any light on the matter. With the murderer still at large, gentlemen were advised to take great care on the streets at night.

Thomas put aside the news sheet and closed his eyes. He pictured a whiskery old face, a soft smile and a Hampshire voice. Montford Babb had been a harmless old gentleman. May his murderer be brought quickly to justice. And may Thomas Hill's visit to London be a brief one. Already he missed his books, his friends and the Hampshire countryside. Even for a coronation, London was no place for a man who valued his peace.

At the southern end of the bridge the coach pulled up. Thomas alighted, and his bags were handed down. He paid the coachman, tried not to look at the heads impaled on spikes over the gate and, followed by two boys carrying the bags, set off on foot across the bridge. He did not care to take a river wherry up to Westminster Steps, nor was it worth attempting the bridge in a coach – both sides of it were lined by tall buildings which met in the middle and formed a narrow tunnel through which all traffic had to pass. It would be quicker and easier to make the crossing on foot.

As he walked, Thomas thought of the extraordinary man whom he had come to see crowned king and who had ridden across this same bridge almost twelve months earlier. The future Charles II had stood, aged twelve, beside his father when the royal standard was raised at Nottingham, had fled the country in the summer of 1647, had returned to Scotland and marched south, only for his army to be routed at Worcester, had famously escaped again after spending a day hiding in an oak tree on the Boscobel estate, and had returned eight years later to reclaim his throne. And, astonishingly, he had done so without a shot being fired or a drop of blood being spilt in his name. Charles had agreed to an Act of Oblivion, and spoken of peace and reconciliation, of forgiveness and goodwill, and waited for the way to be cleared for his return. No fighting, no army, no invasion.

Mind you, the blood was flowing now. If his own father had been unjustly executed, Thomas wondered, would he have taken his revenge by promising his enemies clemency, only to hunt them down and execute them with single-minded ferocity? Would that not make martyrs of the executed and increase the risk of a backlash? Or would it terrify the malcontents into submission? Old comrades were now sitting in judgement on each other, condemning each other to death and hoping the king would not turn his wrath on them. The country's politics were every bit as complex as one of the mathematical problems with which Thomas liked to wrestle, and a good deal more dangerous.

A hundred thousand people, it was said, had lined the route from Dover to Canterbury and thence to London. A hundred thousand men and women, many of whom had supported, even fought for the cause of Parliament, but now wanted nothing more than the return of their monarch. The Black Boy, some people called him, for his dark complexion. A clever boy, too, to have survived eight years of exile and to have returned in triumph.

At the north end of the bridge, Thomas agreed a fare for the journey to Piccadilly and climbed into a hackney coach while the jarvey loaded his bags. The coach lurched forward and they were off, along the north bank of the river, up to Ludgate Hill, along Fleet Street and the Strand to Charing Cross, the very place where a number of the king's enemies had died under the executioner's axe, their entrails extracted and burned before their eyes, their heads sliced off and their bodies quartered and displayed around London. The stench had been so bad that the local people asked for the executions to be moved to their traditional place at Tyburn.

The further west they travelled, the wider and cleaner the streets and the grander the buildings. Both sides of Piccadilly were lined with elegant, brick-built town houses — a different world to the narrow, dark alleyways no more than a mile to the east, where thieves and whores plied their trade and rotting beasts and dung heaps assailed the senses. Mounds of filth and reeking drains were not fit for prosperous merchants and landowners. Their money bought space and comfort.

Outside one of the finest houses on the south side of Piccadilly, they pulled up and the jarvey jumped down to open the door. Thomas stepped out. It was a lovely April day, the chestnuts in St James's Fields were coming into leaf and there was neither a severed head nor a dangling corpse in sight. His spirits restored, Thomas breathed deeply and knocked on the imposing door. It was opened immediately by a liveried servant.

'Thomas Hill, sometime bookseller, indentured servant and cryptographer, and devoted admirer of Mrs Carrington.' He announced himself with a broad grin.

The servant returned the grin. 'Good morning, sir. I am John Smythe, Mr and Mrs Carrington's steward. They are expecting you in the sitting room. This way, if you please.'

Thomas was shown into a large, sunlit room where a tall man, his thick black hair lightly streaked with grey and his waist only a little thicker than Thomas remembered, stood beside his elegant wife, their backs to the window. Before Thomas could say a word, Mary Carrington rushed forward and engulfed him in an embrace. When she eventually released him and stepped back, he could see that she was every bit as beautiful as he remembered. Her green eyes shone and her skin, unblemished by the Caribbean sun, glowed. In a flowing emerald gown with white lace at the neck and cuffs and with her black hair tied back with a matching ribbon, Mary was still ravishing.

'Thomas Hill,' she said, hands on his shoulders, 'what a delight. I've been looking forward to seeing you for months. A little greyer at the temples, perhaps, but just as handsome and not a pound heavier. Are you as well and prosperous as you look?'

'Apart from occasional gout, both, happily. As are you, I hope,' replied Thomas, delighted that Mary had taken such trouble with her appearance, although she was a woman who would look beautiful in an old sack.

'I too have been looking forward to seeing you, Thomas,' interrupted Charles Carrington, hand outstretched, 'and if my wife would be good enough to release you, I would like to make my own inspection.' Charles looked Thomas up and down. 'Well, my friend, you seem to have cleaned up rather well. Very well, in fact. Bright of eye and clear of skin. Come and sit and tell us how you've managed it. Alas, plantain juice is not to be found in London. Would you care for a glass of Madeira instead?' While in Barbados, Thomas had become fond of the juice of the plantain mixed with a little sugar, which had sustained him through many a long day of torment. Now he much preferred Madeira.

Having filled three glasses from the bottle on a side table, Charles proposed a toast. 'To Thomas Hill, without whom I might still be a miserable bachelor.'

'To you both, without whom I might still be miserably indentured to the brothers Gibbes,' replied Thomas, raising his glass. For nearly three years the barbaric Samuel and John Gibbes had been his masters in Barbados.

Despite the warmth of the day a fire had been lit in the grate. For a minute the three friends sat unspeaking around it. Mary broke the silence. 'Well now, this is a fine thing. We haven't seen you for nine years and none of us can think of a thing to say. You first, Thomas. Tell us everything you didn't put in your letters. Everything, mind. Warts and all, as the late Lord Protector would have said.'

'Did say, by all accounts,' replied Thomas, 'and I really haven't much to tell you. As you know, my sister Margaret died of a fever at Christmas two years ago. It was a sad time and I miss her terribly. My nieces are well. Polly has just turned twenty-two, she's married — happily, I think — and, as I mentioned in my letter, Lucy is two years younger, and here in London at the behest of the Duchess of York. She is a guest of Lady Richmond in Whitehall.'

'Indeed you did mention it. What an honour for her. She must be an exceptional seamstress to have been appointed to make the Duchess's coronation gown.'

'I believe she is. And an embroiderer, too. We are very proud of her. I just hope London does not turn her head. She is a lovely child, but unworldly and easily led.'

'I am sure you will keep an eye on her while you are here,' said Mary. 'And what about you, Thomas?'

'I live a quiet and virtuous life in Romsey with my books and my writing. I seldom venture far from my own bed and it was only your invitation that persuaded me to travel to London.'

'Are you still living in the house you built by the school?'

'I am, and happily the school thrives. It has thirty pupils and two teachers. I read my books, enjoy my cellar and bore my friends with earnest talk of philosophy and mathematics.'

'Is that it, Thomas?' asked Charles. 'Nine years, and that's really all you have to report? No affairs of the heart, no literary triumphs, no narrow escapes from the jaws of death?'

'None. I fear that I'm really the dullest of men.'

Mary refilled his glass. 'Nonsense, Thomas. No gentleman who has saved my life twice could possibly be dull.'

Thomas smiled. 'You returned the favour, Mary, as I recall.' He paused. 'And what of Barbados? Does it still grow rich from its sugar?'

'Much of it does,' replied Charles. 'We've been fortunate, although not as fortunate as some. You remember James Drax, I expect. His estate is now over a thousand acres and he makes as much from trading slaves as he does from his sugar. Extraordinary that an island with a population of no more than a tenth the size of London's can generate such prosperity.'

'And how is Adam, Mary?' asked Thomas.

'My brother is well. Fat and wealthy, and still unmarried. He did not care to leave the estate for the voyage. And he takes his responsibilities as a member of the Governor's Council terribly seriously.'

Once the dam had broken, conversation flowed freely and they talked until the evening of Barbados and London, sugar and land, king and Parliament, peace and war.

Having been taken to Barbados by her brother at the age of twelve, Mary had never before visited London. She had spent the three weeks since their arrival for the coronation entertaining and being entertained.

'I do so love the theatre,' she declared. 'Mr Moone was wonderful in *The Traitor* and so was Mr Betterton in *The Bondman*. Of course we have nothing like it at home. I would go to a new performance every night if Charles would escort me but, alas, the theatre is not to his taste.'

'I can't see the sense in boys pretending to be women. A

fellow can hardly admire Ophelia's bosom if she hasn't got one. It was bad enough Mary dressing as a boy on the ship.'

Thomas raised an eyebrow. 'Mary, why did you dress as a boy on the ship? Or would you rather not tell me?'

'All the passengers had to put on a little entertainment. I wrote a short play. Charles played my father and I his prodigal son. It went down very well.'

'Perhaps you'll put on a second performance in London. I'd very much like to see Charles on the stage.'

'Certainly not. Once was enough.' Charles sounded horrified at the idea.

Mary turned to Thomas. 'Would you escort me to the theatre, Thomas? *The Changeling* is playing in Salisbury Court. I should like to see it.'

'Of course, my dear. When would you like to go?'

'Go on Thursday next,' suggested Charles. 'I am dining with Chandle Stoner. He wants to tell me how well our investment is doing.'

'Then that's settled. The theatre for us, Thomas, and business for Charles. Perfect.'

'By the way,' went on Charles, 'I have invited Chandle and his sister to join us for dinner after the coronation.'

'His sister? I did not know he had one.'

'Neither did I. I gather Louise is married to a Frenchman and lives in Paris. She is in London for the coronation and Chandle asked if she might accompany him. I could hardly say no.'

'Of course not. No doubt she is charming.' Mary turned to Thomas. 'Did I mention that we are giving a small dinner party after the coronation? Joseph Williamson, who has arranged our seats in the Abbey, is coming, and his cousin Madeleine Stewart.

And now Chandle Stoner and his sister. I do hope you will join us, Thomas.'

Thomas hesitated. Dinner with four strangers was not all that appealing but Mary might be offended if he made an excuse. 'Of course. I should be delighted.'

'Excellent. Joseph is an old friend of Charles. Not a great conversationalist but a man of influence. He has the ear of the king. I think you'll find him interesting.'

'I am sure I shall. And shall I find Miss Stewart interesting?'

Charles stirred himself. 'You might, Thomas, you might.'

CHAPTER 3

The eight years since the new king had fled to France had been a strange time. While Thomas had been quietly establishing his school in Romsey, there had been no monarch, and for some of the time no Parliament, when the Lord Protector, Oliver Cromwell, and his Council had ruled the land. By dissolving Parliament, the great republican had alienated some of his staunchest supporters, and had made himself doubly unpopular by introducing new taxes to finance his war with Spain and appointing major-generals to collect them. Not only that, but he had allowed himself to be addressed as 'Your Highness'.

Thankfully, Oliver's successor, his son Richard, had quickly proved himself worthy of his nickname 'Tumbledown Dick' and had been bullied out of power and out of the country after a few months of dithering incompetence. But now everything had changed again. The new king would take his revenge on his father's enemies and then, God willing, the country would begin to smile again.

As if to reinforce this hope, St George's Day, 23 April 1661, had been chosen as the day of the coronation, and high up in the scaffold built for the occasion at the north end of Westminster Abbey Thomas Hill and Charles and Mary Carrington watched Charles II being crowned King of England and Ireland. It was a long ceremony, very long, and Thomas's attention at times wandered. He found himself comparing the day to the one just over twelve years earlier when he had heard the news of the execution of the king's father while he was indentured in Barbados. On that day, he had been dragged to the Mermaid Inn in Oistins to hear Colonel James Drax announce the king's death and had seen and heard the landowners arguing about what the news would mean for them. It had been a loud, rough meeting, fuelled by ale and rum, which had ended for his tormentors, the Gibbes brothers, when Charles Carrington had deposited both of them on the floor with no more than an outstretched leg and a helping hand. Thomas smiled. Even now, he enjoyed the memory.

Westminster Abbey was rather different. As indeed was the new king. Unlike his limping, stammering, charmless father, the tall man in blue and gold who strode up the red carpet that ran the length of the aisle to a raised throne gave every appearance of being outgoing, relaxed and cheerful. The royal smile looked genuine enough, at least from where Thomas sat, as did the delight of the people in their new monarch. Like many, they had arrived at the Abbey to take their seats in the early hours of the morning. By the time the ceremony finished they had been sitting there with only occasional breaks for more than twelve hours. They watched courtiers, officials, lords, ladies, bishops and musicians proudly playing their parts in the spectacle, they listened while the king knelt to take the oaths and held their breath when asked if they knew of any reason why Charles Stuart should not be proclaimed King of England.

Thomas strained to see the Duchess of York's gown, sewn and embroidered by Lucy. He was too far away really to appreciate it, and consoled himself with the thought that it would certainly be more beautiful than the duchess herself. The daughter of the Lord Chancellor, Lord Hyde, was not renowned for her looks.

When at last it was over, they made their way through the cheering crowds outside the Abbey — Thomas guessed at ten thousand people — and hurried back to Piccadilly, while the king and his bishops and lords set about the feast laid out for them in Westminster Hall. Thomas had seen no sign of any demonstration against the new king. The die-hard Puritans and non-conformists must have wisely stayed at home.

'Well, Thomas, what did you make of it?' asked Mary, on their way back.

'I found it impressive, if a little long.'

'I do agree. Still, all those fiddlers will be able to tell their grandchildren about the day they played at the king's coronation.'

'Let us hope that he proves a more successful king than his father,' said Charles. 'Another war we do not need, nor indeed wars against the French or the Dutch or anyone else. Peace and prosperity are what we need now.'

Thomas descended the Carringtons' staircase for dinner as their long-case clock struck six and an enormous clap of thunder erupted overhead. The gods, it seemed, having blessed the day of the coronation with fine weather, were about to demonstrate their impartiality with a huge storm. He heard laughter from the library. A guest must have arrived early. The library door opened and

Charles emerged, grinning broadly, his arm around the guest's shoulders.

'Well, Chandle, things seem to be going splendidly. Well done indeed.' Charles sounded delighted. He looked up and saw Thomas. 'Ah, Thomas, perfect timing. Allow me to introduce my good friend Chandle Stoner. Chandle, this is Thomas Hill, about whom I have told you.'

Stoner was a man of medium height, with an abundance of black hair, a sharp nose and a neat pointed beard. Thomas noted his dress — silk shirt and trousers and a short velvet coat embroidered with ribbons, all well in keeping with the spirit of the day — and wondered if he might himself be rather underdressed for the occasion. He had thought that a white shirt with black breeches and silk stockings would suffice.

Stoner bowed low and smiled widely. 'Mr Hill, a pleasure. Charles has indeed told me much about you and I look forward to hearing more.'

Thomas returned the compliment. 'And he has spoken highly of you, sir. I trust we shall soon be well acquainted.'

Charles was in a jovial mood. 'Excellent, excellent. Come into the drawing room, gentlemen, and let us take a glass while we wait for the other guests. Mary has taken Louise upstairs to attend to her hair. They will be down shortly.'

Fortified by Charles's French brandy, the three men talked amiably while they waited. They spoke of the new feeling of hope in London, theatres and taverns reopening, dancing no longer banned, and their new king. They agreed that Charles II showed none of the debilitating lack of confidence of his father and shared the hope that he would soon tire of bloody reprisals. They were optimistic for the future. With Charles in such good humour and

Stoner a man of easy charm and wit, conversation flowed and Thomas found himself warming to his fellow guest.

Mary and Louise soon appeared. They could hardly have been more different. While Mary was as striking as ever in pale blue silk and silver slippers, Louise was a plain woman, a little plump, with mousey brown hair and a sallow complexion. Her dress and shoes matched the colour of her hair. When Mary introduced her as Chandle's sister, Madame Louise d'Entrevaux, Thomas bowed and took the proffered hand with a polite '*Enchanté, madame.*' He was favoured in return with the thinnest of smiles and a slight inclination of the head. On first acquaintance it was hard to believe that she was Chandle Stoner's sister.

When the other two guests arrived, they were both a little bedraggled by the rain now beating down, which must surely have put paid to the fireworks. Joseph Williamson was no more than thirty, tall, with dark eyes and thick eyebrows. He wore a long black wig to his shoulders and a fashionably long silk coat over his shirt. An indoor man, thought Thomas; probably never sits on a horse and seldom sees the sun. It took him a while to realize that Williamson's left eye did not move as it should, which gave him a disarming way of peering at people. He greeted Thomas and Stoner courteously enough but of Stoner's natural charm he too had none.

No one could have said the same about his cousin Madeleine Stewart. One look at her and Thomas knew at once what Mary was up to. Slim, with a face too angular to be conventionally pretty — it would take a Rembrandt to do justice to its planes — thick brown hair piled high on her head, china-blue eyes and modestly dressed in cream and pink, Madeleine Stewart would have turned heads in the grandest of circles. Only the fine smile lines at her eyes suggested her age as more than twenty. When she offered her hand to Thomas, she looked directly into his eyes and said something about the pleasure of meeting Mary's brave friend at last. Thomas's educated nose caught the fragrance of roses. He managed a feeble bow.

At dinner Chandle Stoner dominated the conversation. He alluded once to his 'dear late wife', but offered no information about her. He described himself as a financier and philanthropist and spoke earnestly of the importance of integrity and discretion in business. He was clever and witty, if a little self-important, and vague on what exactly he financed or to whom he was philanthropic. Charles clearly held him in high esteem and when he rose to propose a toast to all those present and 'even greater prosperity', it was to Stoner that he raised his glass.

Stoner's plain sister, however, made no effort to contribute, confining her conversation to monosyllabic replies to Charles's gallant efforts to draw her out. She said only that she lived in Paris and was married to a Doctor of Theology at the Collège de Sorbonne. Thomas was lucky that Joseph Williamson sat between them, although he too was no Ben Jonson. Other than to confide that he worked in the office of the secretary of state, Sir Edward Nicholas, on matters of security, Williamson too revealed little about himself. It was only when Mary mentioned Thomas's skill with codes and ciphers that he became animated. He asked how Thomas had come to have an interest in such matters and what he knew about them. Thomas allowed himself to be drawn on his methods of decrypting intercepted parliamentary despatches when with the late king at Oxford and how he had found a way to break the Vigenère square. And at Mary's prompting, he confessed to having used his knowledge to decipher a despatch from Sir George Ayscue to Colonel Thomas Modyford, which alerted the governor of Barbados, Lord Willoughby, to Modyford's intention to desert the cause of the king and join Ayscue's invading force.

He did not mention that in the one case he had prevented the queen and her unborn child from being captured and held to ransom by Parliament or that in the other he had helped avert what would have been a catastrophic battle on a small island. Williamson listened carefully, then asked about the latest developments in cryptography and whether Thomas had retained his interest in it. When Thomas assured him that 'once a cryptographer, always a cryptographer', he nodded wisely.

On the other side of the table Stoner turned his charm on Madeleine Stewart, and in between answering a question from Williamson on the analysis of the relative frequencies with which letters of the alphabet typically appear and another on the use of mis-spellings and nulls, Thomas wished that she would stop smiling at the man and turn her attention to him. Why had Mary placed him beside the educated but dull Williamson and not the lovely Miss Stewart? Was it one of her tricks or had he been mistaken? Cruel woman. He would have words with her later.

After an eel and oyster pie and an enormous shoulder of mutton, the diners talked of rising levels of crime in the city. Despite a general mood of relief at the end of the dreary republic, the news sheets were full of reports of robberies, housebreakings and assaults. And the brutal murders of Matthew Smith and Sir Montford Babb, both respectable gentlemen, had caused widespread alarm in coffee shops and salons all over town.

'I know Lady Babb,' said Madeleine. 'Montford was such a kind man. It was a dreadful thing.'

'It certainly was, my dear,' agreed Mary. 'An elderly gentleman attacked, robbed and killed in the street, and all for the contents of his purse. Let us pray it is not a sign of things to come or we shall be wishing for Cromwell to return from his grave to restore order.'

'I doubt that,' said Charles, 'though that part of the city, so I'm told, is singularly nasty. I can't imagine what either of the victims was doing there.' He looked around the table. 'Did you know them, Joseph?'

'I knew Smith.'

'I knew Sir Montford,' said Thomas. 'The Babbs once lived near Winchester. The murders were foul affairs, by the sound of them. What about you, Chandle?'

Stoner stroked his beard. 'I may have met them. It's hard to be sure. One meets so many people in the course of business. In any event, I don't remember them. The crimes were robberies, weren't they?'

'The coroner thinks so,' replied Williamson, 'although the man's about as much use as a piss-pot with a hole in it, so I doubt we'll ever know.'

Mary pretended to be shocked. 'Really, Joseph, it's not like you to say such a thing. Can he be that bad?'

'He can. Seymour Manners has always been incompetent. Now he's a hopeless drunk as well.'

'Don't you think they were robberies, Joseph?' asked Charles.

'I daresay they were, and by the same man. Both found in Pudding Lane and both with their throats cut. But if there was some other motive for either of them, the murderer would still have taken his victim's purse, just to make it look like a robbery. That wouldn't have occurred to Manners.'

Thomas heard something in Williamson's voice that hinted at more than he was saying. He was searching for the right words to enquire further without giving offence, when Stoner chimed in.

'Oh, come now, sir, Manners cannot be that bad, and in Pudding Lane after dark what motive could there be other than robbery? Why Smith or Babb was there I could not begin to guess, but robbery it most certainly was.'

They were about to tackle a large cheesecake and an even larger bowl of fruit when Smythe came in carrying a letter on a silver tray. He looked embarrassed. 'Excuse me, Mr Carrington, this letter has just arrived for Mr Williamson. I was reluctant to interrupt you but the messenger said it was most urgent.'

'Then you had better give it to Mr Williamson,' replied Charles with a frown.

Williamson broke the seal and unrolled the letter. 'My apologies, Mary. I always let the duty clerk know where I am in case of some emergency. He would not have sent this unless it was important.'

'We quite understand,' she replied, with the tiniest hint of disapproval.

He read the letter quickly. 'You must forgive me. There has been another murder. A man named John Winter who worked for me. I must go at once.'

All four men were on their feet. Charles spoke first. 'Smythe will fetch your carriage to the front door, Joseph.'

'I am so sorry,' said Madeleine. 'Another murder. And of one of your own men. How dreadful.'

Thomas and Charles accompanied Williamson to his carriage. 'John Winter was a good man,' he said quietly. His voice trembled and he was clearly shaken.

In the dining room Chandle Stoner was gallantly offering comfort to the ladies, none of whom needed much comfort.

Indeed, Louise d'Entrevaux looked positively uninterested.

'I have never seen Joseph so flustered,' said Charles. 'Do stay, though. There's no point in letting this cheesecake go to waste.'

'Yes, do stay,' agreed Mary. 'The cake was made with rose-water. I'm sure you'll like it.'

Charles cut thin slices for the ladies and thicker ones for the gentlemen. 'There you are. Eat up and then we'll share a bottle of brandy. A new consignment arrived yesterday from France. I am keen to try it.'

An hour later they were sitting around the fire with the brandy bottle to hand. Thomas had learned much about Chandle Stoner, nothing about his sister and very little about Madeleine Stewart. Other than that she was unmarried and lived with her housekeeper in a small house near Fleet Street, he was none the wiser. He made one last try. 'Have you relatives in London, Miss Stewart?'

'Only Joseph.'

'Perhaps I shall have the pleasure of meeting you again while I am in London.' This, at least, produced a smile.

'I expect so. London may be large but we all move in such small circles that I daresay we shall run into each other again.' Madeleine turned to Mary. 'I think I should be getting home now, Mary.'

'Would you like one of the gentlemen to escort you?'

Thomas opened his mouth to speak. He was too late.

'We will escort you back with pleasure,' said Stoner. 'Why not travel in our carriage? Yours can follow behind and we will go on after seeing you home.'

'Thank you, Chandle. That would be kind. These murders have made me quite nervous.' Thomas bit his tongue. Beaten to it by Stoner. Damned irritating.

'Well,' said Mary, when they had left, 'a day that starts with a coronation and ends with a murder does not come along all that often. It has quite exhausted me and I shall leave you gentlemen to the brandy.'

When she had retired, Thomas asked Charles about his fellow guests.

'Madeleine Stewart is a dear friend of Mary,' said Charles. 'She must be about thirty-five, despite looking twenty, and no one can understand why she has never married. She has never said a word about it. Chandle Stoner is a sound fellow. A little pompous, I grant you, but very astute in business. He's done well for us. His dull sister I can tell you nothing about. I wonder he asked to bring her. Joseph Williamson is much more important than he chooses to admit. The king holds him in high regard. What did you make of him?'

'An intelligent man. He seemed most interested in my work with codes. I thought Madeleine Stewart delightful. You should tell Mary, however, that if the lady has resisted all approaches so far she's unlikely to take much notice of one from me.'

Charles laughed. 'You're right, my friend. Why would she be interested in an ageing cryptographer who's been imprisoned twice and deported once?'

'Why indeed?'

Chapter 4

Thomas and Mary arrived at the Salisbury Court Theatre a few minutes before the performance was due to begin. They hurried past the press of beggars, cutpurses and urchins who had gathered to take their chances with the theatre-goers, to the theatre entrance, where a plaque on the wall informed them that it had been known previously as the Whitefriars Theatre and before that had been the site of a Carmelite monastery. Thomas grinned at the thought. Players for prayers — a sign of the times.

He produced the money to pay for their seats — while most of the audience would stand, a few would pay the extra cost of a seat — and Mary took his arm. They wriggled and elbowed their way through the crowd to their places in the middle of a row of raised chairs at the back.

It was a small theatre, big enough for no more than a hundred or so, and unlike the open theatres in the city, protected from the weather by a roof. Candles had been lit and placed on sconces around the walls. 'Intimate' and 'noxious' were the words that occurred to Thomas. Even from the back they would see the features of the players clearly, but a hundred bodies packed together like stalks of corn in a field were producing a fearsome stench. Thomas hoped the play would make up for it.

It did not. He managed to pay attention for the first two acts but by the middle of the third his mind was wandering. Three brutal murders — one victim a harmless old man, the others Williamson's employees. Could there be more to them than robbery? Was there a connection between them, and if so, what? Or was the murder of Babb just a coincidence?

He was jolted back to the present by a sudden commotion in the audience below them. On the stage Deflores had cut off Alonzo's finger to get at his ring and was holding up the bloody digit for the audience's inspection. A woman in the middle of the pit had fainted at the sight and those nearby were trying to clear a space around her. At such a dramatic moment, however, the audience behind her did not care to be cleared away and were standing their ground. A scuffle broke out and in no time fists were flying and women were shrieking. A fat man was pushed from behind and fell. Two or three others stumbled over him and were struggling to get up. In seconds, the play was forgotten and all semblance of order had disappeared.

While the actors quietly left the stage — perhaps being accustomed to such things — the commotion turned to panic. The audience surged towards the back of the pit where a narrow gang-way between the raised seats led to the front entrance. Bodies desperately tried to push through spaces that did not exist and were shoved back by other bodies. Some of those with seats left the platform and joined the melee, getting nowhere and making matters worse. 'Better stay put,' breathed Thomas into Mary's ear, putting an arm around her. Mary nodded and they stood together on the platform, waiting for the crush to ease and the panic to subside.

The crush, however, did not ease. Panic became chaos. A tall man reached over the rail and grabbed a chair from the platform. He smashed it on the floor and flayed those around him with a leg. Two others turned on the man, knocked him down and kicked him about the head. There was no sign of the crowd thinning and Thomas realized that the front entrance must in some way be blocked. If so, things could only get worse. Theatres with wooden walls and ceilings were notorious fire traps and if a candle fell or the ash from a pipe was tipped out, chaos might become conflagration.

'Don't let go,' shouted Thomas, taking Mary by the hand and leading her to the end of the platform furthest from the door. He hopped over the rail and reached back to help Mary do the same. Without hesitating, she hitched up her skirts and clambered over. The fight for the door had left a narrow gap along the wall. They inched their way along it towards the stage, Thomas using his feet and elbows to widen the gap, while Mary hung on grimly to the collar of his coat. They had almost reached the stage when a flying fist caught Thomas in the eye and sent him sprawling, leaving Mary unprotected. Thomas took only a few seconds to recover his senses and get to his feet, but in those seconds Mary had disappeared, swallowed up by the press of bodies trying to get out. He backed against the wall and strained to catch a glimpse of her. A few determined kicks and he would get to her. But there was no sign of her.

He forced his path to the stage, jumped up and found his way around the back to a narrow passage with two doors leading off it.

The first door opened into a room full of costumes, the second into a tiny bedchamber. He followed the passage to where it turned sharply to the right, and saw a weak light coming from under another door. He pushed it open and found himself in a small courtyard surrounded by a high wall, in which there was a single, very low door. He crouched to get through it, and ran round behind a short row of houses to Fleet Street and back down to Salisbury Court.

A small crowd had gathered outside the theatre entrance, where a man with a large ring of keys was trying each of them in turn in the lock. Although the cries from the audience inside could be heard clearly, the man appeared to be in no hurry. A few of the players had joined the onlookers but there was nothing much they could do other than stand and watch. Thomas tapped a player on the shoulder. 'Could we not get them out through the back?' he asked.

Alonzo shrugged theatrically. 'If you've seen the back way out, it's not worth trying, even if they can be made to listen. Audiences are the same everywhere. Herds, flocks, swarms, audiences. Just the same.'

'Why is this door locked?'

'I do not know. It should not be.'

The man with the keys was still trying each one in turn and showing no inclination to hurry. Thomas stepped forward and grabbed the keys from him. 'For God's sake, man, there are women in there. We must make haste.'

Thomas tried a key which did not turn in the lock. He tried another. That too would not turn. The third, however, did and he heard the lock slide open. But when he pushed the door it barely moved. The press of bodies against it was too great. Two burly men from the crowd came forward and put their shoulders to it. Thomas shouted for those inside to make way and gradually the door opened enough for the first person to slip through. Once a few were out, it became easier and a trickle of dishevelled theatre-goers soon became a steady stream.

Thomas stood to one side, watching them leave and waiting for Mary to appear. He saw nothing more serious than cuts and bruises and frayed tempers, and expected her to be in one piece. But when the stream dried up, she had not appeared. He rushed inside and looked around the empty theatre. He clambered on stage and around the back. He looked in the bedchamber and the costumes room. Still no sign. He turned back and went outside. Perhaps he had missed her.

By then the only people left in the court were the group of players and Mary, looking not the slightest bit put out and chatting happily to Alonzo. 'There you are, Thomas,' she said when she saw him. 'Oh dear, I fear your eye will spoil your looks for several days.'

Thomas had forgotten his eye and put his hand to it. It was swollen and tender. 'Never mind my eye, madam. Where have you been, may I enquire?'

'*Calme-toi*, Thomas. I left by the back door as I imagine you intended me to. I could not reach you and I knew you would follow me.'

'Mary . . .'

'Tush, Thomas, all's well that ends well.' She gestured to Alonzo. 'This gentleman tells me it is not uncommon for his finger to cause problems in the audience and the players have agreed that if it does, they will leave the stage quietly until order has been restored.'

'On this occasion, however,' said Alonzo, 'order was not restored, so we all left through the yard. God knows why the door was locked.' That reminded Thomas of the man with the keys. He had struggled to find the right one, but Thomas had got it at only the third attempt. Surely even a drunken oaf could have done better. He looked around. The man had disappeared.

'Come along, Thomas,' said Mary brightly, 'we must take you home and bathe your eye. Charles will be most amused to hear of our adventure. Goodbye, sir. Perhaps we shall come to the play again and hope to see it all.'

Alonzo swept off his hat and bowed extravagantly. 'I do hope so, madam.'

'Another conquest, Mrs Carrington,' muttered Thomas as they walked back to Piccadilly, 'and if you so much as hint that I was knocked down and lost you, your husband will hear of it.'

Mary laughed. 'Be assured, sir, that he will indeed hear of it, because I shall tell him myself. It does him good to be jealous from time to time.'

They found Charles sitting in front of the fire, a glass in his hand. 'How was the play?' he asked, slurring his words a little. 'You're home earlier than expected.'

'I found the first half a trifle slow,' replied Thomas, 'but it warmed up later.'

'And you, my dear, did you enjoy it?'

'It was unexpected.'

Charles beamed at them. Then he noticed Thomas's eye. 'Are you sure it was the theatre and not a prizefight? Your escort appears somewhat the worse for wear.'

'Quite sure,' replied Thomas, with a glare at Mary. 'There was a minor disturbance, nothing more.'

Charles nodded, refilled his glass and patted his stomach. 'I, too, had a good evening. Chandle is full of confidence about the venture. He even suggested that we increase our investment.'

'What did you tell him?' asked Mary.

'I said we would consider it.'

That night, after soothing his eye with a cold compress, Thomas thought of Plato. *Life must be lived as a play*, the great philosopher had said. Surely he had meant a play with a beginning, a middle and an end, not one cut short by fear and panic. If Thomas's visit to London was an act in his own play, he hoped it would be a good deal less dramatic than a Greek tragedy.

CHAPTER 5

Three days later, Thomas decided to visit an apothecary who offered an efficaceous remedy for gout; having tried potions and salves supplied by any number of charlatans — so far with little success — he hoped for something better from an apothecary in Cheapside, of whom he had heard good reports. He sometimes thought that gout was the one thing he had in common with the late Lord Protector. At least the walk would give him an opportunity to see the city for himself, to buy a news sheet and perhaps to visit one of the new coffee houses.

Lavender handkerchief pressed to his nose and purse tucked safely inside his shirt, he strolled slowly along the Strand and Fleet Street, the better to take in the noise and bustle. In the Strand, he was accosted by a pair of well-dressed young gentlemen, neither of whom could have drawn a sober breath since the eve of the coronation, and forced to toast the new king with a drink from their bottles. Halfway along Fleet Street, he passed a couple noisily copulating in a doorway, and on Ludgate Hill he stopped to buy a stick of sugar from a street vendor. The coins were barely out of his purse before he found himself surrounded by insistent vendors of pastries, herrings, garlic, milk, ale, daffodils and the Lord only knew what else. He shouldered his way past them, up the hill and through the narrow streets towards Cheapside.

In Bread Street he declined an offer from a girl who could not have been much more than twelve years old. Partially covered in filthy rags, her face and hair streaked with the grime of a hundred coal fires, bare-footed and bare-headed, she would be lucky to see another Christmas. As the Puritans had abolished Christmas fourteen years earlier, she could never have seen one. He was reminded of the filth and squalor he had witnessed in Oxford at the start of the war. Beggars and whores, mutilation, disease, death. Not wishing to dwell on that terrible time, he put it out of his mind and hurried on.

Streeter's Apothecary stood at the junction of Cheapside and Bow Lane. Thomas paid for a small jar of Master Streeter's mixture of honey, rosemary, goat droppings and his 'particular ingredient, imported at great cost from the island of Jamaica', put it in his pocket and set off along Poultry and Cornmarket to Threadneedle Street. There he bought the day's news sheet from a vendor and found a seat at a small table in Turrell's coffee house near the church of St Katharine Cree. He ordered a dish of Turkish coffee for a penny and spread the news sheet on the table.

The murder of John Winter was reported on the front page. His body had been found in the evening of the day of the coronation, in the graveyard of St Olave's church. The coroner, Seymour Manners, had inspected the body and judged the cause of death to have been strangulation. The deceased's identity had been established by an inscribed silver watch found in his coat pocket. As the dead man carried no money the coroner had expressed the view that robbery was certainly the motive, the thief having been disturbed before he could remove the watch.

The writer of the article speculated about the reason for Mr Winter being in such a place, suggesting that he might have overdone his celebrations on coronation day and lost his way among the tangle of streets in that part of the city. He made no mention of the murders of Matthew Smith or Sir Montford Babb.

Thomas was surprised that the coroner had not suggested a possible connection between the three murders — all the victims being well-to-do and respectable men, robbed and killed in unsavoury parts of the city — and wondered if Williamson's damning description of Seymour Manners might be on the mark. He finished the news sheet, left the coffee house and made his way back to Piccadilly. This time he did not stop to buy a sugar stick or a pie and was in the Carringtons' sitting room within the hour. He had just sat down and was about to apply the salve to his foot when Smythe came in with the silver letter tray.

'A letter arrived for you no more than a few minutes ago, Mr Hill. The boy was instructed to wait for your reply. He's in the kitchen.'

Thomas broke the seal and read the letter. It was brief.

For the personal attention of Thomas Hill Esquire
I should be much obliged if you would call on me tomorrow morning. At ten o'clock, if that is convenient. I have a matter of importance to discuss and upon which I should value your opinion. Please inform the courier if this will be convenient.
Your respectful servant,
Joseph Williamson, Chancery Lane

Thomas could think of no reason why it would be inconvenient. 'Thank you, John. Please tell the boy that I shall call as requested.' Smythe bowed low and went to do so.

Well now, Thomas, he wondered, what could Joseph Williamson, officer in the department of the secretary of state and adviser to His Majesty King Charles II of England, Scotland and Ireland, want to discuss with the likes of you?

When he arrived at Joseph Williamson's house in Chancery Lane at five minutes before ten o'clock the next morning, Thomas was shown by a steward into a large room which evidently served as both library and study. Books covered three walls from floor to ceiling, two library chairs stood either side of a coal fire and heavy curtains, half drawn back to allow some light into the room, hung at the windows.

Williamson rose from his seat behind a wide oak desk and offered his hand. The desk was precisely organized, with neat stacks of papers and a box of quills placed exactly between pots of black and red ink. Thomas noticed that the files open on the desk had even been given names. One had AUGUSTUS written in large letters on it, another CALIGULA. He was just able to make out that the AUGUSTUS file concerned Parliament. It was the desk of an orderly, precise, even obsessive man. 'Good day, Mr Hill. I am greatly indebted to you for coming at such short notice. Do be seated.'

He indicated a chair, politely sitting only when Thomas was seated and at an angle which favoured his right eye. 'Like you,' he began without preamble, 'I studied mathematics at Oxford. Now, as you know, I serve Sir Edward Nicholas in the office of the secretary of state. While Sir Edward is travelling, His Majesty has appointed me to deputize for him in all matters of security. That includes our work at the Post Office, as he considers it essential that a close watch is kept on correspondence that might pertain to the defence of his realm. We have many enemies abroad and at home. London is brimming with spies and malcontents, not all of them ruffians and vagabonds. Some masquerade as professional men. The medical profession is the most popular, possibly because a sick man is thought more likely to be indiscreet. This is a continual source of anxiety. I'm sure you understand.' Thomas nodded gravely, wondering when Williamson was going to get to the point.

'Our situation has been made worse by the re-emergence of some of the more extreme groups of dissenters. The Fifth Monarchists I believe we have finally dealt with by executing their leader, Thomas Venner, but there are still Levellers and Quakers, not to mention the so-called Diggers and Ranters, who are capable of the Lord only knows what. Unholy alliances are being forged under our very noses.'

Williamson went on. 'Not only that, but the king's arbitrary extensions to the list of those excepted from the Act of Oblivion do not sit well with the people.' He lowered his voice. 'Some of us wish His Majesty had stuck to his promise and executed only those who signed his father's death warrant. As the king himself said, he could not pardon them. But I believe it is unwise of him to hunt down others who did not sign the warrant and to deal with them as traitors. And if they must be punished, hanging would be enough. Quartering and disembowelling are unnecessary. And the digging up of bodies so that they could appear in court and be found guilty of treason before being displayed in public was, to be candid, absurd. Some of those put to death — Colonel Harrison, for instance — showed great courage and spoke with passion on the scaffold. Their words have had an effect. In my opinion, the king was badly advised to act as he did and we are now having to face the consequences.'

'Why has the king done this, I wonder?'

Williamson cleared his throat. 'The king's mind is subtle. I believe that he imagined that, without some reassurance, all those upon whom he wished to take revenge would disappear to Italy or Switzerland, or even the American colonies, as indeed some have. So he promised clemency to any surrendering themselves within two weeks, only to renege on the promise once he had them safely locked up. By such actions His Majesty is fuelling the flames. If the king can do this, the people ask, what else might he do? My informers are reporting growing unease and there have been unexplained disturbances.'

'Mary Carrington and I experienced just such a disturbance at the theatre.'

Williamson looked up in surprise. 'Were you at the Salisbury Court?'

'We were. It was most odd. A simple scuffle turned into a panicking bolt for the door. Which was locked.'

'So I understand. It was fortunate no one was badly hurt, although I notice you did not escape entirely unmarked.'

'Was it the work of dissidents?' asked Thomas.

'Probably. It fits the pattern of some other incidents without obvious purpose except to spread alarm. We are investigating the troupe of players. Now, my purpose in asking you here. Do you know of Dr John Wallis?'

Thomas knew the name well enough. Wallis had served Pym and Cromwell as a cryptographer and was highly regarded for his work. He nodded.

'Dr Wallis is yet another Oxford mathematician — we do seem to be rather a multitude — and until recently was a senior member of staff at the General Letter Office, the department of the Post Office which deals with the good ordering of public correspondence. As he has just been appointed chaplain to His Majesty and therefore has other duties to detain him at present, I must find a competent replacement. I had rather despaired of doing so until we chanced to meet at the Carringtons' dinner. Your name appears on none of my lists.'

'Possibly, sir, because it is eighteen years since I served the king's father at Oxford and I have taken no part in politics or society since. There must be many better qualified to serve than I.'

'I doubt it. Having made certain enquiries, not least of the king himself, I am satisfied that you are as well qualified as anyone to undertake the work I have in mind.'

'And what might that work be?'

Williamson cleared his throat. 'Before we speak of that, sir, have I your word that this discussion will remain confidential?'

Thomas raised an eyebrow. 'If that is your wish.'

'Very well. From the General Letter Office, which was restored four years ago, we despatch correspondence to our agents overseas. Much of this has to be encrypted and their incoming correspondence decrypted. We also look out for anything which might help us to identify threats to our own security. It is an embarrassment that our enemies use our Post Office for their own ends, believing it safer than a common carrier or special courier, either of whom might be arrested and searched when entering the country. Dr Wallis has been in charge of the decryption of intercepted correspondence.'

'And you would like me to take his place while the king requires his services as chaplain.'

'Exactly. You are a skilful cryptographer and your loyalty and discretion can be counted upon. You would be rendering a valuable service to your country.'

'I am obliged, sir, but I have not decrypted anything for years. Is there really no one better suited to the task? And I am not at home in London. The New Forest is more my natural habitat. I plan to return there within the week.'

'I quite understand. I have often thought of returning to Bridekirk, where I was born. The hills and the lakes are lovely. Somehow, though, I have just stayed put. It's the importance of the work we do and the challenges it presents.'

Thomas said nothing. He had half guessed that Williamson might come up with something like this. At dinner his interest in Thomas's experience with codes and ciphers had been more than mere courtesy. He was flattered, of course, but did he really want to stay in London and devote himself to this sort of work? Wouldn't forest oaks, fields of wheat and barley and brown trout from the river be more agreeable?

'I cannot force you to accept,' said Williamson, reading the doubt in Thomas's face, 'and I'm sure you can think of a hundred reasons not to. Bear in mind though that, as I have said, for all the gaiety and rejoicing, there are those in London who seek to overthrow our new king and replace him either with a new republic or with an interloper from across the Channel. I myself served Cromwell, as did many of my colleagues, but the last thing England needs now is to be thrown into another bloody war.'

'Do you believe that this could happen?'

Williamson nodded. 'I do. And there is more. John Winter and Matthew Smith were two of my intelligencers. I had hoped that Smith's murder was no more than a matter of his being in the wrong place at the wrong time, and when Montford Babb was murdered that seemed likely. Babb had no connection with our service. It looked like a vicious thief at work. With Winter's death, however, that has changed. Two of my men murdered, albeit in different places and by different methods, does not look like a coincidence.'

'How was John Winter murdered, if I may ask?'

'He was found strangled under a bush in the graveyard of St Olave's Church.'

'And Sir Montford Babb?'

'I do not know. Mistaken identity perhaps or plain misfortune.'

'Are there many like Winter and Smith?'

'Many, both here and overseas. They are essential to our security.'

'So you believe that the deaths of Smith and Winter were connected to their work?'

'I fear so. Both were sober and reliable. I would not have expected either of them to be in such mean places after dark. The best explanation is that they were lured there. On what pretext, I do not know.'

'Would Winter not have taken greater care in view of Smith's murder?'

'He did not know that Smith also worked for me. My agents operate independently of each other.'

'And after Smith's death, you did not tell him?'

'I did not.'

'And you see no connection with the murder of Sir Montford Babb.'

'I have considered it, naturally. There were similarities. But, as I have said, Babb had nothing to do with any government department. I believe he was merely the unfortunate victim of a robbery.'

'Yet the other two deaths have alarmed you.'

'I confess that they have. If our enemies knew about the two men, what else might they know?' Seeing a tiny smile play across Thomas's face, Williamson asked, 'You smile, sir. May I know about what?'

'I was thinking, as I often do, about something said by my favourite philosopher, Michel de Montaigne.'

'And what might that be?'

'*The public weal requires that men should betray, and lie, and massacre.* It's as true of one side as another, don't you agree?'

'That may be so. But you will not be asked to betray, lie or massacre. Merely to decrypt intercepted letters which may provide intelligence about threats to our king and to our national security. Will you do it?'

Thomas hesitated. 'This has come as a surprise, sir. Kindly allow me a little time to consider. You shall have my answer tomorrow.'

'So be it. I shall await your reply. If you accept, we will agree a suitable fee and I shall be able to tell you more. Would the Carringtons allow you to stay on while you are carrying out the work?'

They would, of course, although Mary would have something to say on the matter when Thomas told her what he was going to do. 'I should have to ask them, sir.'

'Naturally. Thank you for coming.' Williamson rang a bell on his desk and the footman came in. 'Please show Mr Hill out.'

'Yes, sir. And Miss Stewart has arrived.'

'Madeleine? I wasn't expecting her.'

'No, sir. She has called with some fruit for you.'

'Then I had better thank her.' He turned to Thomas. 'You remember my cousin Madeleine, of course. She keeps an eye on me. Always telling me to eat better food and to drink less claret.'

'It will be a pleasure to see her again. And most unexpected.'

In the hall Madeleine stood with a large basket of oranges and apples. She smiled warmly at Williamson. 'Good morning, Joseph. I trust I'm not disturbing you. One can find so many different fruits and vegetables in the markets now and I thought I would bring you some. And Mr Hill. What a pleasure.' She curtsied to Thomas, who bowed in return. 'Shall we have the pleasure of your company in London for long?'

Thomas caught the look that passed between the cousins. The artful young devil, he thought. Not as unworldly as he pretends. Well, two may play that game. 'I am not yet decided, madam. London has its attractions, but my home is in Hampshire. Good day, Mr Williamson, Miss Stewart.'

'Good day, Mr Hill.'

When he arrived back in Piccadilly, having taken a longer but quieter route from Chancery Lane, Thomas found that he had visitors. His niece Lucy, accompanied by a well-dressed young man with long fair hair, was sitting by the fire with Charles and Mary. The young man rose and bowed politely. Lucy jumped up and held out her arms to her uncle.

'There you are, Uncle Thomas. Arthur and I thought to pay

you a visit after our walk in St James's Park.' Lucy kissed him and turned to her companion. 'Arthur, this is my uncle, Thomas Hill. Uncle Thomas, this is Arthur Phillips.'

Thomas stepped forward and took the outstretched hand. Arthur Phillips smiled. 'An honour to meet you, sir. Lucy has told me much about you.'

Thomas raised an eyebrow. 'And how are you enjoying London, Lucy?'

'Until the coronation, I saw nothing of it. The duchess's gown kept me occupied, and Lady Richmond insisted that I go out only with an escort and for no more than an hour at a time.'

Unbeknown to Lucy, when Lady Richmond, a lady-in-waiting to the Duchess of York, had requested that she come to London to work on the duchess's coronation gown, Thomas had agreed only on condition that his niece was very closely chaperoned at all times. Much as he adored her, his niece was a spirited young lady, and especially since the death of her mother quite capable of thumbing her nose at custom and propriety. 'I am relieved to hear it. And since the coronation?'

'I have been asked by Lady Richmond to stay on for a while. She wishes me to embroider some furnishings for her new house.'

'I see. And do you wish to stay on?'

Lucy glanced at her companion. 'I do.'

Thomas stroked his chin. 'I am not sure, Lucy. Perhaps—'

'Nonsense, Thomas,' boomed Charles, 'of course Lucy must stay on. One cannot have too many pretty girls around if one wishes to stay young. And Arthur will take good care of her, won't you, Arthur?'

'I should welcome the opportunity, sir, if Mr Hill agrees.'

Handsome, polite and charming, thought Thomas. I'll

never drag the girl away. 'Tell me more about yourself, Arthur.'

Arthur Phillips made short work of it. His family were from Wiltshire, as was the Duchess of York's father, now the Earl of Clarendon. His lordship had graciously procured for young Arthur a post in the Navy Office in Seething Lane, where he was clerk to Mr Temple, supervisor of the refitting of the Navy's warships. The Duke of York being Lord High Admiral, it was through Lady Richmond that Arthur met Lucy.

'And do you hope to make a career in the Navy Office?' asked Thomas.

'If I am considered suitable, I do, sir.'

Damn me, thought Thomas, modest as well. Not that Thomas generally thought very much of modesty. An overrated quality, frequently false, usually boring and often confused with humility, which was quite a different matter. Still, pleasing enough in this young man.

For an hour or so they talked, and only after Lucy and her new admirer had left did it occur to Thomas that his niece had been without a chaperone. When he mentioned it, Charles looked sheepish. 'Sent her home. Looked like a painting I once saw of Guy Fawkes. Enough to give a fellow nightmares. Told her Mary would do the chaperoning. Hope you don't mind.' Charles clapped Thomas on the back and described Lucy as 'perfectly charming' and Arthur Phillips as 'an excellent young fellow'. He made it sound as if they were to be married the next morning.

CHAPTER 6

Thomas waited two days before sending his reply to Williamson. It was a discourtesy he would not normally have countenanced, but he reckoned it evened the score between them. Oranges or no oranges, Madeleine's arrival at her cousin's house had been no coincidence, although he would have agreed to deputize for Dr Wallis anyway, just as he had agreed to travel to Oxford all those years ago. Williamson was right. It was the challenge. Much as he disliked London and missed Romsey, he could not resist it.

And this time it was also the thought of seeing more of Madeleine Stewart, for all that his eligibility was as doubtful as Charles had pointed out. Despite the uncomfortable feeling that he was being drawn into a play in which he had no business taking part and which might well end unhappily, he sent Williamson a letter agreeing to carry out the work asked of him until the end of the year, unless Dr Wallis was released earlier from his chaplaincy duties.

When Thomas was met by Williamson at the entrance to the Post Office in Cloak Lane, beside him stood a man of about fifty who reminded Thomas of a suspicious spaniel — long black wig, large brown eyes and mouth turned down towards his chin. Williamson greeted Thomas warmly and introduced his colleague. 'Mr Hill, may I present Mr Henry Bishop, Master of the King's Post.' Bishop bowed politely, but said nothing. Thomas immediately sensed antipathy between them.

Inside, it was surprisingly silent. The good ordering of public correspondence was evidently carried out very quietly indeed. Clerks with bundles of letters and packets emerged from one door and disappeared without a word through another. Thomas wondered fleetingly if Post Office staff were obliged to take a vow of silence.

Bishop led them down a short passage and opened a door into his rooms at the end of it. 'Come in, gentlemen,' he said. 'My servant will bring us refreshment.'

When they were settled, Williamson took charge. This time he did not bother to hide his lazy eye. 'Thomas,' he said — it was the first time that he had used Thomas's given name — 'I am grateful to you for agreeing to come here. I know you would rather be elsewhere.' He smiled thinly. 'While you are here, please treat me as your primary point of contact, although of course Henry will always be available if necessary.' He glanced at Bishop, who politely inclined his head. 'Henry is responsible for everything that goes on in this building and at the Foreign Letter Office in Love Lane and for the safe delivery of all mail at home and overseas. He will explain how the Post Office is organized.'

Williamson studied his Madeira before continuing. 'As you know, I am employed by the king to gather intelligence pertaining to national security and as such often have occasion to work closely with Henry. Correspondence to and from our agents overseas is usually encrypted. You will be responsible for its encryption and decryption. In addition, intercepted correspondence, particularly to and from overseas addresses, is a fruitful source of information. Some of it is encrypted. The decrypting was carried out by John Wallis and will also now be your responsibility.' So far, everything was as Williamson had told him. Thomas said nothing.

'Henry has arranged for you to meet Sir Samuel Morland. Do you know him?' Thomas did not. 'Morland, as we did, once served Cromwell. He's a brilliant man — a fellow of Magdalene College, Cambridge, inventor, cryptographer and a distinguished linguist — but not easy to work with. To put it plainly, he's bombastic and rude.'

Thomas risked an interruption. 'If Sir Samuel Morland is as you describe him, he will be less than enthusiastic about my arrival, will he not?'

'Indeed. That is why we have asked him to carry out a special commission — the development of a new family of ciphers — while you deal with the day-to-day work.'

'Is he more enthusiastic about that?'

'Not very. He believes himself capable of both jobs. However, I think we have reached an accommodation.'

'It would perhaps be best if I did not do my work here.'

'I have thought of that. A room for you to work in has been prepared at my house. You will have everything you need. I suggest you call as a matter of course twice each week — shall we say Tuesdays and Fridays at ten o'clock — and I will send for you if anything urgent comes to hand in between visits. Would that be convenient?'

'It would.'

'Good. In that case, Henry will describe the organization of the Post Office while I drink his Madeira and then you will meet Morland.'

'I have also arranged for Lemuel Squire to join us,' said Bishop. 'I thought Thomas should meet him too.'

The name meant nothing to Thomas. 'Lemuel Squire?'

'Squire is responsible for the opening, copying and resealing of intercepted letters,' explained Bishop, 'and now that we use my mark, he has to work fast. All letters are stamped when they arrive. If their delivery is too long delayed, there are complaints. Squire and Morland are my two most senior officers.'

Thomas knew that Henry Bishop had introduced the 'Bishop Mark', which recorded the date of receipt of every letter at the Post Office and made the sender rather than the recipient responsible for the postage price. 'So copies must be made quickly?'

'They must.' Bishop paused. 'The mark helps prevent unwanted tampering, but it also affects our own activities. That is another matter Morland is addressing. Now the Post Office. All correspondence sent from London is either handed in here by the sender or delivered from one of our collection points in the city. It is sorted and stamped by our clerks, who come in at six in the evening on Tuesdays, Thursdays and Saturdays. Much of our work is perforce carried out at night. Indeed, the Clerks of the Road — there are six of them — who are in charge of the record and accounts books are provided with lodgings in the building.'

Thomas had never given much thought to the intricacies of the Post Office. Like everyone else, he took his letters to the Postmaster's office in Romsey and collected those addressed to him at the same time. But, of course, it took a large and complex operation to make such a service work.

'We have thirty officers and clerks working here,' went on Bishop, 'and thirty-two letter carriers in London alone. The Clerks of the Road and the local Postmasters are responsible for safe delivery of all letters and packets outside London.'

'What about overseas correspondence?' asked Thomas.

'Outgoing letters are taken to the Foreign Letter Office in Love Lane, where they are sorted by country and delivered by mail coach to the appropriate office — Yarmouth for Denmark and Holland and Dover for France, for example. From there they go by packet boat.'

'And incoming letters?'

'These are sorted in Love Lane and brought to us for onward delivery. We extract all letters which might need our, er, attention, as indeed we do from the inland post. They are given to Lemuel Squire, who decides what to do with them.'

'How do you know which they are?'

'We don't always know, but letters to and from Holland and France are routinely checked and we are aware of certain names and addresses here which require scrutiny.'

'Yet innocent letters must be opened in the course of the work.'

'That is so. If a letter is clearly harmless we simply reseal it and send it on its way. With our new techniques this is seldom noticed by the recipient. As Joseph knows, I do not condone this tampering with the mail, but I am obliged to accept it as a necessary intrusion.'

'Is there anything else you wish to know, Thomas?' asked Williamson.

'Let me be clear about this. Suspicious letters are intercepted by one of the clerks and given to Lemuel Squire, who opens, checks and reseals them. If necessary, a copy is made by hand.'

'Yes,' replied Bishop. 'An encrypted letter is always copied and the copy passed to Dr Wallis, that is until now. In future, encryptions will be brought to you at Chancery Lane.'

'In both cases are the originals sent on?'

'Other than in very unusual circumstances, they are. We do not generally want our enemies to know that we have read their correspondence and Squire is singularly adept at resealing it.'

'Quite so. And Morland – what exactly does he do?'

'Morland speaks and reads ten languages. He is in charge of translations and also assists with decryptions when the volume of work demands it. In addition to which, he is working on a machine which will greatly reduce the time needed to make copies of intercepted correspondence.'

'A brilliant man indeed. I wonder you need my services as well as his.'

'Morland's hands are full,' replied Williamson quickly. 'We need another pair.'

'Very well, gentlemen,' said Thomas, 'I have agreed to carry out this work and I shall do so, albeit with some reluctance.'

'Then it's time you faced Morland and Squire. Have a sip of Madeira and prepare yourself.' Bishop rang a bell, and asked his servant to show the gentlemen in. They must have been waiting out- side the door because they appeared before Thomas had taken his sip.

The two men were startlingly different. Sir Samuel Morland was in his mid-thirties, with long brown hair, a thin moustache of the type Thomas always distrusted and an even thinner mouth. He was dressed in the black coat and breeches of a Puritan and looked thoroughly dyspeptic. Only the silver buckles on his shoes offered the slightest nod to fashion.

Lemuel Squire, on the other hand, was a head shorter and might have been constructed from two spheres – the larger for his torso, the smaller for his head. There was no evidence of the connection between the two. A thick brown wig fell in ringlets to his shoulders and his eyes were hidden somewhere between bushy eyebrows and deep folds of skin. Thomas could not recall having ever before seen a purple coat matched with turquoise breeches. Only his enormous smile saved Squire from looking grotesque. He waddled forward and greeted Thomas warmly. 'Thomas Hill. A pleasure to meet you, sir. Lemuel Squire at your service. We've heard much about you and how you served the late king so gallantly. Have we not, Samuel?' Morland did not reply. 'Welcome indeed to our little world.'

'I'm obliged, sir,' replied Thomas, suppressing a grin. He was struggling to take this extraordinary man seriously. Morland still said nothing. Thomas turned to him. 'And it is a honour to meet you, Sir Samuel. I'm sure I shall learn much from you.'

Morland looked down his long nose. 'Doubtless you shall. Remember, sir, that Machiavelli himself said that a skilful prince makes a watchtower of his Post Office. Now if you will excuse me, gentlemen, I have important work to do.' And with that, he was gone.

Squire's laugh started in his ample stomach and erupted through his whole face. 'Don't mind Samuel, Thomas. He means no harm. Just a bit short on manners and fond of dramatic exits, that's all. Ah, is that Madeira I see? Excellent.' He helped himself to a glass and held it up to Thomas. 'To you, sir, and a successful outcome to your work.'

'I understand that you are in charge of opening and resealing intercepted letters, Mr Squire?'

'Lemuel, if you please. I so hate formality. Indeed, I am. We have excellent techniques for opening and resealing — far more advanced, though I say it myself, than those of the Dutch or the French — and Samuel is perfecting a machine for copying a page without damaging the original. It is most ingenious and will spare us having to employ armies of clerks to copy by hand at speeds which defy accuracy.'

'I should like to see it.'

'And you shall, Thomas. I shall show it to you myself.' Again Squire's plump face was split by the gigantic smile. It was impossible not to warm to the man. 'The king's dalliances in Holland and France are well known and there is talk of a Portuguese queen. The people fear a return to Catholic intolerance and there are continual threats from abroad. The Dutch and the French are invariably up to something. We have much opening and copying to do.'

So far neither Williamson nor Bishop had said anything. Mind you, with Squire in the room, thought Thomas, there's scant need for anyone to say anything. He talks enough for all.

'Well,' said Williamson, 'now that we've all met each other we'll let you get back to work, Lemuel, before you finish off the Madeira.'

Squire pretended to be put out. 'As you wish, sir. Good day to you all. I look forward to our meeting again soon, Thomas, and to demonstrating our work. Rest assured that I am at your service at all times.'

'And I look forward to seeing you again, Lemuel.'

'What a pair,' exclaimed Thomas when he had gone, 'an insulting inventor and a garrulous gargoyle.'

The corners of Bishop's mouth turned up slightly. 'Don't underestimate them, Thomas. Morland looks and sounds like a righteous Puritan, I grant you, and Squire has acquired a certain notoriety for his manner and habits, but both men are brilliant at their work.'

'I don't doubt it, sir. I shall treat them both with the utmost respect.'

'That would be wise, whatever you think of them. Although Squire has been with us for no more than a year, he has shown himself to be shrewd and reliable. He has an instinct for our work. Morland, like me, worked for Cromwell. I inherited him when I took over at the Post Office from John Thurloe, knowing him to be quite brilliant.'

Thurloe's name brought Thomas up with a start. He had been Cromwell's chief of security. 'I wonder then why you did not give Dr Wallis's work to him,' he observed.

'Allow me to answer that,' said Williamson. 'As you have observed, Morland is rude and arrogant, the kind of man who works best alone and in a locked room. He has no time for even the most basic social graces and I do not wish to work any more closely with him than I must. In addition to which, he is permanently short of money and demanding more. Does that answer your question?'

Thomas laughed. 'It does, sir. I shall treat Sir Samuel with respect.'

Back in his room at the Carringtons' house, it occurred to Thomas that spies and actors alike seek to hide behind a mask. He sat at a small writing table and scribbled idly on a sheet of paper.

Plato: 'Life must be lived as a play.'

The Post Office
Dramatis Personae

Joseph Williamson: spymaster for the new king
Henry Bishop: suspicious spaniel and master of the king's Post
Sir Samuel Morland: taciturn inventor, linguist and cryptographer
Lemuel Squire: spherical letter-opener and oenophile
Matthew Smith and John Winter: murdered intelligencers

He looked at his list, and added

Thomas Hill: ageing cryptographer and reluctant player

'What would the bard have made of that?' he said out loud.
'All we need is the murderer and we'll have a full cast.'

CHAPTER 7

The Dutchman did not have to wait long for his fourth task. The two in the lane and one in the graveyard had been simple enough. This mark, he was told, made a habit of visiting a brothel in Swan Lane every Friday, arriving at eight o'clock in the evening and leaving between ten and eleven. He was described as well built and answering to the name of Henry. His body was to be dumped in the river.

Before carrying out a job the Dutchman always familiarized himself with what he called 'the killing ground'. In Swan Lane he had identified the brothel and found an excellent spot behind a heap of rubbish from which to observe it. By sitting with his back to a low wall behind the heap he could watch the brothel door without the risk of being seen.

For this task he had been instructed not to use his hands and to use a different weapon. He had chosen a heavy iron bar, tapered at one end to make a handle and short enough to be hidden comfortably under his coat. The smith who had fashioned it for him had cut rows of nicks on the bar and prised up their sharp edges, so that it resembled a thick rose stem. It had never let the Dutchman down.

He had taken up his place behind the rubbish heap in time to see a man who matched the mark's description enter the brothel, and had sat there for a little more than two hours. Soon after ten o'clock, the door of the brothel opened and the man emerged. He was tall and broad-shouldered — a different proposition to the other three. The Dutchman touched his maimed face. Being careful to keep his head down, he rose silently to his feet and took the iron bar from inside his coat. He stepped out from his hiding place and was about to follow the mark up the lane when the brothel door opened again and another customer emerged. The Dutchman ducked down quickly. He would not risk an attack on two men.

The second man followed the mark up the lane. The Dutchman swore under his breath and was about to abandon the job — the first he had ever abandoned — when the second man turned down an alley off the lane. Without conscious thought, the Dutchman made a decision. Still holding the iron bar, he ran up the lane until he was just a few yards behind the mark. But the mark had almost reached the top of the lane where the streets were likely to be busier. He called out, 'Henry. Is that you?' The mark stopped and turned. The Dutchman raised the iron bar and leapt forward. But he had lost the advantage of surprise and this was no easy opponent. The mark was alert enough to parry the strike with his arms and aim a kick at his attacker's knee. The Dutchman sensed it coming, swivelled on his left leg and used the mark's momentum to push him face down on to the cobbles. He was on the prostrate man at once. One hard blow with the iron bar and blood gushed from the back of the mark's head. He lay still.

The Dutchman had to move fast. He might have been heard and someone might appear at the top of the lane. He would have left the body where it was and disappeared, but his orders were to dump it in the river. He stuck the iron bar back in his belt, picked up the dead man's ankles and dragged him back down the alley. He was a big man and it was hard going over the cobbles. It was also noisy. More than once he was tempted to abandon the effort, but he prided himself on always completing a task exactly as instructed, so he pressed on, ready to let go of the ankles and run if he had to. He was lucky. No one had heard the commotion and no one appeared in the lane. When he reached the bottom of the lane, he dragged the body over a narrow strip of shingle littered with empty bottles and rotting food, and heaved it into the river.

It was done. Not even stopping to recover his breath, the Dutchman walked briskly back up the lane and set off for the house in Wapping.

CHAPTER 8

For the first two weeks Thomas had been proved right. He spent his time encrypting dull messages to Williamson's agents in Holland and France and decrypting their equally dull replies. The few intercepted letters were easily dealt with, the most difficult being a nomenclator — a mix of letters and numbers — and he had been able to return every original with its transcription within twenty-four hours.

Despite not having used his skills for years, he quickly rediscovered what his old tutor, Abraham Fletcher, had called 'Hill's magic'. It was like riding a horse. Once you knew how, you never forgot, and his knack of visualizing the encrypter of a message soon yielded gratifying results. By seeing the man as young or old, short or tall, fat or thin, he could often divine what type of encryption he would have used. He found himself wishing for something more demanding. What was more, not one of the letters revealed anything more alarming than an enquiry about the date and strength of the next spring tide in the Thames and Thomas wondered why anyone had bothered to encode them. And he had heard nothing more about the deaths of Smith or Winter, or indeed of Babb.

On the day of Thomas's fifth visit to Williamson's house, however, matters took a new turn. He was awoken from a nap in his room just off the entrance hall by a loud knock on the front door and the arrival of a man with a loud voice.

'Josiah Mottershead, 'ere for Mr Williamson. I must see 'im at once.'

'Mr Williamson is upstairs and has asked not to be disturbed,' replied the steward.

'Tell 'im Mottershead's 'ere. 'E'll want to be disturbed for that.'

'I'm not sure, sir . . .'

'Mottershead. Just tell 'im.'

'Very well, sir. Kindly wait here.'

While the steward went to find Williamson, Thomas wondered whether to make himself known to this insistent visitor. The day's work had been particularly dull and he could do with a little excitement. He opened the door of his room and stepped into the hall. Josiah Mottershead was sitting in an upright chair, his hat in his hands and his hands on his lap. A stout stick rested against the chair. He jumped up when he saw Thomas.

'Josiah Mottershead, sir, to see Mr Williamson.'

'Yes, Master Mottershead, I know,' replied Thomas. 'I am Thomas Hill, an aide of Mr Williamson.'

For several seconds, the two men stared at each other, neither knowing what to say next. Despite being six inches shorter than Thomas, Mottershead was a powerful-looking man with muscular shoulders and thick legs. He had a nose that had been in more than one fight, a mangled right ear and a scar on his left cheek. He wore his hair tied back with a black ribbon and a short black coat and breeches, both of which had seen better days, and he held the stick not by the knot which formed its handle but six inches down the shaft. It took Thomas a moment to realize that Josiah Mottershead had unusually long arms for his height. While his right arm held the stick, the left reached almost to his knee. He did not immediately strike Thomas as a likely employee of the Post Office.

Williamson came bustling down the stairs. 'Mottershead. What the devil brings you here during the day? I see you've met Mr Hill.'

'Yes, sir,' replied Mottershead, 'I 'ave. Did you want me to speak in front of Mr 'Ill, or shall we be private?'

Not a man to mince words, thought Thomas. I wonder what he does.

'Both, I think,' said Williamson. 'May we use your room, Thomas? Do join us.'

'Of course,' said Thomas, holding the door for them, and thinking, Now I shall find out.

Mottershead did not stand on ceremony. 'Copestick's dead, sir. 'E's at the coroner's. I came at once, soon as I 'eard.'

Williamson's face was black. 'What do you know about it?' he growled.

'Not much, sir. 'E was found in the river a little upstream from the bridge. A wherryman pulled 'im out.'

'Did he drown?'

'Don't know, sir.'

Williamson stared at the floor. 'The devil's balls,' he said so quietly that Thomas barely heard him. 'Another one.' He looked up. 'We'd better go straight to the coroner's office before that fool Manners does something stupid again. He made an impossible mess of poor Winter before I got to him. Every shred of evidence destroyed. Drunken clod. Come with us, Thomas. We can talk on the way.'

Thomas was unsure. 'Is that wise? I have work to do here.'

'Nonsense. Another pair of eyes can't hurt.'

They were soon loaded into Williamson's carriage and trundling over the cobbles up Ludgate Hill towards Moorgate, where the coroner's office was located.

Williamson was visibly agitated. He rubbed his hands together nervously and tapped his foot on the floor of the carriage. 'This is very bad,' he said. 'Henry Copestick worked for me in the Post Office. His job was to look out for suspicious behaviour and to report privately to me on the conduct of his colleagues. If he too was discovered, we are in grave danger.'

'And what do you do, Mr Mottershead, if I may ask?' enquired Thomas.

Williamson replied as if the little man was not there. 'Mottershead is employed by me to gather intelligence. He's adept at judging the mood of the common man and reports anything he hears which has to do with our national security. His face is well known in the alehouses and taverns of London, is it not, Mottershead?'

'It is, sir, although only you know my real purpose in being there. I make sure no one else knows where I live or 'ow I earn my living.'

'Does no one ever ask?' enquired Thomas.

'If they do, sir,' replied Mottershead with a lopsided grin, 'I wink and do this.' He rubbed his finger and thumb together in the sign for money. 'They think I'm a thief and leave me be. It suits me that way.' Copestick's murder seemed to have affected him rather less than it had Williamson. In his line of work, he would have become accustomed to violent death.

'John Winter,' went on Williamson, 'performed much the same service as Mottershead but at a different level. Coffee houses and barbers' shops were his milieu.'

'So now we have four deaths,' Thomas observed. 'Sir Montford Babb, whom nobody seems to care much about, Matthew Smith, John Winter and Henry Copestick — all employees of yours, sir. It seems your concern was justified.'

'It is not a matter of caring, Thomas. I simply cannot see a connection between Babb's death and those of the others. Babb did not work for me in any capacity. He was an elderly man who kept his own company.'

'Yet, like Smith, he was found with his throat cut in Pudding Lane.'

'A coincidence, nothing more. Smith, Winter and Copestick were connected. Babb was not.'

Sensing that Mr Williamson was in no mood for further discussion, Thomas let it go.

When their carriage pulled up outside the coroner's office, Mottershead jumped out and rapped on the door with his stick. It was opened by an ancient clerk who peered suspiciously at them. 'Mr Joseph Williamson to see Mr Seymour Manners on a matter of urgent business,' said Mottershead, standing up to his full five feet.

The clerk looked down his nose at Thomas. 'And this gentleman?'

'Mr Hill is a senior member of my staff,' replied Williamson, 'and must be admitted with me. Mr Mottershead will remain with the carriage until our business is concluded.'

'Very well, gentlemen. I will see if the coroner will admit you. Kindly wait here.'

After five minutes on the doorstep, Williamson had had enough. 'Hand me your stick, Mottershead, if you please. We'll see if we can wake the drunken oaf.' Taking the stick, he hammered so hard on the door that Thomas thought he might break it.

The door opened and the clerk appeared again. 'The coroner is engaged, but asks you to wait inside.' He held the door open for them. Thomas and Williamson entered, leaving Mottershead to keep an eye on the carriage. They were shown into a small antechamber.

'Engaged, my liver,' muttered Williamson. 'Lying in a drunken heap, more likely.'

It was twenty minutes before the door opened and the coroner appeared. Seymour Manners had packed eighty years' worth of drinking into his fifty years on earth and it showed. Thomas assessed him from the top down — medium height, straggly hair to his shoulders, bulbous nose, broken veins, red eyes, black teeth, protruding stomach, stork's legs and a limp — and knew at once that Williamson's opinion of the man was justified. What was more, he smelt like an alehouse.

'Good morning, gentlemen,' croaked the coroner. 'My apologies for keeping you waiting. My stomach is troublesome today. How may I be of service?'

'We understand that you are holding the body of Henry Copestick. We wish to see it. That is, if you haven't already had it cut into small pieces.' Williamson's voice was brimming with distaste.

'And why, pray, would you wish to do that?' Manners' eyes narrowed.

'Henry Copestick worked for me.'

'Did he now? And what exactly did he do, sir?'

'That is none of your concern, Manners.'

'It is, sir, if you wish to see the body. I cannot allow just any-one to come in off the street and insist on seeing a body.'

'I am not just anyone, Manners,' thundered Williamson, 'I am employed by the secretary of state and, as such, I have every right to examine the body of a member of my staff found in the river.'

'And by whom was this right bestowed? I know of no law granting it.'

Williamson's temper snapped. 'Enough, Manners. We will see the body now or you will shortly be explaining yourself to the king. His Majesty will wish to know why you obstructed one of his officers and why you reeked of drink during working hours.'

Manners shrugged. 'If you are so anxious to see the body of a drowned man, sir, I will permit it. It is intact. Follow me.'

He led them down a passage towards the back of the building and across a small courtyard, where he unlocked the door to what might once have been a storehouse. Inside, Henry Copestick was lying on a low table, only his face showing from under a dirty sheet that covered his body. They approached it gingerly. Manners turned back the sheet. Copestick's clothes had been removed and no doubt the pockets had been checked for anything valuable. The body was pale and bloated, its eyes had gone and there was no mistaking that it had spent some time in the river. Thomas swallowed hard and took out his handkerchief to cover his mouth and nose. Williamson swore under his breath.

'Here he is, gentlemen,' said Manners smugly. 'Quite comfortable and waiting for a decent burial.'

Thomas squirmed at his tone. Despite the state of the body,

he could tell that Copestick had been a handsome man, well made and by the look of him more than capable of taking care of himself.

'Thank you, Manners,' said Williamson. 'You may leave us to carry out our inspection.' Manners stifled a protest, left the room and shut the door.

There had been no incisions, so Manners had not bothered to check for signs of drowning. They walked slowly around the table, looking for anything unusual. 'He must have been a strong man,' observed Thomas. 'He would not have been easily overcome.'

'He was. And he seldom drank. I cannot think that he would have fallen into the river.'

'What are these?' asked Thomas, pointing to a row of puncture wounds on his arms.

Joseph peered at the wounds. 'It's hard to say. If they were made by a weapon it was an unusual one.' They turned Copestick on to his front. The hair on the back of his head was thick and matted. When Thomas carefully parted it they could see a deep lacerated wound stretching from his crown to the nape of his neck. The dead man had been hit from behind with a heavy, rough-edged weapon and would have been dead before entering the water.

'Even Manners must have seen this,' said Williamson. 'Let's see what he's got to say about it. Fetch him in, Thomas, please.'

Manners was waiting in the courtyard. 'You noticed this, of course, Manners?' asked Williamson, indicating the wound.

'Naturally. I inspect all bodies brought to me.'

'And what did you make of it?'

'The wound is consistent with the deceased having hit his head on a rock or other sharp object when falling into the river. It probably killed him. If it didn't, he quickly drowned.'

Thomas and Williamson both stared at Manners. Could he be serious? This wound could only have been made by a blow with a sharp, heavy weapon. It was not made by a rock. 'Is that your opinion?' demanded Williamson.

'It is, sir. I saw no reason to suspect a crime.'

'Did you examine the wounds on his arms?'

'Of course. I could make nothing of them.'

'And what of his clothing? Did it show any traces of a struggle?'

'None. The clothing has been disposed of.'

There was no point in continuing the discussion. Manners was wholly incompetent.

'Then we shall bid you good day,' said Williamson brusquely, and marched back across the courtyard and down the passage to the front door. Thomas followed him. Mottershead was waiting with the carriage and opened the door for them.

'Why in the name of all that's holy is that man still a coroner?' exploded Williamson as soon as they were on their way. 'He should have been removed years ago.'

'Why would he choose to ignore what is obvious to us?' asked Thomas.

'Indolence. Plain indolence. If he suspects a crime he has to investigate it. That means work. Manners hates work. It interferes with his drinking and whoring. That's why, if he can get away with it, he reports every suspicious death as an accident. The man's a dangerous idiot.' Williamson's lazy eye had come to life and was fixed on Thomas. 'I cannot get rid of Manners, nor can I force him to investigate Copestick's death. Three of my agents have been murdered and he has not a single clue as to who murdered them. We shall have to make our own enquiries.'

'We?'

Williamson ignored the question. 'Mottershead, redouble your efforts. Visit every alehouse and brothel in London. Discreetly, of course, but fast. I want the culprit caught and questioned.'

'Count on me, sir.'

'Thomas, will you also keep your eyes and ears open? Visit coffee shops and barbers' shops. They're the places for gossip. See if you can find out anything.'

'Mr Williamson, I agreed to act as cryptographer for you while Dr Wallis is away. I did not agree to anything more, yet now I find myself inspecting bodies and being asked to stand in for a murdered man. With respect, you're not being entirely fair. You have agents all over London. Could you not find someone else for this?'

Williamson looked put out. 'Of course, if you're not of a mind to assist I cannot force you to. A man must live with his own conscience. I shall find someone else. He will not be as suitable as you, as few have your perception and experience, and his face will be better known than yours. He might even be a traitor. Still, if you would prefer not to serve at this sensitive time, that's an end to it. Will you be good enough at least to carry on with the inter-cepted correspondence? And please call me Joseph.'

Thomas was trapped. Agree to Williamson's – Joseph's – request or be made to feel disloyal. Shame and flattery. Twin blades in the hands of a very capable swordsman. He gave up. 'Very well, Joseph, if you put the matter like that I will do as you ask. No more, mind. I will simply watch and listen and report anything I learn to you. Nothing more.'

'Excellent. Whoever murdered Matthew Smith, John Winter

and Henry Copestick knew or guessed that they were agents of mine and has managed to leave not a clue as to his identity or the source of his intelligence. Between the three of us we must find him.'

'There is something else,' said Thomas. 'My instinct is still that Montford Babb's murder was connected to those of the others. I would like to find out.'

'I disagree, but in the circumstances I can hardly refuse you. My cousin Madeleine is acquainted with Lady Babb. I will ask her to arrange for you to meet her. Would that be a good start?'

I can think of none better, thought Thomas. 'Thank you. That will do well enough.'

That evening Thomas faced Mary's ire. 'How could you, Thomas?' she demanded. 'You promised me it would be no more than some simple work on codes, yet now you tell me that you have inspected the body of another murdered man and are to act as intelligencer for Joseph Williamson. What in the name of heaven are you thinking of?'

'I could hardly refuse,' replied Thomas. 'Joseph made it plain that in his eyes to do so would make me little better than a traitor.'

'And in my eyes, Thomas, you are little better than a fool. Why not go home to Romsey and carry on just as you were before?'

'Surely you are being a little over-dramatic, Mary? I am not being asked to take up a sword and slay a dragon, merely to gather information for Joseph.'

'You have a habit, Thomas, of putting yourself at risk. Oxford, Barbados and now London. I despair of you. Just don't come to me with a bloody nose and broken bones, even if you did save my life.'

'Mary, I assure you that there will be neither bloody noses nor broken bones. May I continue to stay here while I am carrying out the work?'

Mary shook her head and for a moment Thomas thought she was going to refuse. 'Very well. Stay here and keep out of trouble. I do not wish to see you hurt.'

'Thank you. I shall take care.'

CHAPTER 9

Three days later, Thomas was tucking into his breakfast when Smythe handed him two letters. The first was from Madeleine Stewart, requesting that Thomas call for her at ten o'clock the following morning when she would escort him to meet the recently widowed Lady Babb.

The second was from Lemuel Squire, inviting him to the Post Office to see the new copying machine in action. Squire mentioned that Sir Samuel Morland was away and suggested that an early visit would thus be wise. Thomas had planned a walk to Cornhill to take a cup or two of Turkish coffee at one of the coffee houses there. It would be his first effort at intelligence gathering. Armed with Squire's invitation, he would go to Cloak Lane on his way back.

The coffee house he chose this time was on the corner of Cornhill and Finch Lane. Two large windows on either side of the door allowed passers-by to see into a panelled room with one long table in the middle and several smaller ones around the walls.

Chairs had been set at each one. In mid-morning it was very busy and he had to wait until a table became free. He did not want to sit at the long 'common table' for fear of having to answer questions about himself. From where he sat he could read a news sheet, observe the room and hear much of what was said. He did not expect to learn much, if anything at all, but at least he was doing as he had been asked. He ordered a small dish of coffee from the *dame de comptoir*, a fearsome lady in an enormous wig and a flowing green gown, and looked about. A dozen well-dressed men sat around the common table, some talking business, others declaiming about the state of the country. News-sheet readers occupied the smaller tables. All were drinking coffee and many were smoking long clay pipes.

Their conversations were hardly the stuff of spies and traitors – complaints about the state of the roads and the price of corn, and gossip about friends and enemies. Thomas heard a young man talking about the problems of finding adequate stabling for his horses and an older one expressing the hope that he would never again be called upon to sit on one. He picked up a few remarks about the new king. His youth was a concern to some, his mistresses to others. But that was it. Gossip and banter only. Not a treasonable word.

Thomas was about to leave when Chandle Stoner arrived. When he saw Thomas he came over immediately to greet him. Stoner was in excellent spirits.

'Why, Thomas Hill if I'm not mistaken. And what brings a scholar to this place of vulgar commerce and common merchants?'

Thomas rose to shake Stoner's hand. 'I thought merely to sample the pleasures I have heard about. "Coffee, conversation and comfort" is how Charles Carrington described these new houses.'

Stoner laughed. 'Did he now? An admirable fellow, Carrington, and the lovely Mary, of course. Now, may I buy you another cup? I don't care for the common table today.'

'That would be most agreeable.'

Stoner ordered the coffee and took a seat at Thomas's table. 'And how have you been occupying yourself in London, Thomas, since we last met? Are you fond of the theatre?'

'I am fond of Shakespeare's plays, especially the comedies.'

'Ah yes, *The Merry Wives*, *Twelfth Night* – I do enjoy them. Thank goodness the theatres are open again and the players can earn an honest living. I gather many of the poor wretches were forced to take to crime during Cromwell's rule. The Lord Protector, indeed. The Lord Destroyer would have been more apt. While you are in London, you must accompany me as my guest to a performance.'

'That is most generous of you,' replied Thomas politely, thinking that after his recent experience he would prefer to stay clear of theatres for the moment.

Stoner enquired about Thomas's family and mentioned that his own family came from a small village in Yorkshire. Thomas thought it best not to ask about his late wife, and when he asked about his sister, Stoner said simply that she had returned to Paris. Then he asked whether Thomas had any interest in business affairs.

'Very little. I am fortunate enough to be adequately provided for and I have never sought wealth.'

'Fortunate indeed, sir. Most of us have to work hard to earn our daily crust. I myself am always trying to find profitable investments for myself and my friends. All very discreet, of course, and I choose my clients with care. Good opportunities are best kept confidential. If you should be interested, Thomas, of course I would be happy to advise a friend of the Carringtons.'

'Thank you. I do not wish to give offence, but I find that while it is sometimes wise to entrust another man with one's health, it is wiser not to do so with one's wealth.' He knew Stoner was being modest about his circumstances. Mary had told him that the Stoners were considerable landowners in Yorkshire.

Stoner laughed. 'As well not everyone agrees with you or I should be hard put to find a single client. And if you should change your mind, be sure to contact me. I have one especially promising venture in which I have myself invested and which I expect to produce an unusually high return. Do bear it in mind, won't you?' He looked at his watch. 'Now I must be away. Business calls. Good day, Thomas. And remember what I said.'

'I certainly shall,' replied Thomas. 'Good day.' A decent enough man, charming even. Land in Yorkshire and business in London. Clever, too.

At the Post Office, Lemuel Squire's welcome was effusive. Resplendent in sky-blue satin and silver-buckled shoes, he bustled out to greet his visitor.

'Thomas, my dear fellow, this is indeed an unexpected surprise. I had not thought you would call so soon.' He grasped Thomas's hand with both of his and shook it vigorously enough to dislodge his curled wig, which slipped over his eyes. Unabashed, he pushed it back on to his round head. 'Have you come from Piccadilly?'

'No, I've been sampling the delights of a coffee house in Cornhill. I thought I would return by way of Cloak Lane.'

'Splendid. What was the name of the coffee house?'

Thomas scratched his head. 'I fear I have quite forgotten. They are all so alike.'

'Was it comfortable?' asked Squire.

'Comfortable enough, and I happened to meet Chandle Stoner there. Do you know him?'

Squire took a small gold box from his pocket and made a show of opening it and taking a pinch of snuff before answering. He sneezed loudly and offered the box to Thomas, who declined it. 'Stoner? Chandle Stoner, you say? An unusual name. No, I don't believe I know him.'

'He's a friend of Charles and Mary Carrington. A man of business.'

'Ah, business,' sighed Squire. 'Quite beyond me, I'm afraid. Words I can manage, numbers remain a mystery. Now, let me show you the wonderful workings of our Post Office. Come and I shall lead.' Thomas followed him through the door by which he had entered and down a corridor with doors on either side. He stopped outside the last door on the right and with a theatrical sweep of the hand ushered Thomas inside.

It was a large square room, with a long counter down one wall and neat rows of wooden boxes lining two others. The counter was marked with each letter of the alphabet. Six clerks were busy taking letters and packets from the boxes, checking their addresses and that they had been stamped and putting them into leather bags or on to the counter. No one spoke or interrupted their work when Thomas and Lemuel came in. The atmosphere was one of hushed concentration and efficiency.

A bespectacled little man with a thin, pale face sat at a desk by the window on the far side of the room. He took a letter from the small pile on his desk, peered at it and put it to one side. When he glanced up and saw the visitors, he jumped to his feet and scurried over to greet them. 'Mr Squire, good morning, sir. Is all well?' The little man sounded nervous and Thomas noticed that his hands shook.

'Quite well, thank you, Roger. This is Mr Thomas Hill, who is deputizing for Dr Wallis.' He turned to Thomas. 'Thomas, this is our chief clerk, Roger Willow, who makes the Post Office run smoothly.'

Willow extended a limp hand. 'Welcome to our little world, Mr Hill. Mr Squire of course exaggerates. I merely oil the wheels, as it were.'

'Good morning, Mr Willow,' replied Thomas with a grin. 'Have you time to explain briefly how the wheels work?'

Roger Willow beamed. 'Certainly, sir.' He pointed to the counter. 'These letters are marked to be collected from here rather than delivered. As you can see, we sort them alphabetically. The clerks are putting outgoing correspondence into bags, which will be checked and labelled by a clerk of the road and sent on their way in a mail safe. Each bag carries a brass label with the name of the town to which it will be delivered. There are now over one hundred and fifty such towns along the post roads. The service grows every week.'

'I understood that the clerks work at night, Mr Willow. Yet here they are hard at it in broad daylight.'

Willow looked sheepish. 'When the volume of post is such that we find ourselves a little behind, we do also work by day. I fear this is such a time.'

'And suspicious letters?'

Willow removed his spectacles and wiped them on the sleeve of his coat. 'These are handed to me by one of the clerks or brought over from Love Lane. I take them to Mr Squire, who performs his mysterious arts on them, and then we send them on resealed.'

'You make it sound easy, Mr Willow, but mistakes must surely be made.'

'Alas, sir, they are. But we select our clerks most carefully and train them fully before allowing them to work unsupervised. A clerk who did not know where Wisbech is, for example, might put a letter addressed there in the Bristol bag.'

Thomas laughed. 'And that wouldn't do at all.' Throughout Roger Willow's descriptions, Lemuel Squire had said nothing and the clerks had taken no notice of them. Their work clearly demanded total concentration. 'Well, I am grateful, Mr Willow. My eyes have been opened and I am most impressed by your operation.' It seemed the right thing to say to a man who evidently took such pride in his work.

'Thank you, sir,' replied Willow. 'Do call again if there is anything else.' And with that, he inclined his head and went back to his desk.

Outside the sorting office, Lemuel put a hand on Thomas's shoulder and asked, 'What did you make of it, Thomas?'

'A swift and efficient business. And in Roger Willow you seem to have a most capable chief clerk.'

'Willow. Yes indeed. Most capable.' Thomas glanced at him. Had there been something strange in Lemuel's voice? 'Now let us examine the copying machine. Morland, as I said, is away this morning, so we shall not be disturbed. If he could, I fancy he would refuse ever to let anyone else near it. A brilliant man, but he can be most disagreeable.'

'So I've heard. And once a formidable supporter of Cromwell. Not a man to be taken lightly.'

Squire led him down a narrow corridor lined with doors. At the end, he took two keys from his pocket and opened two locks on the last one. 'Here we are now,' he announced grandly. 'Morland's copying machine.'

Thomas followed Squire into the room, which was empty but for a single table on which the machine stood, together with two piles of paper, a linen cloth and a small bowl of water. He walked round the table, examining it.

'Now, Thomas, allow me to demonstrate.' Squire patted the machine as if it were a favourite child. 'Bear in mind, however, that it is not yet perfected. Morland is working on an improved version. Still, this will give you a good idea of what we can do.'

He carefully laid a sheet of paper half covered in a closely written script face up on a metal plate which formed the lower half of the machine. Then he took another sheet from the other pile and held it up. 'This is tissue paper, made from good rag pulp.'

He laid the tissue paper on top of the first sheet, dipped the cloth in water and very gently pressed it on the papers until the top sheet was damp. Then he closed the top half of the machine by means of a handle at the side so that the two halves were held firmly together with the papers between them. After perhaps ten seconds, Squire raised the top half to reveal the papers. So carefully that Thomas found himself holding his breath, he lifted the top sheet to reveal that it had absorbed a mirror image of the writing on the bottom sheet. He replaced the original with the damp sheet and put a clean sheet from the first pile on top of it. He closed the lid again and waited another ten seconds. Then he reopened the lid, removed the upper sheet and, with a flourish, turned it over for Thomas to see.

'Now what do you make of that, sir?' enquired Squire. 'Ingenious, is it not?'

Thomas examined the paper and held it against the original. The mirror image had been reversed and it was clear and easy to read. 'Indeed it is, Lemuel. And how many copies can you make of one original?'

'As long as we keep changing the tissue paper, an unlimited number. One paper, however, will begin to mark an original after about six copies. Happily, we seldom need more than one immediately. We can always make more copies later from the first copy if we need to. And Morland is working on improvements.'

'So you can unseal a letter, make a copy, reseal it and send it on its way without any noticeable delay.'

'Exactly. You've put your finger on the matter. Those with access to this room can be sure of copying intercepted correspondence undetected. Now that we have Bishop's Mark, if the post is delayed there are complaints and questions are asked.'

'And who has access to this room?'

'At present only Morland and I. And Bishop himself, of course.'

The door to the copying room was thrown open and Sir Samuel Morland, his face a mask of furious disbelief, stood in the doorway. For a long moment all three men stared at each other. It was Morland who broke the silence. He pointed at Thomas.

'And what, may I ask, is the meaning of this? Who has given permission for this man to be here?'

'Now, now, Samuel, calm yourself,' replied Squire, taking a step towards him. 'We did not expect you to return so soon. I merely thought to show Thomas how your excellent copying machine works.'

Morland was not placated. 'To what end, pray? So that he can steal my invention or so that he can inform our enemies of it?' His voice had risen to a bellow.

'That is absurd, Samuel, and you know it. Thomas has been appointed by Mr Williamson to assist us in the absence of Dr Wallis. He is not a thief and he is as loyal to the crown as you or I.'

'He has no business being in this room. It is bad enough that I have been forced to relinquish my duties as cryptographer to an inferior man. That such a man who is not even an officer of the state should also be privy to our unique method of copying is intolerable. I shall inform Williamson at once and will lodge the strongest possible protest. No doubt he will reconsider Hill's position.'

Thomas spoke quietly. 'Your opinion of my competence as a cryptographer is your affair, Sir Samuel, although I would point out that it was I who broke the Vigenère cipher. However, your insinuation that I am anything other than loyal to the king is insupportable. I demand that you retract it at once.'

'And if I do not? Will you go whining to Williamson or will you challenge me to a duel?'

'Neither. I shall simply mark you as a ridiculous bag of wind whose feeble mind cannot grasp a simple fact and whose own loyalty is questionable. You did, after all, serve John Thurloe, Cromwell's head of security.'

Morland balled his hands into fists and took half a step into the room. Thomas thought that Morland was about to strike him.

Squire stepped between them. 'Gentlemen, please. Enough of this. Let us put our differences aside and repair to the Queen's Head.'

'Hold your tongue, Squire. This ignorant intruder needs to be taught some simple facts himself.' Morland rounded on Thomas, head thrust forward and eyes blazing. 'For your information, Hill, it was I who was sent to Breda to meet the king and I who helped pave the way for his return. I was warmly welcomed by His Majesty, who graciously conferred a baronetcy upon me for my services to him. Those are the facts and it is you, not I, who should withdraw your allegation.'

Thomas was on the point of asking why Morland had changed his allegiance from Commonwealth to Crown when Henry Bishop arrived.

'For the love of God, what is all this noise about? They can hear you in the post room.'

Squire held up his hands. 'It is nothing, Henry, just a minor altercation. We were about to visit the Queen's Head. Would you care to join us?'

Bishop looked incredulous. 'It sounded like rather more than a minor altercation. What have you to say, Samuel?'

To Thomas's relief, Morland had decided that this was not the moment to pursue the matter. 'It was nothing. I shall return to my work.' And with that, he was gone.

'I do not believe you, Lemuel,' said Bishop, 'but I shall let it pass. In future, however, be so good as to see that no further opportunities for such a disturbance arise. As far as is possible,

Thomas and Samuel are to be kept apart. That is why he has a room at my house in which to carry out his work. Lemuel, I look to you in this.'

'You may depend upon me, Henry. Now, will you accompany us to the Queen's Head?'

'I think not, thank you. Good morning, gentlemen.'

While devoting his attention to the finest the Queen's Head had to offer, Squire said very little. He even looked rather miserable, perhaps regretting having invited Thomas to Cloak Lane. Thomas watched him swallow cutlets of lamb, half a chicken and a thick slab of bread, all washed down with a pint of claret, and wondered that the sky-blue satins could take the strain.

Eventually, adequately refuelled, the little round man sat back and belched loudly. 'Far better out than in,' he announced with an angelic smile. 'Have you had sufficient, Thomas?'

'Quite sufficient, Lemuel, thank you,' replied Thomas, who had done no more than pick at a chicken leg.

'Splendid. Thomas, I do apologize for Morland's behaviour. Really, the man can be quite insufferable.'

'Think no more of it. You said that Morland is working on improvements to the copying machine. What might they be, if I may ask?'

'Certainly you may ask, my dear fellow. Some inks resist our method of copying. A letter written in such an ink must first be copied using a different ink. That, of course, rather defeats the object of the exercise. Morland is experimenting with crêped papers which will absorb any ink.'

'For all his temper and ill manners, Sir Samuel is an extra-ordinary man.'

Squire tapped the side of his nose. 'Extraordinary, yes. But *cave artem*, as my dear father was fond of saying.'

Thomas looked quizzical. 'What do you mean, Lemuel? Is Morland's loyalty really in doubt?'

'Good Lord, no. Dear me, no. Heaven forfend such a thing.' Squire mopped his brow with a large red handkerchief. 'It is merely the odd story about his change of allegiance which I have always found hard to believe.'

'And what story is that?'

'Morland claims that he overheard Richard Cromwell and John Thurloe plotting to lure the king from France to England — Sussex, I think it was — and to assassinate him there. He did not wish to be party to such an act and began sending intelligence to the king. It sounds unlikely to me.'

'Then why would he have changed sides?'

'Money, I expect. Morland's always complaining of not having enough. Perhaps he was paid.'

If Morland could be bought once, he could be bought twice. Thomas would have to take care. 'And you, Lemuel, what dark secrets do you have?'

Squire chuckled. 'None, alas, my friend. You see all of me before you.'

'But you cannot always have worked at the Post Office.'

'Ah, no. I was an actor, you know. A member of a travelling company of players until the theatres were closed. That is what convinced me that Cromwell was mad. Banning dancing and closing theatres, for the love of God. What on earth for?'

'Some misguided Puritan nonsense, I suppose. A man may not make up his own mind about what he believes in and how he conducts his life. He must be told.'

'Quite so. Absurd. Thank God all that is behind us now and the country can move forward. It was a dreary time.'

'Indeed it was.'

'And how goes the decrypting?'

'It's been easy enough so far. I would wish for something more demanding.'

'That's not very loyal, is it, Thomas? Wishing our enemies had better weapons, the more to test us? What would the king say?'

Thomas changed the subject. 'How well did you know Henry Copestick?'

'Copestick? Oh, not very well. Distant colleagues, you might say. He seemed a very correct sort of person to me. Not at all the man to be near the river after dark. I can't think why on earth he was there. None of us can.'

'What about the other murders?'

'The coroner thought they were robberies and I daresay he was right. All too common, I'm afraid. Why do you ask?'

'Idle curiosity. Just the devious mind of an ageing cryptographer at work. I'll stick to my codes.'

'Very prudent. It doesn't do to wander too far from home, if you take my meaning. The wise man sleeps in his own bed.'

Thomas laughed. 'Nicely put, sir. And now I must be on my way. Thank you for your company and for showing me the copying machine. Most impressive.'

'Do call again at any time, Thomas. I'm usually to be found earning my daily crust in Cloak Lane. We will avoid Morland.'

At exactly ten o'clock the next morning, Thomas walked briskly down a narrow lane running from Fleet Street to the river and knocked on the door of Madeleine Stewart's house. It was a small, single-storey house in the middle of a row of larger ones with over-hanging upper storeys in the manner of the previous century. Exactly the sort of house a single lady of modest means might live in with her housekeeper.

The door was opened immediately and Madeleine emerged dressed to go out — a broad-brimmed bonnet on her head and a short cloak over her gown. In deference to the newly widowed Lady Babb, the bonnet and cloak were a dark shade of blue.

She took Thomas's arm for the ten-minute walk to Lady Babb's house at the top of Ludgate Hill, where they found the old lady waiting for them in her mourning clothes — a black shawl over a black gown and a white cap.

Madeleine sat beside her with Thomas opposite. She offered her condolences, introduced Thomas and explained that he would like, with Lady Babb's permission, to ask her some questions about her husband. When Lady Babb asked why, Thomas told her that he fondly remembered Sir Montford from when he lived in Romsey. He apologized for disturbing her at such a time and said that he was in the employ of Joseph Williamson and had been given the task of gathering information about the recent murders to see if any connection between them could be established. It was vital that the culprit be apprehended before he could strike again.

'Very well, Mr Hill,' replied Lady Babb, 'but you must speak clearly. My hearing is not what it was. I doubt if I can tell you any-thing to help you as my husband was an unexceptional man and what he was doing in that part of the city after dark I have no idea.'

'Did he say anything about where he was going or for what purpose on the night he died?'

'He merely said that he had business to attend to and would be late home.'

'Was it his habit to be out late?'

'No. It was unlike him, but I thought no more about it.' She took a white linen handkerchief from her sleeve and dabbed at her eyes. 'I suppose I should have.'

'Nonsense, my dear Lady Babb,' said Madeleine, taking her hand. 'You couldn't possibly have foreseen such a terrible thing.'

Thomas allowed her a moment to compose herself before he continued. 'Lady Babb, did you notice anything strange or unusual about your husband's behaviour in the weeks before his death?'

'I have thought about this. Montford was a kindly man, not given to complaint or criticism. Yet he had started asking me about the cost of our household and pressing me to be less extravagant. He even suggested that we might manage with fewer servants. As you can see, we hardly lived in a palace.'

'Was he a wealthy man?'

'Comfortable, I should say, rather than wealthy.'

'Do you know what his business interests were?'

'He never talked of them. He inherited when his father died and, as far as I know, we lived on the income from the inheritance.'

Thomas tried a few more questions, but the old lady was tiring and had nothing more to offer. 'Just one more thing, Lady Babb, and we will leave you in peace. Did Sir Montford keep a journal or an accounts book of any sort?'

'He did keep a journal. It's in his study. He never told me what he wrote in it and I haven't touched it.'

'May I see it?'

Lady Babb glanced at Madeleine. 'It was his private journal. I don't know if anyone else should read it.'

'It might help us find his murderer.'

'How? The coroner said he was attacked and robbed.'

'Indeed he did, madam. But we would like to know why he was in Pudding Lane that night. Perhaps the journal will tell us.'

Lady Babb dabbed her eyes again and looked at Madeleine. 'The coroner did not ask to see it. Is it really necessary, my dear?'

'I believe it might be important. But only with your consent,' replied Madeleine gently.

'Then with your word that it will be returned just as you found it, you may take it. Please take great care of it.'

'Thank you, Lady Babb,' said Thomas, rising. 'You may rest assured that I shall take the greatest care of it and return it to you as soon as I am able.'

On their way out, Lady Babb fetched the journal and handed it to Thomas. 'Here you are, Mr Hill. I trust it will help.'

'Allow me a moment with Lady Babb, Thomas, if you please,' said Madeleine.

Thomas waited outside until she appeared, her cheeks flushed and her eyes red. 'I knew she was uncomfortable about your taking the journal,' she said as they walked down the hill. 'I just wanted to reassure her that you could be trusted. You can be trusted, Thomas, can't you?'

'To keep my word, naturally. To discover his murderer, I don't know. I'll start on the journal today.' Thomas escorted Madeleine home and returned directly to Piccadilly.

Thomas started on Sir Montford Babb's journal that evening. The pages were bound in soft black leather, the first entry dated

1 July 1656, so Sir Montford had been keeping it for nearly five years. Lady Babb had given no suggestion that there were any earlier journals.

To Thomas's relief the entries were in plain text, albeit with odd abbreviations and in Babb's spidery, sometimes illegible hand. Penmanship was not a skill Babb had mastered and he had been less than careful to ensure that the ink was dry before turning a page. Numerous blots and splodges obscured what he had written.

He had made an entry twice each week. Thomas did not try to decipher the illegible ones and concentrated only on those he could read with comparative ease. He chose a page at random. It was dated July 1658 and would do as well as any. But two hours later, having ploughed through a year of visits to friends and relatives, meals consumed, sermons listened to, tradesmen favoured with the Babbs' custom and detailed records of the author's health, Thomas wondered why the old man had bothered to keep a journal at all. Until his sudden death he had lived a wholly uneventful life and had held opinions on nothing. Other than his fondness for eels and his dislike of his cousin Prudence, he revealed very little of himself.

The next day, unable to face four more years of cutlets, constipation and communion, Thomas did something he used to do when faced with a stubborn cipher. He started at the end. Without knowing what he was looking for, it would have been more sensible to have done so in the first place.

The last entry was dated 16 April 1661, three days before Sir Montford's death. It dealt with breakfast and dinner, the cancellation of an order with his tailor for a new coat and Lady Babb's increasing deafness. The final sentence revealed that he was in despair about something he called 'AV'.

Working his way back through the year, he found no mention of Matthew Smith, Henry Copestick or John Winter and nothing to suggest any knowledge of activities at the Post Office. Not that he had really expected any. Life was seldom as simple as that. If there was a link between Babb's murder and those of the others it would surely not reveal itself so readily. The only entries to catch Thomas's eye referred to an investment in AV.

The first mention of it was on 30 June 1660, when Sir Montford declared himself delighted with some recent news of the enterprise. A number of entries continued in similar vein until January 1661, when he had been disappointed to learn that he could not sell part of his interest in AV because he had been planning to buy a house in Cheapside which was available at a good price.

By March, Sir Montford's disappointment was turning to worry and in April almost every entry mentioned AV with increasing alarm. Thomas remembered Lady Babb saying that her husband had started complaining about the costs of the household. Whatever AV was, it had not turned out well for the Babbs. Perhaps poor Sir Montford had been drowning his sorrows on the night he was murdered in Pudding Lane.

Having followed the AV trail backwards to its first appearance, Thomas had had enough. Sir Montford had made an unwise investment, he had lost money, he chided himself for his stupidity and it might have led indirectly to his death. He had not discussed the matter with Lady Babb and there was nothing to be gained by troubling her further. He would ask Madeleine to return the journal to her.

The Carringtons made a habit of spending an hour or two each morning in their sitting room, drinking coffee, reading the news sheets and exchanging views. It was a simple pleasure which plantation life in Barbados did not permit. That was where Thomas found them the next morning. The day was already warm and no fire had been lit, but the fireplace was still the focal point of the room and library chairs had been set on either side of it.

'Well now, Thomas,' said Charles in his cheerful way, 'we've seen little of you these past few days. What have you been up to and how is the gout?'

Thomas hesitated. Of course he could trust the Carringtons, but Williamson had impressed upon him the need for secrecy. 'Where the safety of the kingdom is concerned,' Joseph had said portentously, 'one must take not the slightest risk. Who knows where an enemy may lurk?' Well, no enemy lurks around this fireplace, decided Thomas, and I need to confide in someone.

'The gout is much improved, thanks to Streeter's mixture. I've been doing the encrypting and decrypting they bring me and going about Joseph's business as he instructed. And I've been reading Sir Montford's journal.'

'A good story, was it? Well up to Shakespeare's standards?' Charles was not much of a reader.

'Not exactly. As far as I can tell, Sir Montford led a dull and blameless life. I wonder that he took the trouble to record it.'

'No mistresses, no gambling debts, no secret confessions?'

'Alas, none of those. There was only one unexpected thing.'

'And what was that? He wasn't a French madame in disguise, was he?'

'No. Last year he made an investment in a venture he called AV. He didn't say what it was and at first it seems he was delighted with it. Then earlier this year something went wrong, he couldn't get his money out and he became worried and depressed. He didn't tell Lady Babb about it and I think he must have lost it all. It might explain why he was in Pudding Lane the night he was murdered. Drowning his sorrows, perhaps.'

'AV, did you say?' asked Mary. Thomas nodded. 'Have you heard of AV, Charles?'

'Don't think so,' replied Charles thoughtfully. 'We could ask Chandle, though. He knows what's going on in the world of business and he's done very well for us.'

'So you tell me, Charles. I know little of such affairs, as befits a lady.'

'Befits a lady? A lady who struck fear into the black hearts of the revolting Gibbes brothers, saved a wounded man's life, rescued one Thomas Hill from certain death and who knows at least as much as her husband about matters of business. What nonsense.'

'May I enquire how Chandle Stoner has been of service to you?' asked Thomas.

'Of course you may,' replied Charles. 'Thinking of making an investment yourself? Could do worse than take Chandle's advice.'

'Not exactly, Charles. Just interested.'

'Well, Chandle has his fingers in lots of pies, so to speak, and he knows where there's money to be made. We put a thousand guineas into an enterprise he recommended. He tells us our share is now worth five times as much and he expects it to go higher. Possibly much higher.'

'And what is the enterprise, if I may ask?'

'We swore not to reveal its name. Chandle prefers to keep his best ideas pretty quiet. Damned sensible if you ask me. We don't want the whole world clamouring for a share.'

'We can tell you it's a mining venture in the Americas,' said Mary, 'but that's all.'

'Mining for what?'

Charles laughed. 'Gold, silver, emeralds, rubies, and plenty of them, by all accounts. Should keep a man happy in his old age.'

'Isn't that what I'm for, my dear?' asked Mary.

'Of course, of course.' Charles cleared his throat. 'Helped by the money, that is.'

Thomas was intrigued. The Carringtons were not gambling types. They must think very highly of Stoner. 'How did you meet Chandle Stoner?' he asked.

'He was recommended to us by James Drax, a man who knows a thing or two about making money.'

'Indeed, and not a man to be taken lightly.'

'Anything but. James did well from another of Chandle's enterprises and suggested we contact him when we came to London.'

'Which you did, and I'm delighted it has proved so successful for you. Do ask him if he has heard of an enterprise known as AV, won't you? It may be something or nothing, but I'd like to know out of curiosity.'

'I will, next time I see him.'

Mary changed the subject. 'Did you have a chance to converse with Madeleine, Thomas?'

'Not really. The streets of London do not lend themselves to polite conversation.'

'So at least you did not bore her with talk of that damned Frenchman,' spluttered Charles.

'If he was mentioned at all it was but briefly, as I recall.'

'Good,' said Mary. 'A lady might not be all that interested in a man who speaks only of ancient French philosophers.'

'And she might not be interested in an ageing bookseller with little hair and a sensitive nose. Are you match-making, Mary Carrington?'

'I? Certainly not. Although I can't help feeling that you have much in common. Perhaps you should call on Miss Stewart again.'

'Perhaps. I'll give the matter some thought.'

'As you wish, Thomas, but don't take too long. Ladies can become disobliging if not attended to promptly.'

CHAPTER 10

Montford Babb's journal had revealed nothing and Thomas's efforts to bring Joseph useful intelligence from the coffee houses and barbers' shops of the city had so far proved futile. He resolved to try harder and spent the next two days in and around Fleet Street, Cheapside and Holborn, drinking numerous cups of Turkish coffee, listening to gentlemen in long periwigs earnestly discussing affairs of business and of the heart. And still learning exactly nothing which he might usefully report to an adviser to the king.

The men who sat at the common tables in the coffee shops took little interest in politics or at least did not reveal their opinions in public. They much preferred to boast of their latest conquests, lay wagers on whatever took their fancy from horse races to the colour of the coat of the next man to walk in, and to press each other for advice on how to invest their money to best advantage. It was talk with which Thomas quickly became thoroughly bored.

The barbers' shops were no better. At Fossett's he had his teeth painfully scraped and polished, at a filthy establishment on Ludgate Hill his nails were pared and his face shaved, and while sitting on an uncomfortable wooden stool in the shop of Samuel Gill (barber-surgeon) he allowed a little of his blood to be let. Blood letting was not a treatment in which Thomas had the least faith — it had never helped his gout — and he submitted to it only out of duty. Fortunately, Mr Gill's knife had been sharpened that morning and his incision was neat. The bruising on Thomas's arm would be gone in a day or two.

When Thomas left Mr Gill to attend to the needs of his other customers — needs which he noted included treatment for the pox, the provision of opium imported from the east and tobacco from the west, and advice on the use of a range of devices designed to prevent a lady from becoming pregnant — he imagined himself, blood let, close-shaved, teeth cleaned and nails trimmed, to be as well turned out as any London gentleman. Yet still he had learned nothing. Josiah Mottershead might fare better in low taverns and alehouses but from coffee drinkers and pipe smokers there had been not a word worth reporting.

Turning right down Fleet Street, Thomas set off for Piccadilly, thinking that a short sleep before dinner would be in order. He walked briskly, anxious to be away from the sounds and smells of that part of the city. The Fleet river carried a good deal of London's effluent to the Thames, where with luck it was swept out to sea. Usually, however, the tide that came up the river ensured that the city's waste matter remained where it was.

On the corner of Bell Yard his progress was halted by a noisy brawl blocking the street. Such disturbances were common enough and he waited patiently for one man or the other to prevail and for the crowd to disperse so that he could continue on his way. Happening to glance behind him as he waited, he glimpsed a man ducking into a doorway. He was a short man carrying a stout stick. Why was Josiah Mottershead following him?

Thomas elbowed his way through the crowd watching the fight and turned into a narrow lane, intending to double back until he was behind Mottershead. He would steal up on the man and demand to know what he was doing. Either Joseph Williamson did not trust Thomas or Mottershead was up to no good.

Trying both to keep an eye out behind him and to avoid the piles of muck that lined the lane, Thomas did not see the hag who leapt out from the shadows and tore at his face with her nails. Taken quite by surprise, he stumbled backwards and tripped over a raised cobblestone. Lying on his back, dazed and bloody, it took him a moment to realize what had happened. He pushed himself to his knees and looked about. The woman had disappeared, leaving him with no more than a wound on his cheek and a pair of filthy breeches. He felt his pockets and found that nothing had been taken. Nor was there any sign of an accomplice. A mad woman escaped from the Bedlam, perhaps. He stood up and speedily retraced his steps. His plan had gone awry. He would face Mottershead another time.

At the end of the lane, however, he ran straight into the little man. Josiah Mottershead was no runner but, stick in hand, he was doing the best he could along Fleet Street. His face was red and he was breathing hard. When he saw Thomas emerge from the lane he came to an abrupt halt. Hands on knees, he tried to regain his breath while Thomas stood and watched.

Eventually he was able to speak. 'There you are, sir, thank the Lord. I thought I'd lost you.'

'Lost me, Mottershead? What do you mean? I am not a sheep.'

'No, sir. And I see you've 'ad a little trouble. That scratch looks nasty.'

Thomas reached up and felt his face. Blood was dripping down his cheek where the woman's nails had torn the skin. He wiped it with his handkerchief and tried not to wince. 'It's nothing, Mottershead, just a mishap. More importantly, I want to know why you have been following me.'

Mottershead looked as if he might cry. 'Mr Williamson's orders, sir. 'E said I was to keep an eye on you to make sure you didn't come to any 'arm.'

'Did he say why?'

'Just a precaution, 'e said, sir. I wasn't to trouble you unless I 'ad to.'

'I see. A precaution against what, I wonder.'

'I couldn't say, sir.'

'No, Mottershead, nor could I.' He paused. 'Now I shall return to Piccadilly, where I shall be quite safe. Would you care to accompany me?'

'I better 'ad, sir, just in case.'

Outside the Carringtons' house, Thomas invited Mottershead in. The little man followed him nervously into the sitting room. To Thomas's relief the Carringtons were out so he did not have to explain himself. He fetched Mottershead a tankard of ale from the kitchen and asked him to wait while he cleaned himself up.

Having sluiced himself down with water from the jug in his room, washed away the blood from his face and changed his clothes, he found Josiah, his feet only just touching the floor, perched on one of Charles's big library chairs. With a restorative glass of Charles's French brandy, he sat down opposite the little man. 'Now, Josiah,' he began, 'I should be pleased to know exactly what Mr Williamson told you.'

'Told me? 'Ow do you mean, sir?'

'What exactly were your orders and why did he think I needed following?'

'As to why, sir, I couldn't say, except that Mr Williamson said 'e'd 'ave my balls for 'is breakfast if you came to any 'arm. Not like 'im, sir. Always such a correct gentleman. Very emphatic, 'e was. Must 'ave thought you were likely to come to some 'arm. Seems 'e was right.'

Thomas ignored the barb. 'Nothing else?'

Mottershead thought for a moment. 'Not really, sir. I was to keep you in my sight and make sure you got 'ome safely, wherever you went.'

'So you've been waiting outside the front door for me to emerge and then following me? Sounds a dull job.'

'The waiting's dull, sir, but all in the line of duty for men such as me. We're used to waiting and watching and listening. That's what we're paid for.'

'Are there many like you, Josiah?'

'Not many, I fancy. But Mr Williamson makes sure we don't all know each other. It's safer that way.'

'I daresay it is. So you can't tell me why Mr Williamson is so anxious to keep me safe?'

'Afraid I can't, sir.'

'Well then, Josiah Mottershead, I believe that I can make your job easier. I'm tired of drinking coffee and being shaven and polished and I've learned nothing whatever of any use to Mr

Williamson. Tomorrow I shall accompany you to some of the places you usually visit.'

Mottershead jumped off the chair. 'Oh no, sir. You don't want to do that. They're nasty places, most of 'em, and only nasty people use 'em. All kinds of evil things go on. They're not places for a gentleman like you.'

'Josiah, I've spent time in Oxford gaol, been an indentured servant to a pair of murderers and killed two men in cold blood. I can manage an alehouse or two.'

If Mottershead was surprised, he did not show it. 'Perhaps you 'ave, sir. But not in my care.'

'Are you worried about being seen with me, Josiah? Is that it?'

'Well, sir, as you mention it, perhaps I am. Wouldn't do my reputation no good to be seen with a man of quality and we'd likely 'ave to answer some awkward questions.'

'In that case I shall dress and speak appropriately and pass myself off as your cousin from Hampshire, come to London to help you with a few jobs. How would that be?'

'It wouldn't be good, sir, unless you're the finest actor in London. And my balls won't be the only things Mr Williamson 'as for breakfast, if 'e finds out.'

'Then we'd better make sure he doesn't find out. Just as he won't find out about my little misadventure today.' He coughed lightly. 'As long as we have an understanding, that is.'

Mottershead looked miserable. One accident was bad enough. Another would be a disaster. But if he did not agree, Mr Hill would offer him up on a plate to Mr Williamson and that would be the end of his work. And well-paid work it was too. 'Very well, sir, if you insist. But for the love of God, please keep your mouth shut and look as poor and 'orrible as you can.'

Thomas laughed. 'Poor and 'orrible, it is. I'll meet you outside St Bride's Church at noon.'

'St Bride's at noon. Right, sir.'

'And one more thing. If I am to be your cousin, you'd better call me Tom and I shall call you Josiah.'

'As you wish, sir, Tom.'

When a disconsolate Mottershead had left, Thomas returned to his room. He needed to think and he wanted to put off the inevitable questions about his face for as long as he could. At dinner, he was going to feel the sharp end of Mary Carrington's tongue again and he was not looking forward to it.

He took out his cast of characters and added

Josiah Mottershead: Williamson's man with a stick
Sir Montford Babb: murdered investor in AV. Connection unknown
Chandle Stoner: businessman and friend of the Carringtons
Madeleine Stewart: unmarried friend of Charles and Mary

Now there were four victims, two eccentrics, a spymaster, the inventor of the Bishop Mark, a man of business, a little man with a stick, a beautiful woman and himself. And there would be other characters waiting to make an entrance. A *deus ex machina* perhaps, or even a *dea*. As he would have to stay in London to find out, he might as well amuse himself in low taverns with Josiah Mottershead. It could only be an improvement on tedious barbers' shops and coffee houses.

Thomas went apprehensively down to dinner, his efforts to hide the marks on his face having been as good as useless. When Mary saw him her hand shot to her mouth. 'Thomas, what have you been doing now? Who has done this to you?'

Not for the first time, Thomas dissembled. 'It's not as bad as it looks, my dear. An unfortunate accident. I slipped in the street and landed on my face. Entirely my own fault. A glass of wine too many, I fear.'

Mary got up from her chair and peered at his cheek. 'I don't believe you, Thomas Hill. Someone has scratched you. I knew this would happen. Were you attacked?'

He stuck to his story. 'No, no. I fell, nothing more.'

'You're a poor liar, Thomas. I know you've been attacked. Kindly tell me why and by whom.'

Charles came to his rescue. 'Really, Mary, if Thomas says he fell then he fell. He's not a schoolboy. Leave the poor wretch alone. Come and sit down, Thomas, and have a glass of claret.' He held up his glass. 'It's rather good.'

Much relieved, Thomas took a glass and changed the subject. 'I plan to call on Madeleine Stewart the day after tomorrow. I still have Sir Montford's journal and I had thought to ask her to return it when she next visits Lady Babb.'

That cheered Mary up. 'I am pleased to hear it. And remember what I said. Spirited ladies such as Madeleine do not care to be kept waiting. Do not procrastinate.'

'I have no idea what you mean, Mary,' replied Thomas, suppressing a grin, 'and I shall of course behave with the utmost decorum.'

'Nonsense,' exclaimed Charles, 'decorum will get you nowhere. Just say what you think. It's never done me harm.'

'Only because I'm so forgiving,' said Mary. 'Thomas is a good deal more tactful. Still, do be brave, Thomas, won't you?'

'I'll try.'

Except for his stinging face, Thomas passed the rest of the evening comfortably enough until he asked leave to retire. 'Of course, my dear fellow,' said Charles, 'you must be tired after your accident. Sleep well and do try not to fall out of bed. We don't want any more accidents, do we, my dear?'

'We do not,' replied Mary. 'Do not fall out of bed, Thomas, and do not scratch yourself. My credulity is strained enough.'

The next morning, refreshed in body by a breakfast of egg pie and boiled sausages but still unsettled in mind, Thomas set off in good time to meet Josiah Mottershead at noon, outside St Bride's Church at the eastern end of Fleet Street. He had put on an old shirt, deliberately ripped around the collar, a pair of trousers which he had rubbed in the dirt, and the ancient, much repaired boots he had worn on the journey from Romsey. Having neither shaved nor washed, he reckoned that he looked about as inconspicuous for the day's work as he could, particularly with the marks on his face.

Josiah, stick in hand, was waiting for him outside the church. The poor man still looked miserable. He tipped his hat as Thomas approached. 'Good morning, sir. 'Ere I am, though I'd rather be 'aving a tooth pulled. I was 'oping you'd reconsidered but I see from your attire that you 'asn't.'

'Why would I reconsider, Josiah? I'm your cousin Tom from Romsey in Hampshire come to London to assist you in your work. Whatever that might be.'

Josiah sighed. 'As you like, sir. At least your face looks the part.'

'And my name is Tom. There'll be more than eyebrows raised if you call me sir.'

'Right, Tom. Best keep your mouth shut, though. You don't sound much like a working man.'

'I shall. Now where will you take me?'

'Don't know, Tom. Where'd you like to go?'

'Let us start in Pudding Lane, where Matthew Smith and Sir Montford Babb were murdered. Do you know an alehouse there?'

'I do. The Honest Wherryman.'

'Have you been there recently?'

'I 'ave, sir, in the course of my enquiries. Didn't learn anything. It's a rough place. Not many honest men to be found there, despite the name.'

'Perfect. Lead on, Josiah.'

Pudding Lane was one of the narrow streets running from Eastcheap down to the river and it was where much of the offal from the butchers' shops in Eastcheap ended up. The lane was swimming in it.

The upper storeys of the wooden houses on either side of the lane overhung so much that in places they almost touched each other and so little light penetrated that the inhabitants lived in perpetual semi-darkness. It was a horrid, miserable place, known for its bakers' shops, but home also to pickpockets, beggars, whores and drunkards. Thomas could not believe that either victim had been there willingly, especially at night.

The Honest Wherryman stood at the lower end of the lane, near the river. It was a narrow building, with grey slates on the roof, many of them broken, and wooden walls roughly daubed with lime and clay. Thomas had to duck as he followed Josiah through the door and into the dark, cave-like room that served as the alehouse.

As his eyes grew accustomed to the darkness, he made out

small groups of drinkers seated on stools around low tables littered with bottles, mugs and the remains of whatever they had been eating. An emaciated dog lay unmoving under one of the tables. In one corner a game of dice was in progress, but otherwise the place was quiet. The customers of the Honest Wherryman evidently did not frequent it for company or conversation. They sat in silence, drinking, smoking their clay pipes and eyeing suspiciously any newcomer arriving in their midst.

Thomas shivered, although whether from apprehension or the damp he was unsure. Josiah went to a hatch in the far wall and called for a jug of ale and two mugs. Armed with these, he found them stools at an unoccupied table near the door. Thomas sat with his back to the wall and a good view of the room. Josiah sat to his right facing the door. They each took a sip of ale and looked about.

Only the dice players had carried on without taking much notice of the new arrivals. By every other eye in the room they were being examined either openly or furtively. Thomas did his best to look unconcerned, carried on sipping his ale and wondered if any of his fellow drinkers was ever going to speak. He had more or less decided that none of them was, when the door opened and another new arrival entered. A tall man, he had to bend very low to avoid hitting his head on the door frame, especially as he wore a narrow-brimmed hat decorated with half a goose feather. Once inside the room, the tall man straightened his back and peered around. He raised a hand in greeting to two of the men in the opposite corner, went to the hatch and ordered a mug of ale.

Turning back to the room, mug in hand, he spotted Josiah and came over to their table. 'Josiah Mottershead, if I'm not mistaken. Here again? How's business?' His voice was deep and surprisingly well spoken. Unlike Josiah, he had a use for the letter 'h' at the start of a word.

Thomas noted the quality of his clothes — ruffled shirt, short waistcoat and trousers tied neatly at the knee with black ribbons — and his intelligent face. Hair tied back like Josiah's, sharp blue eyes and a long, thin nose. He reminded Thomas of a schoolteacher who had once taught him Latin and Greek. A man who did not suffer fools gladly.

'Oh, up and down, Woody, if you know what I mean,' replied Josiah, tapping the side of his nose. 'Up and down.'

Woody smiled knowingly. 'And who's this, if I may ask?'

'This is my cousin Tom, come to 'elp out with a job I've got.'

'Good day, Tom. Woody's the name. Come to help Josiah, have you? Where're you from?'

Before Thomas could reply, Josiah said 'Tom's a bit simple-minded, Woody. Doesn't speak much, often not for days on end. Never blabs. Wouldn't know 'ow, would you, Tom?' Thomas shook his head and tried to look simple-minded. ''E's good with 'is 'ands, though. Clever with locks and suchlike.'

'Sounds like a useful cousin to have in your line of work, Josiah. Could do with one like him myself.'

Josiah grinned. 'Only got one cousin, Woody. Can't 'elp, I'm afraid.' He paused and leaned forward to whisper, 'Very quiet in 'ere today. Suspicious looks, too. Most of 'em 'as seen me before. What's going on?'

'It's probably Tom they're looking at. Since those gentlemen were found with their throats cut in the lane, there've been coroner's men about asking questions. Not too popular hereabouts, coroner's men.' So Seymour Manners had not been entirely idle; covering his back, probably.

'Tom doesn't look like a coroner's man, does 'e, Woody?'

'He doesn't. Except his hands are very clean for a man who's good with them. Might have been noticed. Best tell Tom to hide them away if you don't want any questions.'

Josiah was as quick-witted as he was broad-shouldered. ''Adn't thought of that. It's a thing with Tom. Always washing 'is 'ands. Must be to do with 'is mind being funny. Put them under the table, Tom.' Thomas did so. 'And what's the story about the gentlemen whose throats were cut? What was the last one's name?'

'Bebb, I think. No, Babb. Sir something Babb. Murdered and robbed and not a sign of who did it. Nor the other one — Smith. Both in Pudding Lane.'

'No word at all on it?'

'None that I've heard. Strange that, there's usually a rumour or two. Not the sort of murder we expect round here. Proper gentlemen, by all accounts. If it was any of the usual suspects, we'd have heard.'

''Ave there been any strangers about?'

Woody looked up sharply. 'You're very interested in it, Josiah. You sure your cousin isn't a coroner's man?'

'No, 'e ain't. Mottersheads don't work for the law. Never 'ave, never will.' Josiah sounded affronted.

'Then why the questions?'

'No particular reason. Just wondered who did it. Might be the same fellow who did for the other man — Winter, 'is name was. Found by the bridge. I met 'im once in a sort of way.'

'Did you? What sort of way?'

'I 'appened to be on 'is property one evening when he came 'ome. 'E didn't see me but I saw 'im, and I remembered the name from something I found there. It was on a silver cup.

John Winter. Same name, same man. I sold it on, of course.'

Astonished at Josiah's facility for instant invention, Thomas sat and stared at him, looking as simple-minded as he was supposed to be. What an extraordinary little man. Tough as old oak and quick as a rat. A hard man to best in a fight and an even harder one to trap.

Woody swallowed the story. 'Trust you, Josiah. Another lucky escape. Can't help you with names, though. I haven't heard a thing.'

'Ah well. Never mind. We'd best be off, Tom,' said Josiah, 'we got work to do.'

But before they could move, one of the men whom Woody had greeted came over to their table. 'Morning, Woody,' he said. 'I see you got company. One I recognize, not the other.'

'Josiah Mottershead and his cousin Tom, come to help him with some work. Tom doesn't speak much. Or at all, in fact. At least I haven't heard him. This is Jeb Jones. We were boys together up in Clerkenwell. Eh, Jeb?'

'We were. Done well for ourselves, haven't we, Woody?' Jones's laugh was more of a cough. It started down near his navel and ended at his tooth. Thomas could see only the one. 'Hands like a girl's, the silent one's got. Where'd he get those?' he asked suspiciously.

Josiah explained his cousin's odd habit and rose to leave. 'Come on, Tom. Time to go to work. Goodbye, Woody, Jeb.'

'Goodbye, Josiah,' replied Woody.

'Have a drink before you go,' said Jeb. 'Like another drink, Tom?' It almost worked. Just in time, Thomas bit his tongue and shook his head. In the Honest Wherryman, being caught out would not have been a good thing.

They turned left out of the alehouse and walked briskly up Pudding Lane to Eastcheap. Josiah did not speak until he was sure they were not being followed. 'Better rub your 'ands in the dirt, sir. I should 'ave thought of it before.'

Thomas bent down and did as Josiah suggested. 'How's that, Josiah?' he asked, holding up his hands.

'Better, sir. And what do you 'ave in mind now?'

'Well, we didn't learn much there. How about a stroll down Drury Lane?'

'Drury Lane, sir? You don't want to go there. Even I don't go down there unless I 'as to.'

'Nonsense, Josiah. You'll be quite safe with me.'

Josiah looked doubtful. 'If you say so, sir. It's an 'orrible place, though. Don't go wandering off on your own, will you?'

'Of course not. My place will be at your side.' Thomas strode off in the direction of Drury Lane. They passed St Paul's, walked down Ludgate Hill and along Fleet Street to Wych Street, where Josiah stopped and planted his stick firmly on the ground.

'Couldn't we just go down the Strand, sir, or up to 'Olborn? There's plenty of alehouses around there.'

'No, Josiah. Drury Lane it is. Lead on.' A heavy-hearted Josiah led on, with Thomas close behind. The lane ran along the north side of Covent Garden and up to the western end of Holborn. It was a narrow, stinking, winding street, lined with filthy drinking houses and filthier brothels. Its inhabitants could disappear in seconds into the maze of alleyways, tunnels and passages that ran off the lane, quite safe from constables or trained bands who might be looking for them. Honest men did not visit Drury Lane or its offshoots alone.

Despite being aware of the lane's reputation, the moment

they set foot there Thomas was shaken by what he saw. At every turn, poverty, disease, squalor. On the corner of Coal Hole Lane, a man with a face ravaged by pox held another by a rope around his neck. The roped man, eyes crossed and tongue hanging from his mouth, stared blankly at Thomas and Josiah. 'A penny to see 'im dance. Straight from Bedlam, 'e is. Dances as good as a bear. A penny for the pleasure, sirs,' called out the man with the rope. They hurried on.

A little further on, a huge man with one eye and hair down to his waist stepped out from a dark doorway and blocked their path. He did not speak, merely held out one hand and bunched the other into a fist. His meaning was clear. Thomas reckoned that, armed with his stick, Josiah would have been able to deal even with this giant, but, to his surprise, the little man pulled a coin from his pocket and handed it over. The giant tested the coin with his teeth and stepped aside.

'Couldn't you have bested him, Josiah?' whispered Thomas, as they passed.

'Yes, sir. But not the six others who'd 'ave appeared if I 'ad. Now where did you want to go?'

'Anywhere we might learn something. What do you suggest?'

Josiah suggested that they went immediately to Piccadilly. The longer they were in Drury Lane, the more likely they were to meet trouble. And it would be double the trouble for Josiah Mottershead when Joseph Williamson found out. But Thomas was in a determined mood and Josiah had seen that look in a man's eye before. It signalled a mind made up, which no amount of persuasion would change. The good Lord alone knew why. If he were Thomas Hill, he'd be sitting safely at home in Romsey, enjoying a glass of something sweet and fortifying. Not risking his life on the streets of London. Especially not these streets. 'There's an 'ouse in Wild Street, sir. Might be worth a visit.'

'A house? What kind of house?'

Josiah coughed and wiped his mouth with the back of his hand. 'You know, sir. An 'ouse for gentlemen.'

'Do you mean a brothel, Josiah?' Josiah nodded. 'Then for the love of God, say so, man. I haven't spent all of my forty-seven years in church. I know what a brothel is.'

'Yes, sir. Course you do. It's just that this one's rougher than most. 'Enrietta — that's the owner — takes a bit of 'andling. If she takes against you we'll be in trouble.'

'Why would she take against me?'

''Enrietta's sharp as a nail. Might see through you. Don't open your mouth, sir. We'll use the same story as before. Leave the talking to me. And don't show nothing when you see 'er. Very touchy about 'er appearance, 'Enrietta is. Knows what's going on, though. Not much she doesn't 'ear, in 'er line of business.'

'My lips are sealed, Josiah. Not a word shall pass them.'

They arrived at a tall, narrow house in Wild Street. 'Is this it?'

'Yes, sir, 'ere we are.' Josiah knocked three times on the door with his stick. Thomas guessed the knock was some sort of signal. Not every caller would be welcome at Henrietta's house. A small panel in the door slid back to reveal a pair of dark eyes.

'Josiah Mottershead and 'is cousin Tom to see Miss 'Enrietta.' Evidently satisfied, the owner of the eyes closed the panel and opened the door. His skin was as dark as his eyes, he towered above Thomas and Josiah, he was dressed from head to toe in yellow satin and he wore a curved knife in his belt.

'Good day, gentlemen. I am Oliver. Pray come in and I shall

advise Miss Henrietta of your arrival. Mr Mottershead and cousin, did you say?' Josiah nodded. 'Please be seated.' He indicated two chairs in the entrance hall, placed there for just such a purpose.

'An unexpected doorman,' whispered Thomas when he had gone. 'Looks like he was born on the Barbary coast, sounds like he was educated at court.' Josiah frowned, put his finger to his lips and shook his head. Seated on the chair, his toes just reaching the floor, the little man twiddled his stick in his fingers and looked about nervously.

It was not long before Oliver returned, his smile displaying the whitest and largest teeth Thomas had ever seen. 'Miss Henrietta will be pleased to see you, gentlemen,' he announced. 'Kindly follow me.'

They were led down a passage to the back of the house and shown into a room with a window looking on to a small courtyard. Miss Henrietta was waiting for them, a man who could have been Oliver's twin standing beside her. He too was dressed in yellow satin and had a curved knife at his belt.

Only with difficulty did Thomas manage to do as Josiah had instructed and keep his expression neutral. Arranged on an enormous padded chair, the owner of this brothel was a woman who might have been anything from forty to sixty, must have weighed almost as much as Thomas and Josiah put together and wore a wig the colour of an orange. Her cheeks were decorated with black patches in the manner of ladies at court and her mouth was painted to match her wig. In one hand she held a large glass of port, in the other a long clay pipe. Her chair was set so that she could see both the door and into the courtyard, where some customers were unashamedly taking their ease with her ladies.

Henrietta took a puff on her pipe and looked them up and

down. When she spoke her voice was deep and throaty. 'Well, well. Josiah Mottershead, if I'm not much mistaken. We haven't seen you since the king was returned to us. Found another house to visit, I daresay. And who have you brought to meet me?'

''Allo, 'Enrietta. You're looking very fine. This is my cousin Tom. 'E's come from 'Ampshire to 'elp me with a job I've got. 'Is 'ead's not right. Doesn't speak 'ardly ever. Dependable, though, and don't tell tales.'

Henrietta examined Thomas, who tried to look simple-minded. After his practice in the Honest Wherryman, he thought he was making a decent job of it. 'Yes,' she said, 'I can see he's not right. Not like you, Josiah. You're as right as a silver guinea, the ladies tell me.'

For some reason, this brought on a fit of coughing, terminated only by her hawking loudly into a bowl set at her feet. 'Don't want any gentlemen slipping on the floor, do we?' she asked innocently, taking a gulp of port. 'And what can I do for you gentlemen today? Something special? There's a girl from Morocco arrived only last week. A princess she is and knows the things those Moroccan princes like. One of my gentlemen could barely walk home, another one wants to marry her. Makes up for the ones I've been losing. It's always the pretty ones who go off with my gentlemen. Doesn't last long. They're back soon enough when his lordship has had enough of them. Lost Molly not long ago and don't even know who she went off with. Remember Molly, Josiah?'

'I do, 'Enrietta. Red 'air and a viper's tongue. And I'd like to meet the princess, but I don't think we shall today, eh, Tom? Got work to do, 'aven't we?' Tom shook his head and rolled his eyes. Josiah affected not to notice the histrionics. 'Just wanted to intro-duce Tom so's you'd know 'im next time.'

'Pity. Still you'll take a drink with me, eh?' She smiled at her tall servant. 'Rupert will fetch it, won't you, my lovely?' Oliver and Rupert. The late Lord Protector and the king's cousin — no sign of Henrietta taking sides.

Josiah was hoping for this. Henrietta consumed enormous amounts of wine and ale and much preferred company while doing so. Next to money, she most loved an audience.

'Be pleased to, 'Enrietta. Mug of ale, Tom?' Tom nodded enthusiastically. 'Same for me, if you please.'

Thomas studied the room. It was as large as the Carringtons' sitting room, oak-panelled, oak-floored and with a fine portrait of a lady aged about twenty adorning one wall. The subject was a striking woman and the artist had skilfully captured a devil-may-care look in her eye.

Rupert returned with mugs of ale and a fresh bottle of port for Henrietta. 'I see you're admiring my portrait, Tom,' said Henrietta. 'Pretty, wasn't I? Know who painted it?' Thomas hoped it was the last time he would have to shake his head and look simple. 'Sir Anthony van Dyck himself, it was. Not many London ladies had their portraits painted by Sir Anthony. Lovely man. Gave it to me for a present. He used to visit me when he was in London painting the new king's father.' Astonished at this information, Thomas managed, just, to look blank.

'Don't suppose Tom knows who you're talking about, 'Enrietta,' said Josiah. Deftly, he changed the subject. ''Ow's business, now we've a king again?'

'And thank the Lord we have, I say. Gentlemen were too frightened to come here when Cromwell's lot were telling us all what to do and what not to do. Spent too much time on their knees in church and not enough on their elbows at Henrietta's.' Fearing another cough, Thomas looked away. Happily it never came. 'Business has been much better since the coronation and the king himself sets a good example. They say there's scores of little royal bastards running around Paris and Rotterdam. I wish His Majesty would call here, though. Trade's fallen off again since those murders. Bad for business, murders. Especially murders of four respectable gentlemen. Some of our regulars have been staying at home. Hope they catch whoever done it quick.'

This was promising. 'You mean the gentlemen in Pudding Lane and the other in the graveyard? Was there a fourth one, 'Enrietta?'

'Course there was. They said he'd jumped off the bridge. Jumped off the bridge, my arse. Pushed he was and most likely by the same man who did for the other three.'

'Why d'you say that?'

'No one who really wants to top himself jumps off that bridge. More often than not they get washed up safe and sound. He was dead when he hit the water, you mark my words. And there's talk.'

'Is there? What sort of talk would that be?'

'What's it to you, Josiah Mottershead? You got something to do with it?' Henrietta spoke sharply.

Josiah grunted. 'Me? Course not. Not my game, murder, nor robbery, as well you know. Just interested, that's all.'

'Well then. There was talk of a foreigner, Dutch or German perhaps, come over to do it for money. He was seen about the place. Here and there, as you might say. Came and went. Didn't say much, but he was marked by his face. Sliced lip and half a nose, he had. Hasn't been seen since the last murder.'

'Took 'is money and went 'ome, I daresay. Any word on who paid 'im?'

'Not that I've heard. Nor why.'

Josiah decided he had gone far enough. Henrietta had been helpful, but any more probing and she'd be suspicious. He rose to go. 'Better be off, Tom. Thanks for the ale, 'Enrietta. 'Ope business picks up.'

Thomas took his lead and followed Josiah to the door. As he did so, he glanced out of the window. In the courtyard he caught a glimpse of long fair hair and a handsome young face. He swallowed an exclamation and sneaked another look. There was no doubt about it.

'Come again, Josiah. And before you do, tell your cousin not to go getting into fights and to wash his hands. They're filthy.'

At Charing Cross, they parted company. 'Thank you for introducing me to your friends, Josiah,' said Thomas. 'We learned more today than I have in a week. In more ways than one.'

'You're welcome, sir,' replied Josiah. 'Only I 'ope you won't be wanting to meet them again. Made me quite jumpy wondering if you were going to open your mouth and give the game away.'

'We could always say I had suddenly gained the power of speech following the king's touch. I hear His Majesty believes he can heal all manner of diseases with his hand.'

'We could, but I'd rather you stayed at 'ome and left it to me. I like to work alone. Always 'ave.'

'Very well, Josiah. But if you hear anything, anything at all, be sure to let me know at once. If the lovely Henrietta is right, someone might have hired the murderer and brought him here from Holland or Germany. We need to know who hired him and why.'

'I will, sir. You can depend on it. And don't get in no more fights.'

'I won't. And when you report to Mr Williamson, there's no need to mention me.'

'No, sir, I'll just tell 'im about the Dutchman.'

As to the other matter, it had been a shock and Thomas would need to think carefully about what to do for the best. Indulging his niece was one thing, but this was quite another.

Chapter 11

Just as the church bells struck two the next afternoon, Thomas knocked on the door of the little house in the lane off Fleet Street, Sir Montford's journal under his arm. The scratch on his face had dulled to a yellowy brown.

Madeleine's housekeeper, a stout woman with a cheerful, open face, answered the door and introduced herself as Agnes. She showed him into a cluttered room which served as sitting room and parlour. The furniture consisted of just four plain chairs and a table; one wall was lined with books, the others adorned with paintings of rural scenes. The room was saved from being oppressive by the afternoon sun which shone through a large window and bathed it in light.

While he waited for the housekeeper to fetch Madeleine, Thomas studied the paintings. He thought they were rather good. Skilful draughtsmanship and fine brushwork combined to produce interesting and unsentimental scenes of cottages, harvesting, a village square and a tiny church. To his surprise, each one was discreetly signed 'M. Stewart'. Charming, intelligent, beautiful and artistic too.

He was still studying her work when the artist herself, brown hair tumbling on her shoulders and blue eyes smiling, entered the room. 'This is a pleasant surprise, Thomas. I have few visitors.' He turned and returned the smile. Her hand went to her mouth. 'Oh. What has happened to your face?'

'An accident, nothing more.'

Madeleine looked unconvinced. 'If you say so, Thomas. And I see your visit is not a social one. Would you like me to return the journal to Lady Babb?'

'That would be kind. Apart from an unwise investment, I have learned little about him.' Thomas hesitated. 'I had wondered also if you would care for a stroll in St James's Park. We could inspect the king's works there.'

Madeleine smiled. 'A most agreeable idea. I hear the king's menagerie is growing daily and he often walks there himself. I'll fetch my hat and we'll be off.'

The route from Fleet Street to St James's Park took them along the Strand to Charing Cross, and then south down King Street to Westminster Hall, where they turned right past the Abbey and into the park. They passed Somerset House, Worcester House, and the king's palace at Whitehall.

'They say there are so many rooms and passages in Whitehall Palace,' said Madeleine, gazing at it, 'that there are men and women wandering about unable to find a way out. Some have even died of starvation, their bodies unfound for years.'

'Do they now?' asked Thomas. 'Then let's hope the king is always accompanied by a reliable guide. I doubt the country wants another coronation just yet.'

'No. Especially not until His Majesty has a legitimate heir. His brother James, I fear, would command little respect.'

'James has not proved a good name for the king of England. The only one so far was Scottish, preferred boys to girls and took advice from no one but God. Another might be as bad. We need another William or Henry, don't you think?'

'Or an Elizabeth?'

'Indeed. Or a Queen Madeleine, perhaps.'

Madeleine pretended to be shocked. 'Hush, Thomas. You'll have me in the Tower for saying such a thing.' She slipped her arm through his. 'You will come and visit me there, won't you?'

'If time allows, certainly,' replied Thomas, getting a punch on the arm for his trouble.

They strolled through the park to the canal and along the towpath beside it. They were about to turn and retrace their steps when a large party swept towards them. Both men and women were dressed at the very height of fashion — the gentlemen flamboyant in their loose shirts, skirts and voluminous trousers, feathered hats and ribbons, the ladies rather less so in muted skirts, short jackets and simple shawls. At their head was a tall man in a long black wig, swinging a walking stick as he strode along the path and accompanied by three small spaniels. His entourage were struggling to keep up with him. Six soldiers of the King's Lifeguard marched alongside the party. Mary grabbed Thomas by the elbow and dragged him off the path. 'Hat off, Thomas,' she whispered, 'and your finest bow. The king approaches.' As the king passed them, Madeleine curtsied low and Thomas bowed low from the waist. They waited for the whole party to go by before standing upright again.

'That was unexpected. Come to inspect his new canal, perhaps,' said Madeleine.

'Or his ostriches.'

'At least he must feel he can walk freely in the park.'

'Freely yes, but not alone.'

'Quite. Have you noticed how the male of the human species has recently adopted the habits of his counterparts among the animals and birds?' asked Madeleine.

Thomas asked her what she meant. 'In nature, Thomas, or perhaps you hadn't noticed, it is the cock pheasant and the stag who like to show off their finery. The hen and the doe are more modest in their appearance.'

'Quite so, my dear. I fear, however, that I hardly come up to standard in that respect.'

'Nonsense, Thomas. You look as fine as any man in the park.'

Thomas felt himself blush. 'Even His Majesty?'

'Especially His Majesty.'

To hide his embarrassment, Thomas changed the subject. 'When did you come to London, Madeleine?'

'My father died five years ago. I came the following year, as soon as the estate had been settled.'

'Did you say that your father was a parson?'

'He was, as Joseph's father was. A kind man, but not the strongest. Weak in both body and mind, I suppose. He found it difficult to stand up for what he believed in and against his enemies.'

'He had enemies? Catholics, do you mean?'

'No, not religious enemies. There were those in the village who treated him badly.'

'Why would they treat a country parson badly?'

'It's in the past, Thomas. I'd rather not talk about it,' said Madeleine, gently squeezing his arm.

In the park an ancient, one-armed beggar stepped out from behind a tree. 'Spare a shillin' for an old soldier, sir,' the old man croaked, holding out a battered hat.

He was ragged and filthy, and not wishing to provide a new home for the man's lice and fleas, Thomas's first instinct was to ignore the wretched fellow. To his surprise, however, Madeleine pulled a coin from her purse and dropped it into the hat. He mumbled something which might have been thanks and disappeared back behind his tree.

'He will only drink it away,' said Thomas as they walked back.

'I know. It was just the shock of seeing him here among all this wealth and finery. I ignore beggars in the streets.'

'As you should. Charity may be a virtue, but begging is too close to theft for my liking.' Thomas paused. 'Poverty and filth alongside wealth and extravagance. Perhaps it will always be thus.'

'Our new king certainly has much to do if it is to change. Yet the mood of the people is for change.'

'And they must have it. Despite the war, London is thriving. Merchants and financiers are becoming rich. Some of their wealth should be used for the common good.'

'And how is this to be accomplished, Thomas?' asked Madeleine, slipping her arm through his again and smiling sweetly.

'Good Lord, madam, that is a matter far beyond the wit of a humble fellow like me. Questions I can manage, it is the answers I find difficult.'

Madeleine laughed. 'In that, sir, I believe you to be much like most other men.'

'And women.'

'And women.'

'Chandle Stoner describes himself as a philanthropist,' said Thomas thoughtfully. 'I wonder to whom he is philanthropic.'

'He also describes himself as a financier, so I expect his philanthropy is chiefly to himself.'

'Madeleine, I should never have thought you so cynical.'

'Then you must get to know me better, Thomas.'

'Indeed I must.'

As they walked back beside the canal, Thomas looked up. Coming towards them but some distance away were Lucy and Arthur Phillips, arm in arm and deep in conversation. They had not seen him. He quickly steered Madeleine away from the towpath and into the park. He was not ready to speak to Lucy, nor was this the time.

Within thirty minutes they were back at the little house off Fleet Street. Seated on the plain chairs in the parlour, they each took a glass of Spanish sherry brought by the housekeeper. Thomas raised his glass to Madeleine. 'To you. May life bring you everything you wish for.'

Madeleine smiled a little sadly. 'If it's not too much to ask for, may it do the same for you.'

One hour passed, then two, while they talked of this and that — food, books, London, the countryside, music — carefully avoiding politics, religion and philosophy. Even Montaigne was ignored while they explored each other's tastes. A little before five o'clock Thomas rose as if to take his leave.

'Thank you for your company, Madeleine,' he said, 'but

now I must be on my way. I have much enjoyed our afternoon.'

Madeleine also rose, and took his hands in hers. 'As have I. I hope there will be other afternoons.' And, reaching up, she brushed her lips against his.

Thomas's arms went around her. Feeling her relax and respond, he moved closer to her, his hands on her waist. Her hands reached for his shoulders and she pressed her lips to his. He breathed in the scent of roses. Then suddenly, without warning, she pushed herself away from him.

Thomas stared at her. There were tears in her eyes, and her hands were trembling. He was at a loss. 'Madeleine, what's wrong? Have I hurt you?'

Madeleine wiped her eyes with a lace handkerchief. 'No, no. It's my fault. Do forgive me, Thomas. I'm unused to such attention.'

Thomas stepped towards her and held out his hands. 'I am not exactly practised myself.'

Madeleine laughed. 'That I find hard to believe, Thomas Hill. A handsome and intelligent man of substance. Do the ladies of Romsey not come calling at your door every day?'

'Alas, no. If you were to call, however, I would of course throw the door open at once.' Again, he took her hands, drew her to him, and gently placed his lips on hers. This time, however, she did not respond: her back went rigid and she pushed him away. He went cold. Mary was wrong. This woman had been toying with him. He quickly released her.

'Thank you for calling, Thomas,' she said quietly. 'I will show you to the door.'

Not waiting to be shown, Thomas turned and left.

*

He walked quickly back to Piccadilly, taking the same route as they had earlier. He noticed neither the bewigged gentlemen in their skirts walking with their spaniels, nor the urchins playing in the street, nor the traders hawking their wares. He passed Somerset House and Worcester House without seeing them and for once the smells of the city went unnoticed by his sensitive nose.

By the time he arrived at the Carringtons' house he was hot and angry. Angry at Madeleine Stewart for rejecting him, angry at Mary Carrington for giving him false hope, angry at himself for his stupidity.

Unable to face the Carringtons, he went straight to his room. He sat at the table and, as he used to do when wrestling with a difficult cipher, he cleared his mind before allowing it to wander. He was a fortunate man, but there was one thing missing in his life. And now it would remain missing. Despite Mary's encouragement, Madeleine Stewart had rejected him. Just as she said she had rejected the handsome soldier who wanted to marry her. That Thomas could understand. Soldiers seldom made good husbands or good anything much except soldiers. What was harder to grasp was why there had been no more suitors. The young men of Hertfordshire must be a feeble lot to have let Miss Stewart get away. But was she telling the truth? Perhaps there had been others and she had rejected all of them, just as she had rejected him. Perhaps there was more to her than met the eye. Perhaps, perhaps.

Here he was in London, a city he disliked, recruited by Joseph Williamson to deputize for the absent Dr Wallis and now involved in four murders and a possible nest of spies. He had visited coffee shops and barbers' shops, alehouses and brothels — well, one brothel — and apart from rumours of a mysterious foreign murderer at large he had learned practically nothing. He had been attacked in the street and had the remains of an ugly scratch on his face to show for it. What was more, his niece was enamoured of a young man who was not as virtuous as he seemed and he would have to do something about it.

And now Madeleine had spurned him. So much for retreat being cowardly. His advance had been repelled with ease. It was time to go home, agreement with Williamson or not. His Majesty's adviser could find someone else to deputize for Dr Wallis. London was no place for Thomas Hill. His own bed in his own house was where he should be. Tomorrow he would tell Williamson his decision, suffer the inevitable rebuke and go back to Romsey. Decision made, he lay down on the bed.

When at last he went to sleep, he did so with Montaigne whispering in his ear. *My life has been full of terrible misfortunes, most of which never happened.* Was Madeleine Stewart a 'terrible misfortune'? She had certainly 'happened'. Forget her, Thomas, go home and take Lucy with you. And you, monsieur, bugger off back to your cabbages.

CHAPTER 12

When Thomas woke, however, Madeleine was still there. Damnable woman. In the park, she had taken his arm, asked about his family, spoken about her own and hinted at a relationship closer than mere friendship. In St James's, she had told him he was 'as fine as any man in the park'. In her house, she had taken his hands, kissed him and smiled into his eyes. Then she had turned to stone. What was he supposed to make of all that? In the early hours of the morning, Thomas knew only that Madeleine Stewart had embarrassed him and he did not take kindly to being embarrassed.

Not bothering with breakfast, he set off for Williamson's house soon after dawn. If he was still in his bed, that was just too bad. At that hour few other than milkmaids and pure collectors filling their buckets with dog shit were about, and he walked briskly along the Strand and Fleet Street to Chancery Lane. He knocked loudly on Williamson's door, which was opened, to his surprise, immediately and by Williamson himself.

'Good Lord, Thomas, you've made good time. I sent the messenger no more than half an hour ago,' exclaimed Williamson, his head turned to the side to favour his lazy eye.

'Messenger?'

'Yes, man, messenger,' and seeing the blank look on Thomas's face, 'Don't tell me he missed you. Then how did you know about the letter?'

'Letter?'

'Thomas, it's too early for games. Make haste, now. We must go at once to the Post Office.' And with that, he swept out of the house and set off at speed towards Cloak Lane. Thoroughly confused, Thomas hesitated and then followed him.

At the Post Office they were met by Henry Bishop. 'Joseph, Thomas. Good morning. I thought it best to ask you to come at once.'

They were ushered in and led straight to Bishop's room. There Samuel Morland and Lemuel Squire were waiting for them. Morland looked even more irascible than when Thomas had last met him.

'Ah, Samuel,' said Bishop, 'here they are. Have you the copy?'

Morland produced a sheet of paper from inside his coat and handed it carefully to Bishop, who handed it equally carefully to Williamson. Thomas wondered fleetingly if, like the silent clerks he had noticed on his first visit, this might be some sort of arcane Post Office ritual and whether, if Williamson handed it to him, he should hand it to Squire. Fortunately, Williamson kept hold of it.

'Do be seated, gentlemen,' went on Bishop, 'and let us discuss what should best be done.'

Still having no idea what they were going to discuss, Thomas took a seat between Squire and Williamson around Bishop's table and awaited developments. What he really wanted to say to Williamson would have to wait. This was probably not the time to announce he would be leaving London for Romsey that very day.

'The letter is addressed to A. Silver Esq, Aldersgate, London, and was sent from Holland. We open every letter that comes from there. It arrived two days ago from Yarmouth,' explained Bishop. 'Lemuel was indisposed that day so his chief clerk put it on his desk, unopened.'

'I opened it and had it copied as soon as I returned. Then it was sent on to the collection office in Star Court,' said Squire. 'I would normally have had the copy delivered directly to Thomas, but decided to show it to Mr Bishop first.'

'Was the collector at Star Court not apprehended or followed?' asked Joseph.

'Unfortunately not. My warning was not, it seems, received in time.'

'A pity. Is there any significance in the name Silver?' asked Thomas.

'Not that we are aware of. It is the code that interests us. It is entirely numeric. We haven't come across that before, have we, gentlemen?' Williamson inclined his head in agreement. Morland remained impassive. 'Does that suggest anything to you, Thomas?'

'When a new code or encryption appears, it is invariably because the contents of the message are too sensitive for an old one to be used. This is especially the case when the message is travelling along an established route.'

'That is common knowledge,' observed Morland drily. It was his first contribution to the discussion. 'Can Mr Hill offer any other advice?'

'May I see the copy?' Williamson passed it to him. Thomas opened it and spread it on the table. There were eleven and a half lines of numbers, grouped in fours. Each number was separated by a stop and consisted of one or two digits. There were no three-digit numbers.

There were too many different numbers for the code to be a straightforward substitution. He noticed a number of repetitions and such a code would have been quite inadequate against a competent cryptographer. There was more to it and it would require hard work to find out what.

'This is a complex substitution cipher,' he said, almost to himself. 'It can be broken, but it will take some time.'

'How much time?' demanded Morland imperiously.

'A few days, I think,' replied Thomas, still studying the letter.

Morland was unimpressed. 'Come now, Master Hill, it is clear to anyone with eyes to see that these numbers represent not letters, but syllables and words. It is a code, not a cipher. That is why there are so many different combinations. How do you intend to break such a code within "a few days"?'

Morland was wrong. There were too many repetitions. Syllables and words did not feel right to Thomas, just as a bream biting on a hook did not feel like a trout. You could not be entirely sure until the fish was safely in the net, but you would wager a shilling or two as soon as you felt it bite. 'Hill's magic', dear Abraham Fletcher used to call it — an uncanny ability to divine the nature of a code or encryption just by looking at it and by conjuring up an image of the encrypter. This message had been written by an educated hand with elaborate neatness. The encryption would be clever but straightforward. There was no point, however, in arguing with Morland.

'Sir Samuel may well be right, gentlemen. It might be a code and complex codes can take time to unravel, especially with only one document to work on. I suggest that he sets to work without delay.'

'That is one of Master Hill's more sensible suggestions,' said Morland, with a smirk. 'If anyone can decode this, it is I.'

Williamson and Bishop exchanged glances. 'We would prefer you to continue with the important work you are engaged in, Samuel,' said Williamson tactfully. 'Your new family of ciphers is keenly anticipated and much needed.'

Morland looked furious. 'Nonsense. The decoding of this message is much more urgent than the new ciphers and I am by far the best man to do it.'

'Do you not think that Thomas is as well qualified? He did break the Vigenère square and he knew the double vowel substitution cipher when he saw it.'

'Tush. The vowel substitution is simple and he broke the square with a lucky guess.'

Just as they had at their last meeting, Thomas's hackles rose. The second message encrypted with the square he had indeed decrypted with a guess — inspired rather than lucky, he liked to think — but the first one had been the result of a vital insight and logical thought. How dare this unpleasant man suggest otherwise? With difficulty, he kept his tone measured. 'Sir Samuel doubtless has his reasons for holding such an opinion of me, but he is mistaken about this message. It does not use codes for syllables or words and I can decrypt it within two days.'

A tiny smile played across Williamson's face. 'If Thomas says he can decrypt the letter within two days, I am inclined to believe him. What do you think, Henry?'

'I agree.'

'Then he must have the chance. You won't let us down, Thomas, will you?'

I had better not, thought Thomas. Morland is a pig and I want to go home. 'You may rely on me, gentlemen.'

'Ridiculous,' spluttered Morland and stormed out of the room.

Lemuel Squire, who had sat quietly and said nothing, took a pinch of snuff and sneezed loudly. 'Really, that man is quite the rudest in London. I do apologize, Thomas. His behaviour was unforgivable. I shall go and tell him so.' And he followed Morland out.

'You are sure of this, Thomas, I hope?' asked Bishop.

Sure? Not even half sure. A complex substitution cipher in two days? It would take all of Hill's magic and a hatful of luck. 'Quite sure, sir.'

'In that case take the copy and start at once. There is no time to lose,' said Williamson.

Then I'd better be right about it, thought Thomas, or I shall look a fool and Morland will love it.

'How did you come to arrive at my door this morning, Thomas?' asked Williamson, on their way back to Chancery Lane. 'Was it mere chance or had you a reason for calling so early?'

'I had a reason, Joseph. But now it must wait until I've decrypted this letter.'

'Only a day or two, then? This might be just the stroke of luck we need. It could lead us to the heart of the enemy.'

'To be sure. Only a day or two.'

In his room at Williamson's house, Thomas spread the copy of the encrypted message on his table.

48.39.28.5.	34.14.0.11.	6.1.49.83.	7.37.55.36.	30.4.13.48.
35.45.50.19.	56.33.22.83.	48.73.67.24.	12.8.82.16.	97.53.86.59.
52.26.17.46.	10.28.57.18	89.38.62.65.	14.25.77.30.	21.84.19.95.
35.33.85.60.	68.88.46.58.	91.66.2.32.	90.15.64.5.	43.11.28.20.
47.30.23.36.	42.71.51.55.	45.35.81.50.	6.78.72.83.	12.0.1.13.
48.86.46.29.	56.16.52.89.	0.26.27.17.	70.73.13.37.	90.82.28.40.
76.44.84.68.	79.87.75.59.	85.21.62.86.	61.92.83.93.	64.88.38.55.
91.30.4.80.	39.0.1.6.	37.22.5.35.	33.10.24.46.	89.59.65.28.
43.11.74.32.	42.71.9.49.	47.30.13.66.	53.35.16.34.	51.89.81.57.
46.6.61.67.	36.28.8.72.	89.75.86.62.	76.20.64.45.	30.90.23.31.
22.35.50.46.	55.26.77.28.	14.90.93.19.	3.56.18.24.	27.2.97.39.
0.7.42.21.	15.73.48.32.	79.40.		

The letter had come from Holland and might shed light on the suspected spy ring. If so, and assuming it had been written in English, it might contain such words as England, London, agent, king, or even invasion.

Thomas closed his eyes and tried to visualize the man who had encoded this letter. He saw a middle-aged man, precise in word and dress, an orderly man not given to flights of fancy or expansive gestures. A man in control of himself and his life. A man who wrote in an educated hand with elaborate neatness. There were no corrections that Thomas could discern and the numbers were set out in tidy groups. This was not a man who would use tricks or deliberate mistakes to confuse his enemy but would rely upon his art and technique. He would favour a straightforward cipher. A Caesar, not a Cicero.

He turned his attention back to the message itself and started counting. In decryption much time was spent in counting. There were two hundred and thirty numbers in fifty-seven and a half groups of four. The spaces between groups were certainly irrelevant. No message of this length had ever been written using only four-letter words. Then he counted individual numbers. Ninety-one numbers between 0 and 97 had been used with frequencies varying from seven (28) to one. Numbers 41, 54, 63, 69, 94, 95 and 96 had not been used, either because the letters they represented had not appeared in the plain text message or because they had not been allocated to a letter. The same might be true of numbers 98 and 99. Ninety-seven numbers for a maximum of twenty-six letters meant that at least some letters were represented by more than one number. The question was: had they been allocated randomly or was there some pattern to be found?

All day, without food or drink, Thomas laboured away. By the time his stomach started complaining he had got through ten quills, the floor was littered with discarded papers and his fingers were stained with ink. And he had learned very little. Concentrating on the most frequent numbers – 28, 30, 35 and 46 – he had counted and recounted, attempted a few guesses, tried in vain to gain a foothold by examining the juxtapositions of the numbers, hoping to find two that might represent TH, CH, OU or another common pair, and he had searched in vain for possible vowels and double letters. He had found no hint of pattern. At five o'clock he stood up, stretched his aching back, rubbed his eyes and walked to the window. It was a lovely summer evening and he needed to breathe fresh air. Having carefully locked the door of his room behind him, he let himself out of the house and went for a walk.

Just like Oxford eighteen years ago, he thought, as he made his way towards the new park. Stuck in a room with a wicked cipher, no food, no drink, sore eyes and an aching head. Not to mention Williamson's displeasure and Morland's delight if I fail.

Why didn't I hold my tongue and let the wretch try himself? He'd have done no better, the odious toad. *Because*, whispered Montaigne in his ear, *the man who seeks to establish his argument by noise and command shows that his reason is weak. You know Morland's reason is weak and I expect you to prove it.* And you are not alone, replied Thomas silently.

At that time of day the park was busy. Elegant couples in silks and satins strolled beside the canal, noisy children ran about on the grass or played games among the trees, and the king's gardeners, armed with an array of spades and rakes and hoes, tended His Majesty's plants. The last time he had been here was with Madeleine and on the very day she had spurned him. The witch. He really had dared to hope that his feelings were shared and that she would be receptive to his advance. Well, at least not as cold as a hoar frost in February, especially after her initial show of warmth. But she'd been playing a game and he'd fallen for it. How else to explain the smile, her arm through his, the compliments, followed only by cruel rejection?

On the west side of the park with the sun behind him, Thomas found a quiet spot under an old oak. His back against its trunk, he sat down and closed his eyes. Oxford, Barbados, back to his quiet life in Romsey, and now where was he? In London, that's where, up to his neck again in murder and intrigue, desperate to go home, but trapped by his own vanity into attempting to decrypt yet another disobliging encryption. And rejected by the impossible Madeleine Stewart. What might he look forward to next?

'Enough of this, Thomas,' he heard Abraham Fletcher say quietly. 'Get some food inside you and you'll feel better. Empty your mind and think clearly, just as I taught you, and as you yourself have taught others. Stop feeling sorry for yourself and take some of your own advice. And don't delay. Morland is counting the hours.' Thinking that very few teachers have the power to go on teaching long after they are dead, Thomas got to his feet and walked briskly back to Chancery Lane.

Once Williamson's cook had provided him with an excellent mutton stew, bread and cheese and a bowl of fruit, doubtless brought for her cousin by Miss Stewart, Thomas lay down on the floor and stared at the ceiling. It was an old trick of his — a way of clearing the mind of all unwanted thoughts.

He concentrated on the letter. He still thought Morland was wrong about coded words and syllables, so twenty-six possible letters were represented by ninety-one numbers, with a very even distribution which disguised their normal frequencies. He did not believe that this encrypter had allocated numbers randomly, but systematically, in a way which disguised the letters with particular effect. If Thomas could divine that way he would have taken the first step towards decryption. He went back to the letter and asked himself what he would have done in the encrypter's place.

Before he could come up with an answer, however, he heard a key turn in the door and in swept Williamson. 'Good evening, Thomas. What progress have you to report?'

Thomas rose slowly and chose his words with care. 'I am still sure that Sir Samuel is wrong in believing that it is words and syllables which are represented by the numbers. All my instincts tell me otherwise. But I am not yet in a position to prove it.'

Joseph frowned. 'Yet? Does that mean progress or no progress?'

'I have made progress by eliminating a number of possibilities. I know certain things that this cipher is not. I do not yet know what it is.'

'So should I take your repeated use of the word "yet" as encouraging or not?'

This was becoming uncomfortable. Thomas did not want to lie, but nor did he want to sound less than confident. 'This cipher can be broken and I will break it. Our enemy is time.'

'A time, as I recall, Thomas, set by yourself.'

'Indeed.'

'And one to which Henry Bishop and I expect you to keep. Neither of us likes Morland but, more importantly, we have the safety of England at stake. Am I clear?'

'Quite clear, Joseph.'

Williamson's tone softened, as if he had just remembered that Thomas was fifteen years his senior and was not one of his employees. 'In that case, is there anything you need?'

'I shall continue working through the night. If your cook could provide something to sustain me until the morning, I should be grateful.'

'I will arrange it. Let us hope that the morning will bring better news.'

'I am confident that it will.'

Once a plate of food and a jug of wine had arrived, Thomas took up a quill and started again. Strangely, it came to him almost at once. This precise, orderly encrypter had allocated numbers according to the frequency with which each letter typically appears, using each allocated number in turn, which would level the distribution. If E were represented by twelve numbers, for example, and appeared thirty-six times in the text, each of its allocated numbers would appear three times. And if D had been allocated four numbers and appeared twelve times, each of its numbers would also appear three times. That was why there were so many repeated numbers and why he had known instinctively that Morland was wrong.

On a new sheet of paper he wrote out the alphabet with the typical weighting for each letter below it. In a standard English text each letter might be expected to appear approximately that number of times relative to all other letters. Twice as many As as Ds, for example. In each row he hoped to be able to compile a list of the numbers the encrypter had allocated to it.

a b c d e f g h i j k l m n o p q r s t u v w x y z
8 2 3 4 13 2 2 6 7 1 1 4 2 5 8 2 1 6 6 9 3 1 2 1 2 1

From the hundreds of texts he and Abraham Fletcher had studied thirty years earlier he knew that these frequencies were about right, but only about right. Of course, any single text might throw up anomalies and the rarer letters such as X, Q and Z might not appear at all. He was still working more on instinct than logic, and a liberal dose of Hill's magic would be needed.

By dawn he had filled dozens of sheets with rows of numbers, his head was protesting and his eyes were closing of their own accord. He had made no more progress and, without rest, he was not going to. He lay down on the floor intending to rest his eyes briefly. Four hours later, however, he was woken by voices outside the door of his room. Rubbing the sleep from his eyes, he pulled himself painfully up on to one elbow and listened.

He recognized her voice at once. 'Good morning, Joseph. I've brought oranges and cherries. They're delicious. Do try one.'

'Thank you, my dear.' Thomas could see in his mind's eye Williamson reaching out and taking a cherry from her. He struggled to his feet and stretched his back.

'Is Thomas working here today?'

'He is, but I'd rather you didn't disturb him. He's engaged on a most urgent task.'

'Oh? What's that?'

Williamson laughed. 'You know very well I can't tell you, Madeleine, and I wouldn't if I could.'

'My goodness. It must be very important. Never mind. I only wanted to wish him good day.'

Wish me good day? After showing me the door at her house? What does the witch think I am? Some sort of servant? His hand was on the key and he was on the point of opening the door and confronting her when Abraham spoke again. 'Leave her, Thomas. Emotion is your enemy. You have work to do.' To hell with her. He went back to his work table, where there were a few drops of wine left in the jug and a crust of bread on the plate. He swallowed them and took up a quill.

For two hours he worked away at more combinations of numbers, ignoring the spaces between groups and hoping to alight on a clue. If he could find just one possible combination it would be a start upon which he should be able to build.

The start, when it came, was unexpected and thanks to the number 28, which appeared seven times, followed by seven different numbers. He guessed at the letter N, a medium-weight number, followed, at least in some cases, by T. NT was a very common pair — urgent, agent, interest — and likely to appear several times in a text of this length. And T would have about nine numbers allocated to it. The pair also had the characteristic of usually requiring a vowel before the N. From this tentative beginning, he slowly — very slowly and with many corrections — started to ascribe numbers to letters and to write them on his chart.

There was no great pleasure in this. He knew that he should have found the letter N sooner. It was Madeleine Stewart's fault. She had unsettled him.

An exercise like this always reminded Thomas of a race he had once run. Each year on Midsummer's Day, some of the more athletic scholars had competed for a cask of ale by running ten times around Christ Church Meadow. Naturally they ran as the ancient Greeks had — naked — and there was invariably a good crowd of boisterous onlookers of both sexes. Most of the competitors set off as fast as they could and hoped to get too far ahead for anyone to catch them. They quickly tired each other out. Thomas had won the race easily by starting slowly, accelerating a little in the middle and finishing at a sprint. Complex decryption was much the same. Start too fast and you would regret it later. Take your time and check your work carefully before moving on; and as each letter revealed itself the next one became a little easier.

During the afternoon and evening he found the vowels, then T, S and M. All fatigue disappeared and he was accelerating. At six o'clock he sent for more fuel, gobbled down half a chicken and prepared himself for the final mile.

The mile took longer than expected, however, because there turned out to be as many as twenty-five instances of N, the very first letter he had identified, and only twelve of D, which should have occurred about the same number of times. Reminding himself that if such anomalies did not sometimes occur cryptography would be easy, he continued patiently on his way, until he had a complete list of letters and numbers.

When he was satisfied that the actual number of appearances of each letter was close enough to what he expected, Thomas tried writing out the message. Soon he had:

MONEY DUE FROM ARGENTUM NEEDED IMMEDIATELY. OUR PLANS
NOW FAR ADVANCED AND EXPENSES HIGH. RECENT INTELLIGENCE
FROM AURUM UNHELPFUL. TAKE URGENT STEPS TO RECRUIT MORE
AGENTS. OUR FRIENDS IN FRANCE WILL JOIN US ONLY IF CONFI-
DENT OF OUR STRENGTH IN ENGLAND. GOD BE WITH YOU.
ALCHEMIST.

So the name *A. Silver Esq* was significant. Argentum and
Aurum — silver and gold. And all, it seemed, in the hands of an
Alchemist — not, presumably, Ben Jonson's *Alchemist*. If proof
were needed of a dangerous spy ring run from Holland, here it was.
The Dutch and the French. Plans far advanced. More agents.
Time to wake the acting secretary of state.

Despite the anticipation of finding out in the morning
whether or not Thomas had been successful, Williamson had
retired early and was sound asleep when his servant woke him just
after midnight. Within minutes he was alert and presentable and
down the staircase, where he found Thomas waiting for him, paper
in hand.

'Thomas, good news I trust.'

'Good news, Joseph, in that I have decrypted the letter. The
contents, however, are not so good.' Thomas handed over the
paper. Williamson took it and read it twice.

'No, not so good, although it might have been worse if you
had not decrypted it. The sender of this letter did not expect it to
be intercepted and certainly not to be decrypted. It confirms what
we have suspected for some months. The Dutch are trying to
persuade the French to join them against us, possibly even launch
an invasion. The Dutch fleet is already stronger than ours, and if
supported by the French . . .' He let the thought hang in the air.

'And Argentum and Aurum? Have you any idea who they are?'

'None. One apparently a source of finance, the other of intelligence. Two traitors acting together against us — one wealthy or with access to wealth, the other with information valuable to our enemies. I am sure the murders of Matthew Smith, John Winter and Henry Copestick were connected to them and that we are dealing with a formidable foe. A ruthless foe who has penetrated our intelligence network. Has Mottershead told you about the rumour of a disfigured foreigner?'

'He has mentioned it. He said there is talk of the man being the murderer, but there are no witnesses and no clues. It's merely conjecture.' Only a white lie, thought Thomas.

'Quite so. Copestick's death worries me the most because he worked in the Post Office itself. I know there have always been suspicions about Morland. The man was an ardent republican and has all the charm of a dung heap, but there is not a scrap of hard evidence against him.'

'What about Squire?'

'Ha. Too busy stuffing himself, drinking too much and falling ill. Surprisingly clever, but he was never a republican. In fact, like many travelling players, he claims to have carried royalist messages from place to place. I always suspected that was why Cromwell closed the theatres, rather than out of principle. And Squire's sexual inclinations make him an unlikely Puritan. The theatre was his home and his pleasure. I daresay the precious metals are outside the Post Office after all. The Foreign Office, perhaps.'

'Perhaps. But there are two of them, it seems. Twice as easy to catch. And what about the Alchemist himself?'

'As you no doubt know, there are agents scouring Europe for those who signed the late king's death warrant. I will instruct them to keep their eyes and ears open, but I suspect we'll only discover the Alchemist's identity if we can catch Aurum or Argentum and force it out of them. Even then, he'll be safe in Holland.' He paused. 'I think we will keep this to ourselves for now, Thomas. Much as I would like to see Morland's face when presented with your decryption, it will be safer if no one else but His Majesty knows that we have read this letter. Meanwhile we will redouble our efforts.'

'We?'

'I hope you will assist me, Thomas.'

'I had intended to return to Romsey immediately.'

'Immediately? Why so sudden?'

'I do not care for London. I wish to go home.' And I wish to persuade my niece to do the same, he thought, before disaster strikes. I have neglected my duty as her uncle and I have no more excuses for doing so.

Joseph peered at him with his good eye. 'I quite understand. You have done enough. Now I must dress and leave at once to see the king. Go and find a comfortable bed, Thomas. You look as if you need one.'

Thomas awoke in his bed at the Carringtons' house twenty-four hours later. Just before waking, he had dreamed that Madeleine Stewart was speaking to him in a language he could not understand. The more she spoke the angrier he became, until he picked up a pot of ink and threw it at her. But instead of the ink covering her, it turned itself into letters and numbers which hovered in the air. When he opened his eyes, the room was dark and it took him a minute to remember where he was.

Thomas could never see a summer dawn without thinking of Homer's 'rosy-fingered dawn, child of the morn', and when he looked out of his window, he did so again. A cloudless sky, streaked with red, was lightening as the sun rose, the birds were singing their chorus and the chestnuts in the square were as green as the oaks in the New Forest. A perfect day to begin his journey. In three days he would be home. First, however, he must pay his respects and make his explanations to Charles and Mary, of whom he had seen little since taking on the work for Williamson. More's the pity. Charles and Mary, quite apart from having saved his life twice, were people he loved dearly. Excellent company, caring, open, honest. The very people a new colony like Barbados needed. Having spent nearly four wretched years on the island, Thomas knew just how demanding a life it was, even for the now-wealthy planters. Disaster lurked around every corner – heat, disease, storms, violence, crop failure – each one could bring a man down and often did. The Carringtons, of course, would take whatever fate threw at them with courage and good humour. That was their way.

When Thomas appeared, Mary and Charles were at break-fast. 'Ah, Thomas, come and sit down,' said Mary with her customary warmth, 'and tell us what you've been doing. We've seen so little of you.' There was no hint of disapproval. Mary must have forgiven him.

'Thank you, my dear. I fear that I've been a poor guest.' Thomas took a chair beside her and helped himself from the dishes on the table.

'Yes, you have,' agreed Charles, 'very poor. Hardly a morsel of gossip from you, no hint of a scandal, no maids knocking on the door weeping tears of unrequited love, no cuckolded husbands demanding satisfaction, and just one little, ahem, accident. Mary was so sure you'd get caught up in something unpleasant. Really, we've been most disappointed, haven't we, my dear?' By Charles's standards, it was a long speech.

'We have not, Charles. And don't speak with your mouth full of bread. The crumbs go everywhere.' She turned to Thomas. 'I am glad to see that your face has healed, Thomas, and that you have suffered no more accidents. I only wish that we had seen more of you. How is the work going?'

'That is what I want to tell you both. My work is finished and I plan to leave with my niece for Romsey tomorrow.'

'This is bad news indeed.' Charles scattered more crumbs over the table.

'Have you informed Madeleine Stewart of your plans?' asked Mary. 'I'm sure she would like to know.'

'I have not had the opportunity,' replied Thomas stiffly, 'and I doubt if Miss Stewart would be interested in the matter.'

'Ah, lovers' tiff, eh?' exclaimed Charles with evident enjoyment. 'Excellent. Gives a man the chance to show the lady his chivalrous side. Down on one knee, abject apology, her hand in his, kiss, bedroom, everything back to normal. Never fails.'

Despite himself, Thomas smiled. 'Alas, Charles, Madeleine and I are not married. I doubt if the approach would work.'

Charles looked disappointed. 'Shame. It's what I'd do. Still, if you're too frightened . . .'

'It's not a matter of frightened, Charles,' said Mary. 'Thomas is the best judge of what to say to Madeleine. You will go and see her, Thomas, won't you?'

'I had not intended to — unless you think I should.'

'Of course you should. It would be most rude not to. Madeleine would be furious.'

'I must also speak to my niece. I have little time, but I will call on Madeleine if I can.'

Mary looked stern. 'Be sure that you do, Thomas Hill, or I shall never speak to you again.'

'In that case, I shall make every effort.'

'Good,' said Charles, 'and don't forget to go down on one knee. Essential.'

Thomas had no intention of calling on Madeleine Stewart even after the Carringtons' entreaties. Much better to slip away quietly. If he had to explain himself to his hosts, he would say that when he called the lady was not at home. Breakfast over, he returned to his bedroom intending to begin packing his bags, but before he had started Smythe arrived with a letter.

'This has just arrived for you, sir,' he said, holding out the silver tray. Thomas took the letter and knew the hand at once. Her previous letter had been an invitation to visit Lady Babb. He sat on the bed and read it.

My dear Thomas
   I hope you will find time to call upon me again soon. Our last meeting has left me unhappy.
   Your respectful friend
   Madeleine Stewart

No words wasted there, thought Thomas. And I have no time to waste if I am to make a start to Romsey. I must call on Lucy at Lady Richmond's house and tell her we shall be departing tomorrow. Then his old friend whispered in his ear. *It is desire and hope that push us on towards the future.* Desire and hope? Desire and hope for what, monsieur? For another rebuff? For a long journey home with three days to do little but regret even more foolishness? Come now, may I not be left in peace? He would take Lucy home and put Miss Stewart from his mind.

Lady Richmond's door was opened by a footman, who showed Thomas into a small reception room and went to inform Miss Taylor that her uncle had called to see her. Thomas did not have long to wait. Lucy came skipping into the room like a small child and almost threw herself at him. 'Uncle Thomas, this is a fine surprise. I did not know you were coming.' Her eyes were shining.

'Nor did I, my dear, until yesterday. Er, may I sit down?'

'Of course. Sit there,' she pointed to a tall library chair, 'and I shall sit opposite you.' They made themselves comfortable. 'There. Now, how are you and how are you enjoying London? Have you been to the theatre?'

Thomas cleared his throat. Best get it over with. 'That is why I have called, Lucy. I shall be returning to Romsey tomorrow and I wish you to accompany me.'

'But why? Lady Richmond is happy for me to be here as long as I wish and I am enjoying London. Romsey is so dull in comparison. Why must I go home?' The shining eyes were flashing. Thomas knew his niece's temper well enough.

'I would not be happy if you were here without me.'

'Uncle Thomas, that is absurd. I was here without you before the coronation.'

'I know, but it is time we went home.'

'Why? I am quite safe and Lady Richmond always insists that I am chaperoned.'

'Always?'

'Of course, always. Well, almost always. She allows me to walk alone with Arthur, because she knows he will take good care of me. He's such a fine young man, Uncle Thomas. I do hope you will get to know him better.'

'As a matter of fact, I have been making some enquiries about Arthur Phillips. Are you quite sure he is a suitable companion for you?'

'Uncle Thomas! Whatever do you mean and why have you been making enquiries about Arthur? He comes from a good family and works in the Navy Office. He is a most suitable companion for me and I like him very much.'

'He is certainly charming. I merely wonder if you are a trifle carried away by his charm?'

Lucy stood up. 'I do not know why you have taken against Arthur, Uncle Thomas, but I can assure you that he is decent and honourable. I will not return with you to Romsey tomorrow and if you try to make me I shall disappear into the streets of London where you will never find me.'

Thomas also stood. 'Don't be silly, Lucy. I only—' It was too late. Lucy flounced out of the room and ran up the stairs. Thomas shook his head. Well done, uncle, a fine performance.

Four murders, the murderer still at large, an unholy pact between the Dutch and the French, encouraged then rejected by Miss Stewart, and now Lucy attended on by a young man who visits brothels and refusing to go home. Why had he not stayed in Romsey?

CHAPTER 13

T he voice would not be silenced. It badgered and cajoled and wheedled and eventually Thomas surrendered. He would call briefly on Miss Stewart. Then he would return to Lady Richmond's house and, if necessary, bundle Lucy, kicking and screaming, into a carriage.

The front door of the little house off Fleet Street was opened by Agnes, who showed him into the room he knew. He amused himself by studying the paintings until Madeleine appeared. This morning, her brown hair had been teased into ringlets, she wore a shade of blue that matched her eyes and she carried about her the fragrance of lavender. When he saw her, Thomas caught his breath. It was as if she had expected him. Or expected someone.

'Miss Stewart,' he began, 'your letter arrived yesterday and as I'm about to leave for Romsey it was necessary to answer your request immediately.'

'Then it is fortunate that it did so. I would have been

disappointed if you had departed without word.' She smiled. 'Do sit down, Thomas.'

'I would prefer to stand.'

'As you wish,' said Madeleine, taking a seat.

'May I know why you asked me to call?'

'Thomas, as I wrote in my letter, I have been unhappy since we last met. I feel you deserve an explanation.'

'An explanation, madam? I recall nothing that requires explaining.'

Madeleine almost leapt out of her chair. Her eyes were blazing and her voice harsh. 'Thomas, how much of this have I to put up with? You know perfectly well why I have asked you here. Kindly make it no more difficult than it already is.'

Thomas inclined his head. 'Very well. I shall listen to whatever you have to say.' Apparently satisfied, Madeleine sat down again. Thomas did the same.

She sat with her hands in her lap, back straight, looking directly into his eyes. 'I have told you that I came to London from Hertfordshire, where my father was a parson. That is true. I have also told you that I once rejected a proposal of marriage and have never received another. That is partly true.' Thomas raised an eyebrow. 'The whole truth is that I have never had a suitor at all.'

'That I find hard to believe,' interrupted Thomas.

'Let me finish, Thomas, please. Then believe what you wish and judge me as you see fit.' Thomas nodded, and she went on, 'In the autumn of 1643 a troop of the king's guards arrived in our village on their way from Newbury to Oxford. I was eighteen, unmarried and largely innocent of the ways of the world.'

She saw his look. 'I know. Eighteen, the country at war, young men fighting and dying and taking their pleasures when and where they could. I find it hard to believe myself. But remember I had no mother and my father was a village parson, unworldly and protective of his only daughter.'

For a minute she was silent, as if preparing herself for the rest of the story. When it came, it came in a torrent. 'I was on my way home from a walk in the fields when the soldiers saw me. There were six of them. Their blue jackets and broad hats are fixed for ever in my mind's eye. Their leader rode a fine chestnut mare. They surrounded me on their horses and taunted me with insults and threats. I couldn't escape. I was terrified and started scream-ing. That's when they dismounted. One of them held me down while the others took it in turns to rape me. When they rode off they were laughing. I lay on the ground, curled up like a baby, bleeding heavily and whimpering with pain. I must have been there for hours. Eventually I was found by a farmer who took me home.'

With a lace handkerchief she wiped away the tears running down her cheeks. 'It was weeks before I could walk without pain and a year before I ventured out alone. And I was told that I would never have children. That is why there have been no suitors and why I left the village as soon as my father died. Everyone in the village knew what had happened. Some were unkind to us. Others tried to help, but who wants a barren wife?' Again, she dabbed at the tears. 'There was no handsome soldier, no proposal, no rejection.'

Thomas sat quietly searching for the right words. Eventually he said, 'Madeleine, you have suffered in a way few have suffered. To have survived and to be able to recount your terrible experience is testimony to your courage.' Madeleine dabbed at her eyes and smiled weakly. Thomas went on, 'Every war brings tragedy and every tragedy is personal. I was at Newbury. It was an unspeakable affair. Thousands dead and maimed — each death a tragedy for someone — and for nothing. Not a thing.'

'You didn't tell me you were a soldier.'

'I wasn't. I was acting as the king's cryptographer. Sending out encoded orders, that sort of thing. I was never in real danger, but I saw some of the battle. It was bloody and futile. The men who raped you would have been part of it. Violence breeds violence and soldiers are violent.'

'When you kissed me, I thought that, at last, I had recovered. Then my courage deserted me. No wonder you were angry. Am I forgiven?'

'No forgiveness is necessary. It is I who behaved badly.'

'I was dreading telling you my story, Thomas. Now that I have, I feel purged of a terrible secret.' She hesitated. 'Would you care to try behaving badly again or are you determined to board a coach?'

'The thought of our behaving badly together is certainly more appealing than an uncomfortable coach, Madeleine, but only if you're sure your courage has returned.'

Madeleine's reply was to lead him by the hand to her bedroom. She locked the door and turned to face him. 'There is one more thing. The scars are not only in my mind. I want you to see this first.'

Her fingers went to the ribbon at her throat. When she untied it, her dress fell away to expose her breasts. She pulled the dress down to her hips. A long, jagged scar ran from her breastbone to her abdomen. 'They said I'd get another each time I screamed. I didn't scream again.'

Thomas moved towards her and held her tightly, his mouth at

her ear. 'It is nothing,' he whispered. 'Can the bad behaviour begin now?'

By midday, Thomas was in two minds as to whether to board the coach that afternoon; by two o'clock he had decided that there was much to be said for staying a little longer in London, and by four o'clock he could see no reason at all to hurry home. Propped up on one elbow, he traced the outline of Madeleine's face with a finger. 'I shall not enquire how you come to speak French when making love, Madeleine Stewart, but for a lady who professes to be innocent of the world you have remarkable skill. And I'm not talking about your painting, fine though that is.'

'It takes two to dance and two to make love, Mr Hill. And, despite being a novice, I find myself in the hands of an expert. Would you care for another carole?'

It was dark by the time Thomas forced himself out of bed and into his clothes. He had left his bags packed for the journey at the Carringtons', and Mary would be wondering where on earth he had got to. 'I must go now, Madeleine,' he said, stooping to kiss her as she lay on the bed watching him. 'I shall call tomorrow. Would two in the afternoon be convenient?'

'It would. Almost as convenient as one. And don't be late. I do not care to be kept waiting.'

'So I've been told. Until tomorrow.'

Agnes had tactfully disappeared, so Thomas let himself out. He walked swiftly down Fleet Street and into the Strand, thinking of the beautiful lady he had just left and would see again the next day. Suddenly, life had taken on a new aspect for Thomas Hill and the future held a good deal more promise than it had at breakfast. Romsey could wait.

CHAPTER 14

A woollen scarf covered the Dutchman's face from the eyes down. It was better that passers-by should think that he was trying not to inhale the city's coal smoke or that he feared an infection than that it should be seen. He was not often on the streets in daylight and he did not want his face to be noted.

He had been watching the house in Piccadilly and had followed Thomas from there to the lane. He had waited patiently on the corner of Fleet Street for him to emerge from the house. If he did not emerge, the plan might be in jeopardy. Hopefully, the woman would soon turn him out as she had last time and all would be well.

But she did not turn him out and it was a long wait. By the time Hill stepped out of the house and into the lane it was dark. The Dutchman knew the name of this mark. He had been told to remember it for the future. It would have been easy to dispose of him there and then, but he had no instructions to do so. That time would no doubt come.

He followed Hill back to Piccadilly, waited outside the Carringtons' house long enough to be sure that he would not be returning to Fleet Street and then made his way back to Wapping. Tomorrow he would visit the inn in Bishopsgate and put his report behind the loose brick.

Then he would await further instructions.

CHAPTER 15

When Thomas returned, Mary asked him if he had visited Madeleine. 'I have,' replied Thomas, 'and if you will have me, I would like to stay in London a while longer.'

Charles roared with laughter, spilling his claret in the process. 'I told you it would work. Down on one knee was it? Humble apology, bedroom, all's well again? Never fails.'

'Something like that,' replied Thomas, unable to hide a sheepish grin.

Mary, too, was delighted. 'Of course we'll have you, Thomas, and perhaps we'll see more of you and Madeleine now that you've made up and your work is finished. We must go to the theatre again. And that reminds me that we haven't given our own little performance yet. We must find an occasion for it. You'd like to see it, Thomas, wouldn't you?'

'Is that the one you performed on the ship, in which you play Charles's miscreant son?'

'It is. I'm sure you'd enjoy it, and Madeleine would too.'

'I'm sure we would.' There was a knock on the door and Smythe came in to announce the arrival of a visitor.

'Mr Stoner is here, madam,' he said.

'Show him in at once,' said Charles, jumping up. 'More good news, I fancy. It's a day for good news.'

Chandle Stoner was immaculately turned out and looking as if he had just been given the crown jewels.

'Chandle, my friend, come in, sit down and share a glass.' Charles was effusive. 'It's good to see you. What news do you bring?'

'Good evening Mary,' replied Stoner, taking a glass from Smythe. 'Good evening, Thomas. I trust I find you both well.' He turned to Charles. 'Excellent news, I'm pleased to say. A ship arrived last week with a letter from my agent in Jamaica. He reports that the new mine is showing great promise and is confident that it will prove to be our best yet. A hundred ounces of silver have already been extracted.'

Charles raised his glass to Stoner. 'Your health, Chandle, and our gratitude for introducing us to this venture. It sounds as if we shall soon be able to retire in ease and comfort. None too soon, mind, sugar planting is not an occupation for old men. Eh, Mary, my dear?'

'Let us hope so. Chandle, when might we expect to receive our first return?'

'Well now, Mary,' replied Stoner, leaning forward in his chair, 'I'm glad you've raised that. The agent tells me that the more men they employ at the new mine, the quicker they will find the deeper seams which are always the richest and the sooner our investors will receive a healthy return.'

'What is to stop them employing more men?' asked

Mary. 'Surely there are plenty of workers to be had in Jamaica?'

'As ever, my dear, money. They need money to recruit men and to pay them until the seams are found and the profits start pouring in.'

'What about the money already invested?'

'Exploration, wages, payments to local officials and all manner of sundry other costs. Only to be expected in a venture of this kind, of course. I've seen it before a hundred times. Initial investment, proof of potential, second investment, revenues, profits. It's how business works.' Stoner laughed. 'My apologies, Charles, of course I don't need to explain that to you of all people. You must have been through much the same experience in Barbados.'

'Much the same, Chandle, much the same,' replied Charles affably. 'What do you advise?'

'I have given this serious thought, Charles, and my advice is to invest exactly the same amount as before. You will then maintain your share of the venture and may hope for an earlier return than might otherwise have been the case.'

'So this investment will be on the same terms as before, will it, Chandle?' asked Mary. 'Is that usual?'

'Oh, quite usual. We would not want to put a higher value on the venture at this stage. Although within a year or so, it will certainly be worth many, many times more.'

'It seems to me to be a matter of trust, my dear,' said Charles. 'I for one trust Chandle and I think we should take his advice. What do you think?'

'In matters of business, Charles dear, I have always trusted your judgement. If you wish to invest more in the venture, let us do so.'

'Very well. Chandle, you may count on us for a further invest-ment of a thousand guineas. Will tomorrow do?'

'Tomorrow would be splendid.' Stoner was clearly delighted at Charles's decision. 'And what about you, Thomas? Are you tempted to follow suit?'

'In matters of business I am little more than a babe in arms,' replied Thomas. 'Such capital as I have came to me from an un-expected source. I try to avoid things I do not understand.'

'Oh, quite, quite. Most prudent, if I may say so. In this case, however, you have Charles and Mary's example to follow. Might that sway you? I do like to see my friends profiting from my advice.'

'It might. I shall think about it.'

'Very wise. Talk to Mary and Charles. Take their advice. And if you do decide to join us, I shall be able to tell you the name of the venture. Until then, it must remain confidential, eh, Charles?'

'Confidential. Indeed. Much the best way. Don't want every tinker and tailor getting wind of it.'

Stoner rose to take his leave. 'It's time I was about my busi-ness. You've made the right decision, Charles. I'll call again tomorrow. Good evening, Mary. Good evening, Thomas. Do think about it, won't you?' Thomas smiled and nodded and Charles escorted Stoner to the door.

'Well,' said Charles when he returned, 'I knew it would be a good day. First Thomas and Madeleine and now this excellent news from Chandle. I shall sleep well tonight.'

'You sleep well every night,' replied Mary tartly, 'and you snore like a forest boar. Still, I expect you're right. It's just that two thousand guineas is such a large amount.'

'Not as much as fifty thousand, which is what it will soon become. I'm quite confident of it. What do you think, Thomas?'

'I think I shall keep to my books. You know where my money came from — the bottom of a foul hole in Barbados. I am much better at spending the stuff than making it, so I shall leave Chandle's venture to you and hope it makes you enormously wealthy.'

'What do you make of him?' asked Mary.

'I found him affable enough, if a little vague on facts. How well do you know him?'

'Not very. We relied on Drax's recommendation. Why?'

'It's just that he described himself as a financier. That strikes me as being like my describing myself as a mathematician. What exactly does a financier or a mathematician do?'

'One makes money and the other counts it,' laughed Charles. 'Mary has reservations, but I trust the man. We'll take our profits when the time comes and go home even wealthier than when we arrived.'

'I am sure you will, Charles. Forgive my cynicism. Money always brings out the worst in me.'

'In that, Thomas,' said Mary, 'you are not alone.'

When Thomas called at a little after two in the afternoon the next day, Madeleine Stewart opened the door herself. 'Agnes is out, so we shall have to look after ourselves,' she said archly. 'Are you hungry?'

'Not in the least.'

'Good.' Taking Thomas's hand she led him straight to her bedroom, where she undressed and slipped under the bed cover.

'Make haste, Thomas, Agnes will be back in a few hours.' With a grin, Thomas did as he was told.

Two hours later, arms and legs entwined, they spoke quietly of their friends and families. Thomas told her about his sister Margaret and his nieces Polly and Lucy, to whom he had been a father after Margaret's husband had died in a skirmish near Marlborough. Madeleine told him about her father, the village parson, whom she had loved despite his weakness. Their intimacy was interrupted by a knock on the door.

'Now who can that be at such an inconvenient time?' asked Madeleine. 'I am not expecting visitors. Perhaps they'll go away.'

But they did not go away. A second, more insistent knock, and Madeleine reluctantly struggled out of bed and into her clothes. 'Stay there, Thomas, and I will deal with this intruder,' she said.

'I shall. Call me only if you are in mortal danger.' Madeleine stuck out her tongue and went to answer the door. Thomas buried his head in a pillow and waited for Madeleine to return. When, after a few minutes, she had not returned, he too forced himself up, put on his shirt and breeches and opened the bedroom door. He stepped into the sitting room and immediately wished that he had stayed in bed. Sitting opposite Madeleine in front of the hearth was Joseph Williamson.

'This is a surprise. I thought you had left for Romsey, Thomas.' Joseph's disobedient eye squinted at him.

'I had intended to but, er, circumstances have detained me.'

Williamson looked him up and down. 'So I see from your dress. Perhaps a little adjustment might be in order.' Realizing that his shirt buttons were undone and his breeches untied, Thomas retreated to the bedroom, sorted himself out and re-emerged trying to look unembarrassed.

'Well, Thomas,' asked Williamson, 'am I to understand that my cousin has chosen to overlook your many faults and now entertains you in her home?'

'Tush, Joseph,' said Madeleine, 'there's no need to mince words. Thomas and I are lovers. I hope you approve, but if you don't, we will still be lovers.'

Williamson smiled. 'I cannot disapprove of a man who got the better of Sir Samuel Morland. But treat her with care, Thomas. Madeleine is my only cousin and I love her like a sister.'

'Be assured that I shall, Joseph. In my hands Madeleine will be as a lamb to its ewe.'

'Then let us hope there are no wolves about.'

'Enough of this,' said Madeleine briskly. 'Would you gentlemen care to share a bottle of claret? Good. I shall fetch one.'

While she was out of the room, Thomas asked Joseph if there had been any developments.

'Other than an uncomfortable audience with the king, very little,' replied Joseph with a sigh. 'Our fears that the Dutch and the French are up to something have been confirmed, but we don't know exactly what. Our agents in France and Holland have been unable to shed any light on the matter. I have found no evidence of a traitor in the Post Office and Mottershead has unearthed not a single clue about the murders. The king thinks we should close the Post Office until we find Aurum and Argentum and force the truth out of them.'

'Do you still think there is a spy in Cloak Lane?'

'There are spies everywhere, as the murders and the letter confirm.'

'Has Josiah heard nothing more about the murders at all?'

'Nothing other than that rumour of a disfigured foreigner. It is most frustrating and I dread each audience with the king. Had you not decrypted the letter, we would not even know about Aurum and Argentum.'

'Aurum and Argentum. Two precious metals about one base task. No wonder the king is alarmed.'

Madeleine returned with a bottle of claret and three glasses on a silver tray. She poured a glass for each of them and sat down. 'Now what have you gentlemen been talking about behind my back?'

Joseph and Thomas exchanged a look. 'Have you told Madeleine anything, Thomas?'

'I most certainly have not. We found more interesting matters to discuss.'

Joseph raised an eyebrow. 'In that case the less you know, Madeleine, the better. Suffice it to say that Thomas has performed a valuable service and that I have rather more on my plate than I had anticipated when Sir Edward left for the north.'

'How is Sir Samuel behaving?' asked Thomas with a grin.

Joseph waved his hand dismissively. 'As you might expect. With bile and venom. I have told him that you are still working on the letter. He is crowing that he was right and you were wrong and is demanding to be given it. He also wants more money for the work he is doing. The wretch is always short of money although we pay him well. I have no idea what he does with it.'

'And what of Henry Bishop?'

'Bishop does not like the work we do and does not understand why his Post Office has not been made entirely secure. Mind you, Bishop himself was a republican, although not as ardent as Morland. And to make matters worse, he is demanding more staff.

He says the volume of work is increasing and, with Squire forever away sick, he needs more men.'

'Is Lemuel still sick?' asked Thomas.

'He's sick more often than not these days. Too much rich food and too many bottles of wine, if you ask me.' Remembering Squire's consumption on the day he inspected the copying machine, Thomas could not but agree.

'By the way, he has mentioned that the seal on the encrypted letter might have been tampered with. Says it slipped his mind to tell us. Clever but unreliable, that man. I may have to think seriously of replacing him.'

Madeleine wagged her finger at him. 'Not with Thomas, Joseph, or you'll have me to answer to. Promise me you won't try to persuade him.'

'Don't worry, my dear,' said Thomas, 'a troop of the king's lifeguards armed with carbines and pikes could not persuade me to go back to work for Joseph. I am much too busy.'

'I shall have to do something soon,' said Joseph. 'We must remove this threat. God knows what damage has already been done.'

When Joseph had left, Thomas said to Madeleine, 'Despite the seriousness of this affair, I find myself thinking of it as a play, with characters and scenes and a plot which will unfold in its own time. Odd, isn't it?'

Madeleine giggled. 'I expect it's that French philosopher of yours who puts such ideas in your head.'

Having agreed that Madeleine would call for him at the Carringtons' the following morning at ten o'clock, Thomas returned to Piccadilly. Delighted as he was at the thought of enjoying Madeleine's company, Joseph's mood had unsettled him and, as he walked back, he found his mind turning again to the play.

In his room, he took out the *Dramatis Personae* again, and added

Disfigured foreigner (murderer?)
Aurum and Argentum: spy ring leaders

What did he know now about the players? Williamson himself was surely above suspicion. Bishop, however, had worked for Cromwell and had been accused more than once of using his position to promote republican sympathizers. If Joseph trusted him he would have told him about the decryption. Could he be working secretly with the Dutch?

As for the ambitious and disagreeable Morland, he too had been a zealous Parliamentarian. Until, that is, he had seen the return of the monarchy coming and quietly changed his allegiance. Lemuel Squire — gluttonous, affable and often in his sickbed. Could there be even more to him than met the eye? Josiah Mottershead — Joseph's man and a most unlikely spy.

And what of Chandle Stoner? Nothing to do with the Post Office, man of business and friend of the Carringtons, he was not really a player at all, and Thomas wondered why he had included him in the cast. Madeleine? Charles and Mary? Impossible.

And there would be other players, some with small roles, others large. Polonius, Gertrude, Horatio, the Prince of Denmark himself? Still no sign of the *deus ex machina*, though. Fortunately I'm only a cryptographer, thought Thomas. Espionage is too complicated for me. And I have played my part. Joseph must take care of the rest.

Thomas appeared the next morning in the clothes he had worn to the coronation, to be greeted by one of Charles's throaty chuckles. 'Off to visit the king, Thomas? Are you sure about the ribbons on your sleeves? Might not be quite the thing for Whitehall Palace.'

'Take no notice, Thomas,' Mary reassured him. 'You look splendid. Pale blue suits you. Are you taking Madeleine out today?'

'I am. She will be here at ten o'clock. She is hoping to see you and Charles.'

'Good. Madeleine will be most impressed by your outfit. Come and have some breakfast.' In London, it was the Carringtons' custom to take their meals as they did in Barbados, where Charles refused to wait until noon for proper sustenance and insisted on a good breakfast before a morning's work on the estate.

Thomas sat at the table and picked at a plate of smoked fish. Despite having spent the previous afternoon with Madeleine, he was strangely nervous — more like a callow youth of fifteen than a gentleman approaching fifty. Mary watched him for a while and then asked where he planned to take Madeleine. 'I am not sure,' he replied. 'Would you care to make a suggestion?'

'Bed,' bellowed Charles, 'that's the place to take her. Much more entertaining than a hanging or the king's menagerie.'

'Be quiet, Charles, and eat your breakfast,' snapped Mary. 'Your advice on this matter is unwelcome.' With a shrug, Charles returned to his food and left them to it.

Mary turned back to Thomas. 'As it's a fine day, Thomas, why not take a carriage to the village of Kensington? The air is clean there and there are good walks to be had in the fields. You could take dinner in a local hostelry and return afterwards.'

Relieved at having the decision made for him, Thomas managed a few mouthfuls before Charles spoke up again. 'No need to be nervous, Thomas,' he said. 'If you're planning anything matrimonial, just remember — one knee and undying love. Never fails.'

'Oh, for the love of God, Charles, let the poor man be. Thomas will do as he sees fit and needs no instruction from you.' Mary's tone was uncommonly sharp.

Thomas took his leave and returned to his room to wait for ten o'clock to strike. Whether or not he attempted 'anything matrimonial' would depend upon Madeleine's mood and how their day went. And upon whether his nerve held. Just to be safe, however, he rehearsed his words in front of a mirror, first on one knee, then standing erect. Unable to choose between them, he decided to leave it until the moment arrived. If it arrived. He sat at the writing table and picked up his copy of Montaigne's *Essais*. But even the great man could not hold his attention for long. When he realized that he was turning the pages without reading the words, he put the book down, closed his eyes and tried to breathe deeply. It was something he had learned years ago. A state of calm comes from clearing the mind and relaxing the muscles.

When at last the clock struck ten, Thomas rose from his chair, smoothed out his coat, checked his appearance in the mirror and went down the stairs to the sitting room. There he found Charles reading a newsbook and Mary sewing a dress. Charles glanced up when he entered, but said nothing. The strictest instructions from Mary, no doubt, and warnings of terrible retribution if he spoke out of turn. Thomas sat and waited, hoping that Madeleine would not be unduly late. He was anxious to leave the house and be off to Kensington.

At half past the hour, Mary looked up from her embroidery. 'Are you sure it was ten o'clock, Thomas? It's unlike Madeleine to be late.'

'Quite sure. Something unexpected must have detained her. She will be here soon.'

Having made a gallant effort to keep quiet, Charles could do so no longer. 'Doesn't want to appear too keen, I daresay. A good sign, Thomas, if you ask me. Shows her true feelings.' Thomas smiled but said nothing. He was willing her to arrive.

When the clock struck eleven, however, she had still not arrived, and he could wait no longer. 'I shall walk to Madeleine's house,' he said, standing up. 'She may have forgotten our arrangement or she may have been taken ill. I shall go and find out.'

'Yes,' replied Mary, 'I think that would be best. If Madeleine is unwell, I will go myself to see that she is being taken good care of.'

Thomas fetched his hat and set off for Fleet Street. As always, the streets were busy. Ladies and gentlemen taking the morning air, milkmaids, pie-sellers, flower girls, coachmen, messengers — all about their business, all playing their part in the daily bustle of the city.

He walked as quickly as he could on his heeled shoes, through and around the crowds, ignoring the cries of the traders anxious to sell him their wares and trying not to collide with other walkers. Near the corner of the narrow lane, the crowds thinned and he was soon outside Madeleine's house. He knocked loudly, waited a minute, then knocked again. He heard footsteps and the door was opened by Agnes. She looked surprised to see him.

'Why, Mr Hill, is Miss Stewart not with you?' she asked.

'Indeed she is not. I was expecting her at ten o'clock.'

'She left half an hour after nine.'

'Could she have gone somewhere else first and been delayed?'

'She said nothing about going anywhere else. She planned to walk directly to Piccadilly.' Agnes's hand went to her mouth. 'Mr Hill, could something have happened to her?'

'I expect there is a simple explanation, Agnes. You stay here and tell Miss Stewart I called if she appears. I will return to Piccadilly.' Agnes wiped her eyes on her sleeve. 'Now don't worry, Agnes, all will be well. I expect we'll both be back here within the hour. You just stay here.'

'Yes, sir. I'll stay here, but please let me know the moment you find her.'

Retracing his steps along Fleet Street, Thomas intended to make his way straight back to Piccadilly. But he soon found himself peering into dark doorways and venturing into mean alleys. It was absurd but he could not help himself. If Madeleine was lying injured, he must find her.

In the alleys and lanes off Fleet Street he was accosted by whores, insulted by beggars and jostled by street urchins. He ignored them all. He spoke to traders and street vendors. None of them had seen a lady matching Madeleine's description and with each shake of the head he became more agitated. By the time he reached Charing Cross his shoes and breeches were splattered with mud and muck and he was covered in sweat. With an effort of will, he pulled himself up and tried to think rationally. It was fear that had driven him to behave so foolishly — fear for Madeleine, fear of what he might find, fear for himself. Calmer, he walked back to Piccadilly.

Charles and Mary were waiting for him. 'What news, Thomas?' asked Mary as he walked in. He told them what he knew from Agnes and that there had been no sign of Madeleine on his way back.

'Damnably strange,' said Charles. 'What's to be done, do you think?'

'I suggest we send a messenger at once for Joseph. He will know what to do.'

'Good idea. I'll tell Smythe to find one.'

When Charles had left the room, Mary put her arms around Thomas. 'You and I have been through much together and we'll get through this. We'll find Madeleine safe and well, and when we do, I shall expect you to propose to her without further ado.'

'My history with people I care for has not been good. I wish I could share your confidence.'

'Nonsense, Thomas. Joseph is one of the most powerful men in London and he is very fond of his cousin. He will move mountains to find her.'

'Let us hope it does not come to that.'

Joseph arrived hot and flustered from Chancery Lane within the hour. 'What's all this about?' he demanded without a greeting. 'The messenger insisted that I come at once. What has happened?'

'Madeleine has disappeared,' replied Mary. 'She left her house at half an hour after nine this morning to walk here. When she did not arrive Thomas went to her house, thinking she might be ill. We cannot imagine where she is.'

'Why was she walking here alone? Why was she not escorted?'

'Oh come now, Joseph,' said Charles firmly, 'it was mid-morning and the streets would have been busy. There was no reason for her to be escorted. No blame attaches to anyone.

And anyway it does not matter now. What matters is finding her.'

'Can you help look for her, Joseph?' asked Mary.

'I'll tell Mottershead to get to work on it immediately. If she's been robbed or attacked in the street, he'll soon find out.'

'If she had been,' said Thomas, 'she would have raised the alarm or made her way here. It must be something else.'

'And if she had been sent for by someone — Lady Babb, for instance — she would have sent word,' agreed Mary.

'Possibly, possibly.' Joseph sounded distracted. 'I'll put Mottershead on it anyway. Let me know at once if you find her and I will do the same.' He turned to leave. At the door, he added, 'You were right to tell me,' and was gone.

Thomas sat alone in his room, going over the events of the day in his mind. On her way from Fleet Street to Piccadilly, in the middle of a fine morning, Madeleine had disappeared. If she had been attacked, why had there been no hue and cry? If she had fallen or been struck by a coach, there would have been witnesses and word would have reached them. There must be more to it and it was not difficult to hazard a guess as to what had happened.

What was more, Joseph's parting shot suggested that he too could guess. It was no secret that she was his cousin and an unseen watcher would also know that she and Thomas had become close. That made her doubly vulnerable and they should not have spoken freely in front of her. Knowing what she did would not help her if she had been abducted and was being questioned. She would suffer until she spoke and then she would die. And her abductors would know that the message had been decrypted and that their plans were no longer secret. They might have to change them and start again, but they would not fall into the trap of assuming they were safe. It was the worst of all possible outcomes, and the most likely.

That evening, after Charles and Mary had tried and failed to lift Thomas's spirits — unsurprisingly, as their own spirits were just as low as his — he could no longer sit and wait. He had to get out and do something — almost anything would be better than waiting for the news that the body of a woman had been found under London Bridge, her clothing ripped, her face cut and a jagged scar running from her throat down her chest. He shook his head to clear the image, made his apologies to the Carringtons and ran out of the house.

An hour later, having aimlessly walked the streets and peered into dozens of dark alleys and doorways, Thomas found himself outside Madeleine's house in the lane off Fleet Street. His knock was answered by Agnes. To his surprise, behind her stood the square figure of Josiah Mottershead, stick in hand and a belligerent look on his scarred face.

When he saw Thomas, Josiah put an arm around Agnes's shoulders and moved her gently out of the way. 'It's you, Mr 'Ill,' he said with some relief. 'Come in and tell us the news.'

'I have no news, I fear, Josiah. I merely thought to come here for want of anything better to do. And you? The same thought?'

'Mr Williamson instructed me to search the 'ouse, sir, just in case there was some sort of clue.'

'And have you searched it?'

'I 'ave, sir, and found nothing. Agnes 'as baked a pie. We were about to eat it when you knocked.'

'Would you care to join us, Mr Hill?' asked Agnes. 'There's plenty.'

Thomas had never felt less like eating, but he needed company and he did not want to return to Piccadilly yet. 'Thank you, Agnes. I'd be glad to.'

They sat around a small table in the kitchen. Agnes cut the pie and gave each of them a large slice. Agnes and Josiah, despite their obvious distress, polished theirs off speedily. Thomas could manage only a couple of mouthfuls.

'Excellent pie,' said Josiah, giving Agnes a smile and a pat on the hand, 'don't you agree, Mr 'Ill?'

'Excellent indeed, Agnes. Although I fear I have little appetite.'

'In times of trouble, I make a point of eating,' said Josiah. 'It keeps the body strong and the brain working. And a man in my line of work can never be sure when 'e might eat again. Eat your share if you can, sir, that's my advice.'

Thomas had another try and swallowed two more mouthfuls before pushing his plate away. 'Agnes, tell me again about this morning. Did Miss Stewart show any sign of worry or distress?'

'None, sir, that I noticed. She was bright as ever and looking forward to seeing you. We talked about where you might go.'

'And you've heard nothing, Josiah?'

'No, sir. But I'll be out again tonight. News often travels faster in the dark. I'll ask about, see if anyone's 'eard anything.'

'I shall come with you.'

Josiah frowned and scratched his head. 'That would not be a good idea, sir. You won't pass as my cousin Tom in those clothes and, if you don't mind me saying, I'll 'ave a better chance on my own. You stay 'ere in case anyone calls and keep an eye on Agnes.'

Josiah was right. Where he was going, Thomas would stand out like a turkey in a hen house. 'Very well. I'll spend the night here and wait until you return.'

'That's better, sir. Agnes'll take care of you, won't you, Agnes?'

Agnes's round face lit up. 'Of course I will. Be a pleasure. And you take care too, Mottershead. I don't want to have to mend that ugly head of yours.'

'Don't you worry about my 'ead, Agnes Cakebread. My 'ead's taken a few knocks in its time and it's still fixed on. You just look after Mr 'Ill.'

When Agnes had ushered Josiah out of the door, Thomas went to the sitting room, leaving her about her business in the kitchen. He needed to be alone and to concentrate on Madeleine. Just thinking about her might bring something to mind, some small clue as to what had happened to her.

He thought about what she had told him of her childhood, about the pain she had suffered, about her coming to London. He replayed in his mind their walks in the park and their whispered words in this house. He concentrated harder. He saw her sitting opposite him, distraught at having pushed him away, and tearfully recounting the horror of her rape. He thought and thought. And found nothing — neither clue nor inspiration. There could be but one explanation for her disappearance — she had the misfortune to be Joseph Williamson's cousin and the lover of Thomas Hill. She had been abducted and would be interrogated for what she knew. Then she would be disposed of. Thomas's gorge rose at the thought and he tasted bile in his throat. He shut his eyes and breathed deeply. It must not happen.

For Thomas there was no possible hope of sleep. He wandered into the kitchen, where Agnes was curled up on a pallet on the floor, and into the bedroom where they had made love, and he looked again at Madeleine's paintings. With a wry smile, he realized that they were not quite as accomplished as he had at first thought — the brushwork in places was a little heavy — but they were good enough and they were hers.

He jumped at the sound of every footstep in the lane, expecting a knock on the door and the return of Josiah or the arrival of a messenger from Joseph. But none came and when dawn broke and Agnes emerged from the kitchen she found Thomas, red-eyed and haggard, sitting and staring at the empty hearth.

'Mottershead'll be back soon, sir,' she said, doing her best to sound cheerful. 'I'll make some breakfast for you both.'

Before long, roused by the sounds and smells of cooking, Thomas shook his head free of the long night, stood up and stretched his legs and back. There was a knock on the door and when he opened it, Josiah came straight in. Thomas knew at once that he had learned nothing. There was not a hint of a smile on the little man's face and, accustomed as he doubtless was to sleepless nights spent in the course of duty, he looked exhausted.

Josiah shook his head. 'Not a squeak, sir. Nothing. If anyone knows what 'appened to Miss Stewart they're not saying, and I don't think they do know. I'd 'ave spotted it if they did.' Thomas did not know whether to be relieved or dismayed. Neither sight nor sound, but no rumours of a robbery either. And, thank God, no body in the river.

Nothing, it seemed, interfered with Josiah's appetite and he was soon demolishing more of Agnes's pie. Thomas, as he had the previous evening, ate little. They listened as Josiah told them where he had been and to whom he had spoken. He had persevered all night, despite hearing not a word about a lady being robbed or attacked in the street.

'I'll go to Mr Williamson,' he said, wiping his plate with a crust of bread. ''E's expecting me and there will 'ave been other men out last night. Perhaps one of them 'eard something.'

'I'll come with you,' replied Thomas, standing up from the

table. 'Let's be off,' he said, adding, 'Unless you need to rest a while, Josiah,' when he saw the look which passed between him and Agnes.

'No, sir, rest can wait. Thank you for the food, Agnes. I shall be back later.'

'I'll be here,' she replied, 'and praying for better news.'

CHAPTER 16

Joseph Williamson had also been up all night. His shirt and coat were crumpled and his eyes were red. The lid of his left eye drooped over the pupil, giving him the look of a drunk, unable to focus. He led them into his library and invited them to sit. 'What news, Mottershead?' he asked without preamble.

'None, sir, I fear,' replied Josiah nervously. 'Not a sound. I don't understand it.'

'No more do I.' Joseph was tired and short-tempered. 'How can a lady disappear in the middle of the day in a perfectly respectable part of London without anyone apparently having seen or heard anything at all? It beggars belief.'

'So there's been no word from anywhere?' asked Thomas.

'None. I sent four others out as well as Josiah. Not a glimmer from any of them. Three of my men dead and now Madeleine . . . we've lost control of our own city. Whoever these traitors are — Aurum and Argentum and their murdering friends — they must be as cunning as the devil. And I've heard nothing from that drunken sot Manners. I've told him to let me know at once if he has any suspicions.'

'Are you convinced that Madeleine's disappearance is connected to the murders?' asked Thomas.

'I am now. Anything else and we would have heard something. Don't you agree, Mottershead?'

'I do, sir.'

Williamson turned to Thomas. 'Mottershead knows about the letter and the spy ring. I thought it best to tell him in case he picked up a murmur about the names. I do wish we had not said anything to Madeleine, however. Stupid fool that I am, this did not occur to me. It should have.'

'If there's nothing else, sir,' said Mottershead, 'I'll be off. I've still a few places to visit.'

'Of course, Mottershead. Report back this evening, please, or the moment you hear a word.'

'I will, sir. Goodbye, Mr 'Ill. And don't worry, we'll find 'er safe and well. I can feel it in the Mottershead bones.'

Thomas managed a weak smile. 'Do your best, Josiah. If anyone can find Madeleine, you can.'

When Mottershead had gone, Joseph pulled off his long wig and scratched the top of his head. 'God's wounds, but I hope he's right. I'd never forgive myself if Madeleine were to come to any harm on my account.'

'Nor I,' agreed Thomas. 'Is there no more intelligence?'

'None. If it wasn't so serious, it would be comic.' Williamson rubbed his eyes. 'I have never seen the king so angry. "Our entire intelligence service with no intelligence," he said. "Murders, abductions and a Franco-Dutch plot about which we know next to nothing. Get to the bottom of this without delay, Mr Williamson, or we will find someone else to do so." I am going to Cloak Lane to speak to Morland and Squire again, Thomas. Will you accompany me?'

'If you wish it. And if Squire thinks the letter might have been tampered with, perhaps we should also speak to his chief clerk.'

At the Post Office, Henry Bishop was less than pleased to see them. He berated them for yet another intrusion into the daily workings of his Post Office and complained about his lack of staff, Morland's ungracious behaviour and Squire's frequent absences. Joseph and Thomas sat silently until the outburst was over. Then Joseph asked quietly if Morland might be fetched. Without another word, Bishop stormed out.

If anything, Sir Samuel Morland was even less pleased to see them than Henry Bishop. 'I assume you have come to inform me that this man has failed to decode the intercepted letter?' he barked, glaring at Williamson. 'If you now wish me to do so, you will be disappointed. I am much too busy.'

Joseph ignored the bait. 'That is not our purpose. We simply wish to confirm some facts.'

'What facts?'

'That you did not see the original letter, only the copy made by Mr Squire.'

'I have said so. Why do you ask again?'

'So you cannot comment on Squire's view that the seal might have been tampered with?'

'If anyone tampered with the seal it must have been one of the clerks. Or Squire himself.'

'Why would he do that?'

'That is for you to establish.'

Williamson leaned forward in his chair. 'Be sure that we shall, Sir Samuel.' He paused. 'And why did you suppose that you alone could break the numerical code?'

The look that Morland shot at Thomas was so venomous that Thomas felt himself recoil. 'Because I am the most accomplished cryptographer in England. I do not believe that this man has the skill to do it. And it seems that I am right.' Thomas bit his tongue. Much as he wanted to humiliate this hateful man, they had agreed to keep his decryption secret.

'Very well, Sir Samuel,' said Williamson. 'Now please be good enough to ask Mr Squire to join us.' With another look of pure poison, Morland left.

Thomas exhaled. 'That man should hang, guilty or not.'

Williamson laughed. 'You are not alone in that opinion. Let us hope Squire is in a more helpful frame of mind.'

When Squire bustled in, Thomas only just stopped himself from laughing. Even by Lemuel's standards, his outfit that day was bizarre. His ample stomach was encased in a short green jacket with a high collar, over a cream shirt with huge mutton-chop sleeves and a long red skirt. On his feet he wore blue heeled shoes with silver buckles. The whole ensemble was finished with abundant ribbons of assorted colours. In certain circles such an outfit was the very height of fashion. On the rotund Squire it was merely comical.

He adjusted his wig and wiped his face with a pink handkerchief. 'Good day, gentlemen. How can I be of service?' The smile was as wide as ever.

'Just a few questions for clarification, Lemuel. How long was the encrypted letter on your desk before you opened it?' asked Joseph.

'I was away for two days.'

'And you opened it as soon as you returned?'

'I did, and took it straight to Henry. I thought that best.' He sounded apologetic.

'Why did you think the seal might have been tampered with?'

'There was a small mark on it which could have been made by a knife. Perhaps someone changed his mind, or thought he was being observed.'

'Lemuel, who could that have been?' asked Thomas.

Squire clasped his hands over his stomach and took a moment to answer. 'Morland would have had the opportunity and so would Roger Willow, my chief clerk.'

'Do you suspect either of them?'

Another long pause. 'Willow is a loyal colleague.'

'And Morland?' asked Joseph.

Squire held up his hands. 'I have said enough, gentlemen. I should return to my work.'

'Of course. Our thanks for your cooperation. Can you spare Willow for a few minutes? We've seen Morland.'

'I will send him in. We must dine together again soon, Thomas.'

'I shall look forward to it,' replied Thomas with a smile. He could not help liking this overfed, overdressed gargoyle.

Since Thomas had last seen him, Roger Willow looked to have shrivelled. His face was even thinner, his shoulders more hunched and he peered at them over his spectacles with eyes the colour of claret. 'We have some questions, Willow,' said Joseph. 'Nothing to be concerned about.'

Willow scratched his ear nervously. 'Is it about the letter addressed to A. Silver in Aldersgate?'

'Why would you think that?'

'We heard Mr Squire and Sir Samuel arguing about it and the clerks are saying that it must be something unusual and important. Also, Sir Samuel has been particularly ill-tempered since Mr Squire returned from his sickness. He berated me for not showing the letter to him. He knows my instructions are to pass letters to be opened to Mr Squire and no one else, but still he insisted that I should have given it to him. The episode has made me quite unwell.' The words came out in a rush.

'The letter had come from Holland and the address was unknown to you, so perhaps you should have given it to Sir Samuel, or even Mr Bishop.'

'Mr Bishop dislikes the opening of correspondence. He would have told me to put it on Mr Squire's desk.'

'Mr Squire thinks that the letter might have been tampered with. There was a mark on the seal,' said Thomas.

Willow looked up sharply. 'Mr Squire has said nothing about this to me. What sort of mark?'

'One possibly made by the point of a knife.'

'Impossible. Anyone taking a knife to a letter would be observed. And the letter was brought over from Love Lane and given directly to me.' The blood rose to Willow's face. A slur on his clerks was a slur on him. Thomas and Joseph exchanged a look. If Willow was dissembling he was a fine actor. 'I must say, Mr Williamson, that I resent any accusation that I or one of my clerks acted improperly. As always, I carried out my duty exactly as expected of me.'

Williamson stood up. 'Very well, Willow. For now the matter is closed. But we might have more questions in due course. Good day to you.'

Willow's face was set. 'Good day, gentlemen.'

When he had left them, Joseph shook his head and said, 'Well, I do not think we learned much from that.'

'Only confirmation that Morland is uncouth, Squire is a popinjay and Willow looks on the sorting office clerks as his children. Nothing about Madeleine,' replied Thomas.

'Morland's fury at not being given the letter is hard to understand. Willow acted quite properly.'

'Perhaps Morland's self-regard is such that it can affect his judgement. You saw what he was like when you gave me the letter to decrypt. He was apoplectic.'

'But if there is an enemy in our midst we're no closer to finding him. We must redouble our efforts to find Madeleine.'

CHAPTER 17

Thomas was dozing when Mary woke him the next morning. 'A messenger has just come from Joseph. He wants you to meet him in an hour.'

'Where?'

'At the coroner's house.'

'Oh God.' Thomas was wide awake instantly and pulling on his shirt. The coroner's house could mean only one thing.

'Charles will come with you, Thomas. He wants to.'

'If he wishes.'

'And you must eat. The cook is preparing something to take with you. Eat it in the carriage.'

On the way to Manners' house, neither Charles nor Thomas spoke. Thomas managed to wash down a hunk of bread and cheese with sips of warm milk while Charles sat staring silently out of the window. When the coach drew up outside Manners' house, they were out before the coachman could jump down to open the door. Charles knocked loudly on the coroner's door, which was opened by the ancient clerk Thomas remembered from his previous visit.

Williamson was waiting for them inside. 'There you are, Thomas, and Charles too. Good. Manners knows I'm here and I've told him not to keep us waiting this time.'

'What do you know, Joseph?' asked Charles.

'Only that the body of a woman of about Madeleine's age was found under London Bridge this morning. I do not have a description.' Williamson began pacing the room. 'Where is that damnable man?'

A woman of Madeleine's age. Thomas's throat tightened and his legs buckled. He struggled to breathe and grabbed Charles's arm to steady himself. Charles put an arm around his shoulders and helped him to a chair, where he sat head down and in silence. Not Madeleine, surely not Madeleine.

When, after a few minutes, Manners entered through a door at the back of the room, Williamson shouted at him. 'For the love of God, Manners, you're holding a body which might be my cousin and we've been kept waiting again. We will see the body at once.'

What passed across Manners' face was very like a smirk. 'I have been busy, Mr Williamson. A coroner has many important tasks to perform.'

Williamson grunted. 'I daresay. Well, come on, man, take us to her.'

But Manners was not to be hurried. 'Before I do, gentlemen, you should know that the face of the dead woman has been cut with a sharp instrument. A knife, possibly. And there are other matters. Identifying her will not be straightforward.'

Thomas stood up and sat down quickly. 'Would you prefer that Joseph and I see her?' asked Charles gently.

For a moment Thomas was tempted to say yes. An image of Madeleine lying dead and disfigured on the coroner's table would stay with him for ever; it might be wiser to leave it to the others. But he had to see her. It would be a betrayal not to.

'No, I'll come.'

'As you wish,' said Manners pompously, 'but you have been warned. Follow me.' He led them through the house to the room in which Thomas and Joseph had inspected the body of Henry Copestick.

Unlike that of Copestick, this body was covered by a black sheet. Manners strode up to the table and drew back the sheet to reveal the woman's face. Thomas's hand went straight to his mouth and he turned his head away. Again he felt Charles's arm around his shoulders.

For perhaps thirty seconds the room was silent. Joseph was the first to speak. 'Where and when exactly was she found, Manners?' he whispered.

'Under London Bridge at about ten o'clock this morning.'

'Who found her?'

'A wherryman. He sent for me immediately.'

'And she was as we see her now?'

'Naturally.' Manners sounded affronted.

Thomas forced himself to look again at the horribly disfigured face. It was covered in cuts and congealed blood from forehead to chin and across both cheeks, the eye sockets were empty and all hair had been cut off. Manners was right. Identification from the face was impossible. 'Is she clothed?' he asked quietly.

'She is.' Manners pulled the sheet down so that they could see the body. As far as it was possible to tell, she had been about the same height and age as Madeleine. She wore neither rings nor jewellery, as Madeleine did not, and before being submerged in the river, her dress had been a shade of blue that would have matched Madeleine's eyes. 'Do you recognize this woman, Mr Williamson?' he asked.

Joseph shook his head. 'It is hard to say. Thomas, do you recognize her?'

Thomas was conscious of being watched by Manners. He spoke slowly. 'Kindly pull down her dress, Mr Manners, so that I may see her chest.'

'Really, sir, is that necessary? If she cannot be identified from her face, what will you learn from her chest?'

'Just do it, man,' barked Charles.

With a show of disapproval, Manners unfastened her dress and pulled it down to her waist. 'Will that be far enough?' he sneered.

Thomas felt a weight lift from the pit of his stomach. This unfortunate woman had been tortured and murdered, but she did not carry a scar from her throat to her stomach. He turned to Charles and Joseph. 'It is not Madeleine.'

'Are you sure?' asked Joseph.

'Quite sure.'

Joseph spoke to Manners, the relief in his voice clearly audible. 'I fear we cannot be of assistance, Manners, but I am sure you will pursue this poor wretch's killer with your customary zeal.'

Disappointment was written all over Manners' face. The repulsive little man had wanted the body to be that of Madeleine Stewart, Joseph Williamson's cousin. He shrugged and led them from the room. As they were leaving, he said, 'Should you be mistaken, gentlemen, I shall of course have to refer the matter to a magistrate. Impeding a coroner in the pursuit of his duties is a serious business.'

'Hold your tongue, Manners,' thundered Williamson, 'or you'll be getting a visit from Sir Edward Nicholas's men.'

The three of them stormed out of the house and into the waiting coach. 'To Chancery Lane first, coachman,' Joseph shouted, 'then to Piccadilly. And make haste.'

'Thank God,' said Thomas, when they were on their way. 'I suppose one should pity the girl but my only feeling is one of relief.'

'Quite understandable, my dear fellow,' said Charles. 'What we have to do now is find Madeleine and be quick about it. Let's hope Joseph's men have discovered something.'

Joseph said nothing. He seemed lost in his own thoughts.

Outside his house, he alighted from the coach and waited for the coachman to carry on. He had not spoken during the journey and Thomas had not thought to ask him about his meeting with Morland. The coachman raised his whip and was on the point of setting off when Joseph's steward emerged from the house waving a letter.

'This was delivered by hand a few minutes ago, Mr Williamson,' he said. 'I thought you would want to see it immediately.'

Williamson took the letter and examined it. 'Did you see who delivered it?'

'No, sir. It was pushed under the door.'

He signalled to the coachman to wait and carefully broke the seal on the letter. He opened and read it, then passed it through the coach window to Thomas. Thomas read it and passed it to Charles, who read it aloud.

Madeleine Stewart is in a safe place. If there are further attempts to find her, she will die. We require payment of £10,000 for her safe return. Confirm receipt of this letter by placing a notice in Thorpe's newsbook.

Await further instructions.

'Any idea who it's from?' asked Charles.

Joseph exchanged a look with Thomas and said, 'You'd better both come in.'

Thomas closed his eyes and sighed. She must be alive. Ten thousand pounds was a great deal of money, but for Madeleine Stewart, a bargain.

The three men sat in Joseph's library, the letter on a low table between them. Thomas was the first to speak. 'It looks genuine. We know they need money.'

'You two gentlemen have the advantage of me. Who exactly are "they" and how do we know they need money?' From his tone and the look of irritation on his face, Charles did not care for being in the dark.

Joseph cleared his throat. 'You will have to know. A short while ago, we intercepted an encrypted letter which confirmed my suspicion that there is a spy ring operating at a high level in London and that the Post Office might have been penetrated by one of its members. Madeleine's abduction confirms that fear.'

'Do you know who is behind it?'

'It appears that the French and the Dutch are plotting against us. We have feared just such an alliance since the end of the Protectorate. It suits both of them — the French want a Catholic king on our throne and the Dutch want our trade.'

'We believe that the murders of Matthew Smith, John Winter

and Henry Copestick were connected to the ring. They were killed for what they suspected or were about to find out,' added Thomas.

'Do you have any idea who the spy in the Post Office is, Joseph?' asked Charles. 'You must have your suspicions.'

Joseph hesitated before answering. 'I have no evidence.'

'What about a little artful persuasion?'

'If you mean what I think you mean, I would need the permission of the king and that I am not prepared to seek.'

'A pity. In Barbados we wouldn't hesitate if we thought our safety was at risk.'

'Quite. But Barbados has been colonized for little more than thirty years. England is an ancient and, one hopes, civilized nation.'

Charles grunted his disapproval. 'With bits of bodies on display all over London? Hardly. And what about Madeleine?'

Joseph frowned. 'Madeleine is my cousin and I love her dearly, but I cannot allow this country to be held to ransom by our enemies.'

'Joseph, we must put Madeleine first. If she's alive, that is,' said Charles.

Thomas's heart went to his boots. The letter could be a bluff. Madeleine might already be dead. 'We need proof that she's alive and unharmed.'

'And if she is, what then? Ten thousand pounds is a great deal of money.' Joseph sounded doubtful.

'Indeed it is. But I will find it if necessary.'

'Could you find it?'

'I could.'

'I could help if we sell our interest in Chandle's venture,' offered Charles.

Joseph picked up the letter and read it again. 'I really ought to take this to the king. He would expect to be informed of such a development.'

'And if you do, Joseph, what will he do?' asked Charles.

'He will take the matter out of my hands on the grounds that my position is compromised by my relationship to Madeleine. Beyond that, I don't know.'

'Could you justify keeping it from the king until we have proof that Madeleine is alive?' asked Thomas. 'What if we put a notice in the newsbook requiring such proof? They're bound to see it.'

'Perhaps,' replied Joseph, scratching his chin. He walked over to a writing desk in one corner, picked up a quill and wrote on a sheet of paper. He sprinkled sand on it and gave it to Thomas. 'What do you think of that?'

Thomas read it to Charles.

Your letter received and noted. Your request granted. The amount is agreed on condition proof is provided that the subject is not damaged in any way. JW

They argued over whether Williamson's name should be added, and eventually agreed that *JW* would ensure that the notice would be recognized for what it was, without alerting anyone else.

Armed with a fair copy and the price of a personal notice, Joseph's steward was despatched to Thorpe's printing house in Fleet Street. 'If you have any difficulty, use my name,' he told the man. 'I know Thorpe. He's a sound fellow.' It was the business of the head of the king's security to know the publishers of all the London newsbooks.

When the steward had left, Charles returned to Piccadilly to give Mary the news. She would be enraged that this had happened to Madeleine and even more enraged that Thomas had been involved. Reassurances about the ransom being paid would help but little. He advised Thomas to take his time returning.

'Will you really call in your men?' asked Thomas when Charles had gone.

'Except for Mottershead, yes. I trust him not to stir the pot but I will tell him to be doubly careful.'

'Is there still nothing on the murders?'

'Only the disfigured foreigner. Nothing else.'

'And what about the Post Office?'

'We have interviewed every clerk. Bishop is still complaining about lack of staff and Squire is suspicious of Morland, although there's nothing new in that. Morland is still being obnoxious and demanding more money.'

'The man's insufferable.'

'Indeed he is. But also well connected. The more I think about it, the more I believe he's involved. That is partly why I did not give him the encrypted letter and why I have not told him that you were right about it. He is clever enough to have evaded discovery, but I dare not take action without good reason. He would go straight to the king. Then it will be me who finds himself in the Tower, or worse.'

The notice appeared in Thorpe's newsbook the next day. Mr Thorpe had obligingly printed it in a box at the bottom of the front page, where it would not be missed. Thomas read it to Charles and Mary. She had spent the two days venting her fury on Thomas for becoming involved and for putting Madeleine in danger, had told him to pack his bags and go home, only to rescind the order when she saw the misery on his face, and had forbidden him from having anything more to do with the matter.

'You've done enough damage, Thomas,' she shouted at him. 'Leave Joseph to find her. And leave him to deal with his problems at the Post Office himself.' Thomas had nodded meekly and wished the door would open for Madeleine miraculously to walk in.

Joseph's reply to the ransom demand calmed Mary a little. Thomas could only sit alone in his room, staring at the wall and seeing nothing but Madeleine on the rack, Madeleine on the wheel, Madeleine in the scold's bridle. He rubbed his eyes and shook his head, only for the images to return more sharply. He tried reading and he tried writing. Both were useless. Sleep was out of the question, food and drink unwanted intrusions. Any thought other than a thought of Madeleine was shameful. He must concentrate everything on her.

On the third day after their reply appeared in the newsbook, Josiah arrived. Mary showed him up to Thomas's room and left them to it. Thomas needed only to see his face to know that there had been no news. 'Nothing, Josiah?' he asked, without even rising from his chair.

'Nothing, sir. Mr Williamson told me to be careful but I'd 'ave wagered ten guineas we'd 'ave 'eard something by now. If anyone knows anything, they're not saying. Devilish queer, it is.'

'How do you account for it, Josiah?'

'Must be powerful forces at work, sir. The men who took Miss Stewart are no ordinary kidnappers.'

'Let's hope the notice in Thorpe's newsbook gets us somewhere. Is there anything else we can do?'

'We need a stroke of luck, sir. 'Enrietta's been making enquiries. I'm off to see 'er this morning.'

'I shall accompany you, Josiah.'

'Shall you, sir? What about Mrs Carrington?'

'She will not be informed.'

Josiah looked worried. Of enemies armed with muskets, swords and pistols, he was not afraid. Of a woman's wrath, especially Mary Carrington's, he certainly was. 'I do 'ope you know what you're doing, sir. My life'll be as good as over if I bring you back injured.'

'Then you had best keep me safe.' The thought of actually doing something had lifted Thomas's spirits.

'I shall wait here, Josiah, while you go quietly down the stairs to check if Mrs Carrington is in her sitting room. Try not to be seen. If she's engaged, we'll slip out through the kitchen door. Off you go.'

Josiah was soon back. 'All clear, sir. Mrs Carrington's in 'er sitting room talking to a lady visitor.'

Thomas managed the stairs without a sound. Then they were through the kitchen and into the street behind the house. They circled around back into Piccadilly and found a coach to take them to Drury Lane. If the coachman was surprised at their destination, he did not show it. The lane attracted gentlemen from every part of London.

When they arrived in Wild Street, Thomas paid the fare, and just as he had before, Josiah knocked three times. The panel in the door was pulled back and the same pair of black eyes inspected them. The door was opened by Oliver and they were shown to Henrietta's room.

As far as Thomas could tell, Henrietta had not moved since his last visit. She sat in her chair, glass of port in one hand and clay pipe in the other, watching her customers enjoying themselves in the courtyard. She wore the same orange wig and the same black patches on her face. Rupert stood beside her.

'Good day, Josiah. Brought your cousin with you, I see. Washed his hands, has he? And found his tongue yet?'

The time for dissembling was over. 'I have found my tongue, madam,' replied Thomas, 'and I apologize for the deception when last we met. I am Thomas Hill.'

'I know. Josiah's told me. Not that I was fooled. Men pretend to be all manner of things in this house. I see through them all, don't I, Josiah?'

'That you do, 'Enrietta. 'Ave you 'eard anything?'

'There's no rush. Sit down and have a drink with me. Glass of port, Thomas?'

'Thank you. Just the thing,' replied Thomas. This lady would not respond well to being pushed or rushed. He took a glass and handed another to Josiah. 'Your excellent health, madam.'

'And yours, gentlemen.' Henrietta took a gulp of port, belched loudly and lit her pipe. When it was drawing to her satisfaction, she turned her attention to her guests. 'I've done as you asked, Josiah. There's a good few who owes me favours and I've been calling them in. Wouldn't do it for anyone else, you know. Can't imagine why I've got a soft spot for you but I have. Makes no sense to me.' Josiah blushed but said nothing. 'The strange thing is, there's no word of it. No one knows about any lady being attacked or carried off. Not a whisper.'

Thomas's heart sank. Not a word, not a whisper. 'Why might that be, do you think?' he asked.

'There's two possibilities. Either she's dead and the fish are having her for their dinner or she's not in London.'

The first possibility made his stomach heave, the second had not occurred to him. He had simply assumed that she was being held in the city. But she could as easily be elsewhere. 'If you were holding her, Henrietta, where would you hide her if not in London?'

'Well now, if I didn't want to be too far away I'd take her somewhere where no one lives. Epping Forest, perhaps, or the marshes. Very lonely in the marshes. Not many go there. Easy to guard and unlikely to be heard or seen.'

'Which marshes?'

'That's the problem. There's marshes north and south and east. Essex, Lambeth, Kent. Could be any of them. No point in searching. You'd never find her. Better to keep asking around. Want me to carry on, Josiah?'

'Yes please, 'Enrietta. Send word if you 'ear anything, won't you?'

'Of course I will, for you. And drop by if you want another chat. Or anything else. And bring Thomas. The Moroccan girl has proved very popular. Looks like he could do with some entertainment.'

'There is one other thing, Henrietta, if I may,' said Thomas. 'It is not connected to Madeleine, or at least I do not think so.'

Henrietta peered at him over her glass. 'And what might that be?'

'When we were last here I happened to notice a young man in the courtyard. Arthur Phillips. Can you tell me anything about him?'

Henrietta's enormous bosom heaved with laughter. 'Arthur? I can tell you a lot about him. Such a pretty boy, the girls love him. Very regular customer, Arthur is. Plenty of money and unusual tastes.'

'Unusual tastes?'

'Takes more than one girl to make Arthur happy, and the younger the better. Trouble is, he spoils them for anyone else. Can be a bit rough, can Arthur. I only allow it because he pays well. Is that what you wanted to know?'

'Yes. Thank you, Henrietta,' replied Thomas, although it was the last thing he wanted to know. It was worse than he thought. Arthur Phillips led two lives. Charming young gentleman one day, dissolute rake the next. Thank God he wasn't a traitor as well. Mind you, with plenty of money and a post in the Navy Office . . . Heaven forfend. He had enough to worry about without that. He would just have to hope that Lucy came quickly to her senses and went home.

Little was said on the way back to Piccadilly. Josiah was too tactful to ask about Arthur Phillips, and Henrietta's news, or rather the lack of it, about Madeleine had been a blow. Not a word. Might be in the marshes. Any marshes. Might not be. Might be dead. No further forward and time passing. What now?

A familiar carriage stood outside the Carringtons' house. Not bothering to enter as they had left, they let themselves in the front door and found Joseph in the sitting room with Mary and Charles. Mary was furious. 'Thomas, what foolishness is it this time? Where have you been now?'

'My apologies, my dear. It was selfish of me, I know. But I had to do something.' He tried a smile. 'And I needed the exercise.'

'Absurd. I should have sent you home.' Mary peered at him. 'Sit down at once. You look half dead.' Realizing that he felt half dead, Thomas sat. Mary turned to Josiah. 'Why did you permit this, Mottershead? It was insane.'

Josiah's face crumpled like a dead leaf and Thomas thought he was about to burst into tears. 'Don't blame the poor man, Mary. I gave him no choice.'

Mary raised an eyebrow. 'There's always a choice. You haven't heard the last of this, either of you.'

'We have had a reply,' said Joseph, holding it up. 'Like the first letter, it was pushed under the front door of my house. Whoever delivered it ran off without being seen. It's from Madeleine.'

He read it out.

Dear Joseph, all my thoughts are with you, rest assured that I am well, try not to worry for me, fear not for my safety, or for my good health, remember me in your prayers, dear cousin may God bless you. Your cousin Madeleine

'It is her hand,' Williamson assured them, 'and I suppose it proves she is alive and well. Or does it?'

Thomas examined the letter. 'The hand shows evidence of her being under strain, which is not surprising. The paper is good quality. Is Madeleine in the habit of running her sentences together like this, Joseph? She uses commas rather than full stops.'

'I think not. She's careful with her correspondence. Could that also be the strain?'

'Probably,' replied Thomas thoughtfully. 'However, may I make a copy? I should like to study it more.'

'Certainly. Do you think it's trying to tell us something?'

'It's possible. The form is odd. I'll know by the morning.'

'Meanwhile,' asked Mary, 'what should we do now?'

'Nothing, I think,' replied Joseph. 'We await further

instructions, as they directed. Send word if you discover anything, Thomas.'

When Williamson had left, Thomas took the copy he had made to his bedroom and put it on the writing table. The choice of words and the lack of proper punctuation suggested something hidden which he must find. As far as he knew, Madeleine did not have a knowledge of codes and ciphers and, anyway, she would not have had time to use one. The letter was in plain text. What might she have done to conceal a message in it? What would he himself have done? And what would she try to tell them?

For an hour, Thomas sat and stared at the letter, seeing nothing. Then Montaigne spoke. *A wise man sees as much as he ought, not as much as he can.* Thomas turned the letter over and closed his eyes. Among the letters and words, what ought he to see? He ought to see a message, disguised well enough to avoid being noticed by her captors, yet simple enough to reveal itself to him. She would have guessed that he would look for a message; he was a cryptographer.

Then it struck him. The lack of full stops and capital letters had a purpose. It was hiding something. He took a clean sheet of paper and wrote out the message with proper punctuation.

Dear Joseph,

All my thoughts are with you. Rest assured that I am well. Try not to worry for me. Fear not for my safety, or for my good health. Remember me in your prayers. Dear cousin, may God bless you.

Your cousin Madeleine

The capital letters leapt off the paper. You clod, Thomas, he said out loud. There it is. Ignoring the words Joseph, I and God, the capitals spelt out the word DARTFRD and with the inclusion of the *o* of *or*, DARTFORD. Madeleine had cleverly avoided capital letters, which might have revealed the word to her captors, and she had told Joseph the thing he most wanted to know — that she was being held in Dartford.

Thomas knew little of Dartford except that the town had suffered during the war and from regular outbreaks of plague, and that it was noted for the marshes which stretched for miles along the river and were easily big enough to hide a cottage or a hut from searching eyes. Henrietta was right. They would find her in the marshes.

Taking the original message and his version of it, he ran down the stairs and burst into the sitting room, where Mary and Charles were sitting in front of an unlit fire. 'I have it. The clever girl has told us where she's being held. Look at the capital letters.' He handed Mary the messages. She read them and handed them to Charles.

'How ingenious of her,' she said. 'Dartford. An unpleasant place, I believe, surrounded by heathland and marshes and full of plague. A good hiding place.'

'If she's in the marshes, she'll be hard to find,' said Charles, 'and even harder to rescue. It'll be an easy place to guard and defend, even against a troop of militia.'

'We'd better send word to Joseph. He did ask us to,' said Mary.

'Mary,' asked Thomas, 'in the circumstances, would it not be wiser to find her ourselves? Joseph is under pressure from the king and, to be frank, he might not respond as rationally as we might wish. His men all over the place would alert them at once and that would be bad for Madeleine.' Master Phillips would have to wait.

Mary looked shocked. 'Thomas, surely you must speak to Joseph first.'

'If we ask him to wait until we find her, he'll either refuse or agree. He'll send them in or give us time to look. We might just as well start looking.'

'Joseph will be furious when he finds out.'

'Indeed he will. But if we find Madeleine alive he will forgive us.'

Charles agreed. 'Mottershead's the man we need. We'll go to his house first thing in the morning.'

'I know where he lives. Why not now?' asked Thomas.

'It's getting dark. He won't be able to do anything until tomorrow.'

'I know, but I can't sit here and do nothing.'

'Very well, I'll come with you. Mary will stay here in case there is any more news.'

Mary was far from persuaded. 'Charles, why can't you leave it to Joseph?'

'Thomas has explained that, my dear. This is a job for a small platoon, not a regiment.'

'And what shall I tell Joseph if he calls again?'

'Tell him Thomas is studying the message and that we've gone out for refreshment. We'll be back by midnight.' Charles's voice had taken on a different tone in the expectation of action. Thomas half expected him to announce that he would bring his swords. 'Come on, Thomas, no time to lose. We'll find a carriage.'

Josiah Mottershead lived in a tiny house near the north end of the bridge. Their coach took them along Fleet Street and through

Blackfriars. Near the bridge, Thomas told the coachman to stop and to wait for them.

They walked down Swan Lane to where it was joined by a nameless alley, leading nowhere and with just a few rough dwellings on either side. It was a mean place, dark and dank, and reeking of the muck that was thrown every day into the river. They stopped at the last door before the alley petered out into a patch of ground used for dumping waste. Thomas reached for his lavender handkerchief.

'Here we are,' said Charles. 'Let's hope he's at home.'

Josiah opened the door to Charles's knock. He looked at them in astonishment. 'Good gracious, sirs, what are you doing down 'ere at night?'

'Let us in, Josiah, and you shall soon know,' replied Thomas.

Josiah waved them in and locked the door with a key and a heavy chain. 'Can't be too careful around 'ere. Come in, gentlemen, and find a seat.'

They found a plain wooden chair each and sat at Josiah's table. The room must have served for everything except sleeping and cooking. There was no other furniture and no decoration except a makeshift curtain at the window. Thomas could see through a low door to the kitchen, where he guessed Josiah also slept. At least it would be warmer there. There were no other rooms.

'Pardon me, gentlemen, Mottershead's forgetting 'is manners. Would you care for a glass of something?'

They would certainly care for a glass, or even two, of something, but neither knew what might be available and did not want to embarrass the little man. 'Are you having a drink, Josiah?' asked Thomas.

'To be sure, sir. Daresay I'll need it by the look of you. I'll open a bottle of German. Got a dozen as payment for a job I did. Been looking for a chance to drink it.'

'Excellent,' said Charles quickly, 'in that case we'll join you. No point in going thirsty.'

Josiah disappeared into the kitchen and came back with two bottles and three glasses. They ignored the state of the glasses, which showed signs of having recently held some other liquid, and took a sip. The wine was excellent.

'Fine wine, Josiah,' said Charles. 'You must have done a good job.'

Josiah tapped his nose. 'Always do my best, sir. Now what brings you to my palace? 'As there been a reply to the notice?'

'Indeed there has,' said Thomas with a grin, 'and Miss Stewart managed to hide a message in it telling us where she is being held. She's in Dartford.'

'Dartford, eh? And well, I 'ope?'

'It would seem so.'

'Thank the Lord for that. But Dartford's an 'orrid place. Beggars and thieves, very poor folk, plague and pox, and wild country all around. Do we know where in Dartford she is?'

'We don't, but we think Henrietta might have been right about the marshes. That's where we'll look first.'

'They're big, the Dartford marshes. Go on for ever along the river. Won't be easy to find Miss Stewart in there. No one much lives there except a few cottars.'

'Do you know the area, Josiah?'

'A little, sir. Did a job there five years ago. Evil spot, it is.'

'Then that's where she'll be. A place where few people go.'

Josiah nodded. 'Daresay you're right, sir. What's your plan?'

'We haven't told Mr Williamson yet, in case he feels the

militia should be sent in,' said Charles. 'We'd rather spy out the land ourselves. Then we'll tell him if we need to.'

'You and Mr 'Ill, sir?'

'And you, Josiah, if you're willing.'

'Willing or not, sir, you'll need me. Mr 'Ill gets 'imself into trouble when I'm not there.'

'So I do,' replied Thomas, remembering the old hag in the alley. 'Good man, Josiah. This is what we propose. Mr Carrington and I will return now to Piccadilly to tell Mrs Carrington. Best she knows in case of problems. We'll make our way to Dartford tomorrow morning and meet you there at midday. Is there a place we can safely meet?'

Josiah pursed his lips. 'There's a little church at the west end of the village. Can't remember its name, but you'll find it easy enough.'

'The church at midday it is. And Josiah, not a word to Mr Williamson, mind.'

'No, sir. I know you'll speak for me if need be.'

'Of course I shall. We'll be off then. Until tomorrow.'

'She won't be happy,' remarked Thomas on the way back. 'She'll say I'm an irresponsible fool.'

'And she'll say I'm too old to be wading about in marshes. Leave it to me, Thomas. I'll put my celebrated diplomatic skills to good use.' Charles grinned. Thomas raised his eyebrows and said nothing.

CHAPTER 18

Having agreed to set off at four the next morning, Thomas left Charles to exercise his skills and went to his bed. If they were to travel to Dartford and spend hours or even days searching the marshes, he would need some sleep. He had had almost none for three days.

Sleep, however, proved elusive. Thoughts of Madeleine and the anticipation of finding her kept his mind busy long after it should have closed down. Eventually he gave up, lit a candle and tried to read. Well before dawn, Thomas and Charles walked the short distance from the house to the stairs at Whitehall, from where they took a wherry across the river to Lambeth. Charles assured Thomas with a wink that his powers of persuasion had been well up to the task and that Mary was sleeping peacefully. He had buckled on two swords, and Thomas knew from experience that he was equally adept with either hand or both at once.

At that time of the morning the streets and the river were quiet. Even the night-soil men were not yet up and about. The wherryman told them of an inn with stables where horses might be found at a reasonable price and, looking pointedly at Charles's swords, wished them luck with whatever they were planning to do.

The innkeeper was woken and offered a good price for two sound animals, both rested and capable of a hard morning's ride. The normal route from Lambeth would be along the river path past Greenwich and Woolwich and south to Dartford when they reached the river Darent. However, Thomas reckoned that the direct route across country from Greenwich would save a good five miles as long as the road was in reasonable repair. They decided to risk it and set off at a steady trot.

At Greenwich they stopped at an inn to give the horses water and to take breakfast, and from there took the road across country to Dartford. It led them through woodland and over heathland and past three tiny hamlets. The road was rough but dry and they made good progress. They spoke little, each content with his own thoughts.

Outside the church, Josiah was waiting for them. He greeted them cheerily. 'Good morning, gentlemen. How was your journey?'

'Uneventful, thank you, Josiah. And yours? You've made good time.'

Josiah looked sheepish. 'Mottershead and 'orses don't get on very well, Mr 'Ill. I like to keep my feet on the ground, so I set out last night and walked. Easy enough along the river.' He showed no sign of fatigue, despite having walked twenty miles without sleep. 'I've found an inn with decent stables. Best leave the 'orses there if we're going into the marshes.'

Josiah showed them to the inn where they agreed an exorbitant price for fodder and stabling, before setting off on foot towards the marshes to the north of the town. Despite being well situated on the London-to-Dover road, Dartford was much as Josiah had described it. Poor, rough and ravaged by war and disease.

Suspicious eyes watched them go by, the shabby cottages were little more than hovels and there were beggars on the streets and dung heaps on the street corners. A miserable place. Thomas wondered what on earth the king had made of it when he had ridden through it a year earlier. It was a relief to leave the town and enter the marshes.

They took a path between the reeds, running northwards and just wide enough for them to walk in line abreast. Within five minutes they were out of sight of the town. Here and there they saw sheep grazing where the reeds had been cut and grass had grown, but otherwise they had only curlews and gulls for company.

'You were right, Josiah,' said Thomas, 'it's a bleak place.' He shivered. 'And it's much colder here. Have you noticed?'

'Bleak it is, sir. The sooner we find Miss Stewart the better. What exactly are we looking for?'

'Any sign of life,' replied Charles. 'Cottars, habitations, travellers. We know there are cottages on the marsh. One of them may hold Madeleine. We just have to find it. Keep looking around. These reeds could hide a dozen cottages and a hundred men with ease.'

'We may be seen first,' pointed out Thomas.

'Indeed we may. It's a risk we'll have to take.'

They saw nothing until they came to a fork in the path. There Josiah spotted a crust of bread which had been tossed to the side of the path leading to their right. He picked it up and broke it in half. 'Stale, but not mouldy. A day or two, I should think.'

'Right. We'll follow the man who didn't want his breakfast.' Charles was clearly relieved to have found a sign of life, even an old crust, and led them off at a brisk pace.

About four hundred yards further on, he dropped to his knees and signalled to them to do the same. 'A cottage ahead,' he whispered. 'Keep down and I'll take a look.'

They did as they were told while Charles crept forward. He was soon out of sight around a bend in the path and below the tops of the reeds. When he returned he was upright again. 'Just a deserted hovel. No sign of life. Let's go on.'

During the afternoon they came upon three more empty cottages, their owners out on the marshes, and saw a number of cottars with their sheep in the distance. Only once did anyone come close, when Josiah's sharp ears picked up the sounds of approaching voices before their owners came into view. They dropped quickly into the reed bed and watched a party of travellers go past. It was impossible to tell who they were or where they had come from, but theirs were Kentish voices and they were probably harmless.

'Better safe than sorry,' said Josiah, as they emerged wet and muddy from the marsh.

Thomas made a feeble effort to brush mud off his trousers. 'Better dry than dirty. Unless we're going to spend the night out here, we'd better turn back now. We'll stay at the inn and try again tomorrow.'

'It grieves me, but I fear you're right,' agreed Charles. 'We won't find anything in the dark except watery graves.'

Still Josiah showed not a hint of fatigue and led them unerringly back to the town at a fast pace. So fast that by the time they reached the inn, even Charles, whose swords were weighing heavily, needed food and rest. Thomas simply wanted to wash the mud off himself and his clothes and to sit quietly with a bottle of something for company.

At the inn, Josiah went to make sure the horses had hay and water while Thomas and Charles enquired about beds. There was just one — large enough for two but not for three. Josiah would be on the floor. They agreed another outrageous price with the land-lord — a sharp-faced little man with the look and charm of one who has spent much of his life in gaol — and ordered the best he could offer for their dinner. If Josiah was put out by the news that he would be sleeping on the floor, he did not show it. A night without sleep and twenty-five miles or more on foot had dented his good humour not a scrap.

While they waited for their dinner, the weaselly landlord eyed them suspiciously. Thomas doubted if he had ever had three men like them in his inn. His usual customers would be local drinkers and travellers on their way from Dover. They had come from London on two horses. One of them wore two swords and another was as broad as he was tall and carried a stout stick. They must seem an odd little group.

Before long, the man's curiosity got the better of him. 'And what might you gentlemen be doing in these parts?'

Josiah answered without hesitation, as if he had been expect-ing the question. 'Important business. Important and private.'

'Business, eh? And what sort of business would that be?'

'Private, I said. Now go and attend to our dinner.'

'And bring another bottle of this miserable stuff,' said Charles, holding up an empty bottle.

When dinner eventually came, it looked filthy. Three plates of what might once have been parts of an underfed sheep, accompanied by a green mess of turnip and cabbage, all swimming in a brown liquid. It tasted as filthy as it looked and had to be forced down with liberal doses of thin claret.

'Ye gods,' said Charles, belching loudly, 'that was as revolting as anything I've ever been served, even by you, Thomas.'

'I didn't know you was a cook, sir,' said Josiah.

'I am not, Josiah. Mr Carrington is being unkind.'

'I see, sir. Don't forget you're sharing a bed with him tonight.'

'Would you like to change places, Josiah? I could sleep on the floor.'

'No thank you, sir. I'm used to floors.'

Their room was as mean as their dinner. The bed — no more than a dirty blanket and a thin straw mattress on a wooden pallet — Thomas and Charles shared with an army of biting insects. Had they not been too exhausted to care, they would have slept little. Josiah simply curled up under his coat on the floor and in no time was snoring peacefully.

They were awake at dawn and, after a sluice down with rainwater from a butt behind the inn, found the landlord in the kitchen.

'Good morning, gentlemen. Slept well, did we? More important business today?'

They ignored the questions. 'Get us some breakfast, man, and we'll be off. We'll be back for the horses later,' ordered Charles.

'And make sure they get hay and water,' added Josiah. 'I'll know if they haven't been fed.'

Thomas examined his hands, which were covered in red bites. 'I know the lice have been fed. Let's be away before they are hungry again.' Within a few minutes, they had washed down slabs of cold mutton pie with watery ale and were making for the marshes.

They took the same path as far as the fork, where this time they turned left. Early morning mist was rising off the marshes and twice they put up flights of ducks. As the mist cleared they saw smoke from a fire and soon heard voices. Crouching low, they approached as close as they dared and peered through the reeds. Two cottars were cooking their breakfast on an open fire before setting out for their day's work in the marshes. As men hiding Madeleine would not be lighting fires and talking loudly about sheep, they circled the cottage and continued on.

This side of the marsh was more populated than the other and they came across three more cottages, all inhabited by cottars. They avoided these, and after an hour sat down on the path to rest. Already Thomas's spirits were low. He could have been wrong about Dartford. Perhaps it had been no more than coincidence that the letters spelt out the word. Perhaps it was just that he'd been so desperate to find something that he had invented a message. Or Henrietta might have been wrong. Even if Dartford, perhaps not in the marshes. The town itself, or the heathland to the south? Quite possible. This creeping about in the reeds was beginning to look foolish.

Aurum and Argentum — gold and silver. The Alchemist. Three murders. Four if Babb was included. A disfigured man. Bishop, Morland, Squire. A spy ring. A Franco-Dutch plot. Madeleine's abduction. The ransom note. Jumbled thoughts in a jumbled mind. Take stock, Thomas, find the connections and you'll find the murderers and traitors. He got up. 'Two more hours, gentlemen, and then if we've found nothing we'll go back and think again.'

The next cottage sprang out of the reeds before they had a chance to take cover. As soon as they rounded a bend in the path, they were on top of it. It was bigger than the others and better constructed. Stone walls and a roof newly thatched with reeds instead of wattle and straw. They must have been seen by the occupants. There was nothing for it but to brazen it out.

Thomas strode up to the door and knocked loudly. Nothing happened. He tried again. Still nothing. He pushed on the door, which opened smoothly. Well fitted and unlocked. Yet this cottage was surely too sound to have been abandoned. He stepped inside leaving Josiah to keep watch. Charles was close behind.

The room they entered was square, with rough stone walls and an earth floor. There was a hearth on the left and doors leading off both the other walls. A plain table and four chairs stood in the middle of the room. Thomas carefully felt the ashes in the grate. They were warm.

The door opposite led to a kitchen. There they found the remains of a meal on an upturned barrel and a crate of unopened wine bottles in a corner. A back door was open. Behind the cottage was a small yard, from which a path led off through the reeds. In the third room were a narrow straw bed and a low chair set below a tiny window. This cottage had only recently been abandoned.

Thomas sat on the bed and tried to imagine Madeleine there. Had she been held in this room, and if so, why had she been moved? He picked up a rusty nail lying by the bed and turned it in his fingers. He concentrated on the room, trying to envisage Madeleine there. Were you here, Madeleine? Did you lie on this bed? If you were here, where are you now?

As if reading Thomas's thoughts, Charles said quietly, 'Even if she was here, she's not here any more.'

Before Thomas could reply, Josiah stuck his head around the door. 'Men coming, gentlemen. I 'eard 'em.'

'Best make ourselves scarce,' said Thomas. 'The back door, Josiah, and quick.'

They were out of the back door and into the reeds within seconds. Josiah was right. They heard voices and then the sounds of men in the cottage. Thomas peeked out and through the door caught a glimpse of men in the kitchen. They were talking loudly. He heard one swear and the other laugh. He imagined them picking up the crate of wine left in the kitchen and manhandling it to the front door. Signalling to Charles and Josiah to follow, he crept around the cottage. Two men were making their way back up the path with the crate between them. They were finding it awkward to carry and were making slow progress. He waited until they had disappeared around the bend in the path before whispering, 'Our guides, gentlemen, I fancy. Where they lead, we follow.'

Keeping well behind the two men and following them as much by sound as by sight, they retraced their steps up the path for about half a mile. There Josiah spotted a gap in the reeds to their right. It was so well hidden that they had missed it earlier. They followed the sounds of the wine-carriers down a narrow path. It was no more than three minutes before they heard other voices and the sound of the crate being dropped on the ground. A rough voice cursed the men for their clumsiness and ordered them to bring the wine inside. They crept forward along the path until they saw another cottage — this one smaller and shabbier — with two men outside it. They dropped into the reeds and watched. The two men were dressed, like the others, in leather trousers and leather jerkins, and wore high boots and narrow-banded hats. They carried pistols and knives stuck into their belts. In the still air the guards' voices carried clearly to where they were hiding.

'How long will we have to guard the woman?' grumbled one.

'You'll have to ask the Dutchman,' replied the other.

'I don't know why we don't just kill her and be off. I'm sick of this place, it's cursed.'

'She's sick too. Likely to die and save us the trouble.'

Thomas and Charles exchanged a look. She was sick, but they had found her. 'Four,' whispered Charles. 'Any more, do you think?'

'Four to guard one lady is surely enough.'

'It might be a changeover of the guards,' said Josiah. 'Good time to get the wine. We could wait and see if any of them leave.'

'Or we could rush them now and be done with it.' Charles had his hands on the handles of his swords.

Thomas placed his hand on one of Charles's. 'That would be dangerous for Madeleine. We need a plan.'

After two days in the marshes and a night in a filthy inn, Charles was not in the mood to wait. 'I have a plan, Thomas. Attack the swine, kill the lot and rescue Madeleine.'

'A fine plan, Mr Carrington,' whispered Josiah. 'And it would be even better if one of us went around the back to cut off their retreat.'

'Can we manage four, Charles?'

'Shouldn't present a problem.'

'Right. We'll give Josiah time to get to the back, then you and I will march straight in and wreak havoc. Agreed?'

'Agreed.'

'Good. Off you go, Josiah. No escapers, please.'

Josiah grinned. 'Not a one, sir.'

They gave the little man two minutes, then ran up to the door, flung it open and ran inside. Three of the guards were sitting at a table, drinking. Two of them never saw the slashes from Charles's swords that severed their windpipes and sent them crashing to the floor. The third had time to rise and draw a pistol from his belt, but not to fire it. Before he could, Thomas brought the flat of his sword down on the man's arm and heard the bone snap. Charles thrust at his throat and he, too, was dead before he hit the floor.

Like the other cottage, there were two doors off the main room. Thomas followed Charles into the kitchen. The fourth guard, who was struggling to open a bottle and had not had time to move, took one look at the tall man with two swords who burst in, and ran out through the back door. There he was met by the end of a stout stick jammed into his face by a pair of long arms. He collapsed in a fountain of blood from his nose and mouth, rolled over on the ground, convulsed briefly and died.

Josiah stepped into the kitchen in search of another victim, saw only Charles and Thomas and followed them back into the main room where three bloody bodies lay on the floor. While Josiah checked that they were dead, Charles made straight for the other door, opened it and stopped.

Thomas peered over Charles's shoulder. Madeleine sat on a low chair, a long knife at her throat. The man who held it had half a nose and a lip that had once been viciously sliced by a sword or a dagger. The disfigured Dutchman. He spoke quietly, with a guttural accent. 'So, gentlemen. Mr Hill and Mr Carrington, I assume. Unexpected visitors, to say the least.'

Ignoring the knife, Madeleine screamed, 'Kill him, Thomas.' The point pressed into her throat and drew blood. 'Kill him.' Her voice rasped in her throat and sweat ran from her brow.

'If you try, she will be the first to die. You have my word on it.

Now sit down, both of you. Mr Hill and Mr Carrington — it is Mr Carrington, is it not? — you will put your weapons on the floor and kick them towards me.' Charles did not move. More blood trickled from Madeleine's neck.

'At once, or she dies.' The quiet voice would not be denied. Charles slid his swords across the floor and sat down. Thomas did likewise.

'Good. Now let us consider the position. I assume that none of my colleagues is now available to assist me, so you are two and I am one. But I have Miss Stewart — a queen to your knights, one might say. How do you suggest we proceed?' The voice barely rose above a whisper.

'I suggest you release Madeleine and then we discuss your future.'

'Very amusing. My suggestion, however, is a little different. You will stand up and walk backwards into the other room. Miss Stewart and I will follow you. You will then return to this room.'

'Where you will lock us in and depart with Madeleine?'

'Exactly.'

Thomas looked at Charles and saw the faintest twinkle in his eye. A little acting was needed. 'How do we know she'll be safe?' asked Thomas.

'You don't. What you do know is that she will not be safe if you do not do as I say.'

'In that case, Thomas,' said Charles, 'we'd best do as we're told.'

He got to his feet, opened the door and walked backwards into the other room. Thomas let him pass and followed him. A few steps behind, Madeleine emerged, the quiet voice behind her with his knife still at her throat. There was blood on her neck and she was ashen. As she walked through the doorway, a slight movement to her right made her turn her head. Quiet Voice saw it and immediately tried to drag her back into the room. He was too late. Josiah's stick came down on his shoulder with a crack like a musket shot and the knife fell from his hand. Madeleine fell forward and he subsided on to the floor, clutching his shoulder. Josiah stood over Quiet Voice and put his foot on the man's neck. Thomas helped Madeleine to her feet and sat her gently on a chair. She was sobbing.

'Shall I put 'im out of 'is misery, sir?' Josiah sounded keen on the idea.

'Not yet, Josiah. We need a little talk with the creature first.'

'As you wish, sir.' Josiah hauled the man to his feet and dumped him on a chair. When he pushed him down, the man gasped in agony.

'There. Comfortable? Now answer Mr 'Ill's questions like a good boy, or you'll 'ave a pair of broken shoulders.' Josiah stood behind him while Thomas and Charles faced him. The disfigured face was contorted with pain.

'We have information that the man who recently committed several murders in London was disfigured. Was it you?' Quiet Voice said nothing. 'Very well.' Thomas nodded to Josiah, who tapped the man on the shoulder with his stick. He screamed. 'Was it you?' Louder this time. The man nodded. 'That's better. And who told you to carry out the murders?'

He shook his head. Another tap on the shoulder, another scream and the words came out in a rush. 'I don't know.'

'That is difficult to believe. Someone gave the orders. Who?'

'I tell you I don't know. The orders came in writing.' The words were barely audible. Quiet Voice was sinking.

'To where?'

'An inn in Bishopsgate.' An inn used for passing messages — Joseph had said there were many — although Quiet Voice might be lying.

'What inn?'

'The Fox.'

'Were you paid?' He nodded. 'How?'

'Dutch bank.'

'Gold?' Another nod.

'You're a traitor. Why?'

Quiet Voice pointed to his face. 'Naseby. Bluecoats. Fools should have run like the rest of them.'

'Are you English?'

'Half. The better half Dutch.'

'Last chance. Who gave the orders to murder those men and hold Madeleine Stewart to ransom?' Quiet Voice glared at him. 'Do the names Aurum and Argentum mean anything to you?' Was there was a flicker in his eyes? 'Do they?'

'No.'

'You're lying. You are a traitor and a murderer, and someone is giving you orders. Who are they?' Quiet Voice said nothing. 'You have a word with him, Josiah. We'll be outside.'

His arm around Madeleine, Thomas left the cottage and walked a few yards away, where he laid her gently on the ground. Charles followed them. 'Are you hurt, my dear?' he asked, his hand on her cheek. It was burning hot.

'I'm unhurt but I have a fever. It frightened the guards. They thought it might be plague and did not dare to touch me. And that's why they moved me — in case the other cottage was a plague house.' There was a ghastly scream from the cottage, followed by another.

Thomas sat beside Madeleine with her head on his lap and stroked her forehead. Her breathing was very shallow. Charles bent to speak to her. 'It's over, my dear. No need to be frightened now.' There was another yell from the cottage. Charles and Thomas looked up sharply. The voice was different. It was not the Dutchman's, it was Josiah's. Charles leapt up and rushed inside. Almost immediately Josiah emerged, bent double and clasping his side.

'Bugger's out the back,' he croaked. 'Mr Carrington's after 'im.'

'Sit down, Josiah. Charles will catch him.' Still bent over, Josiah sat down painfully. 'Can you tell us what happened?'

'Bloody fool, I am. 'E was play-acting. Not as 'urt as I thought. Grabbed my stick and 'it me in the back. Didn't wait to finish me off. Just ran for it. My own fault. Bloody fool.'

'Calm down and breathe deeply, Josiah. The man is injured and he won't get away.'

''Ope not, sir. Dangerous one, that.' Josiah coughed and yelped in pain. He arched his back and spat out a mouthful of bloody spittle. 'Kidney. 'Urts like the devil, but I'll live.'

'That's a relief, Josiah. There's enough dead bodies in the cottage.' Josiah's laugh was cut short by another stab of pain. 'Apologies, Josiah. This is no time for jokes. Lie down beside Miss Stewart and we'll wait for Charles to bring the Dutchman back.'

By the time Charles returned, Josiah was recovering but Madeleine was barely conscious. Charles was breathing heavily and he was alone. 'Swine got away, I fear. Had to stop to get rid of my sword belt. Would have caught him a few years ago.' The words came out in bursts between lungfuls of air. 'Lost him in the reeds. Thought I'd better leave him and get back here. How is she?'

'Weak and feverish. We need to get her away from here,' replied Thomas, 'and Josiah's hurt too.'

'It's nothing, sir,' said Josiah, standing up and squaring his shoulders. 'Nothing a bit of a walk won't mend.'

'I'll carry her,' said Charles, handing his swords to Thomas. He picked Madeleine up very gently, his arms under her knees and shoulders, and set off. Walking steadily, they were back in Dartford within twenty minutes. 'I think it might be prudent to avoid the inn,' advised Charles. 'That ferret of a landlord is not to be trusted.'

'You're right,' agreed Thomas. 'But we need the horses and we need something for Madeleine. She can't ride or walk to London.'

'Leave it to me, sir,' said Josiah. 'If Mr Carrington would accompany me, I expect we'll find something useful. You wait by the church.'

Charles handed Madeleine to Thomas. She opened her eyes and smiled weakly. 'Can you walk?' he asked. She nodded. He put her down and helped her to the church, where they sat on an old bench by the gate. He felt her face. 'You're very hot. Do you want water?'

She shook her head. 'Stay here with me, please, Thomas. The water can wait.' She rested her head on his shoulder. It was not long before Josiah and Charles appeared. Charles was leading their horses, saddled and ready to go, and Josiah was perched on a flat cart drawn by an ancient pony. He looked unhappy.

'Never did like 'orses,' he grumbled, 'and this one's as old as I am. Still, 'e'll 'ave to do. Put Miss Stewart on the cart, sir, and we'll be off.'

They used their coats to make Madeleine as comfortable as

they could on the cart and set off on the direct road to Greenwich, riding slowly and stopping often for her sake. The route was criss-crossed with streams and brooks, and whenever they stopped Thomas found clear water to cool Madeleine's fever. But each time he felt her forehead it was hotter and by the time they reached the edge of the town, she was barely conscious. Her skin could have been made of paper and her eyes were red and rheumy. Despite the coats, she was shivering. She coughed painfully. Apart from the fever, Thomas could find no evidence of plague — no lumps, no infected sores — but if it was plague, she would not survive the night. The disease killed within days, if not hours. And even if it was not plague, Madeleine was still very sick — burning, shivering, vomiting, unable to speak. Josiah, too, was in pain. Holding the reins in one hand, he held the other to his back and stifled a groan every time the cart hit a hole in the road. Several times he spat out blood and wiped his mouth with his sleeve.

They left the horses and the pony and cart at a stable in Greenwich and hired a carriage to take them to Piccadilly. The carriage driver, alarmed at the sight of an ailing woman, had to be persuaded with an enormous bribe. All the way there — from Greenwich to Southwark, over the bridge and westwards down the Strand and Fleet Street, Thomas sat with his arm around Madeleine, from time to time wiping her face with his handkerchief. Charles and Josiah sat opposite. Not a word was spoken until they arrived in Piccadilly.

When the carriage pulled up outside the Carringtons' house, Charles jumped out and reached in to take Madeleine in his arms. He carried her to the door, which was opened by Mary, and, at her instruction, up the stairs to a bedroom. Thomas and Josiah followed behind and went into the sitting room. Charles soon returned. 'Does Mary think it's plague?' asked Thomas.

'No. If it were, she'd be dead by now. It's probably one of the agues that infest the foul air of the marshes. There will be many there, as there are in Barbados.'

'How does she look?'

'A little stronger, I'd say.' It was a lie.

'Thank you, Josiah, for what you've done,' said Thomas, extending his hand. 'We could not have managed without you. Are you recovered?'

Josiah tried to smile. 'Good as new, sir. I'll go to Chancery Lane now. Mr Williamson must be told about Miss Stewart.'

'Of course. Tell him she's in good hands.'

Josiah nodded and left, still clutching his side.

Mary soon appeared. 'She's very sick,' she told them. 'Feverish and shivering. I'll stay with her tonight. Pray that the fever breaks. Now tell me what happened.'

Between them, they recounted the story of their journey to Dartford, the search for Madeleine and her rescue. Thomas told her about the disfigured murderer. 'He told us nothing about a spy ring or a plot. We still don't know who Aurum and Argentum are. Has Joseph called?'

'A messenger came yesterday, asking you to call at his house. I sent a reply that you were unavailable but would call when you could.'

'He won't have liked that.'

'He will like the real story even less. You'll have to explain why you didn't tell him about the message and why you sneaked off to Dartford, putting Madeleine's life at risk.'

'We'll do it together,' Charles assured Thomas. 'Strength in numbers, don't you think?'

'Quite so. Thank God Madeleine is alive. And we'll need to speak for Josiah.'

'What are you going to do now?'

'Now I'm going to look in on Madeleine and then I'm going to my bed.'

'No, I meant are you going to stay in London or go home?'

'I shall stay until Madeleine is recovered. Then I shall make a decision. As long as you're willing to have me, that is.'

'Stay as long as you want, Thomas,' said Mary. 'Madeleine will need you.'

When Thomas looked in on Madeleine, she was asleep. She was very hot, but breathing easily. It was impossible to say which way the fever would go. Mary would alert him if there was any change. He left quietly and went to his own room.

CHAPTER 19

The next morning, the fever was worse. Madeleine's forehead was on fire, her breathing had deteriorated and, worst of all, an abscess had appeared on her neck. Having sat with her all night, Mary was exhausted. When Thomas went in, her anger had returned.

'Thomas, how could you have been so stupid as to get involved in all that business? I knew it would lead to trouble. Look at poor Madeleine. She's dying. Dying, Thomas, and all because you couldn't leave well alone.' She was crying.

Thomas waited for her to compose herself before speaking. 'If I could undo what has been done, I would. I wouldn't have gone to the Post Office, I wouldn't have decrypted the letter and I wouldn't have done Joseph's bidding. I'd have gone home. As I shall the moment Madeleine is better.'

'Thomas, did you not hear what I said? She's dying. The fever is worse and she has an abscess on her neck.'

'You and I will nurse her, and she will recover.'

Madeleine opened her eyes and groaned. Thomas took her hand while Mary wiped her face. She was trying to say something. Thomas bent over her.

'I am not dying.' It was the faintest whisper. She had heard everything. He squeezed her hand gently.

'Of course you aren't. Now sleep. One of us will be here all the time.' He turned to Mary. 'I'll stay with her. You go and rest.' He pulled up a chair and sat beside the bed. If anyone could survive this, Madeleine Stewart could.

He was still sitting by the bed an hour later when there was an urgent knocking on the front door and the sound of voices raised in anger. He heard footsteps on the stairs and Charles burst in.

'Joseph's here, in a fury and demanding to see Madeleine. You'd better come down. I'll wake Mary.'

Joseph was indeed in a fury. He shook his fist at them. 'I must see her at once. Damned foolish thing to do, taking the matter into your own hands. God knows what might have happened to Madeleine. Damned foolish.'

Charles spoke quietly. 'Sit down, Joseph, and take a glass of wine. Shouting and cursing won't help. We'll take you up to Madeleine when you're calm.'

Williamson ignored him. 'I'd have come last night, but I was with the king. Mottershead only found me this morning. I've a good mind to send the wretch packing. He had no business acting without my authority.'

'No blame attaches to Mottershead,' said Thomas. 'We persuaded him to join us, although he knew he would be in trouble for doing so. He meant well and we would not have succeeded in rescuing Madeleine without him. Mottershead's a good man, Joseph.'

Williamson turned his disobedient eye on Thomas and squinted at him. 'I daresay he is. But I am under extreme pressure from the king and it's my head that'll come off if I fail to find the ringleaders of this plot. I should have been informed of your intentions and that's an end to it.' He took a sip of claret and looked at the glass in surprise. Charles had produced his very best bottle.

'Anything more on the source of the ransom demand?' asked Thomas.

'Nothing.'

'Well, at least it won't be needed now,' said Charles cheerfully. Williamson scowled at him. 'Has Mottershead told you everything, Joseph, or shall we offer our report?'

'I don't know if he's told me everything because I don't know what everything is. I'd better hear it from you after I've seen Madeleine.' An exhausted Mary entered the room. 'Would you take me to her now, Mary?'

They were down again within a few minutes. 'She looks dreadful,' said Joseph. 'If there's no improvement by tonight, I shall have to summon a physician, even though I have little time for them. Now tell me what happened and why you did not inform me of your intentions.'

Joseph sat in silence while they told him about Dartford and the marshes and about the cottages and the guards. He spoke only when Thomas described the man with half a nose and a lip sliced almost in half, who spoke in whispers and had escaped. 'This man, is he English?'

'He told us that he was half Dutch and had been wounded at Naseby.'

'Could he have been mistaken for a foreigner?'

'Yes. His voice was unusually harsh. He did not tell us from whom he took orders, only that they came in writing and were left at the Fox in Bishopsgate.'

'Almost certainly a lie, but I'll have it checked. He's a formidable enemy if he got the better of Mottershead. Anything else?'

'Madeleine may be able to tell us more when she is stronger,' replied Thomas.

'Then we must pray that she recovers quickly. For her sake and our own. In the meantime I shall send Mottershead back to Dartford, wounded or not. He will dispose of the bodies and search the house. Not that I expect him to find anything. I shall return later.'

When Joseph had left, Thomas went back up to Madeleine. For an hour he watched her sleeping, then returned to his room and took out the *Dramatis Personae*. It was time for a new cast.

After rewriting it, he had:

Plato: 'Life must be lived as a play.'

The Post Office, the Murders and the Plot
Dramatis Personae

Joseph Williamson: the king's spymaster
Henry Bishop: suspicious spaniel and Postmaster General
Sir Samuel Morland: taciturn inventor, linguist and cryptographer
Lemuel Squire: spherical letter-opener and oenophile
Josiah Mottershead: Williamson's man
Matthew Smith: murdered intelligencer
John Winter: murdered intelligencer

Henry Copestick: murdered Post Office man

Disfigured Dutchman: murderer

Aurum and Argentum: Morland, Bishop, Squire, others?

Alchemist: Dutch?

Madeleine Stewart: brave and beautiful cousin of Williamson. Very
   sick

Sir Montford Babb: murdered investor in AV. Connection unknown

Chandle Stoner: businessman and friend of the Carringtons.
   Unconnected

Thomas Hill: devoted admirer of Miss Stewart. Soon to exit the stage

That evening, after Charles had gone out to meet Stoner, Williamson called again. Thomas led him up the stairs to Madeleine's room. Mary was sitting by the bed. She stood when they entered and kissed Joseph on the cheek. 'Joseph, she is still very sick.'

He bent to touch her forehead. 'That lump on her neck — are there others?'

'I can find none.'

'What does it signify?'

'I do not know.'

'I shall send for a physician.'

'No, Joseph. No physicians, please. Thomas and I will nurse her. She is better off with us.'

Joseph looked doubtful. 'One more day, then. You'll call for me if there's any change?' He stooped to kiss Madeleine.

'Be sure of it.'

At the door, Joseph peered at Thomas with his good eye and said, 'I have told Mottershead that if such a thing happens again he will be out on his ear. Kindly do not lead him astray.'

'I won't. Has there been anything else?'

'No. We got nothing from the Fox, not that I thought we would. Our enemies are clever. Each link in their chain operates independently, as you found out with the Dutchman. He was hired to murder Smith, Winter and Copestick, but did not know by whom. And the king is losing patience. If I don't tell him exactly what this plot is and who the ringleaders are very soon, I am likely to find myself in the Tower.'

'So what's to be done?'

'I shall call again tomorrow. If Madeleine is able to speak, I shall ask her some questions. She may know something.'

Thomas went back up to Madeleine, where he found Mary still sitting beside the bed. 'Has she woken?' he asked, stroking Madeleine's hair.

'She has briefly. I managed to get a little broth into her. As you can see, the abscess is still there, but no larger, and I can find no others. The fever is also much the same.'

'Joseph will be back tomorrow. He wants to ask her some questions.'

Mary sighed. 'I suppose I can hardly stop him. He is Madeleine's cousin.'

Thomas had to get out of the house. Fear for Madeleine, Mary's anger and, above all, fury at himself were eating away at his mind. The walls were his prison and he must escape them. Although it was past seven o'clock, he put on a coat and left.

From Piccadilly he walked down Haymarket to Charing Cross and past Whitehall Palace to Westminster Stairs. The fresh air revived him. At the top of the stairs he stood and gazed out over the river. Even at that hour it was teeming with boats — wherries, barges, painted galleys — as the watermen went about their work.

On a warm May evening it was difficult to imagine the river frozen so hard that during the winter Frost Fairs games were played and carriages driven on the ice.

Two wherrymen were hurling good-natured abuse at each other. That was the way of wherrymen, as it was the way of the thousands of men and women doing their best to earn a living from the river. From Oxford to Tilbury, whole communities depended upon it. There might be longer, wider rivers than the Thames, but could there be one upon which a nation depended more for its prosperity? The river had carried Romans, Saxons, Danes and Normans. Had it not been for the weather and that fearless brigand Francis Drake, it might have carried Spaniards. Was it now to carry the Dutch and the French? God preserve England if it did.

For more than an hour Thomas stood and watched the river go by, his mind wandering from Madeleine to Aurum and Argentum, to Romsey and back to Madeleine. Then he walked briskly up King Street to Charing Cross and from there to Piccadilly. As he entered the house the clock struck nine. He could hear Charles and Mary talking in the sitting room, but passed the door quietly and went up the stairs.

Madeleine was asleep. He took her hand. It was cold and limp. If only he could make her well simply by thinking her well. If only he could banish the sickness by the force of his will.

If she recovered, would she still want him? Should he stay in London while she regained her strength in the hope that she would? Or should he go home? His work for Williamson was done and there were matters to deal with at the school — books to be purchased, a new teacher to be found, repairs to be made. Madeleine would need time to recover. She would need rest, not

Thomas Hill. And there was Lucy, about whom he realized guiltily he had thought not at all since Madeleine had disappeared. It was clear. He should go home and take Lucy with him, just as he had planned to before Madeleine's abduction.

Joseph arrived early the next morning. Madeleine was still asleep and Thomas was back at her bedside. He came quietly into the room, nodded to Thomas and bent to kiss her. Blunt, even charmless, he might be, thought Thomas, but of his cousin he is very fond.

'Madeleine, my dear, it's Joseph,' he whispered. 'I need to speak to you. It's important. If you can hear me, raise your hand a little.' There was no response.

'Allow me to try, Joseph. She might hear a different voice.'

Williamson stood back.

'Madeleine, it's Thomas. Your cousin is here and must speak to you. Raise your hand if you can hear me.' Nothing.

He tried again. 'Can you hear me, Madeleine? It's Thomas. Raise your hand if you can.' This time, her right hand moved a fraction.

'Good. Now Joseph is going to ask you some questions. Can you try to answer them?' The hand signalled yes. Joseph took the seat by the bed and bent his head very close to Madeleine. Her eyes were closed. He spoke clearly and quietly.

'Madeleine, did they harm you?' A shake of the head. No.

'Did you hear any names?' No.

'Did anyone mention Aurum or Argentum?' She raised her hand. Yes.

'Alchemist?' No.

'Did you hear any talk of a plan?' Yes.

'Did they say what the plan was?' No.

'Did they ask if you knew about the letter?' Yes.

'Did you tell them anything?' No.

Madeleine was visibly tiring. 'Enough, Joseph, don't you think?' asked Thomas.

'Just a few more questions.'

'No, Joseph, she's exhausted. Leave her.' Thomas spoke sharply.

'Very well.' Joseph kissed her again. 'Rest now, my dear. I shall return tomorrow.'

Thomas sat in his room. No names except Aurum and Argentum. There had been talk of a plan and they had asked her about the letter. The disfigured Dutchman had known who he and Charles were, so they had been watched. They must fear that the letter had been decrypted, although very few people knew that it had been. Madeleine had told them nothing. Instead of killing her, they had tried to ransom her. That would be why they had not harmed her. Even if the letter had been decrypted, their plan was intact. Only its existence would be known.

When he went down to the sitting room, Thomas knew something was wrong the moment he saw Charles's face. His eyes were red and his face was drawn tight. 'Charles, is something troubling you? Apart from Madeleine, that is?'

'How is she?'

'Much the same. But what about you? You look as if you have been awake all night.'

A thin smile. 'I have. No sleep for the fool.'

'Fool? Why the fool?' Thomas took a seat opposite Charles and waited.

'Losing money is one thing, being made to look an idiot is another. And I shall have to tell Mary.'

'Tell Mary what?'

Charles let out a long sigh. 'I met Chandle Stoner yesterday. There have been problems at the new silver mine. Heavy rain and flooding. The shaft collapsed. He plans to travel there himself, but thinks it will have to be abandoned.'

'Does that mean you will lose your money?'

'I fear that it does. I should have been more sensible. I know nothing of mining and did not understand the risks. I trusted Chandle's judgement.'

'I am sorry, Charles. I daresay it's the embarrassment as much as the money.'

'It is. I should never have invested in Quicksilver.'

'So that was its name. Quicksilver. How appropriate.'

'More like Nosilver now.'

'Where is Mary?'

'Resting. She's worn out from nursing Madeleine.'

'Then I'll go up to Madeleine. When Mary wakes, please tell her I am with her.'

Thomas spent the rest of the day with Madeleine. She opened her eyes briefly when he held a cup of beef broth to her lips, but otherwise she slept. There was no lightening of the fever and no improvement to her colour. She had whispered that she was not dying. By the evening, it was hard to believe that she was right. When Mary took over the vigil, Thomas went to bed hoping for no more than that she would survive the night.

He heard the long-case clock strike midnight, one, two and three o'clock, before drifting into a restless sleep. He awoke before it was light, arose, and went quietly to Madeleine's room. A candle had been lit and placed on a small table by the window. By its meagre light he could just make out Mary's face. She was smiling. He stepped forward. Then he saw Madeleine. Her head was propped up on a pillow and she was sipping from a glass. He saw immediately that the heat had left her face.

Madeleine smiled weakly and held out a hand. 'Thomas. Did you imagine I'd die?'

'Not for a moment.'

Madeleine poked out her tongue. 'Liar. I heard you all talking about me. It made me determined to live.' The voice was as weak as the smile. 'How are you?'

'Typical. She returns from the dead and enquires after my health. I am quite well, thank you. How is your neck?'

Madeleine felt the lump. 'Greatly reduced. We are at a loss as to what it was. An infection of the blood, perhaps.'

'I shall send word to Joseph. He will want to see you.'

'Tell him he may do so as long as he brings oranges and grapes, and asks me no more questions.'

'I shall do exactly that.' Thomas stooped to kiss her forehead. 'Now rest. I will sit here to see that you do.'

'Thank you, Thomas,' said Mary. 'I too could do with a little rest. Wake me if the patient gives you any trouble.'

The patient, however, did not want to rest. She wanted Thomas to know what had happened. She paused frequently for sips of water and morsels of bread, but an hour later she had told her story.

She had barely left her house on the morning she was due to meet Thomas in Piccadilly when a heavy sack was thrown over her head from behind and her arms were pinned at her sides and tied with rope. She did not see her attackers, but had the impression that there were two of them. They marched her up the lane and bundled her into a waiting coach. When she tried to cry for help, a hand was clamped over her mouth. Even through the sack she could tell that it was dark inside the coach and guessed that curtains had been drawn across the windows. Not a word was spoken.

She knew when they crossed London Bridge by the rattle of the wheels and the shouts of the tradesmen. She tried again to call for help and again was silenced by a rough hand. Frightened as she was, she decided to keep quiet until they arrived at wherever they were going. She assumed her abduction was something to do with Joseph's work and tried to steel herself for what was coming.

When they had crossed the bridge the coach turned left. She lost track of their direction and tried to concentrate on sounds and smells. The only smell she recognized, however, was straw. Bits of it inside the sack rubbed against her face and made her sneeze.

She thought they travelled for about three hours before stopping. When they did, she was dragged out of the coach and, with her arms still tied at her sides, was led off on foot. Still nothing was said. She smelt salt in the air and heard curlews and thought they were in marshland. After about an hour, they reached their destination. Her arms were untied and the sack removed. She was inside a small cottage with a low ceiling and shutters across the windows.

The first face she saw was that of the disfigured Dutchman. He told her quietly that she would come to no harm as long as she obeyed his instructions and did not try to escape. If she did, she would be killed. She was told to sit down and was given food. Then the interrogation began.

The Dutchman wanted to know if a letter encrypted with numbers had been intercepted and copied at the Post Office. She told him that she knew nothing of such matters. He said that he knew about her relationship with Thomas and that he did not believe her. He asked if she had heard the words *aurum* or *argentum*. When she replied that they were Latin for gold and silver she thought he was going to strike her. He raised his hand, then apparently thought better of it.

The questioning went on for hours. The same questions over and over again, sometimes with new ones added. He asked about Joseph, about the work Thomas had done at the Post Office, about Henry Bishop, Samuel Morland and Lemuel Squire. He even asked about Josiah Mottershead. And he kept going back to the letter. She knew he was trying to catch her out and said as little as possible. He did not stop until it was getting dark. Then he told her that he would have more questions the next day, and left. Two guards came in from outside and locked her in a tiny, windowless room with only a straw mattress on the floor. In the morning one of the guards brought her food and she was locked in again.

The Dutchman did not return until the afternoon, when the questions began again. This time he threatened to give her a face like his own if she did not tell him what he wanted to know. He said that he knew she had the answers and would get them out of her sooner or later. She was expecting the torture to start, when he abruptly left again.

The fever began that night and by the morning it was raging. She could not stand and she could not eat the food she was given. She craved water, but there was none. She lay on the mattress, one minute burning, the next shivering, until the Dutchman arrived. He took one look at her and ordered the guards to give her water.

'She's no use to us dead until she's talked,' she heard him say in his strange voice. 'Keep her alive until I say so.'

'These marshes are full of plague, and if it's plague nothing will keep her alive,' grumbled a guard. 'And if this is a plague house, I'm not staying here.'

'We'll move her to the other place,' said the Dutchman. 'Do it now.'

The guards did not want to touch her, but they were more afraid of the Dutchman. They put the sack over her head, carried her to the cottage where she had been found and left her on a narrow bed. She did not know how long she had been there when the Dutchman came in with paper and ink. He made her sit up and handed her a quill.

'Your cousin will want to know that you are well. Write him a letter,' he ordered.

While she was wondering what to write, the idea came to her. Her hand was shaking and it took all her concentration. What was more, she did not know for certain that they were in Dartford. It was only a guess. She was confident that Thomas would see the hidden message as long as the Dutchman did not. Fortunately, he barely glanced at it.

Madeleine had finished her story. 'You know the rest, Thomas,' she said. 'Oddly enough, the sickness may have saved me. The slightest injury could have killed me and the Dutchman knew it.'

'Yes, and rather than kill you, he demanded a ransom for you.'
'Did he? How much?'
'Far too much.'
'How much?'
'Ten thousand pounds.'
'Pitiful. You'd have paid twenty, Thomas, would you not?'
Thomas smiled. 'You'll never know.'

'Find him, Thomas. Find him and bring him to justice. I want the man dead.'

Madeleine's eyes closed. Thomas sat and watched her sleep. A beautiful lady and a brave one. Was he really going to go back to Romsey without her? He thought of their lovemaking. The first time she had surprised him by speaking French. It was a form of intimacy. The language of love, was it not?

Language, words, meanings. Thomas had always seen mathematics as a language — a way of communicating a fact or an idea. Perhaps that was what had led him to cryptography, which called for skill with both words and numbers. Aurum and Argentum — gold and silver — and in French, *or* and *argent*. Thomas *Col*, Henry *Evêque*, Lemuel *Propriétaire*, John *Hiver*, Chandle *Pierre*, well, almost *Pierre*. What would Quicksilver be? *Mercure*? No, *Argent Vive*, that was it. *Argent Vive* — named by the French alchemists for its appearance. Living silver. *Argent Vive*.

Thomas sat bolt upright. French alchemists. Argent Vive, which could be abbreviated to AV. AV was the enterprise Sir Montford Babb had despaired of in his journal. Quicksilver was the name of the enterprise Charles and Mary had been persuaded to invest in by Chandle Stoner. He knew there was a connection between Babb's murder and the other three. AV was Babb's shorthand for Quicksilver. They were one and the same. And that meant Stoner had persuaded Babb to invest. If he had lied about knowing Babb, what else had he lied about? Quicksilver? Himself? What's more, the intercepted letter had been addressed to A. Silver Esq. Aurum and Argentum, A. Silver, AV and Quicksilver, all connected and all run by the Alchemist. And Chandle Stoner was involved. More than involved. He might be Argentum — the financier — and he might well have arranged Babb's murder.

Thomas ran down the stairs and into the sitting room. Charles was there alone. 'Has Joseph been sent for?' he blurted out.

'He should be here soon,' replied Charles, clearly alarmed. 'Why? Is Madeleine worse?'

Thomas realized with a shock that Charles did not know that Madeleine's fever had broken. Mary must have fallen asleep without telling him. 'Madeleine is recovering, thank God. And I know who Argentum is.'

Before Charles could ask who, there was a loud knock on the door. Without waiting for Smythe, Thomas went to open it. It was Joseph.

'How is she?' he asked without preamble.

'The fever has broken. She is asleep. Go up and see her, then come straight down. I have important news.'

Joseph was in the house only as long as it took to see for himself that Madeleine was recovering, and to hear Thomas's explanation of how he connected AV with Quicksilver, and thus with Stoner. At first Joseph was disbelieving, then astonished, then furious. 'I shall order the arrest of the man immediately,' he thundered on his way out. 'We will question him and if he is guilty, he will hang. Not only a traitor but one acting for personal gain. The vilest of creatures who will pay the price for his greed.'

'It's even worse knowing that I was taken in by such a man. I'd willingly draw and quarter him myself,' said Charles when he and Thomas were alone. He, too, was exploding with anger.

'If you do,' replied Thomas, 'kindly wait until he has told us who Aurum is.'

'Who do you think he is?'

'If there are traitors in the Post Office, one of them is likely to be in a senior position. That means Bishop, Squire or Morland.

Morland is by far the most likely of the three. He was a fierce supporter of Cromwell, is permanently short of money and has the brains for it.'

'Why does Joseph not arrest him?'

'Lack of evidence. Morland is well connected. Remember that he was the man sent to Breda to meet the king. If his guilt were not proved, it could go badly for Joseph.'

Charles grunted. 'It's as well for all of them that Madeleine is recovering. If she hadn't, I'd have taken my swords and saved the hangman the cost of three ropes.'

'Stoner did know Babb. Matthew Smith, John Winter and Henry Copestick too, I shouldn't be surprised.'

'A fraudster, a traitor and a murderer. I should have listened to Mary. She never trusted him.'

'You will have to tell her.'

'I know. Thank God for Madeleine. Mary would never have forgiven me.'

The door opened and Mary came in. 'Mary would never have forgiven you for what?'

Thomas stood up and made for the door. 'I shall look in on Madeleine again. Then I believe that I shall go for a walk in St James's Park. No doubt we shall have heard from Joseph by this evening.'

He was out of the house and on his way to the park within seconds.

CHAPTER 20

Animals in cages reminded Thomas of his own imprisonments in Oxford Castle and on the island of Barbados, so the king's menagerie, even his giraffe, did not hold his interest for long. He soon left the park and wandered off in the direction of Westminster Abbey.

Unlike on his last visit to the Abbey, there was no scaffolding and there were no crowds. Thomas walked slowly around the building, wondering at the skill and faith of the men who had given their lives to creating and improving it over the centuries. It had been fortunate to escape destruction when King Henry had been plundering monasteries all over the country. Perhaps the thought of all his predecessors buried there had stayed the royal hand. Oliver Cromwell had enjoyed only a brief rest in the Abbey. He had been buried in great ceremony, only to be disinterred less than three years later, tried and hanged — an act of astonishing stupidity and barbarity.

Kings and queens had been crowned there for six hundred

years. How many more would follow King Charles II? Would any more suffer the fate of his father? Would England ever again be without a monarch? Would the country ever again plunge itself into the anguish and bloodshed of a civil war?

Thomas shuddered at the thought. Never mind all that, Thomas Hill, you have more immediate matters to deal with and there are questions to be answered. Is Stoner Argentum? Who is Aurum? Was it he who alerted the enemy to the interception of the letter, or had they noticed that its seal had been broken and repaired? Who ordered the Dutchman to murder Babb, Winter, Smith and Copestick? Who is the Alchemist? And what exactly are the Dutch and French planning? More important still, what are you going to do about Madeleine Stewart?

Thomas strolled twice around the Abbey before walking back to Piccadilly. The sitting room was deserted and the house quiet. Thomas smiled. If he knew Charles, by now Mary knew about Stoner and was being consoled in their bedroom. He looked in on Madeleine, who was asleep, and went to his own room.

After an hour reading, Thomas's eyes closed, and he was asleep in his chair when Smythe knocked on his door and called through it, 'Mr Hill, Josiah Mottershead and Agnes Cakebread are here to see Miss Stewart. Should I show them up?'

Thomas roused himself and opened the door. 'I will come down, John,' he said, rubbing his eyes. 'Where are Mr and Mrs Carrington?'

'They are in their bedroom, sir. I did not like to disturb them.'

'Very wise.'

Josiah and Agnes were in the sitting room, looking uncomfortable. Agnes was wearing a green bonnet and a thin shawl over her working dress. She held in her hand a wooden box tied with pink ribbon. Josiah hopped from foot to foot and rubbed his hands together nervously. He had placed his stick by the door. 'Good afternoon, Mr 'Ill,' he said. 'We wondered 'ow Miss Stewart is and Agnes 'as baked 'er a fruit cake. It's 'er favourite.'

Thomas spoke gently. 'Miss Stewart is very weak, but the worst is over. Agnes's fruit cake is just what she needs. How are you, Josiah? Recovered?'

'Thank you, sir, quite recovered. Takes more than a poke in the back to do for Mottershead.'

'Good. Why don't we take the cake up to her?'

Madeleine was awake and sitting up. 'How kind of you both to come. I am feeling much better, and if that is a fruit cake in your hand, Agnes, I shall be better still.'

'It is, Miss Stewart,' said Agnes with something very like a curtsy. 'Mottershead told me to bring it.'

'Thank you, Josiah. And thank you also for rescuing me and getting me out of those terrible marshes.'

'It was no trouble, miss, and Mr Carrington and Mr 'Ill did most of the rescuing.'

'Nonsense,' said Madeleine, reaching out to put her hand on Josiah's arm, 'Thomas has told me exactly what happened. Thank you, Josiah.'

How anyone with a face the colour of Josiah's could blush, Thomas did not know, but blush he did. Thomas almost felt sorry for him. 'Shall we leave Agnes and Miss Stewart to gossip, Josiah? Let us go down to the sitting room.'

The moment they were alone, Thomas asked if Stoner had been arrested. 'Afraid not, sir. When we went to 'is 'ouse, 'e 'ad gone,' replied Josiah.

'Hell and damnation. He must have taken fright when he learned that we had found Miss Stewart.'

'Bloody Dutchman. Should never 'ave let him escape.'

'Too late now, Josiah. Did you search Stoner's house?'

'We did, sir. Top to bottom. Not a sign of where 'e's gone.'

'What is Mr Williamson going to do?'

'I'm to find the man, sir. And if the thieving traitor's in London, find 'im I shall. Got everyone I can think of looking for 'im.'

Thomas did not doubt it. But Stoner might very well not be in London. He might not be in England. He might have taken a boat across the Channel and be counting his money in comfort in Amsterdam or Paris. The devil's balls. Why had he not seen through Stoner long ago? The man was too glib and too plausible. Now he might have escaped.

When Agnes came down, Thomas showed them out. At the door he said quietly, 'If anyone can find him, Josiah, you can. Please keep me informed.'

Thomas spent the next two days with Madeleine or walking the streets of the city. He imagined himself finding Stoner lurking in an alley, overpowering him and dragging him off to Newgate. A delicious idea, an absurd thought. Yet if justice was to be done, Stoner would have to be found. He had swindled Charles and Mary and probably been involved in four murders and Madeleine's abduction. The man must hang. Thomas replayed his conversations with him, hoping to remember something that might help — a place, a name, an idle remark. There was nothing.

Madeleine's recovery, meanwhile, continued well and on the third day she left her bed and came down to join them in the sitting room. There had still been no word from Josiah. Since learning from Thomas that Stoner had disappeared, Charles had worked himself up into a rare stew. He paced the room, cursing the man for his treachery and deceit and cursing himself for his foolishness.

'For the love of God, sit down, Charles,' said Mary. 'Acting like a cuckolded husband won't do anyone any good.' Reluctantly, Charles sat. 'Now, Thomas, what are your plans?'

'I had intended to return to Romsey when Madeleine was out of danger, but now I feel I must stay until Stoner is caught and all the spies exposed. If I go home now, I shall find myself pacing about like Charles.' He stole a look at Madeleine. Her face told him nothing.

'If that is what you want, Thomas, of course you shall stay here as long as you wish. And Madeleine will stay until she is fully recovered, won't you, my dear?'

'Thank you, Mary, although I'm sure I shall be ready to go home very soon. I shall have Agnes to look after me.'

There was a knock on the door and in came Smythe. 'Mr Mottershead is here, sir.'

Charles jumped to his feet. 'Show him in at once.'

Josiah came in, hat in one hand, stick in the other. Thomas had never seen him without his stick and wondered if he slept with it. Charles had no time for pleasantries. 'What news, Josiah? Have you got him?'

Josiah shook his head. 'Not yet, sir. We're still searching. I just came to see 'ow Miss Stewart is.'

'As you can see, Josiah, I am much improved,' said Madeleine. 'And how is Agnes?'

'I've been too busy to call, madam. Out all day and all

night. She knows where to find me, though, if she needs me.'

'Has there been no trace of Stoner at all?' asked Thomas.

'None, sir. I'm afraid 'e's gone.'

'I won't have it,' thundered Charles. 'The man must be found and hanged.'

'What do you suggest, Charles?' asked Mary.

'I suggest that Josiah takes Thomas and me to his house and that we conduct our own search. I'll wager there's a clue there somewhere.'

Josiah looked doubtful. 'Mr Williamson did make us lift every chest and open every drawer.'

'Then we'll do so again, won't we, Thomas?'

It would be better than pacing the streets. 'It's worth a try. Come on, Josiah, no time like the present.'

'Very well, gentlemen, if that's what you want I'll take you there. Just don't expect to find anything.'

Chandle Stoner's house was one of the grandest in Cheapside – two storeys high, with glazed and shuttered windows, newly painted walls and beams, and a large oak door. It was the house of a prosperous man.

Josiah produced from his pocket a set of instruments like long nails, tied together with a thin strip of cloth. He chose a nail, inserted it into the lock and twisted gently until they heard the click of the lock opening. He turned the handle and opened the door, taking care to make almost no sound at all. 'Do you think he's done this before?' whispered Charles, with a grin. Picking up his stick, Josiah led them into the house.

When Thomas opened the shutters to let in light, they saw richly embroidered wall hangings and cushions, a fine oak writing table, leather-bound books on the shelves, paintings on the walls, coloured glass bottles and glasses, pewter jugs and tankards and a quantity of plate. There were valuable items in every room — a Flemish tapestry in one bedroom, silk covers from India in another, and a lace tablecloth in the dining room. In the kitchen were dozens of bottles of French and Spanish wine, sacks of flour and sugar and a huge side of beef hanging on a meat hook. Chandle Stoner did not believe in stinting himself or in hiding his wealth. There was no sign of a search having taken place.

'Are you sure the house has been searched, Josiah?' asked Charles.

'Yes, sir. Mr Williamson ordered us to leave it as we found it.'

'Perhaps he thought Stoner might return and did not want to alert him.'

Just as Joseph's men had done, they opened every drawer and looked in every cupboard. They found silk stockings and linen shirts, rows of boots and shoes and a closet full of coats and hats. They even took every book off its shelf and searched it for hidden papers. There were none.

'There are no documents here,' said Thomas. 'No letters, no papers, not even a bill of sale from his tailor.'

'He must have taken anything incriminating with him, or burned it,' said Charles. 'Let's look in the grates.'

The grates in the sitting room and dining room had been cleaned out, but the fireplace in the kitchen was full of ashes. Charles brushed them aside with his boot. Among the ashes were a few scraps of paper. He picked one up. It was the corner of a document, singed but reasonably intact. There was nothing written on it, so he picked up another. Thomas did the same and soon they had a small pile of scraps without a word on them.

'We didn't think to look at the ashes,' said Josiah, a little guiltily.

'If he did take anything, why burn all this?' asked Thomas. 'Keep looking. There may be something.' While Josiah looked again in every possible hiding place, they carried on sifting the ash, taking care not to damage the small pieces they picked up and added to the pile. 'I never have understood the saying about a needle in a haystack,' Thomas said. 'What would a needle be doing in a haystack and why would anyone look for one there? Looking for a fragment in the ashes would be more appropriate.'

Charles held up a small triangle of paper. 'Eureka, if that's the right expression. A fragment in the ashes it is.' He placed it on the floor and together they peered at it. Thomas made out the letters *one*. One what? He looked again. The letters were part of a word, not a whole one. None? Stoner? Money? There was no way of telling. He picked up another scrap. On this one the words *land* and *is* were just legible.

'Could be anything,' observed Charles. 'Land is cheap, Scotland is full of Scots, anything.'

'Quite,' replied Thomas, carefully picking another scrap from the ash. 'Here's another bit in the same hand. I think the word is *rust*. No, *trust*. I can just see the tail of the *t*.'

'*Land*, *is* and *trust*. Not much to go on.'

He found another, larger piece. 'Here's one. I can make out *th* and *Palace*. Has Stoner any connection with Lambeth Palace?'

'Not as far as I know.'

Thomas held up another. 'This is part of the same letter. The paper is thick and hasn't completely burned. I can make out the word *meet*. Meeting someone at Lambeth Palace, do you suppose?'

'Not the place I'd choose to meet an honest man.'

When there was nothing but ash left, they had bits of two documents. One suggested that Stoner might know a man who lived in or near Lambeth Palace, the other nothing at all. 'Let me see the first piece again,' said Thomas. He peered at it so closely that his nose was almost touching the paper. 'Look at that, Charles. Can you make out a letter before the *l* of *land*?' He handed the scrap to Charles.

'Possibly. It could be a *c* or an *r*.'

'I think it's an *r*. *rland*. Morland?'

'Or Netherland?'

'Not followed by *is*.' He paused and looked around the kitchen. 'We're not going to find anything else. We'll take these four pieces to Joseph and see what he thinks.'

'I'll fetch a book to put them in. Wouldn't want to lose them.' With the fragments safely in a prayer book, and the prayer book safely in Thomas's pocket, they left by the back door and went straight to Joseph's house in Chancery Lane.

Joseph was at home. 'We found these at Stoner's house,' said Thomas. He opened the prayer book and showed him the scraps of paper.

'I take it there is something written on them.' Joseph sounded sceptical.

'There is. Two documents, one with the words *meet* and *th Palace,* the other with *rland is* and *trust*.'

'And what are we to make of these fragments?'

'*th Palace* might be Lambeth Palace. If so, Stoner might have met someone there.'

'In the Palace?'

'Unlikely. Probably nearby.'

'It sounds a trifle far-fetched, Thomas.'

'I know, Joseph, but it's all we have.'

'What about the second piece?'

'You may think this even more far-fetched. *rland* might be Morland, and *trust* could simply be trust, or trustworthy, or trusted.'

'Or mistrust.'

'Indeed. But, again, it's all we have.'

Having inspected the fragments for himself, Williamson sat down with his chin on his hand. For some time he said nothing. Then he looked up and said, 'I am more persuaded by Stoner's absence and the lack of documents than by these fragments. I shall arrange another search of the house in the hope of discovering more evidence. Meanwhile, Mottershead will go to Lambeth to conduct his usual enquiries. Quietly, mind, Mottershead. If our quarry is there we don't want to frighten him away. Have you any friends on that side of the river?'

'I 'ave, sir. There's one or two who know me there.'

'Good. Off you go and report back to me the moment you hear anything.'

'Right, sir,' replied Josiah, looking relieved. 'Good day, gentlemen.'

'What about Morland?' asked Charles, when Josiah had gone.

Joseph pointed at the fragments on the table. 'These mean nothing. We still have no evidence that Morland is a spy, despite his manners and his background. He was not the only man to espouse the cause of Parliament when it was prudent to do so and his rudeness does not make him a traitor. I dare not detain Morland without good reason, but I shall have him watched.'

'In that case, Joseph, Charles and I will return home and leave the matter in your hands.'

Mary and Madeleine were still sitting together when they arrived home. Charles told them about Lambeth and Morland. 'It's hardly proof,' said Mary. 'Is there nothing more?'

'It's more than we had before,' replied Charles sharply, 'and it might lead us to Stoner.'

'Mottershead will make enquiries,' added Thomas, 'while Morland is being watched.'

'So again we must wait on Josiah,' said Madeleine. 'Let us hope he does not need your assistance a second time. Tomorrow I should like to be taken out. If one of you is available, that is.'

Thomas grinned at her. 'You know how unreliable Charles is. I shall escort you.'

The hired carriage that called for Thomas and Madeleine the next morning took them past More Fields towards Hampstead Heath. Wonderful views of the city and air free of coal smoke and evil vapours had made Hampstead Hill a popular destination. One would not venture there at night, but on a lovely summer morning it was glorious. They took with them a *pique-nique* prepared by Mary's cook and a bottle of Charles's wine. Under an oak newly come into leaf, from where they could see the Tower of London and beyond, they set out their *pique-nique* on a linen cloth the size of a large dining table, with a cushion for each of them to sit upon.

'Are the French fond of *pique-niques*?' asked Madeleine, in between mouthfuls. 'It does seem to be one of their better ideas.'

'When Margaret and I used to take the girls out to the meadows by the river,' said Thomas, 'we often took our dinner with us. The girls loved it and I always fell asleep under a tree. We'd never heard of *pique-niques*. Typical of the French to think up some fancy name and claim they invented the whole thing.

The Romans were eating mice and snails in their gardens centuries ago.'

'Shall we take a stroll?' asked Madeleine when they had finished.

'We shall.'

They walked slowly along the ridge which formed the hill, stopping from time to time to gaze down at the city. 'It gets bigger by the month,' said Madeleine. 'It can't grow east into the sea, but I suppose it will continue to expand in every other direction. What's to stop it?'

'Nothing, I imagine. Houses, shops, streets, squares, churches, more houses until it reaches Kingston or Richmond.' They were silent for a while until Thomas asked, 'Do you share your father's faith?'

'I pretended to until he died, but now I attend church only when I have to.'

'And I. Worship should be a private matter. Public displays of it I dislike.'

Madeleine looked at him. 'How odd that we should share such views. In the interminable conflicts between Protestant and Catholic, conformist and non-conformist, you and I choose to be neutral. Peace before prayer, one might say.'

'Indeed. And courtesy before creed. I have often thought that there's much to be said for Judaism. The Jews do not try to force their opinions on anyone else and keep themselves largely to themselves. Why they should be persecuted for their faith is beyond my understanding. At least Cromwell showed more tolerance towards them.'

'Have you ever considered that Judaism is easier than Christianity? Or Islam, for that matter?'

'In what way easier?'

'A Jew must only believe in his God. A Christian must believe in his God and that Christ was his son. A Muslim must believe in his God and that Mohammed was his prophet. One leap of faith is easier than two, don't you think?'

'I'd never thought of it like that.'

They had walked half a mile. 'Now that we've dealt with that, shall we return?' asked Madeleine, taking Thomas's arm and steering him back along the ridge to where the coach was waiting for them. Thomas helped Madeleine in and they set off back to Piccadilly. Looking at her, Thomas saw that the colour was returning to her cheeks. She would very soon want to go back to her own home and the care of Agnes. The image of Agnes and Josiah together made him smile.

'Why do you smile?' she asked.

But before Thomas could reply, a front wheel lurched into a hole and there was a fearful grinding noise. They came to a sudden and uncomfortable halt and were jolted off their seats and on to the floor. 'I fear that sounded like an axle,' said Thomas, helping Madeleine up. 'Sit there and I will investigate.'

The coachman calmed the horses and jumped down. They peered under the carriage — not that much peering was needed. The front axle had twisted when the wheel hit the hole and the wheel itself had come loose. They would not be travelling any further in this vehicle.

Thomas stood up. 'If you stay there, my dear, I will go and find another carriage.'

Madeleine climbed down. 'Nonsense. It is no more than a mile to the house. Why don't we walk?'

'If you feel strong enough.'

'Tush, Thomas. Of course I am strong enough.' Leaving the coachman to deal with the problem as best he could, they set off towards Piccadilly.

Madeleine appeared to be enjoying herself. 'I pity the poor coachman, but it has livened up the day, don't you think?'

'Did it need livening up?'

'Certainly it did. A simple *pique-nique* is nothing like exciting enough now that I am well.' Thomas ignored her.

When they reached Piccadilly the street became busier and they had to walk more slowly. Outside Berkeley House, Madeleine stopped and put a hand to her throat. The colour had suddenly drained from her face and she spoke in a whisper. 'Oh dear, I feel quite unwell. Can we sit down for a moment?'

Thomas looked about. Other than on the ground, there was nowhere to sit. 'We are nearly there. Can you not manage to walk?' Madeleine shook her head. Then she turned away and vomited. Thomas put an arm around her shoulders and waited for the retching to stop. When it had, he put his other arm under her knees and gently picked her up. Passers-by made space for them and within two minutes they were at the Carringtons' house. Thomas shouted for Smythe, who opened the door and let them in.

Mary came out of the sitting room. 'What happened, Thomas?'

'I don't know. She was quite well and then suddenly felt ill. I will take her up to her bedroom.'

Mary followed them up. 'Leave her to me, Thomas,' she ordered. 'Ask Smythe to bring brandy and water.'

Thomas did as he was told and then went to sit with Charles. He told him what had happened.

It was an hour until Mary joined them. 'She's asleep. She told me about the carriage, Thomas. Really, you should not have permitted her to walk so far. She was exhausted.'

'How is she now?'

'She will be perfectly well after a rest. But do not on any account allow her to be so foolish again.'

'I have sent for Joseph,' said Charles. 'I thought he ought to know.' There was a knock on the door. 'That will be him now.'

Smythe showed Joseph in. Before he could ask, Mary told him the story and assured him that no lasting damage had been done. Then she took him up to see Madeleine.

They had just come down when there was another knock on the door. 'Good God,' exclaimed Charles, 'is all of London coming to visit the patient? Who can it be now?'

Josiah was shown into the sitting room and stood with both hands resting on his stick. 'They told me I'd find you 'ere, sir,' he said to Joseph. 'Is Miss Stewart well?'

'She will be after a rest,' replied Joseph, 'no thanks to Mr Hill.' Josiah shot a look at Thomas, who shrugged. 'What brings you here, Mottershead?'

'Progress, sir, I 'ope. I didn't get much from my contacts — none of them 'ad seen a new face about — so I visited the trades-people. Often the best sources, the grocers and butchers, seem to know what's going on. There's a baker near the Palace. When I asked 'im 'ow business was, 'e was very keen to talk. Told me all about 'is customers and what they bought. Eat a lot of bread, those churchmen, 'e told me. Thought it must be on account of all the wine they drink in church. So I egged 'im on a bit, one thing led to another, and 'e was soon telling me about a lady who buys a loaf every morning. Insists on one of the first batch out of the oven.

Won't stand for anything less. The baker didn't know why, as all 'is loaves are just the same.'

Joseph was getting impatient. 'Where is this leading, Mottershead?'

'I was just getting to it, sir. The baker said that the lady 'adn't been in the area very long. Thought she must 'ave been set up in an 'ouse nearby by some gentleman. It 'appens a lot these days. 'Enrietta's always losing them.'

'Why would he think that?'

'She dresses like a lady, 'e said, all silks and satins and ribbons, but she can't 'ide 'er voice. Voice like an 'ore, 'e said. And a real lady wouldn't go out to buy bread 'erself. She'd send a servant, unless she 'asn't got one. If she's 'iding someone or something, she might not 'ave one. Not good at keeping secrets, servants, in my experience.'

'And?'

'She's been buying two loaves every morning, instead of one. The baker reckons 'er gentleman is staying with 'er.'

'Is that all?' Josiah's face fell.

'It could be 'im, sir. And I 'aven't got anything else. The baker 'asn't seen 'im.'

'Did you find out where she lives?'

'Yes, sir. I did get that out of the baker. Didn't go there, mind. Didn't want to alert 'im, if 'e was there.'

Joseph turned to the other two. 'We are only guessing that Stoner is in Lambeth. He might as easily be in Paris. It's very little, but all we've got for the moment. We will look into it ourselves. I suggest you take Mr Carrington and Mr Hill, if they're willing, Mottershead, and pay the lady a visit. Quietly, if you please. No need to alarm the neighbours.'

'I'm willing,' said Charles, 'and so is Thomas. Aren't you, Thomas?'

'I suppose I must be.'

'Good. Then we'll go at once. If it is Stoner, Joseph, we'll bring him to you.'

CHAPTER 21

They crossed the river by wherry from Whitehall Stairs and walked along the south bank towards Lambeth. The row of houses that Josiah led them to was no more than a musket shot from Lambeth Palace. The houses were quite new, two storeys high, brick-built, with tiled roofs and latticed windows. It was a quiet, respectable place in which a prosperous man wanting to escape the bustle of the city might choose to live. Here on the outskirts of London there were few beggars and pickpockets. Josiah pointed to the fourth house in the row. 'That's it. The one with closed shutters. She lives there.'

'What's our plan?' asked Charles, fingering the hilt of his sword. Today he had brought only one.

'We should let ourselves in through the back, sir,' replied Josiah. 'An approach from the front might send them running.'

'Or even shooting,' agreed Thomas. 'Do you know what's at the back, Josiah?'

'No, sir, but it won't take long to find out.'

They followed him round to the back of the row, where a narrow path ran between the houses and one of the many streams which meandered down to the Thames, taking with it the waste from the houses and their occupants. The window shutters at the back of the fourth house in the row were also closed, as was the back door. Josiah produced his set of instruments, inserted one of the nails into the lock and twisted. When nothing happened, he tried another nail. With a little persuasion, the second one worked.

There was no one in the kitchen and no sign of anyone on the ground floor. Either the occupants were away or they were in a bedroom. It had better be Stoner. It would be embarrassing to disturb a perfectly innocent couple in their bed. Copying Josiah, they kept to the edge of the stairs where there was less chance of the timbers squeaking. At the top they found a narrow landing off which there were three doors. Josiah signalled to them to listen at each one.

Charles put his ear to the first and shook his head. It was the same with the second door. But when Thomas bent his head to the third door he heard the sound of regular breathing. Someone was asleep in there. He pointed at the door and nodded. Josiah stepped forward, kicked open the door and swept in. Charles, sword in hand, was close behind. Thomas stood at the door to prevent any sudden attempt at escape.

The drapes of the four-poster bed were open, revealing two bodies with their backs to the door, a sheet covering only their lower halves. Charles put the tip of his sword to the neck of the nearer one while Josiah slipped around the bed and held his stick at the head of the other. It happened so quickly that neither body moved and they barely had time to open their eyes.

To Thomas's astonishment, Josiah burst out laughing. 'Well I'll be buggered, Molly Romp, fancy finding you 'ere. 'Enrietta told us you'd cleared off. Didn't know you were living like a lady in Lambeth. She will be pleased to see you again.'

'What the fuck are you doin' 'ere, Josiah Mottershead?' she squawked. 'You won't find no jewels to thieve 'ere. Fuck off and leave us in peace.'

'It's not jewels we're after, my lovely, it's your gentleman friend. Got a bit of explaining to do, 'e 'as. Up you get now and put some clothes on, there's a good girl.' Molly swore mightily, then wriggled off the bed and grabbed a dress from the back of a chair.

'I don't know what you're up to, Josiah Mottershead, but it 'ad better be good. This gentleman ain't done nothing wrong and neither 'ave I.' She's a buxom girl, thought Thomas, watching her dress, and, if I'm not mistaken, with a redhead's temper. Better keep a eye on her.

So far, the other body had neither moved nor spoken. Charles poked it with his sword. 'Turn around slowly. Any sudden move-ment would be a mistake.' Very cautiously, the body turned. 'Well, well. Chandle Stoner. And what have you to say for yourself?'

'I might well ask you the same question, Charles,' replied Stoner, sitting up. 'I daresay the magistrate will want to know why you and your accomplices have broken into this house and held its occupants at the point of a sword.'

'I daresay he might. Not that he's going to find out. Get up and get dressed and waste no more words. Joseph Williamson would like a talk with you.' At the mention of Williamson, Stoner's face betrayed nothing. Watching him closely, Thomas thought that unless the man was innocent he was an accomplished actor. If he had successfully persuaded Charles and Mary to part with their money on false pretences, an actor he must be. Innocence was less likely.

When Molly and Stoner were both dressed, Josiah ripped up a shirt he found on the floor and tied their wrists together. Then he ushered them down the stairs and out of the front door. The moment she was out of the house, Molly started screaming. "Elp, 'elp. Robbers. Murderers. Thieves. Traitors.' Josiah stepped forward and hit her a sharp blow on the head with his stick.

'Shut your mouth, Molly, or you'll get another one, and 'arder next time. Keep quiet and you won't get 'urt.'

Molly rubbed her head. 'You evil little shit, Mottershead. I always knew you was a wrong 'un. 'Itting a lady with that fucking stick.'

'You a lady, Molly? You're no more a lady than I'm a gentle-man. You're an 'ore, and don't forget it.'

'Fuck you, Mottershead.' She spat at him. Josiah laughed and prodded her with his stick.

'I must be the only man in London you 'aven't fucked. Now 'urry along. We've an appointment to keep.'

Charles and Thomas walked behind Josiah, their prisoner between them. Charles's sword was drawn. Mr Stoner would not be running off again. A silent wherryman rowed them back across the river to the stairs at Whitehall, from where they took a coach to Chancery Lane. Molly had learned her lesson and Stoner had also decided to keep quiet. Studying his face in the coach, Thomas still saw nothing. For all that showed in his eyes, Chandle Stoner might have been off to the theatre with friends.

At Williamson's house they were shown into the room that Thomas had used for his decrypting work. Alerted by his footman, Williamson came bustling in and surveyed the scene. Chandle

Stoner and a woman backed against a wall and held there by Charles's sword and Mottershead's stick. 'So. You found him in Lambeth. Was he with this lady?'

''E was, sir,' replied Josiah with a chuckle, 'only a lady she isn't. This 'ere is Molly Romp, who used to work in Wild Street for a friend of mine, name of 'Enrietta.'

Williamson raised an eyebrow. 'Wild Street, eh?'

'Yes, sir. She's an 'ore.'

'And you're a right little bugger, Mottershead, sticking your nose into other people's business. I 'ope you 'ang for it,' screeched Molly, trying to grab Josiah by the throat. Wisely, he stepped back and kept her at bay with his stick.

'And what about you, Stoner?' enquired Joseph politely. 'Have you an explanation for your disappearance, not to mention the disappearance of certain people's money?'

Under pressure, Stoner did what Thomas imagined came most easily to him – he assumed an attitude of high-handed disdain. 'I feel no obligation to explain anything, even to you, sir. A man may go where he pleases. And money invested may be lost as well as increased, as the most gullible of fools must know.' He glanced at Charles. 'However, in the interests of justice and harmony, I will answer whatever questions you have.'

'Good,' said Joseph, and rang a small bell to summon his footman. 'Fetch four constables, if you please. Tell them to look lively.' He turned back to Stoner. 'I will keep you company until they arrive.'

'Where are we to be taken?' asked Stoner.

'The Tower, I think. At present it is full of the king's enemies waiting to learn their fate, but I daresay the Constable will be able to find room for you both. It's where traitors are usually sent.'

'Traitors! I ain't no traitor,' yelled Molly. 'Traitors 'ang. An 'ore I may be, but not a traitor. I wouldn't know 'ow. Tell them, Chandle, for God's sake.' Stoner ignored her. Thomas was inclined to agree, but kept quiet.

'That we shall ascertain in due course,' said Joseph. There were sounds of running boots on the cobbles and the front door being opened. 'Ah, here are the constables. You'd best accompany them, Mottershead, just to be sure. We don't want our birds flying, as the king's father might have said.'

'Very well, sir. Come on, you two, behave yourselves and you won't get into any trouble. Try anything stupid and you'll feel the weight of my stick.'

'Well done, Mottershead. Report back here when you've delivered them safely. Tell the Constable of the Tower that he has my authority to detain them. Then you'll need to return to the house to search it.'

'Yes, sir.'

'I should thank you gentlemen, too,' said Joseph when they had gone. 'Did you have any difficulty?'

'None,' replied Thomas. 'Josiah is a most resourceful soul, and a man who is an expert swordsman with either hand was unlikely to be bested by Stoner.'

'Or his whore,' added Charles with a grin. 'Did you see Josiah's face when he recognized her? I thought he was going to expire laughing.'

'Joseph, may I go back to Madeleine now?'

'And I,' said Charles.

'Of course, of course. You must both do that. I shall take the news to the king and let the prisoners consider their predicament. The Tower can have a salutary effect on its residents. Later I'll go and see what they have to tell us. Would either of you care to accompany me?' The disobedient eye squinted at them as if daring them to refuse.

Thomas and Charles looked at each other. Neither had ever set foot in the Tower, and neither was keen to do so. 'You go, Thomas,' suggested Charles. 'Prisons are more your sort of thing than mine and you're more likely to be some use to Joseph.'

Thomas knew when he had been outmanoeuvred. 'If you don't feel up to the task, Charles, I shall certainly accompany Joseph. I doubt the Tower is any worse than Oxford Castle.' Turning to Joseph he said, 'At what time shall I meet you there?'

'Shall we say nine o'clock? That will give us time for our supper beforehand and the prisoners time to work up a good hunger.'

'Thank you, Charles, you're a good friend,' said Thomas as they left the house.

'Oh come now,' replied Charles, catching the irony, 'it's not like you to be squeamish. You can tell us all about it tomorrow.'

They found Mary sitting beside the bed on which Madeleine was propped up on a pile of cushions. The remains of a meal and two empty glasses were on a tray at the end of the bed. Charles picked up a glass and sniffed. 'Brandy, ladies? May we assume the patient is feeling better again?'

'She is, Charles,' replied Mary. 'Now you and I will leave Madeleine and Thomas here and you can tell me what you found in Lambeth.'

When they had gone, Thomas bent to kiss Madeleine. 'You look stronger, my dear. Not too much brandy, I trust.'

'The merest sip, Thomas. And I do feel stronger, thank you. Did you find Stoner?'

'We did. Hiding in Lambeth with his whore. A lady known to Josiah and who was not best pleased to see him. Neither, for that matter, was Stoner.'

Thomas told her about finding them in bed, about Stoner's protestations of innocence and about Josiah's delight at the prospect of returning Molly to Henrietta. 'They're both safely in the Tower by now,' he said. 'Joseph has asked me to meet him there this evening to question them.'

'Why you, Thomas? Why do you have to go to that evil place? Why can't you stay here and keep me company?'

'Alas, my dear, there is nothing I should like more, but Charles as good as volunteered me for the task. I do not have to be there until nine o'clock. May I stay with you until then?'

'I insist upon it. Then go and threaten to cut Stoner into small pieces if he does not tell you where that Dutchman is.'

A little after eight o'clock, Thomas gently detached his arm from around the sleeping patient's shoulders, slipped out of the room and set off for the Tower. Thirty minutes later his carriage arrived outside the outer wall, where he presented himself to a yeoman warder and was escorted through a gatehouse in the inner wall. At the White Tower, where the Constable of the Tower had rooms, he was shown into an antechamber and asked to wait while the yeoman announced his arrival.

Joseph soon came bustling in. 'Good evening, Thomas. Thank you for coming. I have arranged with the Constable for our prisoners to be brought to us here. I thought we would see the woman first. I doubt she has much to tell us, but a little warning won't hurt.'

'As you wish, Joseph. Is there anything you particularly want me to do?'

'Ask whatever questions you like and watch for signs of dissembling. Extra pairs of eyes and ears are always useful.'

The Molly who was brought into the antechamber was every bit as foul-mouthed and ill-tempered as the Molly whom they had found in bed with Stoner. So far, the Tower had done nothing for her composure. 'Where's that little shit Mottershead?' she screeched. 'Bring 'im 'ere and 'e'll feel the sharp end of my tongue.'

'Mr Mottershead is otherwise engaged,' replied Joseph calmly. 'Now sit down and answer our questions. If you give us any trouble, the warder will bind your hands and ankles.' With a look of pure hatred, Molly sat. 'Good. Now, first of all, how did you meet Chandle Stoner?'

''Ow do you think? 'E came to the 'ouse.'

'The house in Wild Street?' Molly nodded. 'And when was that?'

'Around Christmas time, it was. It was so cold the privy was frozen up and we 'ad to shit on the ice.'

'And when did you leave the house?'

'The day after the coronation. 'E took me to Lambeth and said 'e'd keep me there in comfort, as long as I didn't tell no one about it.'

'And you agreed?'

'Course I did. I'm not stupid. A big 'ouse and plenty of money. Better than spreading my legs for poxy old men for a few shillings. 'E gave me money for clothes, too.'

'But no servants?'

'No, 'e wouldn't allow servants.'

'Did he have any visitors?'

''E did, but I never saw them. I 'ad to go to the bedroom when anyone came. What's this all about? What's 'e done?'

'All in good time. Did he tell you anything about himself?'

'Not much. Said 'e was in business. Spent a lot of time in coffee 'ouses, 'e said.'

'How often did he visit you?'

'Two or three times a week, until 'e moved in for good. Said 'e wanted to be private.'

'When was that?'

'About a week ago.'

Throughout the questioning, Thomas had been watching Molly's face carefully. He had seen not a glimmer of a lie nor a hint of guilt. She was what she said she was — a London whore who had enjoyed a slice of luck. The luck had run out, but she was neither a traitor nor a murderer.

Williamson clearly thought the same. 'That will do for now,' he told her. 'You will be kept here for the present in case you remember anything of use to us. If you do, ask the warder to send word to me. And don't forget that you are still under suspicion of being involved in crimes for which you could hang. Your best chance of release is to tell us everything you remember. Names, events, anything. Is that clear?'

'I've told you what I know, and it ain't much. 'E wouldn't 'ave told me about 'is business, would 'e? I'm just 'is 'ore. Ask 'im yourself if you don't believe me.'

'Not now you aren't, Molly,' said Thomas. 'You won't be keeping Chandle Stoner warm any longer.'

'Piss on 'im then. Never liked the shit.'

'Take her back to her room, warder, please,' Williamson ordered, 'and bring Stoner.'

'She was telling the truth,' said Thomas, when they had gone.

'I fear so. But she might remember something. We'll keep her here just in case.'

Chandle Stoner had evidently decided that his best defence was attack. He stormed into the room and launched straight into a tirade. 'By what authority do you keep me here, may I enquire? I am not unknown in this city and have friends who will want to know why I have been treated like a common criminal.'

'Sit down, Stoner, and answer our questions.' Williamson's voice was icy.

'On the contrary, sir. You will answer my questions.'

Williamson stared at him. 'Bind his hands, warder, and tie him to the chair. If he resists, break his arm.' When Stoner was bound and sitting, Williamson continued. 'Understand that you are in no position to make demands. I have the authority of the king to do whatever I believe to be necessary for the defence of His Majesty and his realm. That includes hanging you if I choose.'

'And on what grounds do you propose to do that?'

'You are suspected of being a murderer, a thief and a traitor.'

Stoner laughed. 'And do you intend to hang me three times for these three crimes, not one of which I am guilty of?'

Williamson ignored the question. 'Have you any knowledge of an enterprise named Quicksilver?'

'I certainly have. A mining venture from which a number of my friends have made considerable profits.'

'And others have made losses.'

Stoner shrugged. 'Business carries risk.'

'Why did you leave your home in Cheapside and go to Lambeth?'

'That is none of your affair.'

Williamson nodded to the warder, who clipped Stoner on the ear with his staff. 'I think you will find that it is. Why?'

'A man in my position needs privacy.'

'What position is that?'

'I am a man of business.'

'Why did you burn all your documents before leaving the house?'

'That is my standard procedure for all confidential documents and correspondence that are no longer needed.'

'Did you know Sir Montford Babb?'

'Possibly. I meet many people in the course of business.'

'Did he have an interest in Quicksilver?'

'I cannot recall.'

'Did you know Matthew Smith, John Winter or Henry Copestick?'

'No.'

'Do you know who murdered them?'

'That is an absurd question.' Another nod to the warder and another clip on the ear. 'No.'

'Do the names Aurum and Argentum mean anything to you?'

'As much as they do to you. Gold and silver. What of it?'

'On one of the letters you burned we found the name Morland. Was this Sir Samuel Morland?'

'Possibly. I don't remember the contents of every document.'

'We think that it was. What business had you with him?'

'None. Now if you have no more questions, kindly release me. I have nothing more to tell you and nothing to hide.'

'You will remain here for the present. You should know, also, that I saw the king this morning. At his request, the Privy Council has authorized the use of the rack if I should deem it necessary.'

Stoner went white. No one could withstand the rack and the Council authorized it only in the most serious cases. 'Keep that in mind when we return tomorrow.' Williamson turned to Thomas. 'Have you any questions, Thomas?'

'Did you have Madeleine Stewart taken to Dartford?'

'I have no idea what you are talking about.'

'Take him back to his room, warden,' ordered Williamson. 'Give him food and water and keep a guard on him. We will return tomorrow.'

'Well, Thomas, what did you make of that?' asked Williamson on their way home.

'The woman knows nothing. Stoner is lying, but about what exactly I am unsure. He knew Smith, Winter and Copestick and I'm sure he knew Babb. The names Quicksilver, Argent Vive, Aurum and Argentum may be a coincidence, but I doubt it. When he learned about Madeleine's rescue, he burned his documents and disappeared. Did he arrange the murders, and if so, why? Was he behind Madeleine's abduction? Is he involved in a spy ring, and if so, how?'

'And most importantly of all,' said Joseph, 'what exactly are the Dutch and the French up to and how are we going to find out?'

'In that connection, has Stoner's arrest been made public?'

'Not yet.'

'May I suggest that it remains confidential for the moment? I have the glimmer of an idea.'

Joseph raised an eyebrow. 'Should I be pleased or alarmed?'

'Time will tell.'

Charles was waiting for Thomas. 'Has the thieving wretch

confessed yet,' he asked as soon as Thomas walked in, 'or is he going to the rack?'

'That has been mentioned. And no, he has not yet confessed. Joseph thought a night of contemplation might change his mind.'

'And what do you think?'

'The man who establishes his argument by noise and command shows that his reason is weak.'

'Sounds like that Frenchman again.'

'It is. And he's invariably right. Stoner's guilty of something. We just have to find out what. The woman knows nothing. I expect she'll be released tomorrow.'

'Anything on Morland?'

'Nothing yet. How is Madeleine?'

'Sleeping like an infant.'

'I'll look in before I retire. It's back to the Tower in the morning. Good night, Charles.'

'Good night, Thomas. Make the bastard sing and we'll feel better about losing our money.'

The procedure at the Tower was unchanged. A yeoman warder escorted Thomas to the White Tower where Joseph was waiting.

'Good morning, Thomas. I thought we would speak to Stoner first. The warder is fetching him.'

After a night in the Tower with thoughts of the rack to occupy his mind, Chandle Stoner looked a great deal less confident. His eyes were red, his skin flushed and his beard unattended to. His clothes had been slept in and, Thomas noted, wrinkling his sensitive nose, he smelt of sweat and fear. Joseph must have seen such transformations before. The rack was a powerful persuader.

'Did you sleep well, Stoner?' he asked cheerfully. 'The rooms are really quite comfortable, are they not? People forget that the Tower was built as a palace, not a prison.' Joseph sat with his good eye towards Stoner.

Stoner ignored the questions. 'I have a proposition to make.'

'Have you now?' Williamson sounded unsurprised. 'And what might that be?'

'In return for telling you what I know of the matters discussed yesterday, safe passage to Denmark.'

'Indeed. And why would I not simply put the rack to work and achieve the same result?'

'I might die before you learn anything.'

'It does happen, admittedly. What do you think, Thomas?'

If this man had stolen the Carringtons' money, been party to four murders and had Madeleine taken to Dartford, Thomas thought he should be hanged without further ado. However, that would not lead them to Aurum and Argentum. 'Perhaps we should give the prisoner the opportunity to prove his good faith by telling us about Quicksilver. He does not know what information we already have, and if he lies, we shall know at once. If he tells the truth, we might decide to accept his proposal.'

Williamson looked approvingly at Thomas, who had guessed that it was just the sort of deception he might have suggested himself. They knew next to nothing about Quicksilver, but then Joseph had no authority to use the rack. 'I agree,' he said. 'Begin by telling us everything you know about Quicksilver, Stoner. Then we'll see.'

Stoner was trapped and he knew it. The only way to save his skin was to do as they wished. 'Very well. Quicksilver was the name of a fictitious mining enterprise. It purported to mine for precious metals and stones in the New World. I raised money from investors in the business.'

'What happened to the money?' Joseph's questions gave Stoner no time for thought.

'Some was paid back to investors in order to create the impression of a successful venture and to encourage more investment.'

'And the rest?'

'Most of it was sent to Holland.'

'Most of it?'

'I kept a small percentage as my fee.'

'Why did you not keep all of it? Why send it to Holland?'

'I have — had — an arrangement.'

'What arrangement?'

'That I would be fully compensated in due course.'

'And you believed this arrangement would be honoured?'

'I did.'

Joseph changed tack. 'Was Quicksilver also known to some as Argent Vive?'

Thomas saw the look of surprise on Stoner's face. That was a question he had not expected. 'I believe it was by some.'

'Such as Sir Montford Babb?'

'Yes.' Stoner squared his shoulders and took a deep breath. 'I have told you what I know of Quicksilver. Before answering more questions, I need your agreement to my proposal.'

'And if we don't give it?'

'You would risk learning nothing more.'

Thomas thought Joseph was about to accept the offer. He was wrong.

'We will think about your proposal, Stoner. You will be quite safe here until we have decided what to do.'

'I am willing to speak now.'

'We, however, are not willing to listen. Warder, take him back to his room and keep a close watch on him. No privileges.'

The warder wrenched Stoner to his feet and led him away.

'Why the delay, Joseph?' asked Thomas.

'I suspect he was planning to tell us only enough to save his own skin. A second day of contemplation might change his mind. We'll have another talk with his whore first.'

When the warder brought her in, Molly looked as dishevelled as Stoner had. Red hair a tangled mess, face streaked with dirt and torn dress slipping off her shoulders. Not as Henrietta would have wished for her customers.

'I've remembered something,' she croaked before she had even been asked a question. ''E 'ad visitors.'

'You've already told us that.'

'I looked out of the window and saw one leaving. Big arse 'e had.'

'Anything else?'

'No. 'E was wearing a long coat. Big arse is what I remember. And I over'eard names. Odd names, sounded like Or Rum and some other Rum. And another name. Norland or Morland, it was.'

Joseph and Thomas were on their feet. 'Are you sure of this?' demanded Joseph.

'Course I'm sure. You going to let me go now?'

'If you are telling the truth, you will be released. If not . . .' Joseph turned to the warder. 'Take her back. Good food and wine.'

Molly screeched at them. 'I don't want no fucking food. I want to get out of 'ere.' She was dragged away struggling and spitting, and cursing them for the shittin' bastards that they were.

'To the Post Office for me, Thomas,' said Joseph. 'I shall have Morland brought here and then go to Whitehall. Morland and Stoner can both spend the afternoon contemplating their future. Shall we talk to them this evening?'

It was a relief to get out of the Tower and back to Piccadilly. Just the thought of the miserable souls delivered by barge to the Traitors' Gate, knowing that their next appointment would be with the executioner, was enough to make Thomas's skin crawl. Two queens of England had been among them.

Madeleine was sitting with Mary and Charles. 'What news do you bring from the Tower?' asked Charles. 'Has Stoner confessed yet?'

'To Quicksilver, he has. It was a fraud. No mine ever existed.'

'I am a fool.'

'Enough of that, Charles,' said Mary sharply. 'It's over and done with. Has he confessed to anything else?'

'Not yet. Joseph is giving him time to consider his position. And Morland has been arrested.'

'Is there proof of his guilt?' asked Madeleine.

'Not proof, but a suggestion.' Thomas told them about Molly. 'I am to return this evening.'

'Must you, Thomas? It is such a dreadful place.'

'It is. I would much rather stay here, but Joseph has asked me to assist in the questioning.'

'Could you not have refused?'

'That would have been churlish. We might have Morland and Stoner, but the Dutchman is still at large. Not to mention the Alchemist, whoever he is.'

There was a brief silence before Mary said brightly, 'We will all take dinner together and there will be no mention of spies, money, traitors or anything else unpleasant. I will go and ask the cook for something special.'

Something special turned out to be a huge venison stew flavoured with nutmeg and ginger, and a rich orange pudding. They washed it down with Charles's best claret and a bottle of Madeira.

Joseph was waiting for Thomas in the White Tower. 'I have had Morland brought here,' he told Thomas. 'Let us see what he has to say.' Morland was sent for and escorted in by two warders. He looked murderous.

'Why am I here and how much longer have I to suffer this outrage, Williamson?' thundered Morland. 'You cannot hold me here without just cause and you know it. I demand to be released at once.'

'This is a matter of national security, Morland, and you will remain here while we make our enquiries.'

Morland glared at Thomas. 'Why is this man here?'

'He is rendering me valuable assistance. Now sit down and compose yourself.' Morland, still glaring, sat down. 'Good. We have detained Chandle Stoner, in whose house a fragment of paper bearing your name was found. He has confessed to being a criminal. How do you explain your name being on that paper?'

'Show me the letter.'

'I think not.'

'Then I deny it. I barely know Chandle Stoner, but if he chooses to write about me, he would not be the first to do so.'

'We also have a witness who has connected you to Stoner.'

'Who?'

Joseph ignored the question. 'You and Stoner are members of a ring of spies centred on the Post Office.'

Morland went bright red and spittle flew from his mouth. 'Preposterous. What proof of this absurd accusation do you have?'

'Let us say that based on the information we have, it is a reasonable inference.'

'Inferences are never reasonable. They are merely inferences. Intuition is always inferior to rational thought, as even you should know.'

'Have a care, Morland. Insults will get you nowhere.'

'Outrageous. You hold me here for no reason and complain of being insulted. May I not complain of your lack of evidence against me?'

'What do you know of Aurum and Argentum?'

'My Latin is certainly superior to your own.' Morland's haughty tone had returned.

'The Alchemist?'

'Alchemy is not a practice in which I have faith.'

'Lemuel Squire has claimed that certain letters given to you for copying disappeared. Why was that?'

'I do not trust actors. They pretend to be what they are not. Furthermore, Squire is an absurd little man. The copying machine is not yet perfected. Mistakes are made. And as long as I am in here, there will be no improvement.'

'Have you anything more to tell us, Morland?'

'About what, pray? I am guilty of nothing and have nothing to tell you. I demand to be released immediately.'

'Take him away, warder, and bring the other prisoner.'

Shrugging off the warder's attentions, Morland rose and stormed out of the room.

'Arrogant and unpleasant, but guilty of treason?' mused Williamson.

'I'm unsure,' replied Thomas. 'His background is against him and he's a hateful specimen, but we have only that scrap of paper and the woman's word that she heard his name. There's no real evidence. I couldn't tell if he was lying.'

'Nor I. Shall we talk to Stoner again?'

Unlike Morland, Stoner looked thoroughly defeated. The Tower had taken no time at all to crush his spirit, as it had crushed so many spirits. His eyes were red and his hands shaking. For several minutes Joseph stared at him in silence. Eventually he said, 'Our conditions are the same, Stoner. If you lie or if we suspect you of lying, you will go to the rack. Is that clear?'

'Yes. And if I tell the truth, have I your word that I shall be given safe passage to Denmark?' Thomas heard the relief in his voice. The man was a craven coward.

'Why Denmark?'

'I have friends there. And I am willing to gather intelligence for you.'

'You are prepared to work for me?'

'I am. It is a simple business proposal.'

'Your proposal is agreed,' Joseph replied in a matter-of-fact way that made Thomas think he must receive this sort of offer every week. He turned to Thomas. 'Would you care to continue? I shall sit and listen for lies.'

Thomas tried not to sound surprised. 'As you wish, Joseph.' He paused. 'What is the connection between Quicksilver and Aurum and Argentum, Stoner?'

'Aurum and Argentum are the code names of two men involved in the plan for which the money from Quicksilver was intended.'

'What plan?'

Stoner smiled. 'If you know about Aurum and Argentum, you know about the plan. Ever since the return of Charles Stuart, our Dutch friends have been talking to the French court. Both countries have reasons to act against England. The Dutch fear an English navy as powerful as their own and the French want a Catholic king on the English throne. An avowed Catholic, not a secret one. You are aware of that.'

'So you are a traitor. Why?'

'It has made me a wealthy man.'

'Where is your money?'

'In Copenhagen.'

'Why were Smith, Babb, Winter and Copestick murdered?'

'Babb was an old fool who threatened to expose Quicksilver.'

'And the others?'

'They had become dangerous. Winter and Smith in the city, Copestick in the Post Office.'

'Who killed them?'

'The Dutchman you met in Dartford. He bore a grudge.'

'How do you know we met such a man?'

'Of course I know. You did not kill him.'

'Did you approve the murders?'

Stoner shrugged. 'I had no say in the matter.'

'Why was Madeleine Stewart abducted?'

'We wanted to know how much you had learned. In view of your close friendship with the lady, we assumed she might know.'

'She did not know. And the ransom?'

'A change of plan, necessitated by her sickness.'

'Who are Aurum and Argentum?'

'That I shall tell you when I have Mr Williamson's written guarantee of my safety.'

Williamson exploded. 'You will not. You will tell us now. Remember where you are, Stoner.'

But having unburdened himself, Stoner had recovered some of his composure. 'No, sir. Your guarantee in return for Aurum and Argentum.'

'You're playing a dangerous game, Stoner. Your life is in my hands.'

'I am aware of that. And the information you want is in mine. Have we an agreement?'

'You will know in an hour. Take him back to his room, warden, and return here.'

When they had gone, Thomas asked, 'Do they always sing like song thrushes, Joseph? The man seemed ready to tell us almost anything. Except the identity of Aurum and Argentum, that is.'

'It is very common. Stoical resistance followed by abject surrender. I have seen it often. The difference here is that he's holding something back which he imagines will save his skin.'

'Will it?'

'It might.'

An hour later, Joseph sent for Stoner again. 'I have a proposal,' he began. 'You will accept it or you will go to the rack. Which shall it be?'

'It seems I have little choice. What do you propose?'

'First, you will reveal the identities of Aurum and Argentum.'

Stoner looked surprised. 'That is agreed.'

'There are other conditions. You will sign a letter to your banker in Copenhagen authorizing the release of all the money to my representative. I will have the letter delivered and the money distributed appropriately.'

There was a slight hesitation. 'Also agreed.'

'You will tell us what you know about the Alchemist.'

Stoner laughed. 'I thought we would come to that. You will not be surprised to hear that I do not know the identity of this man.'

'How did you communicate with him?'

'Through Aurum. I know only that he lives in Amsterdam.'

'Another Dutchman. How long have you been working for him?'

'About a year.'

'How did he contact you?'

'Aurum.'

Joseph nodded. He could not have expected more. 'Very well. You will write the letter to your banker. When the money arrives from Copenhagen, you will be permitted to travel there on terms I shall lay down. Our friends in Copenhagen will ensure that those terms are met.' Joseph paused. 'You are Argentum.' Stoner nodded. 'Who is Aurum?'

'Lemuel Squire is Aurum.' Stoner spoke so quietly that Thomas wondered if he had misheard.

'Squire?'

'Yes.'

Joseph was the first to recover. 'Warder, lock this man up again and put a guard on the door.' He swept out of the White Tower, across the courtyard, through the gate and into the waiting carriage. Thomas had to run to keep up with him.

The journey to Cloak Lane was fast and dangerous. The coach tilted alarmingly as it took corners, bouncing over the cobbles and scattering angry pedestrians. On the way, Thomas asked about Morland.

'He will stay there until we are sure we have not been tricked. The woman will be released,' replied Joseph.

Outside the Post Office, they leapt from the coach and charged in. 'Where's Squire?' shouted Williamson. 'Bring him here at once.' Two guards disappeared into the building to find him. They returned empty-handed.

'Mr Squire has sent a message to say that he is unwell,' said one of them.

Thomas turned on his heel and ran back out of the building. He was just in time to stop the coach from driving off. 'Hold, man. We need you again,' he yelled. The driver pulled on his reins and waited until both men had got in.

'Where does he live?' asked Thomas.

'Near the Charterhouse.'

'Charterhouse, driver, as quick as you can.' The driver cracked his whip and called for a clear road. Thomas shut his eyes and tried not to be sick.

Within ten minutes, they were in Charterhouse Street and outside a timber house of the type built some eighty years earlier. The upper storey overhung the lower, the windows were small and the roof was tiled. Joseph thumped on the door and demanded it be opened. When nothing happened, he tried the handle. It was locked. The door was oak and would not yield easily to force.

'Break a window, Joseph,' suggested Thomas, 'and I'll squeeze through it.'

By this time a group of onlookers had assembled. 'Keep those people back, driver,' ordered Joseph. 'We are about the king's business.' He picked up a stone lying in the street and broke a window. 'Can you get through that, Thomas?'

'I can try. If you would help me up, I'll take it head first.'

Standing on Joseph's locked hands, he pushed his arms through, shut his eyes and forced himself inside. Bits of broken glass showered the floor as he did so. He picked himself up and wiped blood from his hands. A key was hanging by the door. He unlocked the door and let Joseph in.

It was obvious at once that this bird had also flown. The grate was cold, the remains of a meal had been left on a table and his desk was covered in papers. Unlike Stoner, Squire had left in too much of a hurry to burn the evidence.

For a reason he could not explain, Thomas took Squire's seal from the desk and slipped it into his pocket. He picked up a letter. It was short and written in a numerical code. He held it out to Joseph. 'Look at this. What odds that this is the same code as in the Aurum and Argentum letter?'

Joseph examined it. 'Is it?'

'The pattern is the same — groups of four one- and two-digit numbers. It might be.'

'How long to be sure?'

'No more than a few minutes, but I shall need my working papers.'

'Where are they?'

'At the Carringtons' house.'

Another breakneck ride and they were in Piccadilly. Thomas ran up the stairs to his room and took a pile of papers from a drawer. When working on decryptions, he hated being rushed — it was all too easy to make a mistake — but this was different. He laid the letter on his table and found the sheet on which he had written the code. He knew at once that this was the same. The numbers for the letters A and R jumped off the page, swiftly followed by E, O, T and S. Without bothering to decipher the whole thing, he picked up both papers and ran back down the stairs. Joseph was waiting impatiently in the hall. 'It's the same code, no doubt at all.'

'Proof enough that Stoner told us the truth. Squire is Aurum. I'll send out a message at once. We may yet intercept him before he escapes the country.'

Charles had heard their voices and emerged from the sitting room. 'Joseph, Thomas. What's going on?'

'Aurum,' replied Thomas. 'It's Squire. We have proof.'

'Not Morland?'

'Not Morland.'

'Pity. Miserable fellow. Still, Stoner will hang, I imagine.'

'I shouldn't be at all surprised,' said Joseph, 'but perhaps not quite yet. I have plans for Mr Stoner.'

'I'm sure you know best, Joseph, but remember he stole our money. I'd put the rope round his neck myself if I could.'

'As would others,' said Thomas. 'Now what, Joseph?'

'We will go through all the papers in Squire's house. With luck we might find something useful. If there is anything encrypted, I will bring it to the Tower. Please finish decrypting the one you have and meet me there in two hours.'

Thomas shook his head. 'I'm in and out of that place so often they might as well give me a room there.'

When Thomas returned to the Tower he found Joseph and Josiah waiting for him. He handed the decrypted text to Joseph, who read it aloud.

'*Our efforts continue but hampered by recent events. Post Office no longer secure. Will advise new means of delivery. Believe this cipher intact.*'

'So he does not know that you decrypted the letter, although of course he does know it was intercepted. What does he mean by "recent events"?'

'Madeleine's rescue, possibly, and the Dutchman's escape.' Joseph held up the paper. 'The important thing is that the letter was never sent. Squire took fright and fled before he could finish it. He panicked when he heard Madeleine was safe, just as Stoner did.' He looked around the room. 'There are spies everywhere. For all we know, there is one listening now.'

If there is, thought Thomas, we are as good as doomed. Foreign agents in the Tower of London. God forbid.

Joseph sent for Stoner. He came in looking smug. 'I told you the truth, did I not?'

Joseph ignored the question.'Where is Squire?'

'If he is not at home or in Cloak Lane, I suggest you try all the best inns in London. He could be in any of them.'

'I am not in the mood for levity, Stoner. Where is he?'

'France, possibly. He likes French wine.'

'Have I not made myself clear? I want to know where he is. If you choose not to tell us, our agreement will not be honoured and you will suffer.' Joseph was furious.

'I cannot tell you where Squire is any more than I can tell you who the Alchemist is. Give me a letter to my bankers and I will sign it. That is all I can do.'

'The letter can wait. Take him back, warder, and bring the woman.' Stoner was marched, protesting, back to his room.

When the warder returned with Molly, she took one look at Josiah and spat out a stream of obscenities. 'Not you again, you 'orrible little turd. I've told you what I know and I want to go 'ome.'

'You are free to go. Mottershead will escort you,' said Joseph.

'And 'ome is where Mottershead is going to escort you, my

dear. The only 'ome you've got now. 'Enrietta's 'ouse. She will be pleased to see you.'

'Fuck you, Mottershead. I don't want to go back there. Just let me go.'

'Can't do that, Molly. These gentlemen want to be sure you're in safe 'ands. Don't want you walking the streets, do we? Come on now.' Molly knew she had no choice and, still cursing, was led away by Josiah.

'Poor wretch,' said Thomas. 'Not much of a life and a short one.'

'There's hundreds like her. If the pox doesn't kill them, the hangman does. As soon as they're too old to be whores, they have to steal. Sooner or later they get caught and end their days at Tyburn.'

'Do you recall her talking about a visitor with a large backside?'

'A big arse, I think she said.'

'Quite. It might have been Squire.'

Joseph laughed. 'There are not many bigger arses in London. It probably was.'

'I wonder why she hates Josiah so much. I must ask him. What happens to Stoner now, Joseph?'

'He'll stay here at least until we've received the money. In due course, arrangements for his voyage to Copenhagen will be made. A month or two probably.'

'It seems unjust. Murderer, thief, traitor and now off to Denmark.'

'Unjust? I will find work for him and I prefer to think of it as expedient. The world of intelligence is like that.' He paused. 'And how is Madeleine?'

'Much improved. You should come and see her.'

'I shall, as soon as this business is over.'

'What about Squire?'

'I fear we are too late for him. He will have left England by now. I blame myself, of course. I never suspected him and if there were any signs of his treachery, I missed them. The king will not be pleased.'

'Bishop missed them too, Joseph, and with or without Squire the spy ring is broken.'

'Yes. I shall be sure to stress that to His Majesty.'

'And I shall tell Madeleine to expect you soon.'

Joseph took a deep breath. 'I suppose we had better see Morland. Are you feeling strong?'

'Not very.'

'Nor I. Still, it has to be done.'

The warder was despatched again and soon returned with Morland. Beside his fury, Molly's was as nothing. He marched in spluttering with rage and thrashing about with his arms as if he had lost control of them.

'This is monstrous,' he shouted. 'I am being held here on some ridiculous pretext and I demand to be released at once.'

Joseph's voice was icy. 'Be quiet, Morland. You will remain here until I decide to release you. Until then you would do well to guard your tongue.'

Morland pointed at Thomas and bellowed, 'Why is this man here again? What authority does he have?'

'Mr Hill has my authority to be here. He needs no other.'

'I suppose you are going to tell me that he has decoded the intercepted letter and that my name is in it.'

'Would you care to comment, Thomas?'

Thomas looked hard at Morland and spoke slowly. 'The letter

was, as I suspected, a cipher, each letter being represented by one or more numbers. I decrypted it by means of logical analysis and rational thought — two qualities to which you yourself lay claim.'

Morland looked sceptical. 'And what, pray, did this letter tell you?'

Thomas looked at Joseph, who nodded. 'That there is a ring of spies in London and that the Dutch and French are plotting against England.'

Morland stared at Joseph and scoffed. 'Ha. There are spies everywhere. There is nothing new in that. But now you believe that I am one of them, or you pretend that you do.'

'And are you one of them?'

'That is absurd. You find my name on a scrap of paper and lose your wits. You would do better to interrogate this man.' Again he pointed at Thomas. 'Ask him if he invented a decryption to suit his own ends. Ask him if it is my position he is after. Ask him which master he serves.'

'Now that is absurd,' said Thomas calmly. 'There is nothing I should like less than your position, as Mr Williamson knows. And I have shown him how I decrypted the letter. I did it within forty-eight hours, as I said I would. It was not difficult.'

Morland turned his fury on to Joseph. 'This is a plot. A plot to have me removed from my post. I demand to be released immediately.'

'So you have said. However, you will remain here while we continue to conduct our enquiries. You will be released only if your innocence is proven.'

Thomas thought Morland was about to explode. He shook his fists and spittle flew from his mouth. 'That is despicable and illegal. The king shall hear of it and you will pay dearly.' The warder was alarmed enough to draw his sword.

'Take him away, warder, and guard him carefully.' Still bawling, Morland was ushered out at the point of the warder's sword.

'Do you really still think he's involved?' asked Thomas, Morland's threats ringing in his ears.

Joseph smiled. 'No. But I think we can justify keeping him here until Squire is found.'

'What about the king?'

'We will risk the king's displeasure.'

'A risk worth taking for the pleasure of holding him in the Tower.'

Joseph turned his good eye on Thomas and grinned. 'Quite so. My thanks for your assistance, Thomas. Are you quite sure you would not like Morland's position?'

'Quite sure, thank you. May I go home now? I have seen enough of this place today.'

'Go. If we find anything at Squire's house, I shall send word. And tell Madeleine I shall call on her soon.'

Thomas had never seen Mary so angry. 'What on earth is Joseph thinking of,' she thundered, 'sending the man off to Denmark? Why isn't he going to hang? That's what happens to thieves and traitors, isn't it? I've a good mind to go straight to Joseph's house to tell him what I think of him.'

'I agree with you, my dear,' said Charles. 'Justice is hardly served by allowing a traitor to trade the gallows for a life of ease among the Danes.'

'Perhaps there are forces at work of which we are not aware. Joseph spoke of expediency.'

'You are too philosophical, Thomas. Joseph should have sent

Stoner to the gallows and he hasn't. May the thieving wretch rot in hell.' Mary was not in the mood for argument.

'And don't forget they haven't caught Squire yet,' pointed out Charles. 'He's just as guilty as Stoner. Joseph must be furious at himself for not seeing through the man.'

'As we did not see through Stoner,' agreed Mary. 'I can't think what possessed us to trust him.'

'There is nothing to be gained from dwelling on it,' said Madeleine firmly. 'I am recovered and you can afford the loss of a few guineas and your pride. Lady Babb has suffered more.' She paused. 'Now, I am quite well enough to go home. Will you take me tomorrow, Thomas?'

'Of course, if that's what you want.'

'It is. I should never have recovered without all of you, but now I miss my own bed.'

'Quite right, my dear,' said Charles with a grin. 'I much prefer my own bed with my own wife. Nothing else compares.' If Mary's aim had been just a little better, the apple would have hit him between the eyes.

CHAPTER 22

At breakfast the next morning, neither Charles nor Mary looked as if they had slept at all. Mary's face was red and puffy and Charles had black rings under his eyes.

'Are you both well?' asked Thomas. 'You look exhausted.'

'Not much sleep. Things to think about,' replied Charles, barely looking up from his plate. Mary smiled sweetly and said nothing. Thomas thought it best not to ask about their 'things' and to leave them in peace to think about them.

'As I came here with nothing more than I was standing up or, rather, lying down in, it won't take me long to prepare,' Madeleine told Thomas. 'I shall be ready in an hour.'

'And I shall be ready to escort you.'

Charles and Mary had recovered sufficiently to wave the carriage off. 'Do take care, Madeleine,' advised Mary. 'Thomas is terribly prone to unfortunate accidents.'

'Do not concern yourselves. I shall keep him well guarded.'

'Wonderful people,' said Madeleine in the carriage. 'You

must tell me how you came to meet them and about Barbados.'

'Not all of it is fit for the ears of a lady, my dear.'

'I shall want to hear those bits first.'

At Madeleine's house, the door was opened by a beaming Agnes. 'At last, Miss Stewart,' she declared. 'I had fallen to thinking you'd never come back. Are you recovered?'

'Quite recovered, Agnes, thank you.'

'Good day, Mr Hill. Mottershead tells me you and he have had a fine old time together.'

'Does he now?' Josiah's instructions had not included gossiping with Agnes. What else had the little man been up to? 'Has Josiah been doing his job? I asked him to make sure you and the house were safe.'

'Oh yes, sir. Mottershead's been most attentive. Called almost every day.'

Thomas glanced at Madeleine, who raised an eyebrow. 'That's good, Agnes, and how are you?'

'Never better, madam. And Mottershead's done a few little jobs around the house. He's clever with his hands. You'll see the difference.'

When they went in, they did see the difference. Newly painted walls, a broken chair mended, a cracked window replaced, the floor polished. Josiah had done more than a few little jobs.

'I do hope you looked after him, Agnes. Did you feed him well?'

'Oh yes. I told him he had to keep his strength up and gave him a good dinner whenever he was here.'

'Excellent. Now Mr Hill and I have much to discuss. We will be in my bedroom.'

'Very good, madam. Will Mr Hill be staying for dinner?'
'He will.'

In the bedroom, Madeleine wasted no time. She simply undressed and got into bed. Thomas followed suit. 'Now, Thomas,' she whispered, 'it is so long since we last did this that I can barely remember what it was like. Would you care to refresh my memory?'

'Alas, my dear, I too have quite forgotten. We shall have to refresh each other's memories.' He kissed her. 'Does that help?'

'A little. Try again.'

It took several tries before Madeleine fully recovered her memory, but when she did, Thomas found it to be excellent in every particular. Being confined to her bed for so long had some-how increased her vigour, as if she had been storing up her strength for this occasion. After two hours of strenuous work, Thomas pleaded hunger and went in search of food.

He found Agnes in the kitchen polishing a pair of boots. 'Mottershead does like clean boots,' she said.

'He's a fortunate fellow to have you to clean them for him, Agnes. Our discussions are taking longer than expected and we need refreshment. Can you help?'

'Course I can, sir. You go back to your discussions and I'll bring you a plate of chicken and a bottle.'

Hours later, having sampled Agnes's fare and taken yet more exercise, they fell asleep as day became night and did not stir until the morning.

Thomas was woken by Agnes calling through the door, 'Mottershead is here, Mr Hill, and asks to see you at once. Mrs Carrington told him you were here.'

'Now what?' grumbled Thomas, rubbing sleep from his eyes. 'Tell Mottershead I am not yet dressed and he must wait ten minutes.'

Mottershead, stick in one hand and hat in the other, his boots newly polished, was waiting in Madeleine's sitting room. 'My apologies, Mr 'Ill, sir, but I thought I'd better come at once.'

'So I see, Josiah. And what is so urgent that it brings you here at this hour?'

'It's Molly, sir, Stoner's 'ore, if you recall.'

'I do recall, Josiah, and what of her?'

'She came to my 'ouse last night. Said she'd seen Lemuel Squire, or thought she 'ad. Said she'd seen 'is arse, if you'll pardon me, sir. Said she'd know it anywhere.'

'And where did Molly think she saw this arse?'

'Drury Lane, sir. Disappearing into an alley. She followed it, but it must 'ave gone into an 'ouse and she lost it.'

'Hardly a clear sighting, Josiah. Do you think she's telling the truth?'

'Yes, sir.'

'Although the woman was less than pleased to see you when last you met, as I recall.'

Josiah laughed. 'Oh no, sir. Molly loves me like a brother. I saved 'er from Newgate once. It's just 'er way of showing it.'

'So what do you propose that we do, Josiah? I am not feeling at my strongest this morning.'

'I'm sorry to 'ear that, sir, because I was 'oping you'd want to come with me.'

'To Drury Lane, Josiah? Last time you did your best to dissuade me from going there.'

'Yes, sir. But this is different. If we tell Mr Williamson, 'e'll send in the trained bands and it's no place for them. As soon as they're within 'alf a mile of the lane, word'll go out and every thief and murderer 'iding there'll disappear. There's places around the lane that can 'ide a man for ever if 'e wants.'

'So what makes you think you can find Squire if he's there?'

'I know the place as well as anyone, sir, and there's a good few who owes me a favour.'

'Like Molly?'

'That's it, sir. Like Molly.'

'Do you really need me, Josiah? Couldn't you find someone else?'

'Daresay I could, sir. Just thought you'd like to be there when we catch 'im, after all the trouble 'e's caused you.'

'Josiah, I am forty-seven years old, I do not care for violence and I came to London simply to see my old friends Charles and Mary Carrington and to attend the coronation. Yet I have been dragged into fraud, espionage, treachery, abduction and murder. Further-more, Miss Stewart is asleep and would not be pleased to awake and find me gone. I really do not want to accompany you to one of the nastiest parts of the city in the hope of finding Lemuel Squire.'

For a moment Thomas thought Josiah was going to cry. 'That is most disappointing, sir. I 'ad thought that you would want to complete the job before going 'ome. I 'ad you down as a man who likes to finish what 'e's started, and isn't afraid of going nowhere. Seems I was wrong.'

Thomas eyed the little man. Not just a man of action. Just like his master, quite up to a little subtle persuasion and not easy to refuse. Then a thought struck him. A little distasteful but in the circumstances . . . 'Josiah, I might be persuaded to accompany you in return for a small favour.'

Josiah looked alarmed. In his line of work, he must be asked for some strange favours. 'And what favour would that be, sir?'

Thomas took a deep breath and told him about his niece Lucy Taylor and Master Arthur Phillips who worked in the Navy Office. 'My niece appears rather attached to him,' he said, 'although I have reason to believe that he is not the kind of young man with whom she should be consorting. I would be pleased if he happened to leave London, for personal reasons perhaps, or having been posted elsewhere.'

Josiah grinned. 'Is that all, sir? Shouldn't be a problem. I'll 'ave a word with the young man myself. Arthur Phillips at the Navy Office. Consider it done.'

'Thank you, Josiah. No rough stuff, mind, just a little persuasion.'

'Leave it to me, sir,' said Josiah, tapping the side of his nose. 'Master Phillips is about to take a fierce dislike to London. Now what about your side of the bargain?'

'Very well, Josiah. I'll come with you. If we don't find Squire this morning, however, that will be that. No more escapades for me.'

'Understood, sir. We'll be back in good time for our dinner, just you mark my words.'

'And if we're not?'

'Then Agnes will know what to do. Bring your purse and 'ide it under your shirt. We might need money and we don't want your pocket picked.'

Thomas thought better of asking why they might need money. He went to fetch his purse. 'Lead on, then, Josiah. *Once more unto the breach . . .*'

'What, sir?'

'Never mind, Josiah.'

At that time of the morning, Fleet Street was still quiet. They saw only a milkmaid, a baker's boy delivering bread, and on the corner of Carting Lane a whore hoping for a late-night reveller on his way home. They joined Drury Lane near Wild Street. In the lane, the drain which ran down one side was already full of the night's waste, waiting for rain to wash it down to the river. While Thomas kept the handkerchief pressed to his nose, Josiah appeared not to notice. He strode on up the lane towards Holborn until they came to a dark alley which was little more than a hole between two hovels. Josiah stopped there and turned to Thomas.

'This is where Molly saw 'im,' he said, ''is arse disappearing down 'ere.' He pointed to the alley. 'It's a nasty place. More than one on the king's death list 'as 'idden in 'ere. Is your purse safe?' Thomas nodded. 'Good. Stay close to me, sir, and speak to no one. The moment they 'ear your voice, we're in trouble. Let me do the talking.'

Thinking that he would be perfectly happy to go back to Madeleine's bed and let Josiah do everything, Thomas peered into the alley. Other than a few yards of narrow lane, he could see nothing. The houses on either side were so close that it must always be dark down there. And the stench was worse even than in the lane itself. He would not be wandering more than a foot from Josiah and he would not be engaging any of the inhabitants of this hellish place in conversation.

No more than ten steps into the alley and their path was blocked. The same one-eyed giant whom they had met in Drury Lane on their way to Henrietta's stepped out of a doorway and held out his hand.

'A shilling, sir, if you please,' whispered Josiah. He took the coin from Thomas and handed it to the giant. 'We're looking for a friend,' he told the man, 'thought 'e might be staying around 'ere. Plump fellow, big arse. We've another shilling if you can tell us where 'e is.'

The giant held out his hand again, so Thomas passed Josiah another coin, which was grabbed and dropped down the giant's shirt. They waited for him to speak. Without a word, however, and two shillings better off, the giant simply disappeared back into the dark doorway from which he had emerged.

Josiah shrugged. ''Ope you've got plenty of shillings, sir. Looks like we're going to need them.'

They continued on down the alley, their eyes gradually adjusting to the darkness, to a point at which it turned so sharply to the left that it almost ran back on itself. By this time, word of strangers must have spread and Thomas was aware of movement in the shadows and eyes on his back. The dwellings on either side must have been connected by a network of passages allowing people to move around and messages to be passed, unseen by anyone in the alley. The hairs on his neck stood up. To be seen yet not to see — it was loathsome.

Around the corner, the alley became so narrow that they had to walk one behind the other. Thomas kept within touching distance of Josiah. It was impossible to tell where this alley led, if it led anywhere. It might as easily come to a dead end and they would be forced to retrace their steps. Just as Thomas thought that that was exactly what they would have to do, they found themselves in a tiny yard surrounded by old wooden houses. He looked around. It was lighter than the alley and he could see that each house had a low door and two narrow windows. It was a yard that might have been built two hundred years earlier and have been gradually cut off by new buildings until the only way in was through the alley off Drury Lane.

A curtain moved and a young face peered out at them. Then another face and another. Thomas looked at Josiah for guidance. 'Just stay still, sir. Some of them know me and they'll see we've no weapons.' Anyone who had seen Josiah use his stick would certainly count it as a weapon, but Thomas nevertheless did as he was told.

The five minutes they waited seemed to Thomas like twenty. He jumped when a squeaky door opened and three children emerged into the yard. Two were boys, the other a girl. None of them was more than six years old and all three were filthy. They came up to the strangers, as they must have been told to, and held out their hands. Thomas passed three coins to Josiah, who handed them over.

'We're looking for our friend,' he said, 'a short, fat man. We've got an important message for 'im. 'Ave you seen 'im?'

Like the giant, none of the children spoke. The two boys stood and stared at them while the girl went back inside the house. Thomas inspected them. They were feral creatures, half covered by a few rags, their eyes narrow and their faces thin. Their arms and legs were like sticks. Thomas wondered how many more like them spent their lives in this place. Miserable, short lives they would be. Few would see twenty.

The girl reappeared and beckoned them to come in. The two boys stayed in the yard. Lookouts, probably, thought Thomas, in case we've brought reinforcements. They ducked through the door and into the house. Inside, a single tallow candle stood on a wooden box in the middle of a small, square room. There was another door opposite them. A man sat in one corner, out of the light of the candle, a long clay pipe in his hand. They could not see his face.

'Well, well,' said a rough voice, 'Josiah Mottershead. 'Aven't seen 'im in a while. And 'oo's this with 'im? Not the law, I 'ope.'

''Allo, Finn. This 'ere's my cousin Tom. Doesn't speak much.'

'Very convenient. And what brings you 'ere? We don't get a lot o' visitors.' The gruff voice turned into a foul cough. 'Lookin' for someone, are you?'

'A friend. Short and fat. Got a message for 'im.'

''As your friend got a name?'

'Not one 'e'd 'ave told you.'

'What's 'e done, your friend?'

'Don't know, don't care. Just got a message for 'im.'

'What sort o' message would bring you and 'im 'ere?' he croaked, pointing his pipe at Thomas.

'Can't tell you that, Finn. Private.'

Finn sat in his corner, saying nothing. Surrounded by a cloud of tobacco smoke, he was barely visible even from a few feet. Thomas sensed that he was assessing them. Not what their real business was — if he'd been concerned about that, they'd be dead by now — but about their worth. If he knew where Squire was, he'd be working out how much he could get for telling them and how he could get it.

'If I were able to 'elp you,' he said eventually, 'I'd need payin'. Five guineas.' It was a lot. A man could buy a good horse for five guineas. But Finn must have decided that Josiah and his cousin had that much in their pockets and would be willing to part with it. And he was right. Thomas had brought more than a few shillings.

'Five guineas it is, Finn,' agreed Josiah, 'as long as you lead us to the right man and say no more about it.'

''E's your man, all right. The child'll take you. Three guineas now and give 'er the other two when you're there. It's not far.'

'Done.'

Thomas fished three guineas out of his purse and put them where Finn could see them beside the candle.

Finn laughed. 'May not talk much, your cousin, but 'e's quick with 'is money. I don't know what your business is, Josiah, and I don't much care. Just do it and be gone. We don't want the trained men to come calling.' He called for the girl. 'Take 'em to the inn, and show 'em the way out. I don't want 'em coming back 'ere.'

And I am not all that keen to come back here, thought Thomas. An inn, though? Not what he expected.

The girl led them through the other door, into a foul kitchen which reeked of rotten food and outside into another dark alley. They followed her along it to a low door which she pushed open. Yet another alley led directly ahead of them. About ten yards up it, the girl stopped and pointed to a hole in the wall.

''Ere?' asked Josiah. The girl nodded and held out her hand. Thomas took out two more guineas and gave them to her. She pointed down the alley and said, 'Out.' Then she ran back the way they had come. Five guineas to be shown a hole in a wall in a mean alley by a filthy child. For all they knew, the hole led to a sewer.

'Do you think he's in there?' asked Thomas.

''E will be. Finn knows we'd be back if 'e weren't. 'E wouldn't want that.'

'It doesn't look much like an inn.'

Josiah laughed. 'It's not an inn, sir. That's just a word they use for a place where a man can 'ide. For a shilling or two a day, 'e's safe from the law. There's a number of inns around 'ere.'

'Not safe from us, though.'

'No, sir. But we wouldn't 'ave got this far if I 'adn't been recognized, or if we'd been short of five guineas. Are you ready?'

'Ready, Josiah. Let's find the man and be gone.'

Josiah climbed through the hole first. It opened into a space about the size of the Carringtons' sitting room, with three doors off it. An old woman sat on a stool beside one of the doors. Her face had been ravaged by pox, she was almost bald and she smelt like a dung heap. Thomas only just stopped himself from pulling out his handkerchief again. When she saw them, the woman pointed to the door on her right.

News did travel fast. How did she know who they were and what they wanted? Alleys and passages and small children, Thomas supposed. Josiah nodded to the woman, who heaved herself off her stool and scrambled through the hole, leaving them to be about their business.

The door was unlocked. Josiah turned the handle, opened it and stepped inside. Thomas was a pace behind him. The room was bare but for a heap of blankets in one corner. Under the blankets a body was snoring. Thomas walked over and kicked it. There was a grunt of surprise and a head poked itself out of the heap. Thomas started. It was close shaven, hollow-cheeked and dirty. It was not the head he was expecting. He looked again. Yes, it was. Lemuel Squire might have lost his wig and a stone in weight, but he was still Lemuel Squire.

'Good morning, Lemuel. We appear to have woken you. We've come to escort you to more comfortable quarters. Kindly stir yourself and we'll be away.'

Squire peered at him through sleep-encrusted eyes. 'The devil's whores, how did you find me here?'

'Josiah is adept at such matters. It was not difficult.' A lie, but he could not resist it. If Squire had thought he was safe, all the better to rub his nose in the dirt.

Squire pushed himself up and sat on the blankets. 'I under-estimated you, Thomas. I thought you were just a clever cryptographer. Now I see there's more to you.' He was recovering his wits.

'Never mind that. Joseph Williamson is waiting for you. Get up.'

Squire shrugged and made as if to rise. His hand emerged from under the blankets. It was holding a cocked flintlock pistol. 'It is loaded,' he said quietly, pointing it at Thomas. 'Step back against the wall, both of you, and sit on the floor, or I will shoot.' Thomas looked him in the eye. He meant it. He backed away and did as he was ordered. Josiah put down his stick and sat beside him.

'That's better.' The pistol had never wavered from Thomas's face. Squire's voice was steady. 'Now, it is true that I have only one pistol and one shot. If I shoot Mottershead, Thomas will pick up the stick and attack me and only one of us will leave this room. On the other hand, if I shoot Thomas, Mottershead will certainly beat me into a bloody mess. He will, however, have to explain Thomas's death to Williamson. Which is it to be?'

'There is a third way,' said Thomas. 'You could hand me the pistol and come with us. Joseph has spared Stoner the gallows and he will do the same for you.'

Squire scoffed. 'Even if I believed you, why would he spare me? I've deceived him for more than a year, plotted against him and his like and caused him much grief and embarrassment. I doubt if the king is very pleased with him and he'd be even less pleased if I were allowed to live. When I leave here, it will be to go to a place where I cannot be reached.'

Despite himself, Thomas was intrigued. Could this really be the same bluff Squire who dressed like a court jester, ate and drank like a trencherman and had treated him like a brother? 'Why, Lemuel? Why the treachery and deceit?'

A shadow passed over Squire's face. 'Deceit, certainly. As you know, I was an actor until the theatres were closed — not one of the Lord Protector's better ideas. My Falstaff was much admired. But treachery? That I deny.'

'How can you deny it? You betrayed secrets to our enemies and put the country in danger.'

'Your enemies, Thomas, not mine. That is the nub of the matter. As a republican, I am loyal to the principles of republicanism and have done what I could to help the cause. I do not wish to be ruled by a king or by any man who holds his position simply due to an accident of birth. By the same token, I did not choose to be born an Englishman, so why should I owe my loyalty to England? It is principles of equality I have espoused, not geography. A deceiver, yes, a traitor, no.'

'You are a Leveller. I should never have guessed it.'

'Our leader, John Lilburne, preferred the word "agitator". If wanting a Parliament and judiciary free of corruption and believing in religious toleration makes me an agitator, then I plead guilty to the charge. That there are now so few of us does not diminish the strength of my beliefs. I choose to fight for them in the best way I can — by using my skills as an actor. The profession is home to many of my fellow agitators.'

It was no surprise. Squire had falsely claimed to carry messages for the king, but Lilburne was reputed to have had just as many supporters among the companies of travelling players. And actors were deceivers. Squire would have had no difficulty pretending to be one thing while actually being another. Some of the Levellers would still be active. But whatever the merits of their principles they could not excuse murder. 'How do you justify the murders of four men and the abduction of an innocent woman?'

'Pragmatism and expediency — necessary companions to principle and creed, if the struggle is to be won. Just as an alliance with our friends in France and Holland is necessary.'

'What was expedient about the abduction of Madeleine Stewart?'

'We thought she would tell us what you knew. Alas, she became ill and would not have survived more vigorous interrogation.' Squire stared at the two of them, his pistol aimed at a point halfway between their heads.

'We know that Stoner is Argentum. Are you Aurum?'

Again Squire scoffed. 'If you know about Stoner, you know about me. I do hope you've caught the bastard. Not a principle in his body. Money, profit, wealth — Stoner knows nothing else.'

'Was Morland involved?'

'Good God, no. Morland is not as clever as he thinks. He made a convenient scapegoat. You would be surprised how easy it has been to intercept and read correspondence from Williamson's agents without his knowing.'

'You must have had help.'

'Possibly.'

Thomas tried a long shot. 'Roger Willow?'

A fleeting look of surprise might, just might, have crossed

Squire's face. 'Roger's Shylock was as good a performance as I have seen.' So Willow too had been an actor. How unexpected.

Throughout the exchange, Josiah had said nothing and barely moved. His eyes had never left Squire and Thomas sensed that he was waiting for the moment to attack. With a loaded pistol in Squire's hand, that would be suicidal. He put a hand on Josiah's arm to restrain him. 'Then would you care to tell us about a disfigured Dutchman or the Alchemist?'

'Other than that neither is in England, no. Enough questions. I have a decision to make. We will sit here while I consider the matter.' A minute passed, and another, and the pistol moved to Thomas's head. He prepared himself for the bullet. If Squire shot him, at least he would go to the gallows. Josiah would make sure of it. Or would he use the bullet on Josiah, leaving only Thomas between himself and escape? He might. Thomas wriggled forwards and sideways on his backside until he was in front of Josiah.

'How brave, Thomas,' said Squire quietly, 'but pointless, of course.' He paused and ran his free hand over his shaven head. 'It hasn't always been easy, you know, playing the role of loyal eccentric. Skilled though I am, even the finest actor can tire of a part. And now that there are so few of us left in England and Charles Stuart is on the throne, I should have joined my friends in Amsterdam. Alas, loyalty to the cause has kept me here in the hope of being some use. As, I like to think, I have been.' He laughed. 'Actually it has been rather a relief to be in here and not to have to wear ridiculous clothes or stuff myself with food and drink. But I can't stay here for ever. I must move on.'

'I will speak for you if you hand me the pistol and allow us to escort you away from here.'

Squire grunted. 'Even if I thought there was a slender hope of my being spared the gallows, we would never leave here alive. Finn and his people would kill all of us.'

'They might not. Josiah would speak to Finn, wouldn't you, Josiah?'

'I would, sir.' Thomas could hear the doubt in his voice.

'That would do no good,' said Squire. 'Now move over to the corner by the door, Thomas. I have made a decision and I would not want you to be splattered with blood and brains.' Thomas ignored him. 'Do move away, Thomas.'

'I find myself unable to oblige, Lemuel,' replied Thomas. 'My backside seems to be stuck to the floor.'

'Better do as 'e says, sir,' muttered Josiah. 'If 'e shoots me, go for 'is throat or 'is eyes. Then smash 'is 'ead against the wall. That should do for 'im.'

'Very well, Thomas, if you are determined not to move, on your head be it,' said Squire. 'Farewell. The play is over.' Thomas shut his eyes and waited for the bullet. The crack of the shot, when it came, reverberated around the room. For an instant Thomas was stunned. When he opened his eyes, Squire was slumped on the blankets. His finger was still on the trigger and the barrel was in his mouth.

Josiah was the first to his feet. 'Time we were gone, sir,' he said. 'The shot will 'ave been heard. They'll be coming to investigate.'

He helped Thomas up and out of the room. They climbed through the hole and turned left down the alley in the direction the girl had pointed. ''Urry, sir,' he urged, breaking into a trot. 'I can 'ear them already.' So could Thomas. The sounds of running feet and urgent voices were all around them. There must be a passage alongside them and others nearby. If they did not reach a way out before their pursuers they would be trapped.

They came to a flight of stone steps leading downwards. Josiah took them two at a time and waited for Thomas at the bottom. 'Make haste, sir. No time to lose.'

Hearing voices close behind, Thomas was down the steps and beside Josiah in a trice. On they went along the alley, still with no idea where they were heading. Without warning a dark figure stepped out in front of Josiah, a long knife in his hand. Barely breaking his stride, Josiah broke the man's arm with his stick, knocked him to the ground and stepped over him.

He looked back at Thomas and shouted a warning. 'Behind you, sir!' Thomas turned. Another man, this one with a short-handled axe, had appeared from nowhere. The man approached cautiously, his axe raised to strike. Thomas kept his eyes fixed on the man's arm. The moment he saw it move, he stepped outside the blow, grasped the man's wrist in his left hand and thrust the knuckles of his right hand into his throat. With a satisfying gurgle, the man collapsed on to the ground. Thomas turned back to Josiah and rubbed his knuckles. 'Years of practice, Josiah.'

They started running again, following the curve of the alley. Then they stopped. A brick wall blocked their way. They were trapped. Josiah was panting heavily. 'There must be a way out, sir. There's always a way out.'

Thomas looked about. 'There. On your right, Josiah. See it?'

'Got it.' There was a wooden door low down on the wall, well disguised and just big enough for a man to crawl through. There was a key in the lock. Josiah turned it and kicked the door open. 'On you go, sir.'

Thomas ducked through the opening and found himself in a vertical shaft with a wooden ladder nailed to it. Light was filtering down from the top of the shaft. He started to climb towards it, expecting Josiah to follow. But after no more than four rungs, there was a scuffle behind him. A hand grasped his ankle and pulled it hard. Taken by surprise, he let go his hold on the ladder, slid down and landed in a heap at the bottom. Again his ankle was grasped and he was dragged back through the low door. He was kicked in the ribs and ordered by a rough voice to stand up. When he did so, he saw Josiah held by his arms by two men, while a third held a knife to his throat. Josiah's stick lay on the ground.

'Sorry, sir,' croaked Josiah. 'I was too slow.'

Pinned by their elbows, they were marched painfully along the alley, up the steps and back to the 'inn', where they were thrown into the room in which they had found Lemuel Squire. The door was slammed and the key turned in the lock.

Thomas's eyes were drawn to the body. He wriggled as far away from it as he could and sat with his back to the wall. On the opposite wall were splattered Squire's brains, blown to pieces by the pistol shot. He turned away. Hell and damnation. A few seconds more and Josiah would have been through the low door and up the ladder. Now they were locked up with a dead body for company.

'You in one piece, sir?' whispered Josiah.

'I think so. Just a kick in the ribs. And you?'

'Took a fist in the throat, sir.' Josiah was clearly hurting.

'Sounds painful. Best leave the talking to me.' Thomas moved closer to Josiah so that he could see him more clearly. 'Just nod or shake your head, Josiah.

'Does Agnes know where we were going?' A nod. 'Will she go to Mr Williamson? No? Charles Carrington? No? Who then?'

''Enrietta.' It was barely audible and Thomas thought he had misheard.

'Henrietta?' A nod. 'What can Henrietta do, Josiah?'

Josiah was trying to force out his answer when the door was unlocked and in strode a tall man with a shaven head and a scarred face. He was holding Josiah's stick. Two men stood guard at the door.

'Well, Josiah Mottershead, you lied to me. You told me you had a message for a friend. I didn't believe you and it seems I was right. Odd sort of friend who ends up with 'is head blown to pieces by 'is visitors. What 'ave you to say for yourself?' From his voice, Thomas knew it was Finn.

Josiah said nothing. 'He was hit in the throat,' said Thomas. 'He can't speak.'

'Then you'll 'ave to speak for him. And you can start by telling me who you really are and why you've come 'ere.'

'My name is Thomas Hill. I am a friend of Josiah. He asked me to come with him to find this man.' Thomas waved a hand in the direction of Squire's body.

'And 'ow did you know 'e was 'ere?'

'He was seen entering the alley.'

'Seen by who?'

'I don't know.' It was Thomas's first lie and Finn knew it.

'Yes you do, but I'll let it go for now. Who is 'e?'

'His name was Lemuel Squire.'

'Why did you kill 'im?'

'We didn't. He shot himself.'

'Why?'

'He was a traitor and a murderer. He only had one bullet so he couldn't kill both of us.'

Finn laughed and thrust the end of Josiah's stick at Thomas's face. 'I've only got one stick, but I could easily kill both of you and I will if I find you're lying again. I don't like being lied to.'

Josiah tried to say something, but managed only a rasping cough.

'You should know me better than to take me for a fool, Josiah Mottershead. Now 'and over your purse, Mr 'Ill, and both of you take off your boots.'

They did as they were ordered. One of the guards took their boots and Finn put Thomas's purse in a pocket.

'You'll stay 'ere with your dead friend while I decide what to do with you.' Finn turned on his heel and left. The door was locked behind him and they were in semi-darkness again.

Talking was plainly so painful for Josiah that Thomas could not bear to tempt him into it. He closed his eyes and tried to think clearly. Josiah must have had a reason for telling Agnes to go to Henrietta if they had not returned for their dinner. Perhaps Henrietta had influence with Finn. Josiah evidently thought she had a better chance than Joseph Williamson's men. Meanwhile, without boots or Josiah's stick they would not be overpowering their guards and making a run for it, so they had better sit quietly, gather their strength and hope Henrietta could think of something. If not, they were in the hands of Finn. Not a happy prospect.

Mind you, facing the wrath of Miss Stewart was not a happy prospect either. What would she think when she woke up to find that Thomas had sneaked off with Josiah to one of the most dangerous areas of London, leaving poor Agnes to raise the alarm if they did not return. If she washed her hands of him for being stupid and irresponsible, he would have only himself to blame. You clod, Thomas, you should have sent Josiah packing and gone back to bed. He sat miserably and tried not to look at the horribly dead body a few feet away.

When night fell, the little light there was in the room disappeared altogether. The door had remained locked since Finn had left and Josiah had not spoken. Thomas reached out and touched his leg. 'How is your throat, Josiah?'

Josiah answered in a slow, hoarse whisper. 'A little better, sir. Wouldn't mind some ale, though.'

'I doubt if Finn's serving ale today. We'll just have to wait for Henrietta to bring us something. Do you think she'll be able to help?'

''Ope so, sir. Otherwise we're in a bit of an 'ole. Finn's a mean bugger when 'e wants to be.'

'What will he do?'

''E'll try to get money for us. If 'e can't, 'e'll drop us in the river.'

'Then let's hope someone somewhere is willing to pay for us.'

CHAPTER 23

The night was long and foul. Thomas shivered and shook and listened to rats scrabbling about behind the wall. It would not be long before they caught the scent of the corpse and came to investigate. Thomas and Josiah exchanged a few words to keep their spirits up, but otherwise sat in silence with their own thoughts. The longer they were there, the worse their chances of getting out alive. Cold, starvation, thirst, their throats cut, a blow to the head and a watery grave — it would only take one to finish them off.

As they had not returned for their dinner, Agnes would have called on Henrietta. Thomas hoped Josiah had told her to expect two tall men in yellow satins and a large woman in an orange wig drinking port and smoking a pipe. If not, poor Agnes might have taken fright and run. Not that he had any idea what Henrietta would do. He imagined her, Boudica-like, fearlessly leading her girls into the alley, overcoming Finn and his men and rescuing the two prisoners. Molly would certainly be capable of scratching out some eyes. Would she carry them off to Wild Street, there to put them to work as her servants or, worse, have her wicked way with them before putting them out on the street? Thomas shuddered. They would be better off at the mercy of Finn.

He caught himself. Don't be absurd, man. Your mind always plays tricks at times like these, especially when you are hungry. If Josiah trusted Henrietta, he had good reason to do so. With perfect timing, his stomach rumbled in complaint. To take his mind off it, he got up and tried the door. Locked fast. He felt his way around the stone walls. Not a chink or a wobble. He thought about the heap of bloody blankets on which Squire's body lay, decided he could not bear to touch them and made do with jumping up and down. Even in midsummer this dank little cell was cold at night.

Some time during the night, Josiah was racked by a fit of coughing. It was a raw, rough, grating croak, and it hurt Thomas just to listen to it. The coughing went on for several minutes, each spasm making Thomas grit his teeth and screw his eyes closed. Eventually it ended, leaving Josiah wheezing and panting and Thomas drained. He put his hand out to comfort the little man and found that he was grasping his throat as if to stop it bursting through his neck.

'Josiah, you must be in a lot of pain. Can I do anything?' Josiah shook his head and tried to say something. 'I'm sorry. Don't try to talk. Just keep as still as you can.'

Thomas went back to the door, hammered on it with his fist and shouted as loudly as he could. 'Water, we need water. Water. Now.' There was no response. He tried again. 'Bring water, damn you. Bring it now.' Still no response. He thumped on the door and screeched curses, using words he had not heard for years. He gave up only when he felt a hand on his shoulder. Josiah took his arm and gently led him away from the door and back to his place on the floor. There the two of them sat until a little weak light began to find its way into their cell.

When at last the door was opened, it was Finn who came in. He put a pail of water on the floor and glanced at the dead body. 'Rats been at 'im yet? Won't be long before they do, so look sharp if you're 'ungry. Word's out that you're staying with us so we'll keep you alive for a day or two. After that, you'd better 'ope you've got a friend with the money.' He pointed at the body and snorted. 'Otherwise you'll be joining 'im.'

As soon as Finn had left, Thomas put the pail in front of Josiah, who scooped handfuls of water into his mouth. Then Thomas did the same. The water was dirty and smelt of rotting fish and he had to force himself to swallow it, but it did help. Josiah managed a lopsided grin. 'You should 'ave asked for ale, sir.'

'How is the throat, Josiah?'

'I'll live, sir. Never was much good at talking.'

There was no knowing whether the pail would be refilled, so as the day went on they drank sparingly. The cell gradually warmed up and Thomas found himself sleeping in snatches. While he was awake he thought about what had brought him to such a place. Ciphers and spies and murderers. Traitors and plots and greed. At least Aurum was dead and Argentum in the Tower. And if Joseph could find the Alchemist . . .

He thought about Charles and Mary and Joseph, and he thought about Madeleine. What could she have thought when she awoke to find Thomas had sneaked off with Josiah? And what would she be thinking now that they had not returned? That Thomas Hill was an irresponsible old fool with whom she would have nothing further to do? That he deserved whatever he got? That he was dead and good riddance? The chances were that he would never know. And he thought about Lucy. Master Phillips was a frequenter of brothels and admirer of young girls. If she found out, she would be devastated, and that would be his fault. He should have dealt with the matter sooner and better.

The first rats appeared that evening. As it grew darker they came sniffing out of their holes and made for the blood and gore on the blankets and the walls. Josiah broke the legs off the table and chair and threw them at the creatures. The one he hit was immediately set upon and devoured by the others. By the time it was too dark to see, the body was covered in rats. They armed themselves with a chair leg each and hoped the creatures would be satisfied with Squire.

It was pitch dark when they heard voices raised and the clatter of metal on stone. The sounds echoed through the alleys and reached them through the hole in the wall leading to the inn. Thomas could not tell from which direction they were coming. Wide awake at once, they concentrated on listening. They heard oaths and curses and a woman shrieking. 'Intruders,' growled Josiah, struggling to his feet. 'If it's the trained men, we're done for. Finn will 'ide us where we can't be found.'

Thomas also stood up and strained to make out the voices. He heard a man shout, 'Get out,' and a cry of pain. Was it his imagination or were they getting closer? They heard the door being unlocked. It was thrown open and two of Finn's men entered the room. They both held knives. 'Move,' ordered one, 'and be quick. Follow me and don't try nothing.'

The other man got behind them and prodded them out of the room and through the hole in the wall. They turned left, away from the voices and towards the steps. Josiah was right. Unwelcome visitors were in the alleys and the prisoners were being moved to a safer place.

With one guard in front and the other behind, they were led down the alley to the top of the steps. There the first guard stopped and turned to face them. Keeping his knife pointed at them, he took a key from his pocket and opened a narrow door in the wall.

The two tall men in long black cloaks who came out of the shadows and up the steps were so fast and so silent that neither guard saw or heard them until it was too late. Their windpipes severed by wickedly curved daggers, both guards subsided sound-lessly to the ground. Thomas caught a glimpse of yellow satin under a cloak.

'Mr Mottershead and Mr Hill,' said Oliver in his educated voice, 'Miss Henrietta awaits you.'

They could hear men approaching. 'And we must make haste,' added Rupert.

They ran down the steps and reached the low door, which was open. Thomas was pushed through, followed by Josiah. Their rescuers wriggled through the door on their stomachs after them. 'Up you go, gentlemen. We shall follow,' said Oliver.

Thomas needed no urging. He shot up the ladder like a squirrel up a tree and pushed open the trapdoor he found at the top. A bright half-moon lit the night. He clambered out to find himself between a pile of cabbages and a heap of manure. Josiah soon emerged, then Rupert.

'Covent Garden,' said Josiah, looking around.

There was a howl of pain and Oliver, a huge grin on his face, popped his head through the opening. 'He was a foolish fellow to hold on to my leg,' he laughed, jumping out. He closed the trap-door with a bang and stood on it.

There was a screech from behind Thomas, loud enough to make him jump. 'I might 'ave guessed you'd be down some stinking drain, Mottershead.'

''Allo, Molly. Missed me, 'ave you?' Josiah's voice was not much more than a croak.

'No I 'aven't. Just came to see if you found the big arse.'

'We found it and now it's dead.'

'And what 'ave you done with your boots, you little bugger?'

'Stolen, same as my stick. You'll 'ave to buy me a new one.'

'Fuck off. I've 'ad an 'ard night and now I'm off to my bed.'

By this time a small crowd had emerged from the corners of the market and gathered around them. 'Let us be away, gentlemen,' said Oliver. 'We do not want to attract any more attention.'

They walked quickly to Wild Street and let themselves into Henrietta's house. 'Miss Henrietta asked to see you both immediately. I will escort you.' Rupert had already removed his cloak and was brushing down his yellow satin with the back of his hand. Oliver was doing the same.

Despite the hour, Henrietta was in her chair with a glass at her side and her pipe in her mouth. Candles lit the room and the little courtyard outside. She motioned for them to sit and took her time inspecting them. At last she took the pipe from her mouth. 'Caused me a lot of trouble, you two gentlemen have. I had to find twenty brave enough to go into those alleys to divert attention, and send my boys in the back way to find you. They could have been hurt, or worse.'

'Thank you, 'Enrietta,' croaked Josiah, 'I knew you'd 'elp out.'

'Did you now, Josiah Mottershead? And what gave you that idea?'

'Your kind 'eart and the thought of a few sovereigns.'

Henrietta's laugh gurgled up from her enormous belly, erupted through her orange lips and ended in a hacking cough into the bowl at her feet. 'You know me too well, Josiah. Too generous for my own good. And it looks like I shall have to buy you a new pair of boots. Now you just sit there and when Thomas has gone home we'll discuss my reward.' The colour drained from Josiah's face. The thought of rewarding Henrietta clearly terrified him.

'I too thank you, madam,' said Thomas, getting to his feet. 'You have done us a great service. Josiah has been injured in the throat. I daresay a glass of brandy would help.'

Henrietta leered at Josiah. 'It's not his voice I want.'

'Indeed, madam. Now, with your permission I shall return to Fleet Street where a certain lady is doubtless waiting for me.'

'She's a lucky lady,' said Henrietta, licking her lips. 'Be sure to tell her so from me. And take a pair of boots from the rack on your way out. We always have spare pairs left by gentlemen in a hurry.'

'I certainly shall,' replied Thomas, with a bow. He departed with a grin at Josiah, leaving the poor man to his fate.

By the time Thomas knocked on Madeleine's door, dawn had broken. He was let in by Agnes and found Madeleine in her sitting room. 'Good morning, my dear,' he greeted her, trying to plant a kiss on her cheek. 'Here I am and quite unharmed.'

Madeleine pushed him away. 'I have no wish to speak to you, Thomas. Kindly leave this house at once.'

'Madeleine, do you not want to know what happened?'

'Go, Thomas. Now. You are not welcome here.' Her voice was icy. There was nothing to be done. Thomas turned and left.

Agnes was standing by the front door. 'Thank you for your help, Agnes. Josiah is perfectly well. I expect he'll be back soon.' His voice was shaky.

'Where is he, Mr Hill?'

Thomas hesitated. He did not want to upset Agnes but she would know if he lied. 'He is at Henrietta's house. I believe she expects a reward for her part in our rescue.'

Agnes stared at him and a tear came to her eye. 'Oh God. She could kill him. Mottershead's only little. I must go there at once.'

'No, no, Agnes, I wouldn't do that. Josiah will be fine. Cook him a good breakfast for when he returns.'

Agnes dabbed her eyes with her sleeve. 'If you say so, Mr Hill. But I do hope she's gentle with him.'

Thomas wandered slowly and unhappily back to Piccadilly. He was tired, hungry and miserable. He had escaped physical injury but he had been a fool and was being punished. He only hoped that the punishment would not be permanent. If it was he would just have to pack his bags, bid farewell to Charles and Mary, rescue Lucy and creep back to Romsey.

He was let in by Smythe, who looked unusually miserable. 'You look as wretched as me, John. Is something wrong?'

'I'm not sure, sir. Mr and Mrs Carrington have left. They instructed me to inform the servants and to close the house after you've gone. I'm to take care of it until it's sold. They said they wouldn't be needing it any more.'

'When did they leave?'

'Two days ago.'

'How strange. I thought they weren't leaving until next week. Did something happen to change their minds?'

'Not as far as I know, sir. Mrs Carrington has left a letter for you. It's in the sitting room.'

The letter was on the mantel above the fireplace. It was sealed and addressed to Thomas Hill Esquire, in Mary's hand. He broke the seal and unrolled it.

My dear Thomas

Please do not think too badly of us for departing without bidding you farewell. Having learned that there is a ship sailing from Southampton the day after tomorrow, we have decided to leave immediately. We will take the coach to Guildford, and from there travel on to Southampton.

England holds nothing for us now and we have instructed our lawyer to sell this house. Do use it as you wish until the sale is completed. I have sent a message to Joseph and will depend upon you to explain matters to dear Madeleine.

I will write again from Barbados.

Whatever the future brings you will always be in our thoughts, as we hope we shall be in yours.

God bless you.

Your most affectionate friends

Charles and Mary Carrington

Charles has asked me to remind you about going down on one knee. He says it never fails.

Thomas read it twice. How unlike Mary. The Stoner affair must really have unsettled her. 'England holds nothing for us now'

— an oddly blunt expression — and the house to be sold. And 'Whatever the future brings' — most unlike Mary to express such a thought.

Sad as he was not to have been able to make his farewells, Thomas tried to understand. They were tired of London and they did not want to miss the ship sailing in two days' time. He wondered how they had learned about the ship and how they knew there would be a cabin available for them. No doubt he would find out when Mary wrote again from the island.

In his bedroom, Thomas washed and changed. When he came down, the cook had prepared breakfast for him. He wolfed it down with three mugs of ale and told Smythe that he was going to visit Joseph Williamson and would be back soon. He found a carriage and set off for Chancery Lane. Tired and miserable or not, he must inform Joseph of Squire's death and Morland's innocence.

Williamson was at his own breakfast when Thomas arrived. 'Good morning, Thomas. It is early for a visit.'

'I have come to report that Lemuel Squire is dead. He shot himself.'

'What? Squire dead? I imagined he was in Holland by now.' Williamson put down the letter he was reading and stared at him.

'He had been hiding in London, waiting for a chance to escape. We found him two days ago.'

'We? You'd best sit down and tell me about it.' As was his way, Williamson did not interrupt while Thomas told the story. He listened quietly, occasionally nodding as if making a mental note.

'So,' he said when Thomas had finished, 'once again Mottershead has exposed you to unnecessary danger. First the Dartford marshes, now Drury Lane. A foul, evil place, riddled with crime and disease. What possessed you to go with him?'

'God knows. Impetuosity, curiosity, lunacy. All three perhaps.'

'Why didn't you inform me? My men would soon have caught Squire.'

'With respect, I doubt very much if they would have. The area is a warren of passages and alleyways and the moment a trained man had shown his face, Squire would have been spirited away to one of a hundred secret places. Without Josiah, Squire would still be in hiding.'

'Perhaps. But he did not have to take you with him.'

'I insisted.' Williamson would recognize the lie, but he could not refute it.

'Just like Dartford, eh? Your powers of persuasion are considerable, Thomas.' Williamson stood up. 'So. Squire dead and Stoner in the Tower awaiting a ship to Denmark. And Roger Willow has disappeared. I really cannot spare anyone to go looking for him, so whether he has run off from fear or fury we may never know. I have lost three good men, but a dangerous spy ring is broken and the ringleaders are no longer a threat. I should keep my head.'

'Did you know that Willow was an actor, as Squire was?'

Joseph raised his eyebrows in surprise. 'I did not.'

'Squire claimed so. Why do you suppose Squire took his own life?'

'Fear, I imagine,' replied Williamson. 'Being half hanged, drawn and quartered cannot be a comfortable way to die and it is a death the king insists upon for traitors. Squire knew it, decided not to take the risk and shot himself. Any of us might have done the same.'

There was a knock on the door and Williamson's footman came in. 'A messenger is here from the Constable, sir.'

'Ye gods, what now? I've hardly finished my breakfast and already I'm besieged by visitors. Show him in.'

The messenger handed Williamson a letter. He broke the seal and read it. 'The Constable asks me to go to the Tower immediately. He does not say why. Are you up to coming with me, Thomas?'

'Must I?'

'Yes.'

At the Tower, they were met by a yeoman warder and taken straight to the Constable. 'Thank you for coming, gentlemen,' he greeted them, shaking their hands. 'I fear that I have unwelcome news.'

'Don't tell me Stoner's escaped,' exclaimed Williamson.

'He has not escaped, sir. He's dead.'

'By his own hand?'

'I think not. I have asked the guard to join us. He will tell you what happened.'

Williamson was furious. 'It had better be good, or the man will find himself in Newgate before nightfall.'

The guard was shown in and stood in front of them. He looked terrified. 'Now, man,' ordered the Constable, 'tell Mr Williamson and Mr Hill what you told me. Leave nothing out.'

The guard took a deep breath. 'It was last night, sir. The prisoner had two visitors at about six o'clock. An elderly man and a younger one, who I understood to be his son. The older man said he was the prisoner's uncle and that they had brought him food and drink. I inspected their basket, which had a bottle of wine and some bread and cheese in it, and searched them for weapons. They had none so I let them in. Prisoners are permitted family visitors unless I have orders to the contrary. They were with the prisoner for about half an hour. When they left, they said he had drunk the wine and was sleeping.'

'Did they say anything else?'

'No, sir. I checked the prisoner at ten o'clock and found him lying on the bed with his back towards the door. I assumed he was asleep and did not disturb him.'

'Is that your normal practice?'

'Yes, sir.'

'And?'

'This morning when I went to take him his breakfast he hadn't moved, so I went to wake him. He was dead.'

'Were there any signs of how he died?'

'No, sir. No blood, no wounds.'

'Can you describe the visitors?'

'The older one was tall, with a black beard and a limp. The younger one quite slight, also bearded and hooded. They both wore long coats.'

'Did you see their hands?'

'They wore gloves.'

'Anything else?'

'No, sir.'

'Where is the body?'

'It hasn't been moved, sir. The Constable said he would inform you before we sent word to the coroner.'

Given the likely state of Seymour Manners at that hour of the day, Thomas thought that was wise. 'Shall we inspect the body, Joseph?' he suggested.

'Yes. With the Constable's permission, we shall.' The Constable nodded his agreement. 'Thank you. Lead on, guard.'

They followed the guard across a small courtyard, through a door in the innermost of the Tower's walls, and up a winding staircase. The guard opened a door at the top of the staircase with a large key and stood back to allow them to enter. 'Stay there, man,' ordered Williamson, going in.

Thomas went in after him and looked around. It was a more comfortable prison than any he had been in. Light and clean, a decent bed, a washstand and wash bowl, a writing table and a chair. Stoner lay on the bed, just as the guard had told them, with his back to the door. They walked around the bed and examined him. 'No sign of poison,' said Joseph, sniffing, 'no smell, and he looks peaceful.'

'Princes in the Tower?'

'Eh? Oh, yes, probably. Soundless, impossible to detect and there were two of them. It's very difficult for one alone to suffocate a grown man.'

'Cheated investors or hired assassins?'

Williamson fixed Thomas with his good eye. 'I wonder. A father and son, both bearded and in long coats. What does that put you in mind of, Thomas?'

At first, Thomas could think of nothing it put him in mind of except a pair of hooded assassins hired by England's enemies to get rid of a serious risk to their plans. Then it dawned on him. The Carringtons' dinner party. The entertainment planned by Mary Carrington which had gone unperformed when news of Winter's death had arrived. A father and his miscreant son. Costumes and beards to hand and Charles had learned his words. To be sure, the Carringtons had suffered at Stoner's hands, as many had. But murder? Surely not.

'Oh come now, Joseph,' replied Thomas, 'I hardly think so.

And in any event, Stoner died yesterday. Charles and Mary left for Southampton two days ago.'

'So they said. But that might have been a ruse. They could have hidden in London for a day.'

'Joseph,' exclaimed Thomas, 'are you really suggesting that Charles and Mary Carrington, our friends, pretended to leave at short notice for Southampton but instead hid somewhere, visited Stoner last night and smothered him? And that they did so out of revenge for their losses in Quicksilver?'

Williamson's voice was cold. 'I am saying that it is possible. They are suspects, that is all.'

'Charles and Mary are dear friends of mine and of yours. How can you think this?'

'Thomas, I am in charge of His Majesty's security and that of his realm. He does not pay me to let personal feelings interfere with my judgement or my duty. The Carringtons, dear friends or not, had the means and the motive to murder Stoner.'

'As did many others.'

'Possibly. But it is incumbent upon me to find out the truth of the matter and I cannot allow my suspicions to go unchecked.'

Thomas was aghast. 'So what do you intend to do, if I may ask?'

'I shall send urgent word to Southampton. If their ship has not yet sailed, the Carringtons will be apprehended.'

'And if it has?'

'In that case, I shall consider what further steps should be taken. Meanwhile, we will continue our enquiries. I too hope that my fears are unfounded. It would be a hurt of the most grievous kind to see Charles and Mary on trial for murder, albeit the murder of a foul fraudster and traitor.'

Thomas was silent. Williamson, the king's servant, took precedence over Joseph, the Carringtons' friend. He was set on doing his duty as he saw it and that was that. Thomas could only hope that when the ship sailed Charles and Mary would be safely on it. Not that he thought them guilty of Stoner's murder. It would just be better if their fate were not put in the hands of a jury.

Joseph was unusually flustered. 'Can you find your own way home? I must arrange for a message to be taken at once to Southampton and then go to Whitehall. The king must be informed of Stoner's death and of Squire's. I'll tell the Constable to send for Manners. Not that he will be able to tell us anything.'

'I shall be happy to,' replied Thomas. 'It might clear my head and settle my temper.'

At the Carringtons' house, Thomas sat at the writing table, took out the *Dramatis Personae*, laid out a new sheet of paper and dipped a quill in his pot of ink. After rewriting the list once more, he had:

Plato: 'Life must be lived as a play.'

The Post Office, the Fraud and the Plot
Dramatis Personae

Joseph Williamson: the king's spymaster, and clever pragmatist
Henry Bishop: Postmaster General, deceived by Squire
Sir Samuel Morland: unpleasant but innocent inventor
Charles and Mary Carrington: dear friends of Thomas and
    Madeleine
Josiah Mottershead: Williamson's fearless and loyal man

Lemuel Squire: Aurum, spy and traitor. Dead by his own hand
Chandle Stoner: Argentum, fraudster and murderer. Dead
Matthew Smith: murdered intelligencer
John Winter: murdered intelligencer
Henry Copestick: murdered Post Office man
Sir Montford Babb: murdered investor in Quicksilver
Disfigured assassin: whereabouts?
Madeleine Stewart: beautiful and fiery cousin of Williamson
Thomas Hill: devoted admirer and lover of Miss Stewart
Alchemist: unknown
Roger Willow: Post Office clerk

He sprinkled sand on the paper, folded it and put it in his pocket. God willing, the play was nearly over. He lay on the bed and closed his eyes.

When he opened them again it was dark and he heard the long-case clock strike three. He had slept for twelve hours. He lay awake until dawn, when he rose and dressed. Then he went down to the kitchen and helped himself to a large slab of chicken pie. For the task ahead he needed serious sustenance.

He walked briskly down Haymarket to Charing Cross and along the Strand. At the junction with Chancery Lane where Fleet Street began, he bought an expensive bunch of tulips from an early morning flower-seller. 'Good luck, sir,' said the flower girl cheerfully. 'There's nothing like tulips to melt a heart.' He hoped she was right.

The door was opened by Agnes. 'Good morning, sir. You're early. Miss Stewart is still in bed.'

Thomas held out the tulips. 'Please give her these and tell her I am outside.'

Agnes took the flowers. 'Very well, sir. Will you come in?'

'No thank you, Agnes. I shall wait here.'

'As you wish, sir. Mottershead is here. Shall I send him out to see you?'

'Please do.'

Agnes disappeared into the house, leaving Thomas on the doorstep.

It was not long before a dishevelled Mottershead poked his head out of the door. 'Good morning, sir. Come to see Miss Stewart, 'ave you? I 'ope she's in a better temper than she was yesterday.'

'So do I, Josiah. How was Henrietta's reward?'

'My word, sir, it was a close shave. I 'ad to get a pint of brandy down 'er before she passed out and I could slip away.'

'Agnes will have been relieved. She was very worried about you.'

'Yes, sir, she was. And very pleased to see Mottershead, as you might say.'

'Chandle Stoner is dead.'

'Yes, sir, I 'eard. Odd business by all accounts.'

Thomas knew his efforts had been in vain when Agnes returned with the tulips. 'I'm sorry, sir. Miss Stewart won't take them. She said to give them back and to tell you to go home.'

'Is she really that angry, Agnes?'

'She is, sir. You should have heard her when I told her where you and Mottershead had gone. I had to cover my ears.'

'Is there anything I can do?'

Agnes frowned. 'Not yet, sir. Give the lady time. If there's any change, I'll send Mottershead with a message. Will you be at the house in Piccadilly?'

'Not for much longer. Now the Carringtons have left and Miss Stewart is not speaking to me, I shall go home in a day or two.'

'Leave it to me, sir. I'll see what I can do.'

'Thank you, Agnes.'

In Fleet Street Thomas gave the tulips back to the flower girl. Perhaps they would bring another hopeful suitor good luck. A coach stood outside the house in Piccadilly, apparently waiting for someone. Thomas ignored it and went inside. He was met by Smythe. 'Your niece is here, sir. She wishes to see you.'

Ah well, no time like the present. Thomas braced himself and opened the door of the sitting room. Lucy immediately threw herself into his arms. She was sobbing. Thomas did his best to comfort her although he feared that worse was to come. He sat her on a chair and took her hands in his. When she had sufficient control of herself, he asked gently, 'Now, now, my dear, what has brought this on?'

Lucy sniffed and wiped her eyes with a lace handkerchief. 'It's Arthur. He's gone.'

Thomas suppressed an urge to cheer. Josiah had not mentioned it. 'I am sorry to hear it. Where has he gone?'

It took Lucy a while to answer. 'He's gone to Bristol. Urgent business, he said.'

'Did he say when he would return?'

Another sob. 'No. He said he might be away for a long time and I should forget him.'

Did he now? thought Thomas. Well done, Josiah. He tried to sound avuncular and concerned. 'Lucy, my dear, such things happen. You will soon meet another young man.' Lucy's sob was more of a wail. Thomas retreated. 'I understand your feelings. We have all felt the pain of rejection.' Lucy nodded. 'What are you planning to do?'

'I don't know.'

'In that case, I suggest that we arrange for you to return immediately to Romsey.' Another nod. 'Good. Then that is settled. I will send a letter to Lady Richmond telling her that you are needed at home and ask Smythe to book a seat on tomorrow's coach for you. How would that be?'

'Very well, Uncle Thomas.'

'Good. Now take the coach back to Lady Richmond's house and pack your things. I will write the letter and Smythe will bring it round.'

Thomas led Lucy to the coach and kissed her cheek. 'I shall be home soon. Try to forget him.' He knew it was the wrong thing to say the moment the words were out of his mouth. Lucy's wail could have been that of a grieving widow. Thomas hastily waved the coachman away and returned inside. Not much of an effort at comforting the poor child, he thought. Perhaps a little too anxious to send her home. But I have my own problems. Madeleine Stewart for one and Joseph Williamson for another.

For the first time in years, Thomas found himself reverting to his old habit of counting things. He thought it must be the waiting. Waiting for word from Joseph or Madeleine. He counted twenty steps in the staircase, one hundred and six bricks around the fire-place and three hundred and ten words on one page of Montaigne's *Essais*.

When he was not counting, he was worrying. Charles and Mary were determined and fearless, but capable of cold-blooded murder? He doubted it. With luck, their ship would depart for Barbados before Joseph's messenger arrived. At least then they would be on their way home. Surely Joseph would not send a frigate to intercept them and bring them back to be interrogated.

Or would they reach the island only to be apprehended there? He could well imagine Charles's reaction to that. Two swords at the very least and woe betide any man who tried to prise him or his beloved wife from their home.

As for Madeleine, if she really had turned her face against him, what could he do? A letter asking for forgiveness and declaring undying love? Roses instead of tulips? A solitary vigil on her doorstep until she agreed to see him? No, Thomas, none of those. If the lady had a mind to forgive, she would do it in her own way and in her own time. He might as well return to Romsey and wait there. She would find him if she wanted to. As soon as he had news that Charles and Mary had left Southampton for Barbados, he would pack up and go home. If they were apprehended . . . well, that bridge would be crossed if he came to it.

When Joseph next called at Piccadilly, however, he brought with him the news that Thomas was dreading. 'The Carringtons are being held on board their ship in Southampton harbour. It will not be permitted to sail without my authority.'

It was the worst possible outcome, worse even than the pain of Madeleine's rejection. Joseph must have seen the distress on Thomas's face. He went on, 'Thomas, they are my friends too and it grieves me to have to do this, but think of my position. I must act as Sir Edward Nicholas would have acted. Charles and Mary are suspected of murdering Chandle Stoner, who was a prisoner in my charge. I really should have had them brought straight back to London.'

'Why didn't you?'

Joseph opened his hands in a gesture of ignorance. 'I am not certain. Perhaps I am hoping that something will come to light which proves their innocence and I can allow their ship to leave.'

'Stoner was a fraudster and a traitor. He did not deserve to live.'

'I agree. However, I live in a world of opportunity and expediency. I had intended to turn Stoner into an agent of my own and the king knows it. How do I explain to His Majesty that I have allowed his murderers to go free? I shall be in trouble enough when Morland tells the king that I imprisoned him in the Tower without a shred of real evidence against him.'

Espionage, treachery, expediency, opportunism — it was high time Thomas went home. But in addition to the unwelcome news, Joseph had brought something else. From his pocket he took a silver box which he handed to Thomas.

'My men have almost torn Squire's house down. Every floor-board has been lifted and every piece of furniture searched for secret drawers. They found nothing until, quite by chance, this came to light.'

'A box for snuff. I remember Squire taking snuff from a gold box. How does this help?'

'Turn it over, Thomas, and tell me what you see.'

Thomas did so. At first he saw nothing except a few marks of the sort one might expect to find on a well-used object. But when he looked more closely, the marks began to take shape. They were very small and their patterns were regular. He held the box close to his eyes. 'I think they are numbers. I can make out forty-six and ninety-nine.'

'Try this,' said Joseph, handing him a bone-handled magnify-ing glass. When Thomas held the glass over the box, the numbers jumped out.

'Now I can read them easily. How did you find this?'

'It was on a shelf. Josiah took it down and dropped it. It

landed upside down and when he picked it up his sharp eyes noticed the scratches. A fortunate accident, you might say.'

'I will fetch my notes. If it is the same cipher, it won't take a minute.' Thomas ran up to his bedroom, retrieved the paper on which he had recorded the numerical substitutions for each letter and returned to the sitting room.

'You read them out, Joseph, and I will write them down. Ignore spaces. It's just the numbers and stops we want.'

Holding the glass with both hands to keep it steady, Joseph read out the numbers.

46.89.42.95.83.91.26.1.48.39.86.6.89.52.65.
9.90.26.7.0.3.11.37.70.17.71.25.45.78.65.83.

'That is all, Thomas. I do not think I have missed any.'

Thomas laid the paper on which he had written the numbers on the table beside his decryption note and started converting the numbers into letters.

In less than a minute, he said, 'The letters in the first line are NFLAMELRMOUFFPA.' And after another minute, 'The second line is JGLAUBERKALVERAM.' He handed the paper to Joseph, who sat studying the letters.

Joseph shrugged. 'I can see nothing here, although there must be something. What would Squire have kept an encrypted note of?'

'A contact name? An address? But why write them down at all? There are only two lines.'

'Names and addresses change. He might have had previous names recorded elsewhere. Or there might be dozens of them.'

Thomas returned to the letters and tried setting out the first line with different spaces.

NFLAM ELRMO UFFPA

N FLAME LRMOUFF PA

N FLAMEL RMOUFFPA

It leapt at him. Nicolas Flamel was a celebrated French alchemist of the fourteenth century. 'The Alchemist, Joseph. Nicolas Flamel was an alchemist.'

'I have heard of him. What about RMOUFFPA?'

'Could PA be Paris?'

'Indeed it is. Rue Mouffetard is in the oldest part of Paris.' It was almost a shout.

That made the second line easy. Johann Glauber was also an alchemist, a Dutch one, and Kalverstraat was a street in Amsterdam. There had once been a cattle market there.

These addresses were where Squire sent his letters. N. FLAMEL, RUE MOUFFETARD, PARIS and J. GLAUBER, KALVERSTRAAT, AMSTERDAM. He would have slipped his letters into the Dover mail and they would have been collected from a local sorting office by an agent of the Alchemist. Or Alchemists. Two addresses in two countries suggested two alchemists working together. Two men, one code name. Thomas did not remember having come across this before, but it was possible. Indeed, it implied a very close connection between the two of them.

Now Thomas knew why he had instinctively taken the seal from Squire's house. 'This might give us a way of luring the Alchemist to London. And unless you intend to despatch assassins to Amsterdam and Paris, that is the only way you are going to eliminate him.'

Joseph looked doubtful. 'What do you suggest?'

'That we compose a letter, ostensibly from Squire and encrypted with the numerical cipher, which gives him an irresistible reason to come here. I can copy Squire's hand and I have his seal. And now we have an address.'

Joseph did not ask how Thomas came to have the seal. 'Two addresses. But what if Squire or Stoner had already alerted the man to our having broken the cipher?'

'I doubt either of them had the time or the means — remember Squire's unfinished letter — but if they did, we shall lose nothing.'

For a long time Joseph sat and pondered. Thomas could almost see the arguments for and against battling it out in his head. At last he said, 'Very well, we will do as you suggest. But Charles and Mary will have to stay on the ship in Southampton while the plan is carried out and Morland must stay in the Tower. I do not want unwelcome distractions.'

Thomas was on his feet. 'I will fetch what we need.'

To have a chance of luring the Alchemist into a trap, the bait would have to be uncommonly juicy. The fox would not leave the safety of his den without the promise of a feast.

Eventually they agreed to send only one letter — to Amsterdam — on the grounds that if there were a second man in Paris, he would be alerted by his counterpart. They also agreed that the message should be brief, saying no more than was necessary. The trap itself would be set if and when they received a reply.

After numerous false starts, they settled on:

Senior govt officer approached. Wishes to help. Your presence here essential. Aurum

The message contained neither Q nor Z, for which Thomas did not have a number. He fetched Squire's seal and his invitation to the Post Office from which to copy his hand, and encrypted the letter as:

10.5.28.22. 39.1.55.49. 25.4.53.6. 89.24.81.11. 37.7.52.68. 59.57.38.21. 2.85.67.18. 32.58.15.82. 76.20.72.31. 91.71.52.34. 93.13.62.52. 64.45.66.56. 46.81.88.2. 5.1.36.11. 79.80.73.35. 8.24.77.26. 7.0.62.13. 48.

With Joseph's help he checked his work and sealed the letter securely. They decided to write the sender's name above the seal, as most correspondents did, to reassure the Alchemist that a reply via the Post Office would be secure and to give him a return address. In Squire's hand, Thomas wrote *A. Knight, Golden Lane, London*, which had the look of a name and address Squire might have used. It would go by special messenger to Dover, where Joseph's man would ensure it was delivered to the Amsterdam sorting office for collection on behalf of the addressee, J. Glauber.

'I will have a Bishop Mark stamped on it and send it on its way today,' said Joseph. 'Then we can only wait and pray.'

They had agreed that if there was to be a reply it would probably arrive within ten days. That was quite enough time for the letter to reach Amsterdam and for the reply to reach London, and if the plan worked the Alchemist would not delay.

At first the thrill of anticipation made the waiting bearable. The Alchemist would fall into their trap, the king would be delighted and Thomas would carry Madeleine off to Romsey to spend the rest of their lives together.

As the days passed, however, anticipation gave way to melancholy. What exactly was he waiting for? The Alchemist would have been alerted to the deaths of Stoner and Squire and would know at once that the letter was a trap. He would laugh at such a feeble attempt to deceive him. Or the Amsterdam address was the wrong one and the letter would never reach him. Or the names on the snuff box were nothing to do with the Alchemist.

Then he caught himself. Don't give up, Thomas, of course the names were the Alchemist. Nicolas Flamel and Johann Glauber were celebrated alchemists. Be patient. The plan might yet work. There was no point in sitting alone in the house in Piccadilly wondering and worrying. He must go out and exercise the mind and body on something else.

Something else or someone else? Should he call again on Madeleine and risk another rebuff? Or should he be distant and aloof, forcing the lady to come to him? Not enough experience, Thomas, he told himself. Most men of forty-seven would know what to do, but here you are behaving like a love-struck youth. Take a hold on yourself and stop being dreary. You have much to be thankful for — two nieces whom you love dearly, a fine house, friends and more money than you will ever need.

But not Madeleine Stewart.

On the ninth day, Thomas set off on a morning walk. From Piccadilly he made his way northwards to Holborn, then down Shoe Lane and up Ludgate to St Paul's. Although he avoided Old

Bailey, a light breeze that day blew the stench from Newgate towards him. He held his handkerchief to his nose and thought of the wretches locked up inside its walls, most with nothing to look forward to but death from gaol fever or at the end of a rope. Thieves, murderers, dissenters, republicans, men, women, children — Newgate made room for all. And its malignancy spread. In the alleys and lanes nearby, whores, pickpockets and beggars plied their trade. It was as if they had gravitated there to await their turn to go inside.

He had chosen this route for his walk, rather than a stroll in St James's Park or along the river, to take his mind off Madeleine. If the horrors of Newgate could not divert him, nothing could. He wandered around St Paul's Churchyard, stopping from time to time to read the inscription on an ancient gravestone, then walked back down Ludgate Hill to Fleet Street.

What nonsense. Newgate had nothing to do with it. This route took him past the end of the narrow lane in which Madeleine lived. That was why he had chosen it.

The temptation was too great. He turned into the lane and stood outside her door. After a minute, he knocked loudly. There was no reply. He knocked again. Still no reply. Madeleine Stewart was not at home and nor was Agnes. At least that spared him another humiliation. He turned to go. As he did so, his eye registered a tiny movement inside the window by the door. There was someone there and it must be Madeleine. Agnes on her own would have answered the door. Madeleine had seen him outside and left him there. Now he knew where he stood.

Damn the woman and damn London. Smythe had started packing up the house, tomorrow would be the tenth day since the letter had been sent to Amsterdam and he had been in London far too long. He should have gone home weeks ago. This time he really would go home, Alchemist or no Alchemist. Lucy had left, he would not be tempted to call on Madeleine again and he would not be persuaded by Joseph to stay longer. Back in his room he threw his clothes and books into his travelling bag and went to tell Smythe that he would be leaving the next morning.

But when at six o'clock that evening there was a knock on the door, he leapt up from his chair and rushed to open it. He knew it was Madeleine come to forgive him.

It was not. A carriage stood on the street and Joseph at the door, holding in his hand a rolled letter.

'It's come, Thomas. A reply.' Without waiting to be invited, Joseph strode in and handed the letter to Thomas. It was short.

81.2.85.17. 52.10.47.14. 36.30.9.86. 35.73.48.22. 67.28.51.90. 98.87.17.26. 21.15.50.48. 61.80.8.

Thomas retrieved his papers from his bag, found the key and decrypted it. 98, for which he did not have a letter, was easy enough to guess. He read it out.

'CHEAPSIDE N JUNE MIDNIGHT ALCHEMIST'

'What does N June mean?' asked Joseph.

Thomas laughed. 'It doesn't. 30 is not N, it is 30. The thirtieth of June. Two days' time.' So much for going home tomorrow. The capricious fates were playing their games again.

'Of course. And Cheapside can only mean Stoner's house. Two days gives us time to prepare. Come on, Thomas, we'll discuss our plan at my house. I have sent for Mottershead. He should be there by now.' Joseph was in no mood for conversation. He strode out as quickly as he had strode in. Thomas hastily gathered up his papers and followed.

Josiah had already arrived at Chancery Lane so they sat in Joseph's library and thrashed out a plan. It was simple enough and would involve no more than four well-armed men and themselves.

Afterwards, Josiah enquired after Thomas's health and apologized for not calling on him. 'Mr Williamson's been keeping me busy,' he explained, 'and when I'm not working, I'm running to the market and doing jobs for Agnes.'

Thomas did his best not to ask after Madeleine. 'Is Agnes well?'

'She is, thank you, sir.'

'I am glad to hear it.' It was no good. 'And Miss Stewart?'

'A little out of sorts, sir. Not eating properly, Agnes says.'

'A chill perhaps. Offer her my good wishes please, Josiah.'

'You could do that yourself, sir.'

'Perhaps. First, however, let us finally get this business over with.'

CHAPTER 24

The night of 30 June was warm and lit by a half-moon in a clear sky. By ten o'clock the trap had been set. Inside Stoner's house on Cheapside a single candle had been lit and placed in the window to tell his visitors that they were expected. Thomas and Joseph sat by Stoner's unlit fire and in the kitchen four armed guards were ready and waiting. Outside, Josiah stood unseen in the shadow of a doorway opposite. If the Alchemist kept this rendezvous, it would be his last.

It had been agreed that Thomas, dressed as a servant in a plain white shirt and black breeches, would answer the door and let the visitor in. Once he was safely inside, the door would be locked and at Joseph's signal the guards would burst from the kitchen and arrest him. Josiah's task was to keep watch until the arrest had been made.

The two hours to midnight dragged by. In the kitchen four nervous men wished they were enjoying themselves in an inn or tucked up in their beds. Joseph and Thomas sat in silence, wondering if the fox really would leave his den. There was no need for Thomas to be there. Anyone could have played the part of the servant. It was just that he did not want to miss the final act of the play. Now that the moment was approaching, he wished it over. Come, Alchemist, and reveal yourself.

The clock of the church of St Mary-le-Bow struck twelve. Joseph took out his pocket watch and checked it. They had agreed that they would wait for half an hour past midnight. If the Alchemist had not arrived by then, he was not coming.

At ten minutes after midnight there was a quiet knock on the door. Thomas looked at Joseph, who nodded and went to the kitchen door. 'Be ready,' he whispered through it and Thomas heard the muffled sounds of the guards preparing themselves. Joseph stood in front of the hearth, ready to greet their visitor face to face. Thomas walked to the front door and opened it.

On the doorstep stood not one but two hooded figures, their heads lowered and their faces partially covered. Both wore long cloaks to their ankles. One was Thomas's height, the other several inches shorter. He opened the door wider and made a gesture of welcome. When he did so, light from the single candle in the window shone weakly on his face. The smaller of the two figures looked up and for no more than a moment stared at him. Behind the hood, Thomas could see only a pair of pale eyes. So quickly did the figure turn and run that Thomas had not moved before the other one set off behind him. Taken entirely by surprise, he stood and stared. By the time he shouted an alarm and gave chase, the smaller figure was halfway down Cheapside.

At that time of the night, the streets were deserted and there was just enough moonlight for him to make out the running figures. They were heading for Stocks Market at the junction of

Poultry and Cornhill. If they reached Leadenhall, they would disappear into the warren of lanes and alleys around Lime Street. Thomas accelerated and by the time he reached Old Jewry, the taller figure had caught up with the shorter one and they were no more than twenty yards ahead of him. At that moment the shorter one stopped and turned. There was a shot and the pistol ball which grazed Thomas's cheek drew a trace of blood and stopped him in his tracks. He wiped it away, realized the wound was superficial and set off again. Both quarries, however, were now out of sight and he feared that he had lost them when two tall runners hurtled past him. Assuming they were Joseph's men and a great deal younger and fleeter of foot than him, he gave up the chase and left them to it.

He was standing with his hands on his knees, trying to recover his breath, when a puffing Josiah arrived. 'Did the boys come past, sir?' asked the little man in between gulps of air.

'If you mean two men running like stags, yes they did. Who were they?'

Josiah grinned. 'I never trust the militia, sir, so I thought to bring along a little 'elp. Just in case, as it were.'

'As well you did. Let's hope they caught the fugitives.' From the direction of Leadenhall, there was the sound of laughter and, as if on cue, the two tall runners appeared holding two hooded figures between them.

'Ah, 'ere are the boys, sir, and they seem to 'ave caught something,' said Josiah. 'Well done, lads. Miss 'Enrietta will be pleased when I tell 'er.' Oliver and Rupert had shed their yellow satin in favour of black shirts and trousers for the occasion, but there was no mistaking them. As they approached, two of Joseph's men clattered up from the opposite direction, pistols drawn and swords rattling at their sides.

Thomas stepped forward and pulled back the shorter prisoner's hood. He found himself looking at a plump, plain face, red with exertion and exuding fury. The thin lips pursed and spat at him. He wiped away the spittle and stared into a pair of narrow, livid eyes. 'Well, well. If I'm not mistaken, Madame Louise d'Entrevaux. How unexpected. *Enchanté, madame.*'

Louise d'Entrevaux's reply was a look of the most venomous loathing that Thomas had ever seen. If Rupert had not been holding her, she would certainly have leapt at him and tried to scratch his eyes out.

He pulled down the other hood. 'And could this be Monsieur d'Entrevaux?'

One Alchemist would have been a fine catch. Two was more than they could possibly have hoped for. They must be delivered to Joseph without delay. 'If Oliver and Rupert would care to hand over their prisoners, we will escort them back to Cheapside and they can return to Drury Lane with our grateful thanks.' He was rewarded with two deep bows and two enormous grins.

'Thank you, lads,' said Josiah. 'Tell 'Enrietta I'll call in the morning.' The lads handed over their prisoners to the guards and strode off chuckling.

At the house Josiah opened the door and stood aside for the prisoners to be pushed inside by the guards. He and Thomas followed them. At first glance, the room was empty. No guards and no Joseph. But when the door slammed after them two figures stepped from behind it. One was Joseph with an arm around his neck and a knife at his throat, the other the disfigured Dutchman. The Dutchman spoke first. 'You will place your weapons on the floor. Or this man will die.' His eyes never left Josiah.

'Kill him,' croaked Joseph. For a moment no one moved. Thomas was the first to recover.

'Do as the Dutchman says,' he whispered. The two guards barely hesitated before unbuckling their sword belts and placing them on the floor with their pistols.

'And the stick,' growled the Dutchman. 'I know what that can do.' Josiah put his stick down beside the swords. 'Now you will stand facing the wall with your hands against it.' With his head he motioned to the wall on the other side of the room. The four of them did as they were ordered.

For the first time Louise d'Entrevaux spoke. Her voice dripped with malice. 'Idiots. Did you suppose we would come unprotected? *Comme vous êtes foux*. And now you will die for your stupidity.' While they faced the wall, two pistols were cocked and two shots fired almost simultaneously. Both guards slumped to the floor. Thomas and Josiah jumped round. Blood poured from the guards' heads. Louise d'Entrevaux had already thrown the pistols aside and picked up the swords. She glared at Thomas. 'You were fortunate to break the cipher and discover the address, but not, it seems, fortunate enough. We suspected a trap and only came because we were instructed to. We insisted upon our friend accompanying us.'

'Let us kill them and go,' said her husband, shakily. Beneath the hood he was pale as a sheet.

The Dutchman still held Joseph with a knife at his throat. 'They will join the other two in the kitchen soon enough. First I have a score to settle. Pick up the stick, Hill, and break the little man's knees.' Thomas did not move. It was beyond imagining.

'You are evil.'

The Dutchman pressed the knife against Joseph's throat and

snorted. 'Do it. Or Mr Williamson will die and I will do it myself while Madame d'Entrevaux holds the point of a sword in your mouth. Then I will remove your testicles and his eyes. Which is it to be?'

'Let him kill me. Then kill them all.' Joseph's throat was so constricted that he was barely audible.

'That might be difficult,' sneered the Dutchman. 'We three have this knife and two sharp swords while you have a single stick. Do as I say, Hill. Now.' Thomas hesitated, then bent to pick up Josiah's stick. Having never held it before, he had not realized how heavy it was.

'If we are to die, why would I cripple Josiah first?'

'I have explained the consequences if you do not.'

'Indeed. Mutilation and death. And revenge.' Thomas was saying whatever came into his head to gain time. The shots might have been heard and help might yet arrive.

'Enough, Hill. Break his knees. NOW.' It was the closest the disfigured man could get to a shout.

'Go on, sir,' whispered Josiah, 'then kill him.' He stood calmly with his back to the wall, no hint of fear in his eyes.

Thomas hefted the stick in both hands, trying to think clearly. Josiah's knees to gain a little more time? Or refuse and risk Joseph dying with an instant stroke of the knife? He glanced at the woman and saw the spite in her eyes. She took a step towards him and hissed, 'Do it well or you will pay.'

It was the malevolence in her voice that did it. Thomas moved without thought and at a speed of which he would not have thought himself capable. The stick crashed against the side of Louise d'Entrevaux's head, sending her unconscious to the floor and the swords clattering towards Josiah. Without hesitating,

Thomas turned to the Dutchman, expecting to see blood gushing from Joseph's throat. But Joseph had seized his chance and jabbed an elbow into the Dutchman's ribs. It had gained him just enough space to grab the man's wrist and force the knife away from his throat. Another second or two and he would have lost his advantage, but before the Dutchman could react, Josiah was on him. He thrust his knuckles into an eye and twisted. There was a furious scream and the knife fell to the floor. Joseph stepped away and picked it up. Without a word, he turned and slashed the blade across the Dutchman's throat and watched him slide to the floor, blood gushing from the wound. 'No point in interrogating him,' he said quietly. 'We would not have got anything from him. And he's too dangerous to live.' The Dutchman clutched his throat, stared in disbelief at Joseph, spluttered and died.

Monsieur d'Entrevaux was kneeling beside his wife, her head in his hands. He had taken no part in the fight and Thomas reckoned it would have made no difference if he had. He was plainly not a man of action. Madame d'Entrevaux, on the other hand, was dangerous enough for both of them. Thomas bent down and felt her neck. There was a pulse and she was breathing. 'She is alive, Joseph,' he said.

'Good. Two more for a visit to the Tower and a few questions. Are you wounded, Thomas?'

Thomas felt his cheek where the shot had grazed him. There was a trickle of blood. 'It's a scratch. She fired from too far away.'

'And you, Mottershead?'

'Quite well, sir, thanks to Mr 'Ill.'

Thomas grinned and patted Josiah on the shoulder. 'Say no more about it, Josiah. If the woman had not stepped too close, I don't know what would have happened.'

'Right, Mottershead,' said Joseph briskly, 'kindly go and fetch help while Thomas and I keep an eye on these two, and we'll need the bodies removed before morning.'

'Right, sir,' replied Josiah and left them to it.

'The two in the kitchen had their throats cut,' went on Joseph. 'God knows how he did it without my hearing. The first I knew, he had the knife at my neck. He must have seen you give chase, realized it was a trap and slipped in through the kitchen window.'

'A very dangerous man indeed, not to mention a kidnapper and murderer. Let us hope England is a little safer without him.'

Josiah was soon back with three trained men. One was ordered to summon the coroner to collect the bodies of the four guards, the other two to help escort the prisoners to the Tower. Josiah stayed to supervise the coroner's men. 'Tell Manners,' Joseph told him, 'that I will speak to him about the matter later today. Until then he is to say nothing. Then go home. I will send for you.'

One of the militiamen hoisted the woman over his shoulder, the other marched her husband along by the scruff of his neck. Joseph and Thomas walked behind them. Fortunately it was not yet light and there were few people on the streets to stare at them. Those that did were ignored.

At the Tower Gate, Joseph asked for the Constable to be sent for while the prisoners were escorted by yeomen warders to the White Tower. The militiamen he dismissed. Neither prisoner had spoken on the way there, although Louise d'Entrevaux had come round and was able to walk.

When the Constable appeared in a state of some dishevelment, Joseph explained who the prisoners were and requested that they be locked in separate rooms with guards both inside and out. There would be no repetition of Stoner's murder or

Squire's suicide. The two of them were taken off by the warders, leaving Thomas and Joseph with the Constable.

The Constable was a civilized man. 'I am at your service should you need me, gentlemen,' he informed them. 'Meanwhile feel free to question the prisoners as you see fit.' He offered them refreshment, which they happily accepted, and left them to recover from their exertions.

Joseph thanked him and raised his glass. 'A good night's work so far, but for you and me, Thomas, it is not over. Assuming these two are the Alchemists, how do you think we should proceed? Both together or one at a time?'

Judging by her behaviour, the woman would be the more difficult. 'Gentleman first, Joseph, I fancy.'

'I agree. Let us see what we can get out of him before we tackle his charming wife. We will sit here and enjoy the Constable's wine while the prisoners enjoy his hospitality and then we will have a talk with each of them.'

The man who was brought to them an hour later was as un-attractive as his wife. His cloak had been discarded and in a ragged green coat, scuffed shoes and black trousers which barely reached his ankles, he could have been a down-at-heel artist or pamphlet writer. His head and face were roughly shaven and his narrow eyes perched either side of a long, hooked nose. He produced a pair of spectacles and peered at his captors with distaste.

'Are you Monsieur d'Entrevaux?' began Joseph.

'I am Henri d'Entrevaux, Doctor of Theology at the Collège de Sorbonne.' The doctor spoke with a marked French accent but his English was otherwise perfect.

'And Louise d'Entrevaux is your wife.' The man nodded. 'When did you arrive in England?'

'Two days ago.'

'Why have you come to London?'

D'Entrevaux bridled. 'Not that it is any of your concern, but my wife and I have come to visit her brother, Chandle Stoner. That is why we went to his house.'

'At midnight.'

'The journey from Dover was arduous.'

'Why did you run off when the door was opened?'

'My wife ran. I simply followed her.'

Thomas and Joseph burst out laughing. 'Do you always follow where your wife leads?' asked Thomas.

D'Entrevaux ignored the question. 'I am a citizen of France and unless you have proof that I have committed a crime, I demand to be released immediately.'

'Are you the Alchemist?'

The reply was disdainful. 'I am a Doctor of Theology. I believe in God, not magic.'

'Is your wife the Alchemist?'

'I suggest you ask her.' It was a disingenuous, craven reply and it angered Joseph.

'Take the wretch back to his room and bring the woman,' he ordered the warder.

'The man's a liar and a coward,' said Thomas, when the prisoner had been led away. 'The Collège de Sorbonne, however, is a fierce enemy of Protestantism and of England. It is the very place we might have expected to find the Alchemist.'

'Indeed it is. We'll see what his wife has to say.'

At first Louise d'Entrevaux had nothing to say. She simply sat in sullen silence, ignoring every question put to her. Eventually Joseph lost patience.

'As you wish, madam. If you refuse to speak, I shall do so. And you would do well to listen.'

While Joseph described in detail how the names Aurum and Argentum had become known to them and how they had realized that her brother was Argentum, Thomas watched the woman's face for signs of fear or guilt. There were none. It was only when Joseph revealed that her brother had told them that Lemuel Squire was Aurum and had offered to spy for England in return for his own life, that Thomas saw a flash of anger in her pale eyes. She did not react to the news of Squire's death by his own hand but when Joseph told her that her brother was also dead, she finally spoke.

'I thank God. I am pleased that the coward is dead and he was not my brother, he was a half-brother. We shared a father. I hated them both.'

'Yet Stoner did not betray you and he worked for you.'

Once she had started, Louise d'Entrevaux had much to say. She had used Stoner simply as a financier, she had never trusted him and she had feared that he would one day betray them. He was a man who worked for money, not principle. She had only responded to the message and come to London because she had been ordered to by a senior minister in King Louis's government. She had been almost sure they were walking into a trap, but the prize was so great that he had insisted on the risk being taken.

'Who was the minister?' asked Thomas.

'That I shall never tell you.'

'But your husband might.'

'He might if he knew, but he does not.'

'Do you not work together?'

She smiled. 'You will have to ask him.'

'We have. He said that you do.'

'I do not believe you. Not that it matters. His death or my own are of no consequence. It is loyalty to the Catholic faith that matters.'

'Is that how you justify torture and murder?'

'England is doomed. You are surrounded by enemies — our Irish friends to the west, France, Spain, and Holland to the east. You will lose your navy and your new colonies and there will be a Catholic king on your throne.' She spat out the words like poisoned darts.

They got nothing more of use from the woman. She would not answer questions about the Dutchman and when asked if she were the Alchemist, said only, 'There is more than one Alchemist.'

It was enough. 'Take her away,' ordered Joseph, 'and watch them both carefully.'

When they were alone Joseph said, 'They will be kept here while we question them further. I have no doubt, however, that both of them will end up on the gallows.'

'Have we caught the Alchemist, Joseph?'

'I believe that we have caught two of them, but she was telling the truth. There are more. And England is in danger. The Dutch want our colonies and our trade and the French and Spanish want a Catholic king on our throne. And after their sufferings at Cromwell's hands, so do the Irish.'

'So what now?'

'In the morning, I will release Morland and ask the king for permission for the ship to leave Southampton. Now that we have two more in the Tower, Stoner's death can be forgotten and Charles and Mary should go home.'

'Will he grant permission?'

'His Majesty values loyalty more highly than anything. I hope so.'

'As do I. Now, if there is nothing else tonight, Joseph, I shall go to my bed.'

'Go, Thomas. I will bring you news tomorrow.'

CHAPTER 25

Joseph arrived at the house in Piccadilly the following afternoon. He found Thomas reading in the sitting room. 'I have come from Whitehall Palace,' he announced breathlessly. 'The king has instructed me to take no further action in the matter of Stoner's death and to concentrate on recruiting loyal and reliable officers to the security service and the Post Office.'

'Thank God.'

'It was straightforward. After ten days of doing nothing, that drunken sot Manners decided that Stoner had taken his own life, although how he did so Manners could not say. I received his report this morning. This time the man's incompetence proved useful. I passed on his opinion, without comment, to His Majesty.'

'What did His Majesty say?'

'He said that he was happy that both traitors had taken their own lives and that he hoped more would follow their example, as that would save the country the trouble and expense of trying and executing them.'

'Then the matter is closed and I can go home.'

Joseph shook his head. 'Not quite closed, I'm afraid. When Morland was released he went straight to the king and made serious accusations against both of us.'

'How did His Majesty respond?'

'I do not yet know. I am to present myself at Whitehall at nine o'clock tomorrow morning. You are to do so an hour later. A carriage will be sent for you.'

It was a shock. 'Joseph, in view of my part in decrypting the letter and identifying Stoner as Argentum, not to mention finding Squire, rescuing your cousin and arresting the d'Entrevaux, is this not somewhat harsh?'

'Of course it is. But we live in harsh times and the king's temperament is mercurial. He can be easily swayed. And there is another thing. Sir Edward Nicholas returned from York yesterday. He has always favoured Morland and is likely to support him. Who knows what Morland may have told him?'

'Perhaps I should leave London at once.'

'I would not advise that. The king would take it as an admission of guilt and have you hunted down and hanged.'

Something inside Thomas snapped. 'For the love of God, Joseph, this is unjust and absurd. You know perfectly well that I have served the country loyally, and what is more, it was you who dragged me into the whole affair in the first place. I insist that you make this clear to the king.'

Joseph peered at him. 'I shall endeavour to do so. The king, however, might not listen, just as his father did not listen when he would have been well advised to do so.' His voice softened. 'Be prepared, Thomas, that is all I am saying. The carriage will be here before ten tomorrow. Oh, I nearly forgot. We have another body.'

'Dear God, not another. Who?'

'Roger Willow.'

'Was he murdered?'

'Impossible to say. Been in the river too long.' Thomas screwed up his eyes and tried not to picture the bloated corpse of the chief clerk. Squire's accomplice or slighted servant of the Crown? Now they would never know.

How does an innocent man prepare for an audience with the king, at which he is to be falsely accused of he knows not what? Does he devise defences against every possible attack or does he trust to his wits and wait until he can see from which direction the attack is coming? He does neither. He eats a good dinner, drinks a bottle of excellent claret and a glass of brandy and goes to sleep for an hour or two. It was a good plan and Thomas carried it out without difficulty.

When he awoke, however, he had dreamed that Madeleine was a witch who had publicly accused him of betraying her and had demanded his head on a platter. Unlike most dreams, it did not vanish with sleep but stayed with him for the rest of the day. Even while he stretched his legs and cleared his head in St James's Park he saw Madeleine's face, fierce and unforgiving, and her long, sharp finger outstretched and pointing at his heart. He heard her grating voice and stared into her unblinking eyes.

Yet when he returned to the house he half expected Josiah to be waiting for him with news. And each time he heard footsteps in the street he listened in vain for a knock on the door. Smythe brought him a light supper, which he ignored. He sat in silence, from time to time rising to pace up and down the room. The *Essais* remained unopened at his side. That night he did not sleep. He did not even close his eyes.

Morning came eventually. Smythe brushed down Thomas's coronation outfit — long sky-blue coat over a white ruffled shirt, satin breeches tied with ribbons at the knee and black shoes with silver buckles — and Thomas scraped his face with a razor and risked a look in Mary's hand mirror. 'You'll have to do, Thomas,' he said to his reflection. 'Let's hope this king is more agreeable than his father.'

At twenty minutes before ten there was a knock on the door. Thomas put on his coat and answered it. A young captain stood outside. 'If you are ready, sir, the king's carriage awaits you. My orders are to escort you to Whitehall Palace.'

Thomas followed the captain to the carriage. An armed guard opened the door for him, then the captain climbed in beside him and shouted at the driver to be off. 'Have you ever been inside Whitehall Palace, sir?' he asked, as they reached Charing Cross.

'I have not. I hear it's possible to get lost in it.'

'So they say. Lost souls and wandering ghosts, some of the servants believe. Alas, I've never seen one.' Thomas heard no clue about his fate in the captain's voice. He might be going to a royal feast or to his own execution.

The carriage made its way along Whitehall to the Palace Gate, where it turned into a long courtyard. 'This is the Court,' said the captain, 'and in front of us is the Great Hall.' The carriage stopped outside the Hall and the captain jumped out. 'Follow me, sir. There are more than fifteen hundred rooms in the palace and I would not want you going into the wrong one.' Nor would I, thought Thomas, not with many of them occupied by one or other of the king's mistresses.

The captain led him past the Hall, and through a maze of paths and lanes to an entrance guarded by two soldiers. Thomas noticed a walled garden on their left. They went through the entrance and into a room on their right. 'This is one of His Majesty's chambers,' the captain told him. 'He likes to hold private audiences here. He will enter from the royal apartments through that door.' He pointed to a door at the far end of the room. 'He will be accompanied by six courtiers. When His Majesty enters, you should bow from the waist and wait for him to address you. If he offers you his hand, take it lightly. I shall be standing at the door we entered by and will escort you to your destination when your audience is over.'

His destination? The Tower? Newgate? Tyburn? 'Thank you, captain. The last time I met a king it was in Oxford. Had either of us but known it, the country had seven years of war to look forward to.'

The room was bare but for heavy Flemish tapestries on the walls and a large chair upholstered in red velvet with gold braid and tassels in one corner. The high ceiling was vaulted with oak beams and the floor polished to bring out the grain of its timbers. It was a room to impose and impress.

The door to the royal apartments was opened by a servant and the king, followed by his courtiers, swept in. His Majesty wore a sumptuous red silk cloak over a snowy-white shirt with mutton-chop sleeves, and blue velvet breeches tied with gold ribbon at the knee. On his feet were shiny black leather shoes with thick soles and huge silver buckles. He planted himself on the chair with his courtiers arranged on either side and fixed the royal stare on Thomas, who bowed as instructed.

'Thomas Hill,' boomed the king, 'I should not have recognized you.'

Thomas was taken aback. Where had he met this king before?

'My humble apologies, Your Majesty. I do not recall having previously had the honour.'

'You served my late father in Oxford when I was a boy. I used to hide behind a screen in the Great Hall of Christ Church and listen to what went on. I learned a great deal by doing so. And I remember your decrypting the message that revealed Tobias Rush to be a traitor. He died under interrogation, I recall.'

Tobias Rush had not died under interrogation. He was buried in an old privy in Barbados. But Thomas let it pass.

The king's voice became stern. 'Now, Mr Hill, on the one hand, the man responsible for the security of our realm during Sir Edward Nicholas's absence advises me that you have served us with courage and skill. On the other hand, however, Sir Samuel Morland, who is well known at this court, has accused you of treachery and deceit and complained about your part in his unjust confinement in the Tower. What is more, Sir Edward has returned from York and advises me to take Sir Samuel's part in the matter. Consequently, I find myself in something of a dilemma.'

Thomas remained silent and kept his head bowed. Joseph was right. Morland had wasted no time in enlisting the support of Sir Edward Nicholas, who as Secretary of State would carry more weight with the king. He might now be in more danger than he had been in Drury Lane or Dartford. If Nicholas had demanded Thomas's head, no doubt he would get it.

'I have heard what Sir Samuel and Mr Williamson have to say. Before deciding what action to take, however, I wish to hear your version of events. Kindly oblige me with your account.'

At least the accused was being given the chance to speak. Thomas squared his shoulders and took a deep breath. For the second time in his life he would have to persuade the king of

England that he had acted in good faith and was innocent of any wrongdoing.

Throughout Thomas's account the king's gaze never wavered from him and not once did he interrupt. He listened without comment or expression to Thomas's explanation of his decryption of the letter revealing a plot involving Aurum, Argentum and the Alchemist, and to his description of the events leading to the deaths of Stoner and Squire and to the capture of Henri and Louise d'Entrevaux. Thomas explained how the fragment found in Stoner's house had led them to suspect Morland, but he did not attempt to excuse their mistake.

When Thomas had finished the king said, 'Thank you, Mr Hill. Your account is consistent with that of Mr Williamson, although I note that you did not see fit to mention the abduction and rescue of his cousin. Why was that?'

Because it had not occurred to him, that was why. 'It did not seem relevant, Your Majesty.'

'I daresay it was relevant to her.' The king paused. 'I must decide what to do on the basis of the information and advice I have received. Before I do so, have you anything you wish to add?'

'Only this, Your Majesty. I served your father because I wanted to bring an end to war, and I have served you because I do not want to see England at war again.'

'A pretty speech, Mr Hill, and your sentiments do you credit. There is, however, the serious matter of Sir Samuel's false imprisonment. Sir Samuel is a trusted friend and an able man whose talents are valued highly by us. I cannot dismiss his complaint without proper consideration.'

The king paused. The royal expression told Thomas nothing. He held the king's gaze and tried to look confident. When the king spoke his voice was grave. 'Thomas Hill, I hold you in part responsible for the unjust imprisonment of our loyal servant Sir Samuel Morland.' The king leaned forward in his chair. 'My policy is to reward loyalty and to punish those who act against those who are loyal to me.'

'Yes, Your Majesty.'

'In this case, however, there are circumstances that demand clemency. You will not be punished, but you are rebuked. Joseph Williamson has been similarly rebuked.'

A royal rebuke. Thomas wondered if he should thank the king for his kindness, swear his undying loyalty to the Crown, or keep quiet. He kept quiet.

The king went on, 'These are dangerous times. Our enemies at home and overseas would like to see England and its king weakened and defeated. By your actions, you have helped remove a serious threat to our safety. For that, you have our grateful thanks.'

'Thank you, Your Majesty.'

'And what now for you, Mr Hill?'

'I shall return to my home in Romsey, and hope to spend whatever years I have left in peace with my family and my books.'

'We hope your wish will be granted, Mr Hill. Now there is one thing more before you go.' The king signalled to a courtier, who produced a low stool from behind the king's chair and placed it in front of Thomas. A second courtier handed the king a gleaming sword.

'Please kneel for His Majesty,' ordered the first courtier.

With the odd sensation that he was watching someone else, Thomas did as he was instructed. He barely felt the sword touch his shoulders or heard the king say, 'Arise, Sir Thomas.' He managed to stand when told to, and took the oustretched hand lightly.

'Is there a Lady Hill, Sir Thomas?' asked the king with a grin.

'Not yet, Your Majesty, but I am hopeful.' Thomas had not recovered his wits and the words came out in a rush.

'Then we wish you well and may God bless you.' The king and his courtiers turned and were gone.

'Sir Thomas,' said the captain, 'if you are ready, I will escort you home.'

'Thank you, Captain. Did that really happen or was I dreaming?'

The captain smiled. 'That is a most common reaction. It's over so quickly, you want it to be done again just to be sure. Take my word, Sir Thomas, it happened.'

In the carriage, Thomas asked the captain to take him not to Piccadilly but along Fleet Street. At the junction with the narrow lane, the carriage stopped and Thomas alighted. 'Good luck, Sir Thomas,' said the young man.

'Thank you, Captain. I shall need it.'

The door was opened by Agnes. 'Why, Mr Hill, this is a surprise. Shall I enquire if Miss Stewart will see you?'

'Thank you, no, Agnes. I will see her.'

Agnes stepped aside to let him in. 'As you wish, sir. If you would wait in the sitting room, I'll tell her you are here.'

There was no point in procrastinating. When Madeleine entered the room, blue eyes flashing, Thomas took two steps forward, put his arms around her, held on tightly and kissed her firmly on the lips. Then he released her and knelt in front of her. 'Madeleine Stewart, please will you come to Romsey and marry me there?'

He stood and Madeleine took his hands in hers. 'Of course I will, Thomas. But was the kneeling necessary?'

'Charles Carrington advised it.'

'Did he now? And what else did he advise?'

'That I swear undying love and take you to bed.'

'Excellent advice.'

'I thought so too, but first there is something I must tell you.'

Madeleine's face fell. 'Thomas, if there's another—'

He put his finger to her lips. 'Ssh. I have come directly from Whitehall. Would you care to know why?'

'Tell me.'

'I have been knighted.'

'I do not believe you.'

'It is true.'

Madeleine threw her arms around him. 'So you are Sir Thomas Hill.'

'I am. And you will be Lady Hill. So if Agnes would bring a bottle, we will drink a toast to long life and happiness as Sir Thomas and Lady Hill.'

Madeleine fetched Agnes and, with her, a bottle of excellent claret and Josiah, who had been tucking into his dinner in the kitchen. When told the news, Agnes curtsied and a beaming Josiah shook his hand. 'Just as well I took good care of you, Sir Thomas,' said the little man.

'Just as well, Josiah, and I trust the future Lady Hill will do the same.' The elbow in his ribs did not hurt all that much.

Some time later, Madeleine propped herself up on a pillow and ran her finger along the graze on Thomas's cheek. She had not asked how he had come by it. 'Such a pity the king did not see fit to make you an earl.'

'Madeleine! Is the wife of a knight not good enough for you?'

'I'm not thinking of myself. Our son would have inherited an earldom.'

'Our son?'

'I suspected it after the first time. Now I'm sure.'

Thomas sat up and took her face in his hands. 'But I thought . . .'

'It seems they were wrong.'

'And your sickness . . .'

'He must be strong.'

'Is it not too soon to be sure?'

'No, Thomas. I am sure.'

Thomas kissed her. 'What shall we call him?'

'My father's name was Edward.'

'Then he will be Edward Hill.'

ACKNOWLEDGEMENTS

As always, I thank my wife Susan for her patient support. Michael and Tom Swanston offered valuable advice and suggestions for which I am grateful.

Thanks also to my wonderful editor, Emma Buckley, and her colleagues at Transworld. It is a great pleasure to work with them.

And a final thank-you to Penny McMahon at the British Postal Museum and Archive in London.

SELECT BIBLIOGRAPHY

Iris Brooke, *English Costume of the Seventeenth Century*, A. & C. Black, 1934

Tim Harris, *Restoration*, Penguin, 2005

Christopher Hill, *The World Turned Upside Down*, Penguin, 1972

Alan Marshall, *Intelligence and Espionage in the Reign of Charles II, 1660– 1685*, Cambridge University Press, 1994

Stephen Pincock, *Codebreaker: The History of Codes and Ciphers*, Walker & Co., 2006

Simon Singh, *The Code Book*, Fourth Estate, 1999

Jenny Uglow, *A Gambling Man*, Faber and Faber, 2009

and, of course, Samuel Pepys, *The Shorter Pepys*, Penguin, 1985

After reading Law at Cambridge, **Andrew Swanston** held various positions in the book trade, including being a director of Waterstones and chairman of Methvens PLC, before turning to full-time writing. Inspired by a lifelong interest in seventeenth-century history, his Thomas Hill novels are set during the English Civil War and the early period of the Restoration. He lives with his wife in Surrey.